Men at Work

MEN AT WORK

Rediscovering Depression-era Stories from the Federal Writers' Project

EDITED AND INTRODUCED BY

Matthew L. Basso

THE UNIVERSITY OF UTAH PRESS
Salt Lake City

The Defiance House Man colophon is a registered trademark
of the University of Utah Press. It is based on a four-foot-tall
Ancient Puebloan pictograph (late PIII) near Glen Canyon, Utah.

16 15 14 13 12   1 2 3 4 5

Library of Congress Cataloging-in-Publication Data

Men at work : rediscovering Depression-era stories
from the Federal Writers' Project / edited and introduced
by Matthew L. Basso.
    p. cm.
  ISBN 978-1-60781-189-3 (pbk. : alk. paper)
  1. Working class writings, American. 2. Working class—Literary collections.
  I. Basso, Matthew.
  PS508.W73M46 2012
  810.8'09220623--dc23
2012014663

Printed and bound by Sheridan Books, Inc., Ann Arbor, Michigan.

In Memory of

Josephine Wukadinovich Burmeister and Raymond Burmeister

CONTENTS

Section I / Times Have Changed

Section II / Time Stands Still

Section III/Modern Times

ILLUSTRATIONS

Following page 280

1. *Man with Pick*, Leah Balsham
2. *High Lead*, Paul Tyler
3. *Black Country*, Michael J. Gallagher
4. *Slaughter House*, Bernard Schardt
5. *House Painter*, Hugh Botts
6. *Mills*, Salvatore Pinto
7. *Blast Furnace*, Elizabeth Olds
8. *Tapping the Furnace*, Charles Reed Gardner
9. *Last Shift*, Michael J. Gallagher
10. *Miner Joe*, Elizabeth Olds
11. *Locomotive*, Beatrice Cuming
12. *Sign Painters*, Hugh Botts
13. *Construction Workers*, Hugh Botts
14. *Clambake*, Fred Becker
15. *Defense Steel*, Horatio Forjohn
16. *Bacteriologist*, Isaac Soyer
17. *Arc Welder*, Harry Mack

The following illustrations were listed in the original *Men at Work* manuscript, but could not be located:

    Calm Before the Storm, John W. Gregory
    Tomato Pickers, Paul Weller
    Seamen's Mess, Irwin Hoffman

ACKNOWLEDGMENTS

I first learned about the possible existence of *Men at Work* while I was a Bradley Fellow at the Montana Historical Society. Brian Shovers and the rest of the lovely folks at the MHS Research Center not only made Helena a home away from home, but also encouraged me to pursue the project. As is always the case with undertakings like this, other archivists at a number of different repositories, including the Getty Research Library, Los Angeles, and the Merrill G. Burlingame Special Collections of Montana State University Library, also lent me support. I want to especially thank the staff at the Library of Congress's Manuscript Division who, following my phone request, kindly went looking and found the full *Men at Work* manuscript; later, they also assisted my on site research in their Federal Writers' Project holdings.

My work on this project began when I was a graduate student in the American Studies Program at the University of Minnesota. I want to thank the program and the university for a variety of fellowship and research funding. Elaine Tyler May, Lary May, David Noble, and David Roediger helped me see the relationship between labor, gender, and race during the New Deal era much more clearly. Equally important to my education on these matters were the discussions with my friends in the American Studies Program, History Department, and English Department during these years. My time as an organizer for the graduate student unionization effort at Minnesota provided me a different—but just as valuable— learning experience. The University of Richmond, my first faculty home, provided me not just lifelong friends but also financial and human resources that proved critical to completing *Men at Work*. I want to thank in particular Hugh West, chair of the Department of History, and Debbie Govoruhk, administrative assistant extraordinaire and all-around wonderful person who helped coordinate the transcribing of many of the stories.

A number of scholars and scholarly communities have allowed me to kick around my *Men at Work* ideas and provided valuable feedback. The *New Mexico Historical Review*, edited by Durwood Ball, provided the first opportunity to publish my thoughts on where *Men at Work* fits within the culture and politics of the Great Depression. *Montana: The Magazine of Western History*, edited by Molly Holz, welcomed a "Men at Work" story that did not make it into Rosenberg's final manuscript. And Patty Dean and Rick Newby, editors of "Coming Home," an award-winning special issue of *Drumlummon Views* offered an especially valuable opportunity. Brian Cannon and Kent Powell, who served as the outside readers for the University of Utah Press, also provided helpful critiques. My thanks too to audiences at the Western Historical Association Conference, the University of Utah's Tanner Humanities Center, and the Berkshire Conference of Women's Historians for their ideas. George Imredy (whose friendship I deeply value not the least because he spent a day at the Library of Congress copying the *Men at Work* manuscript), Paul Lauter, Thomas Thurston, Peter Ratchleff, and Susan Ferber are among the other individuals whose generosity has benefited this book.

The University of Utah has proved a hospitable home for *Men at Work* as indicated in the first instance by the financial backing for the project from the Dean of Humanities, the Tanner Humanities Center, the Vice President for Research, the Utah Museum of Fine Arts, and Marriott Library Special Collections. My colleagues in the History Department and Gender Studies Program have remained wonderfully supportive of *Men at Work* and my other scholarly projects, even as my propensity to spread myself too thin has sometimes slowed their completion. My work as director of the university's American West Center was the primary inhibitor, but by reinforcing my tendencies toward public history and giving me the experience to develop a model of community-engaged scholarship that has partnership and collaboration as the two principle pillars, it also made *Men at Work* a much more rewarding experience.

Indeed, this book, although the centerpiece, is only one part of a larger effort by the University of Utah to engage the community in a discussion about the place of labor in society historically and today. I very much appreciate the support for this undertaking, and insights about that topic, offered to me by my principal partners in this initiative. Paisley Rekdahl, Craig Dworkin, Barry Weller, and Lance Olsen of the Creative Writing Program and the English Department believed an "At Work" edition of the *Western Humanities Review* might compel among contemporary writers the same sort of artistic innovation championed by the original volume. Jill Dawsey, Donna Poulton, and Gretchen Dietrich at the Utah Museum of Fine Arts thought it was important for Great Recession audiences to see and think about art focused on labor made during the Great Depression. And Greg Thompson, Marnie Powers-Torrey, David Wolske, Emily Tipps, Claire Taylor, and Laura Decker of Marriott Library's dynamic Book Arts Program enthusiastically agreed with my idea to handcraft a book so as to more fully enter the spirit of *Men at Work* and do something about the gender inequity it evidences, even though they knew I had no clue about how much labor it would necessitate. I'm incredibly proud of the result, *Wo/Men at Work*, which is included in the special edition of *Men at Work* being jointly issued by Red Butte Press and the University of Utah Press.

My most important collaborators on this book have been my graduate students at the American West Center. First and foremost is Andy Farnsworth. Andy researched and wrote the helpful definitions that appear in the endnotes of each story and assisted with the biographical sketches. He also played a central part in envisioning, coordinating, designing, editing, writing, and printing *Wo/Men at Work*. The list of Andy's labors on this project is remarkable, but does not adequately convey how much I relied on him. My deepest thanks to him for being a stalwart partner during what was an incredibly difficult period in his life. Besides Andy, Rachel Osborne put her impressive skills as a genealogical researcher to work on finding biographical information about the volume's authors and artists. The inclusion of seventeen of the twenty prints that Harold Rosenberg chose for *Men at Work* is the result of Anna Thompson's dogged labor. Chris Dunsmore lent valuable assistance as copyeditor and did yeoman's work printing and assembling *Wo/Men at Work*. And Emily Johnson, while serving a public history internship at the American West Center, did a splendid job co-curating the "At Work: Prints of the Great Depression" exhibition. I also want to thank Annie Hanshew, John Worsencroft, and Vince Fazzi, the graduate student assistant directors of the American West Center, and Michelle Turner, the center's administrative assistant, whose labor helped shepherd *Men at Work* and the other parts of the "At Work" initiative.

The staff at the University of Utah Press—especially Peter DeLafosse, Linda Manning, and Glenda Cotter—have been excited about the possibilities of this project since the first time I mentioned it to them. I'm very appreciative of their willingness to speed the production process and to collaborate with the Book Arts Program and the other "At Work" partners. I also want to thank Jessica Booth of the press for her splendid design work and Paul Grindrod for his first-rate copyediting.

Angela Smith talked through these ideas with me, checked my writing for mechanical and stylistic errors (any and all the mistakes are thus her fault), and was incredibly supportive during the decade it took to finish this project. That brief summary does not appropriately encapsulate all that she's done, but I hope she understands all that she means to me. Our twins, Eamon and Jack, also deserve a tip of the cap for reminding me, as I wrote about work, to make time to play. This book is dedicated to all my family members who lived through the Great Depression, but especially to my Aunt Josie and Uncle Ray. I miss you.

INTRODUCTION

In early 1935, Franklin Delano Roosevelt, two years into his presidency and fresh from the Democratic Party's midterm election triumph, signed omnibus legislation, the Emergency Relief Appropriation Bill, into law. The "Big Bill," as the president liked to call it, signaled a shift in the New Deal's approach toward providing relief from the devastating effects of the Great Depression which, at that point, had already scarred the nation for half a decade.[1] Principal among the agencies created to administer the government's new assistance programs was the Works Progress Administration (WPA). In one of his famous "fireside chat" radio broadcasts Roosevelt forcefully contrasted the WPA's mandated system of work relief to relief not associated with work. The WPA, according to the president, formed the cornerstone of "a great national crusade to destroy enforced idleness which is an enemy of the human spirit generated by this depression. Our attack upon these enemies must be without stint and without discrimination." Emphasizing the effect of the economic crisis on every corner of the nation, he added that, in implementing work relief, "No sectional, no political distinctions can be permitted."[2]

A wide cross section of Americans, in fact, hoped to find succor within the government's new relief programs. Reflecting the special relationship many felt they had with the president, as well as a rapidly evolving sense of the government's responsibility to its citizens, they let their needs be known.[3] Among them were writers in New York City who felt so strongly about the necessity of work relief for artists that they picketed the WPA's offices. One writer carried a sign that encapsulated the collective sentiment: "Children Need Books. Writers Need a Break. We Demand Projects." Their cry for help, and lobbying by artists' groups and friends of the arts led to the creation of the WPA's innovative and controversial work programs for artists, musicians, actors, and writers, collectively known as Federal One. Of the 8.5 million people who eventually found employment under the WPA (renamed the Work Projects Administration in 1939), a small fraction, 37,000, worked for Federal One.[4] Relief workers associated with the Federal Art Project added murals to post offices, schools, and public buildings across the country; those assigned to the Federal Music Project fostered and preserved the organic sounds of U.S. regional music, and millions of men, women, and children attended Federal Theatre Project productions.[5] Best known of the arts relief programs, though, was that demanded by the New York City picketers: the Federal Writers' Project (FWP).[6]

Some of the most distinguished authors of the era, including Saul Bellow, Richard Wright, Kenneth Fearing, Meridel LeSueur, Zora Neale Hurston, and Ralph Ellison, found relief employment in the FWP. Along with the national office, every state had a writers' project unit. Combined, they annually employed between 3,500 and 5,000 people. Bellow, like many of the men and women who found employment with the FWP, "adored" the work he did. The FWP's projects ranged from the production of state and local guides to the recording of oral histories of marginalized communities, including ethnic minorities, industrial and agricultural workers, and former slaves. The historian Jerrold Hirsch argues the FWP's national leaders—men like Henry Alsberg, John Lomax, Benjamin Botkin, Morton Royce, and Sterling Brown—had an ambitious objective: "They aimed to redefine American national identity and culture by embracing the country's diversity." Their inclusive view of America, which the body of work produced by the FWP reflected, directly countered the circumscribed perspective that had fostered the nativist, racist, and anti-labor politics that largely defined the 1920s. Notably, however, the FWP approach, which Hirsch describes as combining "romantic nationalism" with "cosmopolitanism," also covered over many of the fissures that continued to divide the country, in some ways replacing one conservative myth of America with another.[7]

The opponents of the Administration's broad relief plans, most prominently Republican senators who took the majority following the 1938 elections, had a critical view of the FWP and the other components of Federal One for another reason. Aided by the publicity generated by Congressman Martin Dies's Committee to Investigate Un-American Activities, which particularly targeted the Writers' Project and the Theater Project for alleged Communist ties (and for supposedly pumping out pro–New Deal propaganda), the Republicans eradicated the Theater Project. The Writers' Project survived, but Congress eliminated most of its budget and even removed the name "federal" from the national office.[8] The federally supported state writers' programs were allowed to continue, but only on limited funding, so as to facilitate the completion of local projects, especially the state guides. Writing in the London *Times*, Alistair Cooke opined, "The Federal Writers' Project is doomed to die . . . the Federal Writers, as a group or school, are no more. But they have left in print several million words of penetrating and humane documentation, possessing which some future American generation may well marvel at the civilization recorded by a small library of Government sponsored volumes in those turbulent years between 1935 and 1939."[9]

Of the actual written output of the FWP, the state guides, collectively called the American Guide Series, have received the most attention.[10] Cooke wrote of his desire to "buy, beg, steal, annex, or 'protect' a complete library of the guides before [he] die[d]." Lewis Mumford called them one of the best products of the era's "adversity" and likened them to "Pausanias' ancient guidebook to Greece." Alfred Kazin thought they "resulted in an extraordinary contemporary epic. . . . Road by road, town by town, down under the alluvia of the industrial culture of the twentieth century."[11] But the guides' remarkable effort to "introduce America to Americans" by tracing the history and culture of each state "road by road" and "town by town" had an unexpected consequence. It proved such a monumental undertaking that the project, already hampered by the loss of staff and funding and the desire of state agencies to use Writers' Project authors for other state publications, had to abandon another of its goals: publishing literature that reflected the nation in its entirety instead of in its parts, as the guides presented it. Jerre Mangione, the foremost chronicler and a former member of the FWP, has argued that these never completed national studies "quite possibly . . . would have revealed the nation's soul more tellingly than the guidebooks."[12]

* * *

Knowing this history, I was surprised when, in the course of doing archival research on another topic at the Montana Historical Society Research Center, I stumbled upon a Montana WPA file labeled "Men at Work" that contained six short stories by Montana FWP authors and a number of supporting documents all dating from the last months of 1940 and the first months of 1941. The documents indicated these stories had arrived in Washington, DC, too late to be included in *Men at Work*, a volume being undertaken by the national FWP office that would focus on depicting the jobs done by Americans from coast to coast. Instead of concentrating on the social world and politics of the working classes, the typical terrain of 1930s literature, the national FWP office offered would-be *Men at Work* contributors a markedly different charge: write about the actual work done by Americans. "The author may present his experience in the form of an article, a short story, a descriptive sketch, an autobiographical account, an interview. He may describe an individual at work or a team working together. *But the writers must have seen the work done, or perhaps have done it themselves.*"[13] As I read the Montana stories, excitement replaced surprise. Their detailed portraits of workers and the labor they did were unlike any of the literature I had read from the 1930s. Providing fascinating portraits of six different types of workers, including agricultural irrigationists, hard rock miners, and wildfire watchmen, the Montana stories tantalized by showing just how intriguing stories based on such an unusual prompt could be.

But had *Men at Work* actually been completed? Was there a FWP book out there that spanned the entire nation, reflected the New Deal's focus on work, and addressed the culture of labor from this unique angle? A few days later, after searching secondary sources and archival catalogues and contacting colleagues who also specialized in the history of the era, resignation replaced excitement. *Men at Work* did not register anywhere. I returned to my other research, but *Men at Work* kept gnawing at me. Finally, some months after my initial discovery, I decided to make a last effort and called the Library of Congress's Manuscript Division. My story about "Men at Work" intrigued the librarian who answered the phone and he promised to do some searching for me. A few hours later he called back and announced the library had what looked like a single onion-skin copy of a complete manuscript of *Men at Work*.[14]

Men at Work was meant to be the first part of Hands that Built America, an ambitious six-volume series under Writers' Program staff member Harold Rosenberg's editorship that, along with a number of other proposed initiatives, would politically and artistically revitalize the program following its setbacks over the previous few years. Program leaders went so far as to describe "Hands that Built America" as "the logical successor to the state guides," but saw it also as a contribution to national unity and patriotism. One of *Men at Work*'s objectives was to "catch the spirit of American labor with its pride in craft, satisfaction in accomplishment, and desire to contribute to the national welfare."[15]

Men at Work had nearly been ready for publication when the nation's mobilization for World War II and then the war itself intervened. National office staff, if not already transferred to new government agencies like the Office of War Information, received new war-related writing assignments. The last few that remained turned their attention to boxing all the materials in the national office and hastily transferring it to a dusty corner of the Library of Congress.[16] That is where *Men at Work*, and so much else that the FWP produced, sat for decades. The *Men at Work* manuscript at the Library of Congress proved to be almost exactly what those tantalizing documents in the Montana Historical Society promised. It contained a foreword by Rosenberg, who served as the editor for the collection, and thirty-four stories written by FWP writers living in every region of the country. The manuscript also included a list of twenty prints by Federal Art Project artists—an unexpected and delightful addition—that Rosenberg had selected to illustrate the worlds of work represented in the stories. Several of the artists and authors, like Jim Thompson and Chester Himes, had become famous after their time in the FWP, but the majority represented the ordinary culture-workers who were the backbone of Federal One.

Men at Work's stories—four of which were folk tales submitted by Jack Conroy that approached the realities of work from a different but complementary point of view—offered readers vibrant descriptions of the labor involved in cannery work, logging, oil drilling, shepherding, jazz, commercial fishing, mining, advertising, welding, and a score of other jobs.[17] As they did so they revealed the pleasures, pains, and social politics of each of these jobs. I realized that this was precisely what contemporary readers would also experience in reading *Men at Work*, and that along the way they would get a deeper understanding of the Depression era and, perhaps, of the place of labor in their own lives. As I read the manuscript for the second time, I found in each story new insights about work and society in the 1930s, a subject and period I thought I knew well. By the time I had finished that reading, I had pledged to myself that I would make sure that this marvelous volume was published. It took more time than I expected, but seven decades after it was completed, here, finally, is *Men at Work*!

I have sought to reproduce the stories exactly as they appeared in the original manuscript with two exceptions; I have made the editorial changes that Rosenberg noted in red pencil and corrected some misspellings and minor punctuation issues. And I have added four other features that did not appear in the original version: author and artist biographies, the intended illustrative prints, definitions of obsolete or confusing terms in the endnotes for each story, and this introduction. Rosenberg asked contributors to send in biographical sketches, but only one of those sketches was attached to the manuscript.[18] Driven by a reader's curiosity and by a historian's sense that we know very little about the rank-and-file writers and artists of Federal One, I set about searching for information about each of them. For many, finding details about their lives before, during, and even after the Great Depression proved enormously challenging. In most instances the biographies I have included reflect everything I discovered about each author and artist. Tracking down the twenty prints also was difficult; however, because of Rosenberg's own history (after the war he became one of the nation's most influential art critics) I thought this task was especially important. Ultimately, I was able to find and include in this volume seventeen of the prints.

The purpose of the definitions is to help make legible for contemporary readers occupations and contexts that, in many instances, have receded into the forgotten past. The introduction supplements Rosenberg's original preface, providing another type of context by placing *Men at Work* within a contemporaneous debate that Rosenberg consciously chose to enter. That debate, which has continued, centers on the purpose and aesthetics of Depression-era literature. This introduction has a second purpose: in the final section I discuss a number of the ways in which *Men at Work*, with its focus on the labor involved in a variety of jobs, answers the call made most forcefully by Alan Wald for new sources that will provide a different vantage point to consider the social and cultural politics of the Great Depression and the place of gender, race, and class relations in those politics.

* * *

The received history of Great Depression literature stems, in part, from the first generation of scholarship on the topic. It splits the long decade of the 1930s into two periods. From 1928 to 1935 the emphasis was "on working-class literature, revolutionary ideology, and the creation of venues to give voice to unknown cultural workers from the disenfranchised classes." The second half of the decade saw a shift toward "a people's democratic literature, antifascist ideology, and the development of organizations and conferences with well-known and successful writers." The initial scholarly analysis of Great Depression literature linked different groups of writers and intellectuals with each of these periods. Those that dominated the first period advocated the primary importance of political consciousness in any left-wing literature. Major figures in this camp, like Mike Gold, Granville Hicks, and V. F. Calverton, were associated with the editorial position of *The New Masses* and closely affiliated with the Communist Party USA. Representative of their perspective was Calverton's assertion that "proletarian writers believe that their literature can serve a great purpose only when it contributes, first, toward the destruction of present-day society, and, second, toward the creation of a new society which will embody, like Soviet Russia to-day, a social, instead of an individualistic, ideal." The other camp, which dominated the latter thirties, consisted of intellectuals such as Wallace Phelps, Phillip Rahv, and *Men at Work*'s editor Harold Rosenberg, all writers for the *Partisan Review*. They positioned themselves as centrists in relation to the leftists of the *New Masses*, insisting that the latter's focus on content over form and aesthetic quality, and their emphasis on mechanistic and functional writing, ignored the value of art. Worse yet, the centrists believed the leftists imposed a formula upon writers that stipulated that authors "should deal with the more obvious aspects of the class struggle, melodramatize their characters into good workers versus evil *bourgeoisie*, and end on a carefully affirmative note whether the internal logic of the novel demanded such a conclusion or its opposite."[19]

The assumption that the division represented by the *New Masses* and *Partisan Review* was distinct and absolute, that the judgments and demands of left intellectuals defined the field of proletarian literature, and that the proletarian novel all but expired in the middle of the decade has been effectively challenged by later studies.[20] Reflecting this more nuanced take, Karen Irr contends, "neither the intellectual nor the political culture of the North American left was simply a reflection of a centrally controlled and philosophically dishonest policy." Citing Vivian Gornick, Irr argues "It was rather 'a vast, sprawling, fragmented, intensely various experience.'" She adds, "the ideology of class consciousness made sense to people from a variety of origins, and they experienced their commitment to this ideology in a variety of ways and abandoned it for yet another set of diverse reasons."[21] *Men at Work* bolsters this messier conception, because it gathers mostly unknown writers and shows us that their politics, at least read through their stories, can only be described as diffuse. Perhaps more importantly, it also suggests that as late as 1941 a robustness continued to characterize the search for an aesthetic that spoke for the thirties and represented American pluralism.

Methodologically and topically, the book reinforces the sense that the focal point of much Great Depression writing and art was the drive to represent the lives of ordinary Americans. Rosenberg's *Men at Work* fits more specifically within the documentary impulse for which Louis Hine, James Agee, Richard Wright, and, perhaps most famously of all, Dorothea Lange, were all exemplars and for which the decade's artistic output is best known.[22] In an era that saw the revitalization of the union movement and the centering of working people for the first time in U.S. history, a process Michael Denning has memorably described as the "laboring of American culture," it is, of course, not surprising that writers in their quest to document American life explored Americans as workers. In his preface to *Men at Work*, however, Rosenberg argued that most thirties writing in this vein had failed to consider the industrial work worlds that he saw as defining American industry and the experience of the American worker. The most significant exceptions to that pattern, according to Rosenberg, were the "social novels" of the decade.[23] These novels "have shown the worker's home life, his food, his clothing, his struggle to meet his needs, his organizations, and his friends." But he concluded that they had largely ignored his labor: the "productive, and hence powerful and dynamic, core of his existence." Rosenberg wanted *Men at Work* to change that.

Rosenberg also saw the diverse work done by Americans as an unrealized portal for documenting the realities of modernist America and potentially as the basis for a more effective politics. In the preface to *Men at Work* he wrote, "Jobs take in the landscape surrounding them, and odors, tempos, climates, costumes. They take in the worker's delight in touching things and changing them handily. They take in, too, the special kind of suffering and crippling that comes from toil that is tiresome and infinitely repetitious, and in which the instinct of workmanship is reduced to beggary." He believed the stories in *Men at Work* had succeeded in chronicling these aspects of the American workers' experience. But he also thought that substantially more had been gained by the approach he had mandated for the volume's authors. "A man's work, say the philosophers, is the means by which he stamps his image on nature, and also gives form to his own character. So that the manner of his daily doing is an influence interacting deeply with the future of society and with political ideas and social theories." *Men at Work*, by showing the roots of workers' belief systems in the details of their toil, could potentially offer a new basis for developing a successful progressive praxis.

By choosing to follow the documentary style in 1941, Rosenberg indicated continuing support for the Depression's leading method, but by asking writers to use their own creativity to better capture the lives of workers he openly acknowledged the constructed nature of documentary practice and welcomed the role of the artist in shaping meaning. In his preface Rosenberg underscored his sense that literature and art can reveal work in a manner that "[s]tatistical tables, vocational surveys, and sketches" cannot, for the arts "concern themselves with such values as the skill used in the task, its tensions, color, and formal and dramatic appeal." However, in Rosenberg's view, literature and painting lack descriptions of modern work, as "human action" for itself rather than as an "incident . . . or as a detail." This failure, he posits, derives from the perceived triviality of "the operations performed in the factory," the "literary difficulties" in rendering "the new men and women who each day stand emptily alert for hours within a rigid construction through which incomplete and changing objects keep streaming," and, notably, also because "[a]uthors have not had much personal intimacy with physical labor."

As editor, Rosenberg informs us, he required that the writers of *Men At Work* "know disciplines other than those of literary composition," and he emphasizes that "most of them have had first-hand familiarity with the jobs about which they are writing, or with different jobs in the same locality." (In the authors' biography section I have highlighted the work history of each author to the extent I was able to discover it.) As a result, all the stories according to Rosenberg provide "authentic pictures of people at their jobs in America." In their first-person perspectives the stories, nonetheless, juxtapose the figure of intellectual/artist with that of the worker, the act of writing with the act of manual labor. Avoiding the confrontation and conversion narratives to which, according to their critics, proletarian novels rigidly adhere, dispensing with the moralizing assumption of the working-class's false consciousness, and using a reportage-style fiction in which the worker/writer speaks his own working experience, the short stories of *Men At Work* do offer a different approach to representing the working class.

Yet, although Rosenberg appreciated the contributions to *Men at Work*, it appears that he was ultimately disappointed that the volume did not produce a new literary genre that ventured outside of narrative, creating a compellingly different aesthetic along the way. Paradoxically, given his objectives for the volume, this frustration with ordinary forms of expression was related to Rosenberg's tendency to disdain the effort on the part of artists to reach average Americans. His perspective on this issue crystallized in the postwar period and became well known in tandem with his own growing profile, reflected both in his work for the *New Yorker* magazine and his position at the University of Chicago as one of the nation's leading art critics and cultural commentators. In his 1975 book *Art on the Edge* Rosenberg summarized what had become his evaluation of Federal One: "The aim of reaching the common man resulted in the humiliation of the artists and a costly misdirection of their energies. The Art Project was an important event in American art, but it was not important in regard to style."[24] In contrast, Rosenberg continued to celebrate skilled craftsmen and the place of work in life. In 1964 he argued:

> To many of the critics of contemporary civilization the practice of the crafts is the activity by which the human creature is defined. Man is a maker, homo faber, an artist. Put this proposition in reverse—when man ceases to be a maker he is no longer man—and our present crisis is explained. The fall began not in Eden, when man was condemned to labor, but in the nineteenth century, when the machine first threatened him with leisure. With "soulless manufacture," as Ruskin called it, turning out endless quantities of copies of objects to which the human touch was alien, man-the-maker commenced to lose his skills, through which he also gave shape to himself, and with them his dignity and independence.[25]

If the aspirations of Depression art troubled Rosenberg and distanced him from some of his colleagues, he and they continued to share a view about the relationship between gender and labor. Rosenberg's choice of pronouns was purposeful: *man* was "the maker" and *men* were the ones who did productive work. But despite, or perhaps because of, this gender bias, the relationship between gender and labor during the Depression era is one of the subjects about which *Men at Work* provides important insights.

* * *

The popular mythology of men's experience during the Great Depression, which pictures men as unemployed, stoop-shouldered, huddled against the cold, waiting for a meager free meal, frames this volume and our reception of it. Because they are unable to find jobs and, thus, have difficulty putting food on the table or even keeping a roof over their family, men often emerge as the Depression's principal victims. When Franklin Roosevelt proposed a New Deal to assist "the forgotten man" he was, of course, speaking about these men—and likewise further bolstering a specific image of masculinity during the decade. American women of the period, in contrast, rarely appear in similar guise. Instead, mythology of the era assigns them the role of finding work—any work—so as to keep food on the table and the family together; they pinch hit, so to speak, but by doing so further emasculate out-of-work men.[26]

Scholars have shown the deep inconsistencies between the historical record and the stereotypical image of faltering manhood in the 1930s. Far from forgetting men, federal agencies including the WPA went out of their way to support men's place as the head of the household, often to the detriment of women. In 1932, one of the worst years of the Depression, legislation targeted married women for dismissal from federal jobs, reflecting a perspective shared by most men in government, management, and labor, and by a large number of women. Unions, in their public statements and publications, emphasized the importance of an independent male working-class and claimed that it was principally through wise consumption, particularly the purchasing of union-made goods, that women could support their men busy fighting the forces of capital. Other popular culture texts ridiculed working women for supposedly taking work from men and lionized men as the nation's productive backbone.[27] No artifact better highlights the elevation of working-class manhood to a position as the masculine ideal than another book entitled *Men at Work*, Lewis Hine's 1932 photo collection. Hine, one of the period's most beloved photographers, opened his pictorial tribute to working men by quoting William James:

Not in clanging fights and desperate marches only is heroism to be looked
for, but on every bridge and building that is going up today, on freight
trains, on vessels and lumber-rafts, in mines, among firemen and police-
men, the demand for courage is incessant and the supply never fails.
These are our soldiers, our sustainers, the very parents of our life.[28]

Readers were to understand that Hine's black-and-white photographs did
nothing more than capture men at work, providing the visual evidence to support
James's contention.

Men at Work's stories reference men's Great Depression struggles, but at the
same time propose that the definitive feature of manhood in the era involves men
providing the skilled labor at the core of American industry and the American
ethos. It is in the detailed depiction of that skilled labor and the operation of masculinity actually in workplaces that Men at Work provides a corrective to both
Hine and the stereotype of the forgotten man. For every story like Charles Oluf
Olsen's "Logging in the Rain" that depicts heroic manhood through its description
of skilled lumbermen battling nature to harvest the trees of the Northwest, a counterpoint exists. In fact, Verne Bright's "Shingletown" presents a portrait of the very
same industry through the eyes of a narrator who has done virtually every job in
the woods but is bent on reaching what he has heard is its most masculine rung:
working in a shingle mill. He ends up doing one of the very jobs James celebrated,
working a lumber raft, only to quickly learn the supposed prestige is not worth
the risk the actual labor involves. "Shingletown" indicates that for many men, but
especially those with families, the masculine ideal during the depression primarily involved working a job that allowed a man to fulfill the breadwinner role and to
survive—rather than one that supposedly provided elevated masculinity but a high
risk of injury or death. In fact, Edward Reynolds's "Anaconda" indicates that the
social capital necessary to avoid the most dangerous work in a plant was, in some
places, the preeminent sign of masculine status. Indeed, "Anaconda" suggests the
dirtiest and most dangerous labor in a plant often went to racial and ethnic minorities and other outsiders who saw their masculinity denigrated because they had to
do such work.[29]

While it offers a more nuanced picture of the relationship between work
and masculine formation in the 1930s, Men at Work perpetuates the erasure of
women's reproductive unpaid labor—of which cooking, child care, and cleaning
are three of the major tasks—as something other than "work," and also largely
dismisses women's salaried labor.[30] Women, however, are not completely absent
from the volume's picture of "Americans at their jobs." Thirteen percent of Men
at Work's creative output, both literary and artistic, is by women, and women also

feature in a number of the volume's stories. In those a compelling and complex, albeit very much incomplete, picture of women's toil during the Depression materializes. Only one story, Ned DeWitt's "Sade Duggett," features a woman as its protagonist. Duggett operates a kitchen that feeds male oil workers. The story shows her breaking down gender stereotypes by being in the field and taking control over her own finances, as well as affirming them by cooking and eventually marrying. But most importantly, Duggett's work, whether transgressive or not, plays a major part in defining her character. As it does for the male characters throughout *Men at Work*, work shapes the way she interacts at the interpersonal level and frames her relationship to her historical moment.

Such is also the case in Gail Hazard's "Cannery Row," which includes female characters that, like the story's men, are desperate for work and forced to abide by the company's constant efforts to increase the pace of production. One of the women, Gertie, describes her work in terms that bring to life the stress and monotony of industrial labor—particularly non-union piece work:

> "Push the can through the slot only once," they say. "You'll be fired for cheating." Grab for another can. Hurry! Make your hands work fast. Oh, faster, faster! Fourteen cans pushed through the slot adds two cents to the paycheck. "Don't try to cheat! We're watching you!" Work four hours. Rest. Work four hours. Rest. Work some more. "Fast girls, Faster. Make those fingers work!"

In response, one of Gertie's male coworkers indicates that the shared experience of work can transcend gender and, yet, that when men and women work together they inevitably view each other, and work, through a gendered lens.[31] "Well"— Pete grins—"you're a cannery worker. What do you think you are, a housewife?" Gertie's rebuttal makes concrete her sense of distance from the domestic ideal. "I'm a sardine choker, and I'll always be a sardine choker. When I get to be just a housewife, I'll grow me fins and scales and swim out to sea." For Gertie, just as for Pete and the other men in "Cannery Row," work seems one moment inescapable, another moment endangered, but it always defines them and it is always the key to survival. Like "Cannery Row," the stories in *Men at Work* as a whole, while marginalizing women's labor, reveal the influential role of the actual labor that occurred in Depression workplaces in constructing men and women's gendered identities and politics.

* * *

Besides the way it has shaped our understanding of gender during the Great Depression, the myth of the forgotten man also effectively flattened the distinctions of race by suggesting that all Americans suffered equally. On the contrary, scholars have shown that a person's race greatly affected how they experienced the era's "hard times." African Americans in the rural south, already facing incredible hardship due to the region's Jim Crow policies and sharecropping economy, saw their lives become even more difficult in the thirties. Those among their ranks who had headed to the urban North in search of greater opportunity joined a black community there that was also suffering inordinately. If they secured jobs, they typically received less pay than their white coworkers. They were also the first fired. At the height of the Depression, black industrial workers in Chicago saw over 50 percent unemployment—in comparison to a 31 percent rate for whites. The struggle for jobs and racist violence against African Americans went hand-in-hand. Lynchings, the most hideous manifestation of this violence, increased in the early thirties, after decreasing the previous decade. On average more than twenty a year took place in 1933, 1934, and 1935. After one 1934 attack a white Floridian remarked, "a nigger hasn't got no right to have a job when there are white men who can do the work and are out of work." Both rural and urban white workers aggressively promoted the same message in other parts of the country.[32]

Like African Americans in northern cities, Mexican Americans who had found industrial jobs were paid less and laid off before and at a higher rate than whites. In agriculture, Mexican Americans and Mexicans also faced increased discrimination, particularly in the Southwest. White company, union, and government leaders aided white migrants to the region in their quest to take the jobs of Mexicans and Mexican Americans, as well as those held by workers of Chinese, Japanese, and Filipino descent. What followed was not just the loss of jobs by workers of color, but also one of the most inhumane episodes of the Great Depression: the "repatriation" of approximately half a million Mexicans *and* Mexican Americans to Mexico and a smaller group of Filipinos to the Philippines. American Indians, who remained largely a rural population, continued to struggle with high levels of poverty during the thirties. But, thanks to the 1934 Indian Relocation Act, which partially restored tribal control over land and government, and their own well-honed abilities to live off the land, many tribal communities did not see a diminishment in their quality of life.

African Americans, Mexican and Mexican Americans, and Asian Americans joined unions and other organizations to try and combat Depression-era injustice. By the later 1930s their militancy, and the activism of the Communist Party USA, parts of the labor movement, and a number of other groups, led to some improvements for these communities of color, but they still faced intense racism.[33] Some *Men at Work* stories, like "San Francisco Longshore Gang," which features a workplace where skilled black and white dock workers labor alongside one another and belong to a union that looks after their interests irrespective of race, suggest these improvements. Others, like "The Driller," which openly displays the sense of racial superiority held by a white American manager who worked in Mexico's oil fields, underscore the enormous amount that still needed to be done to secure workplace equality.

Taken as a whole *Men at Work* urges us to consider race relations during the era as complex, dynamic, sometimes contradictory, intertwined with gender and class, and influenced by perhaps unexpected forces. For example, in "Cannery Row" the dearth of jobs coupled with the expectation that men should be the breadwinners for their families hindered both interracial and intraracial working-class solidarity. The narrator of "Cannery Row" puts it this way:

> We stand there watching the unloading boats, but not for long. How can we stand together for long when we are cannery workers, warehousemen, and reduction men—divided, one against the other? One gang of cutters against another gang, maintenance men and would be maintenance men, workers against workers. I almost run to my plant because men will be waiting outside ready to jump my job if I am not there. I scowl as I pass a warehouseman, all slick and cocky, going to his post. "What gravy," I think and sneer at his clean jeans.

Given what we know about race relations in the Great Depression, it is not surprising that another worker, described as "An Okie, green and California-new," says to a Chinese American cannery worker, "Hey, Charlie, you better cut fast today 'cause I got a pal lookin' for your job."[34] Intriguingly, although the "Okie" believes the white racial identity he shares with the narrator makes them natural allies, the narrator feels a closer tie to his Chinese American coworker. Scholarship on the era has illuminated the progressive racial politics that some white workers came to champion in the 1930s. While these politics certainly might play a part in the narrator's sensibility, Hazard indicates the bond between the two men is based on a less recognized dynamic: the local roots they share.

Robert Cornwall's "Pogy Boat" is another of the *Men at Work* stories that demonstrates the vital part played by local and regional racial ideologies in Depression-era race relations. "Pogy Boat" details the labor that takes place on *The Boys*, a boat that catches fish called menhaden (also known as "pogies") along the southeastern U.S. coast. Cornwall tells readers that "The crew of *The Boys* consisted of eighteen men: captain, engineer, pilot, mate, cook and thirteen workmen. The first three were white; the others were Negroes, except for the captain's young brother-in-law who served as a handy man." On menhaden boats and in menhaden processing plants a man's skin color determines where he can work. The same dynamic occurred in workplaces across the country, but it was most ingrained in the South. In places "Pogy Boat" backs this view of the South, and indeed reinforces the southern racial order, by repeating without interrogation stereotypes like that of the happy singing southern black worker. Likewise, in choosing at various moments to depict black workers' bodies as machines, and in making them, in all but a few cases, the backdrop—nondistinct, replaceable, expendable—of the white workers' world, the story seemingly echoes how many white southerners saw black workers. But the story also pushes past the expected narrative in its description of the highly local workspace of *The Boys*. This is particularly evident in the passages that discuss the African American "mate" sharing in the leadership of the boat with the white officers, and those that highlight the skill of the rank-and-file African American sailors in performing the limited jobs open to them. To understand the way race worked in the industry, the story seems to suggest, requires intertwining these regional and local racial strands.

Acknowledging that exceptions like those in "Pogy Boat" occur, perhaps what we should most value about *Men at Work*'s stories is their ability to connect the specific, concrete, and sensory details of labor for men and women of all races to the totality of the Depression-era capitalist system without losing the individual worker. John Delgado's "The Fruit Packers" is indicative. Delgado describes the ways technology shapes labor and how the worker physically and intellectually experiences that labor. The most telling scenes in "The Fruit Packers" occur in the packing shed, where both "white" and "Japanese" workers labor in the company of "the machine," a simple device which "consists of an endless canvas belt which carries the pears under three sets of brushes."[35] The bodily experience of labor appears at several different registers in this story. The machine is anthropomorphized and becomes the central organ of the collective working body, "the heart and nerve center of the fifty-man plant." For all the workers the experience of working in the packing shed involves a common but enforced bodily and sensory engagement with the machine: "When it starts, everybody goes to work. When it stops, everybody quits working." In between the machine makes a "humming, whirring sound that will be dinned into the brain of every man and woman there." Although the machine controls the working day of the packers and sorters, the narrator engages in an ongoing struggle with it that testifies to his and other workers' agency in carrying out and understanding their work:

> The machine becomes an invention of seventeen devils. It keeps me rooted in this oven when my whole body craves a cold, clean bath and starched white clothes.
>
> The machine seems to have conquered me, yet I know that I am its master. I can dump four or five boxes into it at once and choke its gloating roar; I can stop feeding it and laugh at its pleas for fruit.

Paradoxically, while the mechanization of the narrator's labor imposes severe limitations on him, it also provides perhaps unexpected autonomy. As the narrator notes, "feeding the machine is a mechanical task that employs only my arms, back and legs. My mind is completely free." How we should evaluate that freedom—to what degree it really served as a counterpoint to the bondage of the body in mechanized workplaces and how it may have influenced worker politics—is one of the many questions *Men at Work* raises that is as germane today as it was in the 1930s.

Men at Work holds countless other insights about how labor intersects with a wide variety of other aspects of Great Depression culture and society. I feel almost guilty concentrating narrowly on only small parts of the stories I have referenced, and even more so for not at least mentioning some contribution of each and every one of the stories. I am heartened, however, knowing that whether readers are interested in issues of shop-floor control and the traditional tensions between employers and employees, the atmosphere of specific workplaces and the mentality of particular workers as seen through details like the language of tradesmen and the place of food in the world of work, or the complex environmental politics of workers, they will find much on these topics—and many more besides—in the pages that follow. Although it focuses on a small part of the American saga during the Great Depression, *Men at Work* answers Wald's desire for new sources that will provide a different perspective on that most compelling of decades. Of equal importance, it speaks to the way labor shaped lives during the Great Depression and hints to us how our own work shapes our lives.[36] Perhaps it even offers what Mangione hoped for from such volumes—a glimpse into the "nation's soul."

Notes

1. There have been an abundance of histories of Franklin Delano Roosevelt's presidency, the New Deal, and, more broadly, the Great Depression. The following are older field-setting books as well as newer contributions: Arthur M. Schlesinger, *The Age of Roosevelt*, 3 vols. (New York: Houghton Mifflin, 1957–1960); William E. Leuchtenburg, *Franklin D. Roosevelt and the New Deal* (New York: Harper & Row, 1963); Jonathan Alter, *The Defining Moment: FDR's Hundred Days and the Triumph of Hope* (New York: Simon & Schuster, 2006); Eric Rauchway, *The Great Depression and the New Deal: A Very Short Introduction* (New York: Oxford University Press, 2008); Anthony Badger, *The New Deal: The Depression Years, 1933–1940* (New York: Ivan R. Dee, 1989); Steve Fraser and Gary Gerstle, eds., *The Rise and Fall of the New Deal Order* (Princeton: Princeton University Press, 1989); Paul Conkin, *The New Deal*, 3rd ed., (Wheeling, Ill.: Harlan Davidson, 1992); Colin Gordon, *New Deals: Business, Labor, and Politics in America, 1920–1935* (Cambridge: Cambridge University Press, 1994); Alan Brinkley, *The End of Reform: New Deal Liberalism in Recession and War* (New York: Alfred A. Knopf, 1995); Ellis Hawley, *The New Deal and the Problem of Monopoly: A Study in Economic Ambivalence*, 2nd ed., (New York: Fordham University Press, 1995); Jason Scott Smith, *Building New Deal Liberalism: The Political Economy of Public Works, 1933–1956* (Cambridge: Cambridge University Press, 2009); Sarah T. Phillips, *This Land, This Nation: Conservation, Rural America, and the New Deal* (Cambridge: Cambridge University Press, 2007); Richard H. Pells, *Radical Visions and American Dreams: Culture and Social Thought in the Depression Years* (New York: Harper and Row, 1973); Michael A. Bernstein, *The Great Depression: Delayed Recovery and Economic Change in America, 1929–1939* (Cambridge: Cambridge University Press, 1987); T. H. Watkins, *The Hungry Years: A Narrative History of the Great Depression in America* (New York: Henry Holt and Company, 1999); David Kennedy, *Freedom from Fear: The American People in Depression and War* (New York: Oxford University Press, 1999).

2. Reprinted in *The Public Papers and Addresses of Franklin D. Roosevelt*, vol. 2, 1933 (New York: Random House, 1938); Russell D. Buhite and David W. Levy, eds., *FDR's Fireside Chats* (Norman: University of Oklahoma Press, 1992), 68–70. Studies that discuss the New Deal's effect on different regions include Frank Friedel, *F.D.R. and the South* (Baton Rouge: Louisiana State University Press, 1965); Richard Lowitt, *The New Deal and the West* (Norman: University of Oklahoma Press, 1993); Catherine McNicol Stock, *Main Street in Crisis: The Great Depression and the Old Middle Class on the Northern Plains* (Chapel Hill: University of North Carolina Press, 1997); Donald Worster, *Dust Bowl: The Southern Plains in the 1930s* (New York: Oxford University Press, 2004).

3. A remarkable reflection of this special relationship can be found in the letters ordinary people sent both the president and the first lady. Some of these can be seen in Robert S. McElvaine, ed., *Down and Out in the Great Depression: Letters from the Forgotten Man* (Chapel Hill: University of North Carolina Press, 1983). Three other

moving first person accounts are Studs Terkel, *Hard Times: An Oral History of the Great Depression* (New York: Pantheon Books, 1970); Richard Lowitt and Maurine Beasley, eds., *One Third of the Nation: Lorena Hickok Reports on the Great Depression* (Urbana: University of Illinois Press, 1981); Ann Banks, *First Person America* (New York: W. W. Norton, 1991).

4. Depression-era unemployment figures are often debated. The 3.5 million unemployed cited by Roosevelt referred to those on relief and employable. Some 1.5 million more relief recipients were not employable because of age, infirmity, or other reasons, and another 5 million Americans were not working or on relief. See William F. McDonald, *Federal Relief Administration and the Arts: The Origins and Administrative History of the Arts Projects of the Works Progress Administration* (Columbus: Ohio State University Press, 1969); Watkins, *The Hungry Years*, 277–78.

5. Books that discuss each of the elements of Federal One at length, or concentrate on the Federal Theater Project, Federal Music Project, or Federal Art Project include Jane DeHart Mathews, *Federal Theater, 1935–1939: Plays, Relief, and Politics* (Princeton: Princeton University Press, 1967); Paul Sporn, *Against Itself: The Federal Theater and Writers' Projects in the Midwest* (Detroit: Wayne State University, 1995); Ilka Saal, *New Deal Theater: The Vernacular Tradition in American Political Thought* (New York: Palgrave Macmillan, 2007); Kenneth J. Bindas, *All of this Music Belongs to the Nation: The WPA's Federal Music Project and American Society, 1935–1939* (Knoxville: University of Tennessee Press, 1995); William H. Young and Nancy K. Young, *Music of the Great Depression* (New York: Greenwood, 2005); Francis V. O'Connor, ed., *Art for the Millions: Essays from the 1930s by Artists and Administrators of the WPA Federal Art Project* (Greenwich, Conn.: New York Graphic Society, 1973); Matthew Baigell, *The American Scene: American Painting of the 1930s* (New York: Praeger, 1974); Marlene Park and Gerald E. Markowitz, *Democratic Vistas: Post Offices and Public Art in the New Deal* (Philadelphia: Temple University Press, 1984); Bruce I. Bustard, *A New Deal for the Arts* (Washington, DC: National Archives and Records Administration, in association with Seattle: University of Washington Press, 1997); Laura Hapke, *Labor's Canvas: American Working-Class History and the WPA Art of the 1930s* (New York: Cambridge Scholars Press, 2008); Roger G. Kennedy, *When Art Worked: The New Deal, Art, and Democracy* (New York: Rizzoli, 2009).

6. Scholarship specifically focused on the Federal Writers' Project includes: McDonald, *Federal Relief Administration and the Arts*; Jerre G. Mangione, *The Dream and the Deal: The Federal Writers' Project 1935–1943* (Boston: Little, Brown, 1972); Monty Noam Penkower, *The Federal Writers' Project: A Study in Government Patronage of the Arts* (Urbana: University of Illinois Press, 1977); Jerrold Hirsch, *Portrait of America: A Cultural History of the Federal Writers Project* (Chapel Hill: University of North Carolina Press, 2003); David A. Taylor, *Soul of a People: The WPA Writers' Project Uncovers Depression America* (New York: Wiley, 2009).

7. Alan Brinkley, "Foreword" in *Survey of Federal Writers' Project Manuscript Holdings in State Depositories*, by Ann Banks and Robert Carter (Washington, DC: American Historical Association, 1985), v–vii; Mangione, *The Dream and the Deal*.

For employment statistics see Dick Netzer, *The Subsidized Muse: Public Support for the Arts in the United States* (Cambridge: Cambridge University Press, 1978), 55–56. On the slave narratives see George Rawick's nineteen-volume series offering transcriptions and interpretations of the interviews. The first volume is George P. Rawick, *From Sundown to Sunup: The Making of the Black Community* (New York: Greenwood Press, 1973). On the intellectual framework of the FWP and the similarities and differences among its leaders see the excellent study by Hirsch, *Portrait of America,* 1–5, 17–40. For an important analysis of how intellectuals redefined the nation in the 1930s see David W. Noble, *Death of a Nation: American Culture and the End of Exceptionalism* (Minneapolis: University of Minnesota Press, 2002).

8.   Brinkley, "Foreword," v–vii. Conservative Democrats, in large part from the South, also joined the chorus of voices criticizing the Programs. See also Ellen Schrecker, *Many Are the Crimes: McCarthyism in America* (New York: Little, Brown and Company, 1998) and Hirsch, *Portrait of America,* 197–212. In mid-1939 the Federal Writers' Project officially became the Writers' Project. Peter Conn contends in *The American 1930s: A Literary History* (New York: Cambridge University Press, 2009), 53–57, that the Theater Project undoubtedly had a propaganda function. The controversial nature of Federal One continued into the postwar. In 1949, for example, a young Richard Nixon complained about the "subversive" art that had been placed in federal buildings and noted his hope that when the Republicans came to power in the future that art would removed. Notably, while a concerted campaign specifically targeting Federal Art Project art does not appear to have taken place in the postwar, Diego Rivera's famous installation in Rockefeller Center was removed during the thirties and a part of San Francisco's Coit Tower murals was also censored in that decade. In the 1960s some students found offensive the representation of black sharecroppers in a mural in a Brooklyn school. A debate about the mural's removal ensued. Although students voted to keep it in place, the mural was later vandalized. Relatedly, in 2011 Maine's newly elected Republican governor ordered the removal from the state's Department of Labor building of a large mural completed in the 1980s depicting worker activism. Andrew Hemingway, *Artists on the Left: American Artists and the Communist Movement, 1926–1956* (New Haven: Yale University Press, 2002), 169; "Controversy in Context: A Reassessment of James Michael Newell's Evolution of Western Civilization," accessed 14 April 2011, http://newdeal.feri.org/echs/cohen.htm; Steven Greenhouse, "Mural of Maine's Workers Becomes Political Target," *New York Times,* 23 March 2011.

9.   The threat to shift control of Arts Programs to the states had been made repeatedly since 1935. Mangione, *The Dream and the Deal,* 8, 24.

10.   Christine Bold, *The WPA Guides: Mapping America* (Jackson: University Press of Mississippi, 1999). Perhaps the best-received single FWP publication was *These Are Our Lives, As Told by the People* (Chapel Hill: University of North Carolina Press, 1939), a compendium of life histories of blacks and whites from North Carolina and Tennessee. *Time* magazine labeled it the FWP's "strongest claim to literary distinction," and FWP administrator Jerre Mangione had the distinction of having Eleanor

Roosevelt praise it to him in person. Mangione, *The Dream and the Deal*, 12. The life histories FWP workers took of former southern slaves continue to draw scholarly and public attention. Ira Berlin, Marc Favreau, and Steven F. Miller, eds., *Remembering Slavery: African Americans Talk About Their Personal Experiences of Slavery and Freedom* (New York: The New Press, 1998).

11. Mangione, *The Dream and the Deal*, 24, 216. Alfred Kazin, *On Native Grounds* (Garden City, NY: Doubleday, 1942), 393. Quoted in Kennedy, *Freedom from Fear*, 255. Many of the Guides have been republished over the last several decades, with contemporary critics also raving about them.

12. Hirsch, *Portrait of America*, 23. Mangione added, "As more and more books in the American Guide Series rolled off the presses, [FWP Director Henry] Alsberg became increasingly concerned with the task of presenting a more comprehensive portrait of the country than could be suggested by the guidebooks." Mangione, *The Dream and the Deal*, 277, 285. Some FWP regional collections were completed during the period. Other sources like the *Anvil* also published anthologies during the 1930s. Since then a number of scholars, most notably Ann Banks (*First Person America*) and Studs Terkel (*Hard Times*) have edited collections of 1930s writing or developed oral history projects about the era.

13. Emphasis in original. Loren S. Greene to Joseph E. Parker, 3 December 1940, MC 77, box 9, folder 7, Work Projects Administration Records, Montana Historical Society Research Center, Helena, Montana. This folder also contains the six referenced Montana stories. Those stories are archived at Montana State University Library too. United States Work Projects Administration (Mont.) Records, 1935–1942, Collection 2336, Series 10, Box 89, Merrill G. Burlingame Special Collections, Montana State University Library, Bozeman, Montana. I have succeeded in having one of these stories published: Matthew Basso, "Another Look at Burke's Butte: The Great Depression and William Allen Burke's 'Greenhorn Miner,'" *Montana: The Magazine of Western History* (Winter 2006): 16–30.

14. Harold Rosenberg, ed., "Men at Work: Stories of People at Their Jobs in America," folders 1 and 2, box A-852, Writers' Program, Work Projects Administration, 1941, Records of US Work Projects Administration, Library of Congress, Washington, DC. I later found reference to *Men at Work* in Ann Banks's wonderful *First Person America*. Since the late 1990s archives across the nation have placed ever more complete catalogues of their holdings on the internet. One can now, for example, find that the Getty Research Library has a "Men at Work" folder (which also contains a complete copy of the manuscript) in its Harold Rosenberg collection and, of course, that the Library of Congress has a copy of *Men at Work*. The WPA records at the Library of Congress and in Montana indicate several subtitles were being considered for the volume.

15. Hirsch, *Portrait of America*, 222.

16. Hirsch, *Portrait of America*, 219–20, 278n17. Banks, *First Person America*, iv.

17. Douglas Wixson, *Worker Writer in America: Jack Conroy and the Tradition of Midwestern Literary Radicalism, 1898–1990* (Urbana: University of Illinois Press, 1994),

245. On the interest in "folk" culture among intellectuals in the thirties, and its specific ties to *Men at Work*, see Matthew Basso, "Culture at Work: The Federal Writers' Project and Modern Uses of the Pre-modern in Lorin W. Brown's 'Basílico Garduño, New Mexican Sheepherder,'" *New Mexico Historical Review* 77, no. 4 (Fall 2002): 398–427.

18. Edward Reynolds, author of "Anaconda," submitted a biographical statement to Rosenberg. The sketches also do not appear in the copy of *Men at Work* in the Rosenberg papers at the Getty Research Library.

19. Alan Wald traces literary criticism of proletarian literature of the thirties from such seminal works as Walter B. Rideout's *Radical Novel in the United States, 1900–1954* (New York: Columbia University Press, 1956), and Daniel Aaron's *Writers on the Left: Episodes in American Literary Communism* (New York: Columbia University Press, 1961)—both of which established the documentary-style novel as "the most important genre for left-wing writing" and associated it with the political force of the Communist Party—through expansions and augmentations of Rideout and Aaron, such as William Stott's *Documentary Expression and Thirties America* (Chicago: University of Chicago Press, 1973). Wald then considers the more recent "renaissance of critical studies of the 1930s applying the new methodologies that grew out of the 1960s, especially feminist literary theory and a more sophisticated Marxism." In this latter category, Wald cites, among others, Cary Nelson, *Repression and Recovery: Modern American Poetry and the Politics of Cultural Memory, 1910–1945* (Madison: University of Wisconsin Press, 1989) and Paula Rabinowitz, *Labor and Desire: Women's Revolutionary Fiction in Depression America* (Chapel Hill: University of North Carolina Press, 1991). To that list can be added works such as Barbara Foley, *Radical Representations: Politics and Form in U.S. Proletarian Fiction, 1929–1949* (Durham: Duke University Press, 1993); Caren Irr, *The Suburb of Dissent: Cultural Politics in the United States and Canada during the 1930s* (Durham: Duke University Press, 1998); Jeff Allred, *American Modernism and Depression Documentary* (New York: Oxford University Press, 2010). See Alan Wald, "The 1930s Left in U.S. Literature Reconsidered," in Bill V. Mullen and Sherry Linkon, eds., *Radical Revisions: Rereading 1930s Culture* (Urbana: University of Illinois Press, 1996), 19–34. For the quotations in the text, see Wald, 24; Irr, 37; and Rideout, 228.

20. James Murphy in *The Proletarian Moment*, for example, argues convincingly that this received history operates within a limited paradigm which acknowledges neither the inner complexities and shifting viewpoints of those within so-called centrist and leftist positions, nor the broader international framework of some thirties literature. A significant aspect of this overly simplistic conceptualization stems from critics' acceptance of the *Partisan Review's* own revisionist history of the era, offered during that magazine's self-restyling in 1937, which created a straw man entitled Leftism through which it channeled a hostility toward a narrowly defined proletarian literature. James Murphy, *The Proletarian Moment: The Controversy over Leftism in Literature* (Urbana: University of Illinois Press, 1991), 195. Irr also questions the overly hasty division of the radical literary conflict of the early thirties into two poles—one

focused on political content and associated with *The New Masses*, the other focused primarily on aesthetics and "individualist and avant-gardist ideals" and associated with *The Partisan Review*. Irr, *Suburb*, 106.

21. Irr, *Suburb*, 107.

22. Agee famously portrayed the radical desires—and problematics—of thirties documentary method when he wrote, "If I could do it, I'd do no writing at all here. It would be photographs; the rest would be fragments of cloth, bits of cotton, lumps of earth, records of speech, pieces of wood and iron, phials of odors, plates of food and of excrement." He paired this point with a critique that argued virtually all efforts to write about "how the other half lives" were harmful, biased, and even "obscene." James Agee and Walker Evans, *Let Us Now Praise Famous Men: Three Tenant Families* (Boston: Houghton Mifflin, 1941), 7, 13; Lewis W. Hine, *Men at Work* (New York: The Macmillan Company, 1932); Dorothea Lange and Paul S. Taylor, *An American Exodus: A Record of Human Erosion* (New York: Reynal & Hitchcock, 1939); Richard Wright and Edwin Rosskam, *12 Million Black Voices: A Folk History of the Negro in the United States* (New York: Viking, 1941). An array of contemporary scholars have detailed the highly mediated nature of Depression-era documentary projects: Paula Rabinowitz, *They Must be Represented: The Politics of Documentary* (New York: Verso, 1994); Allred, *American Modernism*; Linda Gordon, *Dorothea Lange: A Life beyond Limits* (New York: W. W. Norton, 2009).

23. Michael Denning, *The Cultural Front: The Laboring of American Culture* (New York: Verso, 1998). The University of Illinois Press's Radical Novel Reconsidered Series republished a substantial number of novels in this genre. Among others, see Grace Lumpkin, *To Make My Bread* (Urbana: University of Illinois Press, 1996) and Myra Page, *Moscow Yankee* (Urbana: University of Illinois Press, 1996).

24. For Rosenberg, "The new ideology of art for the community" erred by "cut[ting] the link between painting and sculpture in this country and the advanced art of Europe, which Americans had been engaged in and absorbing in the twenties." Harold Rosenberg, *Art on the Edge: Creators and Situations* (New York: Macmillan, 1975), 199.

25. Harold Rosenberg, *Discovering the Present: Three Decades in Art, Culture, and Politics* (Chicago: University of Chicago Press, 1973), 62. This treatment of the subject was an expanded version of a talk Rosenberg gave at the First World Congress of Craftsmen in 1964. It was published in this form initially in *Partisan Review*, 1965.

26. One significant source for this idea is Caroline Byrd, *The Invisible Scar* (New York: David McKay Company, Inc., 1966). An excellent analysis of gender in work produced by Federal One is Barbara Melosh, *Engendering Culture: Manhood and Womanhood in New Deal Public Art and Theater* (Washington: Smithsonian Institution Press, 1991). On masculinity in the 1930s see Michael Kimmel, *Manhood in America: A Cultural History* (New York: Free Press, 1995) and Matthew Basso, *Meet Joe Copper: Race and Masculinity on Montana's World War II Home Front* (Chicago: University of Chicago Press, forthcoming). For an overview of women's experience during the Great Depression see Susan Ware, *Holding Their Own: American Women in the 1930s* (Boston: Twayne, 1982).

27. Alice Kessler-Harris, *In Pursuit of Equity: Women, Men, and the Quest for Economic Citizenship in 20ᵗʰ-Century America* (New York: Oxford University Press, 2001), 58–62, 64, 76; Elizabeth Faue, *Community of Suffering and Struggle: Women, Men, and the Labor Movement in Minneapolis, 1915–1945* (Chapel Hill: University of North Carolina Pres, 1991); Mary Murphy, *Mining Cultures: Men, Women, and Leisure in Butte, 1914–41* (Urbana: University of Illinois Press, 1997). On labor more generally in the 1930s see Robert Zeiger, *The CIO, 1935–1955* (Chapel Hill: University of North Carolina Press, 1995) and Nelson Lichtenstein, *State of the Union: A Century of American Labor* (Princeton: Princeton University Press, 2003).

28. Hine, *Men at Work*, i.

29. For a fuller reading of the operation of masculinity in "Anaconda" see Matthew Basso, "Context, Subjectivity, and the Built Environment at the Anaconda Reduction Works," *Drumlummon Views* 3, no. 1 (Spring 2009): 125–52.

30. Alice Kessler-Harris, *Out to Work: A History of Wage-Earning Women in the United States* (New York: Oxford University Press, 2003); Julia Kirk Blackwelder, *Now Hiring: The Feminization of Work in the United States, 1900–1995* (College Station: Texas A&M University Press, 1997).

31. For a fascinating adjunct to this see Kessler-Harris, *In Pursuit of Equity*, 51–52. On women in the canning industry during this period, see Vicki Ruiz, *Cannery Women, Cannery Lives: Mexican Women, Unionization, and the California Food Processing Industry, 1930–1950* (University of New Mexico Press, 1987); Kevin Starr, *Endangered Dreams: The Great Depression in California* (New York: Oxford University Press, 1997).

32. James M. Gregory, *The Southern Diaspora: How the Great Migrations of Black and White Southerners Transformed America* (Chapel Hill: University of North Carolina Press, 2005); Harvard Sitkoff, *A New Deal for Blacks: The Emergence of Civil Rights as a National Issue: The Depression Decade* (New York: Oxford University Press, 2008); Lizabeth Cohen, *Making a New Deal: Industrial Workers in Chicago, 1919–1939* (New York: Cambridge University Press, 1990); W. Fitzhugh Brundage, *Lynching in the New South: Georgia and Virginia, 1880–1930* (Urbana: University of Illinois, 1993); Amy Louise Wood, *Lynching and Spectacle: Witnessing Racial Violence in America, 1890–1940* (Chapel Hill: University of North Carolina Press, 2009); Robert S. McElvaine, *The Great Depression: America, 1929–1941* (New York: Times Books, 1993), 187.

33. Camille Guerin-Gonzales, *Mexican Workers and American Dreams: Immigration, Repatriation, and California Farm Labor, 1900–1939* (Piscataway, NJ: Rutgers University Press, 1994); Devra Weber, *Dark Sweat, White Gold: California Farm Workers, Cotton, and the New Deal* (Berkeley: University of California Press, 1996); Dorothy B. Fujita Rony, *American Workers, Colonial Power: Philippine Seattle and the Transpacific West, 1919–1941* (Berkeley: University of California Press, 2002); Erika Lee, *At America's Gates: Chinese Immigration during the Exclusion Era, 1882–1943* (Chapel Hill: University of North Carolina Press, 2003); Josephine Fowler, *Japanese and Chinese Immigrant Activists: Organizing in American and International Communist Movements, 1919–1933* (Piscataway, NJ: Rutgers University Press, 2007);

Robin D. G. Kelley, *Hammer and Hoe: Alabama Communists during the Great Depression* (Chapel Hill: University of North Carolina Press, 1990); James Goodman, *Stories of Scottsboro* (New York: Vintage Books, 1995); Graham D. Taylor, *The New Deal and American Indian Tribalism: The Administration of the Indian Reorganization Act, 1934–45* (Lincoln: University Of Nebraska Press, 1980); Alexandra Harmon, *Indians in the Making: Ethnic Relations and Indian Identities around Puget Sound* (Berkeley: University of California Press, 2000); Colleen O'Neill, *Working the Navajo Way: Labor and Culture in the Twentieth Century* (Lawrence: University Press of Kansas, 2005); William J. Bauer, *We Were All Like Migrant Workers Here: Work, Community, and Memory on California's Round Valley Reservation, 1850–1941* (Chapel Hill: University of North Carolina Press, 2009); Jennifer McLerran, *A New Deal for Native Art: Indian Arts and Federal Policy, 1933–1943* (Tucson: University of Arizona Press, 2009).

34. Bruce Nelson, *Workers on the Waterfront: Seamen, Longshoremen, and Unionism in the 1930s* (Urbana: University of Illinois Press, 1990); Gilbert G. González, *Culture of Empire: American Writers, Mexico, and Mexican Immigrants, 1880–1930* (Austin: University of Texas Press, 2004).

35. Delgado tells readers that his fruit picking and packing protagonists make their temporary home in the orchard's "white" camp. "The 'white camp,'" the narrator tells us "is the melting pot of all Caucasian nationalities, Spanish like ourselves, Portuguese, Germans, Americans—peoples of all nations who annually descend upon California's vast orchards and leave behind them stripped, bare trees." Implicitly "white camp" is defined just as strongly by what it is not: "Japanese camp" or "Hindu camp," the home to the rest of the fruit packers and pickers who work the Blake Ranch. On whiteness and first- and second-generation European immigrants in the 1930s see Matthew Frye Jacobson, *Whiteness of a Different Color: European Immigrants and the Alchemy of Race* (Cambridge: Harvard University Press, 1998); David R. Roediger, *Working toward Whiteness: How America's Immigrants Became White: The Strange Journey from Ellis Island to the Suburbs* (New York: Basic Books, 2005); Ira Katznelson, *When Affirmative Action Was White* (New York: W. W. Norton & Company, 2005); Basso, *Meet Joe Copper*.

36. The subject of how work affects our lives has been of deep interest to scholars and the public. Two exemplary studies are Studs Terkel, *Working: People Talk About What They Do All Day and How They Feel About It* (New York: The New Press, 1997) and Matthew Crawford, *Shop Class as Soulcraft: An Inquiry into the Value of Work* (New York: Penguin, 2010).

ORIGINAL PREFACE

Harold Rosenberg

Methods of labor sometimes remain static for centuries, are sometimes completely revolutionized by the introduction of a single machine. One great source of America's social and cultural variety is that, by the side of the most advanced techniques of the twentieth century, men still work in ways that have descended from the beginnings of human history. The story of Basílico Garduño, New Mexican sheepherder, included in this book, presents an idyllic picture reminiscent of the Bible, old Italy, the slopes of the Alps. "My father and I both worked for Don Mariano, who first owned these springs. He was *muy rico*, a man of many sheep and much land. . . ." Today, a tourist hotel or "dude ranch" or the depot of a transcontinental air line has perhaps alighted not far from Don Mariano's meadows. Yet the *pastor*, and the manner of living built upon his labor, belong as fully to contemporary America, in both its inner and outer aspects, as the golf instructor or the transport pilot.

Jobs as individual as Basílico's exist within the complex routines of modern industry, and the growth of professional and managerial services, and of such institutions as the radio, movies, and experimental laboratory, has even increased them. For the bulk of occupations in the United States, however, the trend is away from the skillful self-sufficiency of the shepherd or the artisan. "The National Research Project studies have shown," testified Corrington Gill, Assistant Commissioner of the WPA, at a hearing of the Temporary National Economic Committee, "that the jobs of factory production workers are steadily becoming more simplified, as machinery is made more automatic and specialized, and as production methods are otherwise improved by management."

Some hint of what this historic trend toward simplification and automatism means, in terms of the daily experience of millions, may be gathered by glancing among the 17,452 job descriptions contained in the *Dictionary of Occupational*

1

Titles, issued by the U.S. Department of Labor in 1939. In an important percentage of these, some small portion of the human organism moves in tight fidelity to the place and turnings of a machine, whose process it helps complete. To quote one job description at random: "KEY-CRIMPING-MACHINE OPERATOR. Attaches can-opening keys to metal containers of preserved foods by means of an automatic or pedal operated key-crimping machine: feeds cans one at a time into machine; presses pedal to actuate crimping mechanism; removes cans with keys attached; loads key magazine at regular intervals."

The brief abstracts in the *Occupational Dictionary* are very suggestive, as if a man sent home a telegram to say what he was doing. But to visualize the creative life to America, more is needed than telegrams. Jobs take in the landscape surrounding them, and odors, tempos, climates, costumes. They take in the worker's delight in touching things and changing them handily.

They take in, too, the special kind of suffering and crippling that comes from toil that is tiresome and infinitely repetitious, and in which the instinct of workmanship is reduced to beggary. A man's work, say the philosophers, is the means by which he stamps his image on nature, and also gives form to his own character. So that the manner of his daily doing is an influence interacting deeply with the future of society and with political ideas and social theories.

Statistical tables, vocational surveys, and sketches telling about training, wages, chances of promotion, cannot convey the immediate living quality, the human "tone," of the individual at work. This can find full expression only in the arts, which concern themselves with such values as the skill used in the task, its tensions, color, and formal and dramatic appeal.

Literature and painting, however, are not rich in descriptions of modern work. Passages crop up in a few great novels and poems, but these usually introduce the labor process as an incident in some moral or social argument, or as a detail in the landscape, rarely for itself, as human action worth looking at, like a battle or a love scene. In the United States some very good stories and chapters of novels have been based on work, especially on the more romantic occupations, like logging, work at sea (*Moby Dick* is unique in its devoted recording of materials and labor processes), river navigating, railroading. Something approaching a "work tradition" might even be said to exist in American Literature, with such writings as Upton Sinclair's *The Jungle* and Frank Norris' *The Octopus*. Of late, the so-called regional novels and paintings have sometimes studied local ways of producing a living, and there have been occasional descriptive pieces in *Fortune, Harper's, The New Yorker*, and other magazines. The only collections of American work literature we have been able to find, however, are a school reader and a slim volume of essays, both compiled more than twenty years ago.

Recent native literature seems interested rather in non-industrial phases of American development, in the plantation, the pioneer, Revolutionary and Civil War society, the small farmer, New England gentlefolk. Even writers who deal with contemporary social problems often ignore the basic relation a man's work bears to his being as a whole. Concentrating on the *conditions* surrounding his labor and his emotional life, they commonly neglect his acts in making things. "Social" novels of the past few years have shown the worker's home life, his food, his clothing, his struggle to meet his needs, his organizations, and his friends, but rarely the productive, and hence powerful and dynamic, core of his existence.

One reason, of course, that actual work has frequently played so small a part in those writings most zealously dedicated to the modern workingman is that the operations performed in the factory appear to be so minute and trivial as to offer very little to the writer. The labor activity can be described in a few sentences, and the same task is performed day after day until broken off by unemployment. To the extent that the action has lost its personality, it ceases to have meaning for the onlooker. The writer turns aside from the monotony of his subject's labor, thus rendering a negative verdict on his creative life.

Literature has not yet perfected its techniques for dealing with the new men and women who each day stand emptily alert for hours within a rigid construction through which incomplete and changing objects keep streaming. The greatest artistic presentation of these strange people and their strange setting has been Charlie Chaplin's movie *Modern Times*. Here the logic of the belt line led to a memorable sequence of farcical scenes—the apparition of the foreman on a television screen in the lavatory, the lunch machine, the final derangement of the worker, the department-store dream of luxury. Effects resembling those of *Modern Times* had been achieved earlier in some Expressionist dramas composed abroad, but Chaplin's masterpiece is superior to anything done in words.

Apart from the literary difficulties of dramatizing modern men at work, there is a more circumstantial reason why writers have done little with the inner rhythms and tensions of industry. Authors have not had much personal intimacy with physical labor. In the main, they have belonged to aristocratic or commercial milieus, and they have been familiar chiefly with the behavior patterns of these groups. Working people, when they have been seen at all, have been seen from a height, for they themselves have never developed a literature of their own experiences and image of the world. Even a writer like Zola, despite his conscientious delineations, has been much criticized as a superficial reporter who paid flying visits to the scene for the purpose of gathering material, but did not stay long enough to learn labor from the inside.

This collection represents a first effort on the part of a group of writers, each working separately, to make literature out of the human activity in the field, factories, ships, and mines in the United States. All the authors in this volume are members of the WPA Writers' Projects in various states, and most of them have had first-hand familiarity with the jobs about which they are writing, or with different jobs in the same locality. They are writers who know disciplines other than those of literary composition.

We have made no attempt to conduct experiments with new literary techniques, since this requires a great expenditure of time and opportunities for consultation not available in the present organization of the WPA Writers' Program. Our proposal to the projects declared that each author might "use any approach he finds suitable to the material." He was urged to observe carefully, interview workers, and "in his writing to give full play to his sense of the sounds, textures, physical sensations, and mental attitudes accompanying the doing." Family backgrounds or social conditions were to be shown only in so far as they were reflected in the image of the man at his work. The one point that was underlined was that the author "must have seen the work done, or perhaps have done it himself."

Though the contributions differ as to literary value, all are, we feel, of great interest as authentic pictures of people at their jobs in America. Human skill is the dominant note, skill that burgeons at times into the unique and complex performance of the fine artist—as in Leonard Rapport's great vocalist of the tobacco belt: "'Twenty. Twenty dollars, gentlemen, for this good lemon leaf; dandy tobacco, gentlemen, dandy tobacco.' You slap your hands together like a pistol shot, a trick picked up years ago to keep the sale alive. 'Twenty dollah bid twenny wenny wenny wenny' up the line, back down, catch Jones' eye inquiringly, he was buying this type yesterday, Jones shakes his head a fraction of an inch, still no bid, so drop it down to nineteen and a half, no bid, nineteen, no bid, eighteen and a half, eighteen, seventeen and a half, you flash a look at the pile and see it's good tobacco but poorly graded, seventeen and Al nudges you and the house takes it at seventeen." This centuries-old trade of auctioning tobacco breathes its aroma into the society that enfolds it, and keeps alive the memory of its masters: Bodenheim with "his splendid tenor"; Crenshaw "coming down the floor sounding like a brass band"; Colonel Langhorne "whose girl, Nancy, became Lady Astor; Herbert Baker, greatest of them all." And "even as you remember you've sold another pile of smoking leaf, Carroll and Mallory carrying the bids and Mallory taking it at nineteen."

The genial personality of the tobacco auctioneer is molded by his craft, which combines something of the singer, the actor, the showman, the prestidigitator, and even the country preacher—people whose skills, like those of the salesman and others belonging to the distribution side of the American economy, are directed upon the human mind rather than toward the production of physical things. The different formative influences of productive jobs are apparent in such stories as Charles Oluf Olsen's "Logging in the Rain," Francis Donovan's "Discontinued Model," and, in an amusing way, among Grace Winkleman's temperamental and humanly sagacious mining mules of Utah.

As Miss Winkleman notes with nostalgia, personal relations are destined to play a smaller part in the work she is describing; and in "Fruit Packers," by John Delgado, and "Cannery Row," by Gail Hazard, both skill and human exchange have all but vanished from the labor process. The fruit packer and the fish canner attend belts carrying food towards containers, jobs physically and nervously exhausting, and which enslave the attention of the worker without engaging his mind. Yet even here the eyes and sensibility of the creative writer distinguish significant variations not visible in the mere vocational outline. "Fruit Packers" retains the pastoral atmosphere of the California orchard, while "Cannery Row" is in a much harsher and darker mood. Allowing for contrasts of temperament in the writers, this difference has much to do with the physical setting of the work itself, which affects the attitude of the workers. In the first story, the texture and odor of the green pears, the somnolence of the fields surrounding the open-air shed, the lightly clothed girls along the belt, though they do not eliminate the torment of the "invention of seventeen devils," diffuse noticeably its pressure on the spirit. While the foulness of the fish-canning plant, the screaming and rattle of metal, the contamination of hands, clothing, hair, join to aggravate the nagging bleat of the checker: "Watch the heads, boys! Watch the guts!"

In his story "Anaconda," Edward Reynolds of Montana makes a notably successful attempt to deal with work in an enormous industrial plant. The author realized the difficulty of his undertaking. In a "sketch autobiography" sent to the National Office of the Writers' Program, he wrote: "It's hard for anyone to comprehend the hugeness of the Anaconda Reduction Works. It's hard for anyone who has spent a lifetime working in only one or two of its many departments. It's almost impossible for one who has never seen it. You can tell people it's the largest non-ferrous smelter in the world. You can tell people that all the ore from the Butte mines—the richest hill on earth—passes through it. But it doesn't mean anything. It's too big.

"It would take a book to tell of the Micks and Slavs and Swedes and Russians; the Cousin Jacks, the Polacks, the Italians, the Germans—all the many nationalities to be found there. It would take a book to tell of the varied occupations, as many in number as the works is huge. Electricians, pipefitters, lead burners, bricklayers, iron workers, smeltermen, millmen, rope men, ditch diggers and many more. It's known for the vast amount of copper it produces, but this is just a part of it. There are zinc, lead, gold, silver, sulphuric acid, arsenic, phosphate, and other byproducts."

A literary device helps Mr. Reynolds compress the scene into a few pages. Pausing on the "high line where they dump the great cars of copper ore from the Butte mines," he visualizes the flow of processes through the various structures. "The great buildings seemed to flow down the mountainside, wrapping themselves around rocky ledges with snakelike purpose. They were built to utilize gravity." In some respects the story reminds us of the famous tale "The Gentleman From San Francisco" by Ivan Bunin, Nobel Prize winner, in which, as from a godlike eminence, the eye of the author followed the routine of a millionaire's vacation.

One or two of the project writers resorted to symbolism in an effort to show the worker as a harmoniously moving wheel of a vast mechanism. As they saw it, a process of creation was in play—e.g., in a bottling plant—of which the factory hand was but a partly conscious agent, but whose workings filled his life with meanings superior to his mere actions as an individual. Unfortunately, these stories failed to come off, and could not be included here. Their approach, however, bears an interesting resemblance to that of certain Italian Futurists, whose striking formulas concerning the "metalization of man," and violent enthusiasm for the beauty of artillery and aerial bombardment, were a direct affirmation of the crushing of the human by the modern division of labor.

Such extremes of thought and sensibility are not customary among American writers, perhaps because industrialization descended here more gradually than elsewhere and with less shock, and found fewer old social forms to splinter. The majority of contributors to *Men at Work* preferred to tell about jobs which, while more important in American production than those of the artisan or handicraftsman, still did not baffle the writer with their lack of human content. Thus they turned to what might be called "transitional" industries, those not yet thoroughly mechanized, like mining, fishing, lumbering. Or they picked jobs which still linger on in smaller plants, though they have been pushed out elsewhere by new methods. As a result the present collection has the added value of being a preserver of

American work memories and a record of fast-disappearing folkways. Scattered through the book, too, are several occupational tall tales, selected from a group gathered on projects by Dr. B. A. Botkin; these are especially rich in recollections of old work methods and colorful indigenous types.

In choosing the prints for this volume from the WPA Art Program's collection, we were struck by the similarity of interest of the artists and writers. Jobs involving the exercise of individual skill, as in fishing, mining, construction, predominated as subjects. As for factories, only a few artists found them suggestive, usually for their abstract force in design and their mystifying shapes. Like the writers, most artists seemed to pronounce negative judgment on labor in which the human action plays a dependent part. In the pictures of large industrial plants there were rarely seen any *men working*, and when human figures did appear, they were too small to be reproduced.

TIMES HAVE CHANGED

DRIFT MINER

Jack Conroy (Illinois)

There had been a time when most of the drift mines[1] in Happy Hollow[2] had been considered pretty fair places to work—almost as good as the shafts. Even after I was a husky lad, some thick veins were left, and not too much clay and sulphur to dirty up the coal.

But as time went on and coal became more scarce, a man who had to go down into the hollow to work was considered unlucky, indeed. The hills were honeycombed with old diggings, and since all of them had been burrowed out in the most haphazard fashion, you could never tell when you'd blast or dig through into old works. The best that could happen to you in that event would be that you'd have to retreat and do much of your work over, but you might be overcome by the deadly "black damp"[3] gas that accumulates in abandoned mines before you could make it to the fresh air pouring in from outside. The veins of coal in the hills lie close to the surface, and consequently are very irregular in height and extent, corresponding to the contours of the earth.

The hollow miners never possessed equipment for preliminary test drilling. The prospector would select a hillside where he judged by the terrain and other natural phenomena that there should be a vein of coal. Then he'd strip the trees, brush and dirt from a space at the foot of the hill and begin to burrow a horizontal passage toward the coal believed to be reposing within. The black leaf humus from innumerable autumns was easy going, and the tenacious white or yellow clay beneath would yield to a tilling spade unless too many rocks were commingled with it. Limestone could be managed with dynamite or crowbar, but dynamite cost money, and using a crowbar or wedges to pry strata of limestone apart consumed a great deal of time.

Before I knew anything about the backache from stooping and the headache from powder fumes and stale air and the raw and smarting knees from kneeling on lumps of rock and coal, I thought that the opening of a new drift mine must be a romantic experience, like digging for buried gold. If the coal turned out to be thick, black, and fat, the miner would be rewarded by a season of moderate prosperity without too much backbreaking work. In the beginning the coal could be pushed quickly in a low car the small distance from face to mouth.

We boys, when early frost had ripened the pawpaws and persimmons growing in abundance in the Happy Hollow bottoms, liked to explore the various branches of the hollow for new diggings. Often we were guided by re-echoing shouts or the ring of axes, picks, or sledgehammers. Sometimes, if the face of the coal were near enough and the miners friendly, we'd creep back into the cave and perhaps wield a pick for a while as the coal diggers, grateful for a breathing spell, looked on with tolerant amusement at our awkwardness and with renewed pride in their own strength and deftness. Blisters acquired in this fashion were borne as a badge of honor and a symbol of honest toil.

Everybody, including the grownups, speculated about the use of the extensive, unmapped network of hollow mines as a hideout for fugitives from the law. That these slopes often accommodated illicit liquor stills was well known to everyone except officers of the law, who officially ignored the situation. Jesse James, Bill Anderson, and other celebrated guerillas had at one time or other infested the neighborhood; and, though the hills encircling Happy Hollow were undespoiled by pick and blasting powder until long after "the dirty little coward that shot Mr. Howard had laid poor Jesse in his grave," a legend cherished by many had it that the James boys, hotly pursued by Federal troopers, had secreted themselves in an abandoned mine and left there some of their bank-robbing loot.

Many of the Happy Hollow miners took their sons to work with them when the boys were twelve or even less. For a long time there had been laws prohibiting boys under sixteen from working in the mines, but it had always been considered a parental right for a coal digger to take his own son into the mines with him, even in the shafts where the state mine inspectors exercise some sort of jurisdiction. Most of the time the mine inspectors left the Hollow mines alone, so that safety restrictions covering air, proper timbering, and other things were totally ignored. The Hollow roads were inaccessible to automobiles in bad weather, and difficult even in summer when drought had dried the creek beds.

I'll never forget my first trip to the mine my father had opened up on one of the last productive hillsides in Happy Hollow. The slopes were heaped with "dirt dumps" of soapstone and burning or burnt-out slag. Some of the mines have been known to live for a decade or more, eating away relentlessly at veins too sparse or too sulphur-streaked for profitable digging. Blasts of smoke and sulphurous fumes belched forth from the mouths of the burning mines, as well as from dozens of crevices throughout the hills.

I discovered that the apprentice miner soon loses whatever fear he may have had, and learns to enjoy the warmth in winter and coolness in summer and the comparative silence of the underground. Mines are full of noises of their own, however. The air rushing in its circuit from mouth to air shaft has a queer, hollow hum; the roof settles down on the stout oaken props supporting it and often they crack loudly, giving a beginner the impression they are about to break. An old timer can tell by the way the roof sounds to the blow of a pick whether there is any immediate danger of a rock fall.

The day passes quickly, too, if you don't have a watch to look at now and then. Few miners have. It's too easy to smash it, kneeling, doubling, wielding a pick, shaking a riddle, hugging a prop, or pushing against a car. Watches cost money, too, and very few Hollow miners have much of it to throw at the birds. There is no sensing of the sun and its transit; time flows along through an even, unchanging blackness.

Of course, the mine monotony palls at first upon the lad who has run untrammelled through the hills, but the oldsters, remembering their own atrophied childhoods, are lenient and don't require too much work until the wild youngster is pit-broken and docile to the turnmill of his days. A boy of ten or less can pick up chunks and throw them in a car being loaded, and he can fetch prop caps or the water deck when his old man is putting in a narrow cutting or using the riddle.

One of the things I liked from the first was making powder cartridges for father. You take any kind of round object of the right circumference, preferably a brass pipe, and fashion a tube of newspapers around it, crimping one end. You keep the pipe well doped with soft yellow laundry soap so that the finished cartridge will slip off easily. One or two cartridges are filled with powder, and these, with a long slow-burning fuse attached, are pushed with a pole or rod to the end of a hole drilled several feet back into the coal. More cartridges filled with drill dust are tamped securely against the powder. If they aren't tamped securely, there's a "windy" shot—one that just blows out of the hole without blasting down any coal. Some of the worst bawlings out I ever had from my old man were when I hadn't laid on the tamping rod heavily enough. It means, naturally, that there's no coal to be loaded the next morning, and if the miner gets any carloads he has to pick them off the face by hand.

One of my first jobs was to shake the riddle, since I was big for my age. The riddle is a coarse sieve through which the finer coal is sifted, the fine stuff falling to the ground to be shoveled later into a separate car. This fine coal is sold as "slack" at a lower price than the coarser lumps, which the man holding the sieve must toss into an adjacent car with a deft movement of his wrists. The riddle man usually sits cross-legged, holding the riddle before him, and for the greenhorn it's an extra tiring job having to sit there and feel the shock of each shovel of coal thrown into it. At first the shock tingles up from your hands to your shoulders like an electric charge, and afterwards your arms get numb for a while until a dull ache spreads all through your arms and back. Some riddlers prefer to kneel, but this is tough on your knees. You can wear canvas knee pads, of course, but they're heavy to pack around and a lump of coal can find a tender spot right through the thickest ones, anyhow.

Mules or donkeys usually haul out the small cars used, and a mule driver has to be a bold and tough man. Mine mules get plenty rambunctious, and may kick the daylights out of you if you don't watch them. When you pass one in an entry, it's best to squeeze tightly against his hindparts so he can't lift his back legs at you.

There aren't many drift miners left now. Strip mines, using huge steam shovels, tear up the whole countryside. And in the shafts too deep for stripping, they use a mining machine run by electricity. Nowadays some of the mines are so spick and span you can almost wear white gloves to work. When I started in, a man had to walk maybe ten miles with his pit clothes on and with the coal dust still all over him. We washed in wooden tubs at home, and now some mines have shower baths and everything. But they're full of machines with few miners tending them. Only trouble is that a machine can pick coal faster than a man and when it ain't working it don't have to eat.

Notes

1. A horizontal tunneling approach (which differed from "shaft" and "slope" methods) to excavating coal veins that were visible on the side of a hill. Eric Arnesen, ed., *Encyclopedia of U.S. Labor and Working-Class History*, 3 vols. (New York: Routledge, 2007), 901.

2. Conroy published a short story, "Down in Happy Hollow" which addresses some of the same subject matter as that found in "Drift Miner." The story appeared in the March-April, 1935 edition of the *Anvil*, a proletarian periodical that Conroy edited. Though fiction, the narrative bears some rough similarities to this vignette. A more readily accessible reprint of the story can also be found in Jack Salzman and David Ray, eds., *The Jack Conroy Reader* (New York: Burt Franklin, 1979), 100–108; 291.

3. A term miners used for toxic levels of carbon dioxide in the air, just one of the many names for airborne toxins in mine work environments. "Choke damp," "white damp," "silicosis," and "miner's lung" were other terms for health hazards coal miners faced

as a result of the dust and chemical byproducts generated by the mining process. The presence of noxious gases and poisonous particulates resulted in a number of chronic illnesses for miners, a fact which mine owners were not eager to admit (Arnesen, *Encyclopedia*, 902). For an extensive treatment of the history of mine-related health complications and the ensuing conflicts between workers and their employers see Barbara Ellen Smith, *Digging Our Own Graves: Coal Miners and the Struggle over Black Lung Disease* (Philadelphia: Temple University Press, 1987).

LOGGING IN THE RAIN

Charles Oluf Olsen (Oregon)

The logging camp lies in a hollow of the hills—a handful of board buildings in a green Northwest wilderness. A logging railroad cuts it in two. On each side of the track are bunk-shacks. A plank-walk pitted and splintered from shoe-caulks fronts them, flanked by rude benches with tin wash-basins.

A commissary building, first-aid shack and a cookhouse head one string of bunkhouses; the other tails out with a toolhouse, black-smith shop, filing shed and, a little to one side, a bathhouse and toilet. Down the track is a pigpen.

Stumps of giant firs surround the camp, brush between them. Back of the camp are forested slopes. In the distance loom the Cascade Mountains, tree-clad, capped with snow.

It is dawn and the November rain is slashing all outdoors. From the cook-house comes the clink of pans and crockery. Breakfast is over and dishes are being washed. The crew hug the stoves and the camp looks deserted.

In the commissary Old Man Tyler, "bull o' the woods," or boss of the camp, looks through the window. The wind blows the rain across the panes. Behind him is a glowing stove, to one side a counter with overalls, gloves and tobacco, at one end of the counter a young timekeeper poring over a ledger. The floor is pitted from caulked shoes, littered with logging gear. In one corner of the room lean ax and peavey handles, in another a blood-spotted stretcher.

The grizzled boss opens the door a crack, and wind and rain fill the place.

"Whew," says the timekeeper. "No day for logging! Guess it'll be 'Turkey in the Straw'."[1]

Tyler grunts, steps outside and closes the door behind him. Massive, square-jawed, tight-lipped, he stands a moment considering the weather. He flips a glance at the Shay-geared[2] locomotive with the "mulligan van" behind it, waiting to take the crew to the woods.

Buttoning his slicker jacket he crosses the streaming railroad track, pushes open the door of the first bunk-shack, and rumbles: "All out!" He continues down the walk, crosses back to the other string of bunk-houses, pushes open doors and repeats his "All out!" The whiffs of air that meet him are thick with the smell of drying woolens, tobacco smoke and shoe-oil; from inside the doors comes the stir of feet, grumblings and the slam of stove doors. He hears snatches of lusty-voiced comment: "Old ginger-face got a gall turnin' us out on a day like this!" "I guess it's 'roll out' or 'roll your blankets for town'." "Come on, you goddam sunshine loggers!"

Tyler grins inwardly and climbs the steps to the cab of the waiting Shay, takes a seat on the fireman's side and nods briefly to the gray-haired engineer opposite. The logging crew pours from bunkhouses, a hard-bitten, husky lot in the habiliments of the big timber: paraffined "tin" pants, stagged below the knees for the sake of safety in the brush; paraffined hats, short black slicker jackets, woolen socks and high-top woods shoes, studded with rows of sharp-pointed steel caulks for the sake of footing.

Some of the crew make for the mulligan van, a box-car with stove and seats, and in the dry comfort roll cigarettes or stuff Copenhagen snoos inside their lower lips. Others sprint for the filing shack, the oil shed, or the blacksmith shop and return with long, limber, shining saws, with gallon tins slopping lubricant, or with axes, wedges, and bits of logging gear, which they stow under benches, amid badinage, guffaws, and sallies of salty wit, their slickers glistening and hat-brims dripping rain.

Tyler glances from the window of the cab, notes the last logger's scramble aboard, and nods to the engineer to go ahead. The Shay's whistle shrieks. The quadruple machinery of the locomotive turns with a volley of exhausts and the Shay clanks over the switch, onto the main line, and towards the loading landing in the green timber.

The country lies dim and indistinct. Night still loiters here and there, under gloomy hemlocks, in clefts and hollows, at the bottom of brushy water-courses. Dawn, dark and brawling, stalks the hills. The railroad right-of-way turns and twists through narrow cuts, over high trestles, along shelves carved from rocky slopes, always climbing. Tyler keeps a sharp lookout. The wind may have thrown a tree across the track. He shudders at a certain memory and glances at the engineer. The silent keeper of everybody's safety sits like a statue, hand on throttle, eyes piercing the murk. He is a veteran of a hundred steep logging roads, rock-staunch to danger.

The locomotive approaches a maze of towering masts and steel cables: the loading landing. Men drop from the mulligan van, singly or in pairs, dive into the dripping jungle. Sure-footed and swift, they pick their way over the jumble of felled trees and saw-logs toward their work. Their shoe-soles flash as the light catches the polished steel caulks.

The loading landing is a sea of mire—a yellow-brown stew of muck, bark, and splinters. The landing skids are submerged. Mud cakes the drums of the donkey-engine[3] sitting off to one side. Cables, logging-rigging, everything, are sticky and plastered.

The Shay stops. The remainder of the crew reclaim their work-gear and vanish into the woods. Tyler stands in the gangway of the Shay, silent, noticing everything. The hooktender or boss of the donkey-crew has a last word with him about some work detail, then splashes after his riggingmen along a rough, miry ditch made by logs hauled in. All stumble and labor through snarls of vine-maple and devil-clubs, over all sorts of debris and uptorn young-growth.

It is daylight now and Tyler nods to himself. The horizon shows a streak of clearing sky. He has used good judgment in rousing the crew out to work. He stares beyond the landing to where the country rises. The top of the slope is draped in mist, but halfway up, tree-fallers are already starting work. A brown wall of clean, straight tree trunks marks their methodical advance. The wall looks like the edge of a gigantic wheat field around which a reaper has cut a swath. At the foot of the brown wall lies downed timber. A close-up would shock an eye unfamiliar with it. Inexpressibly still, vanquished, stripped of dignity and grace, the trees sprawl, limbs driven into the ground, broken off, splintered, reaching helpless stumps in grotesque appeal. Over them hangs the smell of wasting sap and pitch; from every bough water drips and trickles with a melancholy sound.

Tyler sees none of these things. He is accustomed to this devastation. Trees to him are only so much lumber to be logged at a profit and to enable men to build homes, barns, bridges, and wharves.

The pop-valve of the donkey-engine lets go with a roar. Tyler shifts his gaze. The donkey engineer tugs at the throttle and gears begin to revolve. The "chaser" beneath the lofty logging-mast sends him a "highball" signal, and the donkey-drums spin. The main log-hauling line—a crucible-steel cable as thick as a man's wrist—unwinds its mud-caked length, slides snakily two hundred feet in the air to the huge "lead-block" and away to the woods. A sling, called a "choker," thirty feet of massive steel rope with an eye in one end and a hook in the other, dangles from the main-line bight. As it sails through the air it lashes out with its steel tail. A young fir, a foot through, is in its path. A loop of the steel choker wraps it, tightens, hesitates, then uproots it and flings it aside as if it were a toothpick.

The main line glides on, stops at a "Hi!" from the hooktender, conveyed by the "whistle-punk"[4] from the woods to the donkey, by way of the whistle-wire.

Out in the timber the husky riggers throw themselves on the arriving choker, wrestle with its devilish kinks, curse nonchalantly, and by main strength put the "necktie" around a log six feet in diameter and forty feet long. The hooktender again yells "Hi!" and all scramble for safety. The whistle-punk jerks at his wire. The donkey on the landing jumps alive. The six-foot log moves on in.

At the landing the chaser and the un-hook man await it. In a jiffy they fall on it. Gloved hands fumble, arms fly, shoulders wrench. The log is unhooked, the men plastered with mud. They pant, stand up, fling mud from hands and arms. Again the chaser gives the donkey engineer his highball signal and the mainline with its choker goes back to the woods.

Tyler, still in the gangway of the Shay, looks approvingly on, then glances aloft, his sharp eyes noting every detail of rigging. He has seen lead-blocks come hurtling down, killing and maiming, burying themselves in the landing. It is hard for a layman to realize that this block swinging so lightly from its sling, weighs a ton. That its sheave is three feet across, and that its shell holds lubricating reservoirs of five-gallon capacity. It does not appear large. Nor do the guy-wires steadying the logging-mast top, or the buckling-stays at its middle, though they are two-inch cables. The overhead loading lines seem no thicker than telephone wires; the colossal mast itself is dwarfed. The huge proportions of the country throw all comparisons out of gear.

The loading crew busy themselves with the big stick just hauled in. Loading tongs, weighing two hundred pounds, move into the air, hang suspended by their loops, are lowered and hooked into the log. The loading engineer knows all the tricks. The log rises to a level with the loaders' eyes, moves on to the steel bunks of the logging trucks, slips down into place without fuss. But the head loader is not satisfied with its position. He gives the engineer an impatient signal. The great log moves back to the landing, swinging gently to and fro. Suddenly one of the pairs of tongs lets go. The log drops within inches of the head loader's feet. The man stands his ground, though he goes a shade pale, and he lets out a string of curses in savage monotone, wipes his splattered face with his gloves and spits copiously. The loading engineer grins. Tyler's face is non-committal. The head loader signals viciously, the tongs are lowered, the massive stick is again lifted and this time laid to suit.

Tyler climbs from the Shay, turns his back on the landing, and walks up to a new piece of railroad under construction. The wind has died. The rain is now a drizzle. He passes men laying ties and steel, comes to the "chunking-out" crew, clearing right-of-way. At the end of the grade is the chunking-out donkey. Below is a gulch and at the opposite side of it the hooktender and two choker-setters are at work. They have just finished putting a choker over a slippery, leaning stump, and a "slow" signal has been given for the donkey engineer to "jerk it out." The choker tightens, the hauling-cable stands like a taut string across the canyon. Of a sudden the choker slips and with a flip leaves the stump and lands on a slack hauling line in the mud of the gulch.

The hooktender, red-haired, burly, signals the engineer to "skin" 'er back again!" As the choker returns to the stump, flopping from the pull, he gives a stop-signal with such a savage downward chop of his arms that it seems like a malediction. He and his two chokermen seize on the mud-smeared loops of the choker and by sheer awkward strength propel them back up the slope, crawling on elbows and knees, indescribably muddy, digging in toes for foot-holds, swearing and panting. The choker is slammed back in place with more profanity and another "slow" pull-signal is given.

Tyler discreetly veers off and strikes across virgin timber. On a knoll he comes on a gigantic tree, trimmed of branches for three-fourths of its tremendous height to make a future logging mast.

The denuded tree trunk, beautifully tapering, rises majestically from its massive pedestal of roots, a flawless fluted brown pillar, supporting a canopy of misting clouds.

Just below the remaining branches of the fir clings a man in stout leather harness. His long spurs are sunk deep into the rough fir bark; his feet are wide apart. He leans back on a life-belt encircling himself and the tree, and saws with a lazy, rhythmic "swish-swish". The sound descends to Tyler, dulled by the noise of whispering water. It ceases, while the high-climber changes position and calls loudly: "Timber! TIMBER!"

The sawing commences again. The top begins to lean. It is a hundred feet tall, tons-heavy. The high-climber pulls his saw from the cut, lets it drop to the end of the cord suspended from his shoulder. Hands on the slip-knot in his life-rope, head thrown back, he keeps his eyes glued to the colossal mass of branches tottering above him. The top dips, cleaves the air with a foreboding swish, until it is poised at right angles with the tree, when it suddenly leaps clear into space. One of its heavy limbs almost rakes the logger in passing, but he nonchalantly side-steps it with the speed and precision of a trained acrobat. The top lands close to Tyler with a terrific rending and splintering. Its leave-taking sets the beheaded tree trunk swinging in far-flung, vicious circles, as if it were trying to fling the ravaging high-climber into space. The logger clings for life, giddy, dazed, nauseated.

In a moment he descends. He comes slowly at first, then by leaps and bounds, jubilant, with the feeling of victory.

Tyler skirts the knoll and cuts across a depression. He views his crew of "buckers," the men who wield the crosscut saws. He gives his next donkey-setting the once-over, calculates near-by stumpage, figures ways to haul the logs out. Finally, he looks at his watch. Eleven o'clock. Wet and dripping he strikes back to the loading landing.

The Shay has just returned from its trip to the river with logs and has brought the cook and his grub-boxers from camp atop one of its string of empty logging trucks. The landing crew helps him unload his stuff while the yarder engineer pulls the whistle-cord as a signal for the noon meal.

The loggers in the timber hear, and make for the landing. They crowd around the steaming donkey boiler and scrape mud from themselves with splinters of wood, hang soggy gloves to dry on pipes and cylinders, tidy up for eating. The hooktender takes the nozzle of the water-hose from the wooden watertank and begins sluicing the mud off his "tin" pants.

The steel triangle before a long, low shed in the brush across the track rings out. The waiting mob of hungry "timberbeasts" launch themselves in a body toward the sound. Inside is a rough table and benches. The table groans under food—meat, bread, potatoes, vegetables, cake and pie. At one end of the shed is a fireplace with a huge coffee pot before it. Everything is spotless.

The men fill the benches and fall to. Not a word is spoken, outside of the necessary requests for food out of reach.

Two belated woodsmen arrive and the cook frowns at their tardiness.

The last logger satisfies his ravenous appetite and leaves. Frenchy looks ruefully at his once spotless gear and furnishings. The benches, white and clean a moment ago, drip with mire. Along the edges of the table the white oilcloth is sticky with mud. Gobs of it smear the caulk-pitted but well-swept floor.

"By Gar!" Frenchy swears. "Talk 'bout timberbeast! Look at me more lak timber-*hog*! Sacré dieu!"

He grins affectionately.

Notes

1.   It's likely this expression harkens to the early American folk song of the same name. First published in 1834, the rambunctious fiddle tune was originally titled "Old Zip Coon," and though the meaning is open for interpretation, the relevance here seems to be in the song's general sentiment of abandoning work for leisure. Stuart Berg Flexner, *I Hear America Talking: An Illustrated Treasury of American Words and Phrases* (New York: Van Nostrand Reinhold, 1976), 54; Wayne Erbsen, *Rural Roots of Bluegrass: Songs, Stories & History* (Pacific, MO: Mel Bay, 2003), 159.

2.   Initially designed in 1877, Ephraim Shay refined, developed, and patented variations of his highly successful "geared" locomotive. Eventually, three classes of Shay loco-

motives were manufactured for hauling freight and cargo, and the steam-powered engine was widely used across several industries. The "geared" design, as opposed to a direct, rod-driven transmission, generated excellent traction and was therefore well suited for operating on steep grades and moving large timber loads. Alfred W. Bruce, *The Steam Locomotive in America* (New York: Norton, 1952), 36, 111–12.

3. The steam-powered "donkey" was a winch used in the logging industry for hoisting the trunks of large trees such as redwoods and Douglas firs. The invention is credited to John Dolbeer and his patent of the "logging engine" in 1882. Given the description here by Olsen, it seems likely that a later iteration of the "donkey engine" is being used in this logging camp, one that integrates with a geared locomotive for greater hauling adaptability. Lynwood Carranco and John T. Labbe, *Logging the Redwoods* (Caldwell, ID: Caxton, 1975), 41–45.

4. Also "whistle jerk," the colloquialism refers to any person, often a boy or young man, who operated the signal whistle in a logging camp. The whistle punk communicated with the operator of the "donkey engine" by yanking a whistle wire, thereby indicating when the operator should start and stop hoisting. Harold Wentworth and Stuart Berg Flexner, *Dictionary of American Slang* (New York: Crowell, 1960), 576; Stuart H. Holbrook, *Little Annie Oakley & Other Rugged People* (New York: Macmillan, 1948), 225.

SAVE THE PEAVIES

Robert Wilder (Massachusetts)

Sure, I worked for old Van Dyke, God rest his soul in pieces! Perhaps I shouldn't have said that. What I mean is that I hope he's in the blackest part of hell, rolling iron logs with a red hot peavey. And nothing to eat but beans and codfish either!

Sure, I worked on the drives from Connecticut Lake to Mountain Tom. But I generally stopped at Turner's Falls. And don't call us log drivers. We're river men. And you should have ought to have heard the gang cheer when old Van Dyke slipped, and we all seen he was a goner!

I'd go up in the fall and spend the winter in the woods. We'd cut the logs and pile 'em on the bank of a little stream somewheres, if it warn't handy to get them to the river. We had to mark each one with the company mark, kind of a brand, I guess, cut in the end of each log. And they were piled in such a way that when the freshet¹ came in the spring, we could yank out a couple of props, and the whole caboodle of logs would go rolling into the water.

We'd send a small gang on ahead—maybe a couple of boats—to break up the jams, and keep the drive going. Then the bunch of us would come with the horses. And last, would come another small gang with maybe a team or two, to haul in the logs the farmers had stole offen us. And I guess maybe the gang changed the marking on a log once in a while, if they thought it would pay.

The idea was for the first bunch to ride the freshet, and not let the drive get held up. Of course, the water would take the logs over meadows, and when the river went down, we'd have to haul them out with horses. But we knew where it was liable to happen, so we'd have a man at the right place to keep them in the current. And sometimes two or three. And sometimes we'd string a boom—hitch logs end to end. And hitch the ends to trees, maybe—so the boom would steer the logs for us. For the quicker we got the drive through, the cheaper it was for old Van Dyke—he didn't have so big a pay-roll. And that old devil was everywhere. Last part of it he had a car and chauffeur, so's he didn't have to drive, but could keep his mind on swearing.

Such sleep as we got, we got on the ground. And then be waked up by a kick from Van Dyke's boot, if he caught you at it. Guess he never slept at all. And to save time in cooking, the cook of the first gang would bury beans in bean pots in holes dug in the sand and filled with hot coals, so the next bunch didn't need to waste any time.

I got sick of being wet and cold all the time, so I asked for a job cooking. Van Dyke told me that if I'd let rum alone I could stand on a log. And what the L was I cold for? That work would keep me warm. But I told him I thought I could save him money on the grub. So I got the job.

We used to buy our supplies from little stores in the towns along the river that stood in with Van Dyke. And they used to give me a little book with what I'd bought written in it. I bought anything they had that I thought the boys would like. But I made the storekeeper write in beans so much, and codfish so much. But nothing else. I let the storekeeper charge up a pound or so extra for doing this.

One day Van Dyke came running. He'd seen some egg shells in the ashes of one of my campfires up river. "Show me your books!" He yelled. I showed 'em. He couldn't read much. But he knew beans and codfish when he seen it. He looked surprised. But he said, "That's the stuff, Hop, beans and codfish is good enough for peasoups.[2] Sock it to 'em!" But after that I buried my egg shells.

He said codfish helped a man to swim. And that beans was better than dynamite for blowing up a jam. What he meant was he liked them because they was cheap. And that men had to be well fed on something or they couldn't do their work.

One time, in the French King Rapids, the logs jammed. And when a couple of the gang went out to hunt the key log, the jam broke. Then men ran for it, but it was no use, both got knocked into the water. Of course, we ran out on the logs to help. But old Van Dyke yelled, 'Never mind the men, save the peavies!'[3] That was him. Never mind the men, he could get more. But the peavies—the hooks on a wooden handle, that we rolled logs with, you know—was property. And property cost money.

Yes, a peavey is like a cant-hook,[4] except a peavey has a spike on the end.

So maybe we didn't cheer that day at Turner's Falls, when Van Dyke had his chauffeur back his touring car to the edge of that cliff that overlooks the Falls, so's he could stand up in back and wave his arms and swear at us. I was standing on a boom out in the middle of the river, pushing logs that was branded for down the river so's they'd go over the Falls, and steering those we wanted inside the boom, and keeping one eye on Van Dyke, like everyone else. Guess the Falls was making too much noise to suit him, and he wanted to get nearer so's we wouldn't miss anything he was saying. He waved the chauffeur to back more. The chauffeur acted scared and only backed a couple of feet, and stopped so's Van Dyke almost lost his balance—he was standing in back. He turned around and said something to the chauffeur, then stood watching him fumbling with the handles. The man was badly rattled, I guess, with Van Dyke right there on his neck, almost. The car coughed once or twice, and then shot back over the cliff. And, my, didn't we cheer! "Never mind the man, save his matches!" yelled somebody . And we all cheered again.

We were awful sorry for the chauffeur though. And both of 'em were killed deader'n the codfish old Van Dyke used to make us eat.

When you asked me about Van Dyke, I thought I hated him. And was glad he was gone. But now I've been talking about him, I'm not so sure. I was only a kid then. But I see now that old Van Dyke was up against the railroads. He had to do things on the cheap in order to save his job and ours. Sure, he was hard. But maybe we weren't so soft ourselves. People in the Turner's Falls stores didn't like us walking on their hardwood floors in our caulked boots—shoes with spikes in the bottom to keep us from slipping off the logs. We chipped little pieces out of the varnish every step we took. And when they kicked, maybe we didn't take them places apart! Ever see a man who's had the small pox? Face all pitted? Well, if he was a river man, maybe he had small pox, and maybe he didn't. Maybe some boys tromped on his face with caulked boots. If they weren't any ladies around, I could show you where they tromped on me, when I put salt instead of sugar in their coffee by mistake. Believe me, I'm tattooed!

One thing old Van Dyke seemed to like. That was to hear us sing. Not that we ever sang much. But sometimes when the old river was rolling the logs along nice, and we'd finished our grub in the evening, we'd strike up a song. And old Van Dyke never butted in.

No, I can't remember the songs. Wish I could. I mind a verse of one though. It had lots of verses and some of them weren't exactly pretty. But the one I liked went this way—

"Oh, come ye lousy rivermen,
Come on and gather round!
We'll sing a song of French King Rock,
Where the bunch of us was drowned!"

Notes

1.   Prior to the government's procurement of a large portion of the eastern forests dur-
     ing the Great Depression, the freshet, or spring thaw was historically a peak time for
     the logging industry. River transport was an ideal mode for economically transport-
     ing large timbers, but the environmental costs were great, and thus, due to a number
     of regulations regarding commercial access to public waterways, the practice waned
     dramatically. It's possible this story's anxieties about costs and profit margins (embod-
     ied by Van Dyke) in the timber industry reflect the regulatory pressure on private
     industry at the time. Douglas W. MacCleery, *American Forests: A History of Resil-
     iency and Recovery* (Durham, NC: Forest History Society, 1994), 43; Michael Wil-
     liams, *Americans and Their Forests: A Historical Geography* (New York: Cambridge,
     1989), 96–99.
2.   French Canadians. Harold Wentworth and Stuart Berg Flexner, *Dictionary of Amer-
     ican Slang* (New York: Crowell, 1960), 379.
3.   Ibid., 380. Also "peavey." Although the narrator in this story is referring to the long,
     wooden-handled tool in common use by lumber workers at the time, the term can
     also refer to a sort of "green" Civilian Conservation Corps recruit.
4.   The cant-hook is similar to the aforementioned peavey, in that it is also a steel hook
     attached to a long wooden handle, but the cant-hook lacks the steel point at the end.
     Mark Allcutt, *Improvement in Adjustable Cant-Hook for Moving Logs* (US Patent
     16,222, issued December 16, 1856); George W. Lord, *Cant-Hook* (US Patent 303,870,
     filed January 14, 1884, and issued August 19, 1884).

THE FISH ARE RUNNING

Charles Oluf Olsen

It is dawn. The Columbia lies like a river of oil, swift and shining and gray from
the Washington shore to the shadows along Astoria's waterfront. Slips, warehouses, and wharves are black irregular blocks from Tongue Point to Youngs River.
About them and the piling the gray oil invades the tide flats. The main town, huddled on the steep slopes, is still plunged in night. Rows of lights crossing each other
at right angles outline the streets, and here and there headlights of early autos clash
with the dissolving gloom.

In "Oldtown," however, that historic part of Astoria covering the point of land
where the pioneers first settled, dwelling house lights have been shining throughout the night, singly and in clusters. It is May-day morning, opening day. Today
the law lifts the ban on net, seine, trap, and troll,[1] and for a brief span of months
salmon fishing is free again.

Out of a two-story frame house in the lower part of Oldtown come two men—
the young giant, Nels Pederson, whose bronze skin stretches tight and polished
over high cheek bones—and Toivo Wirkula, bulky, bright-eyed and brown, with
his weight so close to the earth that he rolls as he walks. Nels, 26, and with an easy
grin, is married to Toivo's daughter. He is still young enough to believe he might
some day be something else than a fisherman. Toivo is 46 and contemplates the
world without emotion, never questioning the fisherman's proverb that "He who
wets his feet in the Columbia must always return."

In silence the men cross the railroad track onto the stretch of river shore, and
survey its spots of sandy marsh, filled-in land, and docks on piling. Toivo's nostrils
expand as he gets a whiff of breeze wafted in from the Pacific. "I think she's goin'
to blow a little," he says in his soft drawl.

Nels knows Toivo is thinking of their nets and the danger to them if it should
happen to storm. Their favorite fishing spot is a shallow stretch fairly close to

where the breakers lose their force. Toivo never takes a chance on losing the nets. He has spent a lot of time tanning and hardening them. He believes he has the hardest and best-tanned nets on the river. He is probably right. But Nels is different from Toivo. Nels believes in taking a chance, getting fish, and letting the fish pay for new nets. He also sniffs the freshening wind and says, "Let'er blow—we was here first."

Toivo shakes his head. "A smart fisherman uses the wind. He don't argue with it."

They walk down the plankwalk that bisects the strip of beach with the land to their left and the docks to their right. Here, not long ago, wherever there was room, lay the boats of the tuna fleet, the halibut vessels, and the trawlers, pulled up on dry land by a power-slip with stout wire cables. Boats a good deal alike except for their owners' individual ideas about outfitting. Each had a name, usually feminine. All winter, owners had worked about them, scraping, caulking, tinkering, painting and scrubbing—fixing up for the spring and summer trips.

Now they are ready for the trollers. Trollers are gamblers, Nels reflects. Skittering out to sea like a swarm of pigeons after a sardine run. Chugging along with trolling lines dragging like sea rats with hooked tails. And expecting fish to take hold. Maybe they do and maybe they don't. Like angling for trout. Nels disdains the rows of shining craft. He is a born gill-netter.[2] Gill-netting is the only thing. He smiles, thinking how much better the odds are. You swing out your net and drag it in. Sneak up on the salmon. No gamble in that. Not when the fish are running.

Toivo, who was once young and daring, though not many would suspect it, recalls the trolling trips he used to make years ago—when fishing was much better than today. Fish biting like hell. Boat full in no time. He and his partner too busy to eat or sleep. And a good price for chinooks. Money in the pocket and places to spend it. He and Einar. His face, ordinarily so expressionless, tautens until the lines look etched. Einar—best partner a man ever had. Toivo can't help recall that last trip, whenever it freshens from the southwest. Gale fell on them. Couldn't make it in. Had to run for the open sea. And a wave got Einar. . . .

Nels interrupts his thoughts. The young fellow is pointing riverwards where scores and scores of windows are still illuminated in vast buildings perched on piling-supported docks: the canneries preparing for the first salmon catch of the season. Two of them are especially huge. Nels jerks his head in the direction of the first—the Columbia River Packers—and says, "They're gettin' ready for us."

"We don't sell to them," Toivo announces.

"Why not?"

"We sell to them that stand by us." Toivo points to the cannery of the Fishermen's Cooperative.

"We sell where we get the best price, don't we?" Nels says.

Toivo is fanatically cooperative. "We sell to our own people," he announces with finality.

Nels shrugs. Toivo owns a two-third interest in their fishing output.

They come to the municipal "basin" where most of the gill-net boats have anchorage. Gill-netters, unlike the rest of the men of the fishing fleets, fish all the year around, except March and April and parts of August and September, therefore keep their craft in the water the greater part of the time. But now the basin is nearly empty of boats. Toivo's eyes sweep the deserted anchorage and he grunts. "Huh—you thought we was early—look."

Here and there a boat still lies dark and dead, but most have already left for their favorite fishing spots, up river or down river. And right now boats are probably racing for the very place where Nels and Toivo aimed to string nets. Both men jump alive. In no time their *Anna*, a two-and-a-half tonner, is untied and poled away from the dock, her nose turned towards the river. Toivo steps aft of the diminutive cabin-housing to the tiller; Nels thrusts himself through the tiny door of the cabin to the diesel engine in the cockpit below. In a moment there is a coughing and sputtering as the machinery starts, and a whirring of the propeller. Then the *Anna* pokes her blunt nose into the choppy water outside the anchorage, and sets a course down-stream for the vast estuary. Nels stoops for a minute over the rhythmically clattering assembly, speeds up the motor a bit, then steps backwards into the cabin, unconsciously bracing himself against the sharp plunging of the boat.

Nels can span the cabin with arms outstretched in any direction. There's a small diesel oil-stove with two burners, a tiny sink, a little cupboard with coffee, salt, and canned goods. Opposite are two bunks, one above the other, with old quilts bulging from them—bunks so short and narrow that it is a wonder Nels or Toivo can stretch in them. Over the whole hover strong odors of diesel, lubricants, stale food, sweaty clothes, and bilge.

The cabin is smaller than the open hold in the deck forward where the nets lie and where the fish are thrown. Nels has known that hold to spill over with a first spring catch of Chinooks, and wished it was bigger. Good old chinooks! King of all fish! Bluebacks, steelheads and the rest of the salmon are all okay, but chinooks . . . big and best . . . and always a good price. Suddenly he cocks his head and listens. Toivo is calling him from the deck above. He pushes his long body through the cabin door and squints where Toivo points. In the morning light the great spread of the estuary is dotted with black specks emerging from the diminishing gloom. Nels jerks back and speeds up the engine. Slowly the *Anna* crawls up on the specks, till they grow to be the gill-netters' boats, each headed for its favorite drift or "reach" in the watery expanse. Each boat shows a man aft, his head—and sometimes his shoulders, if he is tall enough—outlined against the brightening day over the top of the cabin housing. Like statues, Nels reflects, and wonders at the faint stirring within him.

Toivo peers overside. He hasn't been too keen on casting net this morning. The water isn't quite roily enough for good fishing. Day-fishing might be all right in Alaska where in the spring the mouths of the rivers were nearly always yellow-white with silt from the glaciers. But not here—unless spring freshets inland and storms at sea have muddied the river mouth so that the salmon can't see the mesh of the nets. Toivo favors night-fishing. Nels had wanted to come out today, though. Maybe Nels was right—on account of old Omni. Omni has been batching in a shack two doors below Toivo's house, and Nels claims Omni is after their fishing "reach." Has been saying nobody owns the river or has a monopoly on any part of it. But Nels and Toivo have fished on their ground going on five years now, and everybody else lets the spot alone.

Toivo gauges the tide with practiced eyes. Just about an hour and a half before high. Soon be time to cast net.

He throws the tiller over a bit so that the *Anna*, which has taken the short waves on her port bow, now cuts straight across them. The wind is rising. It's going to blow all right. He squints at the clouds scudding before the southwester. Maybe it won't blow till they're through fishing. The *Anna* rides the water well. Good boat. They're nearing their fishing reach and Toivo brings the boat in line with a point of land on the far, indented shore. Several other craft are almost within shouting distance. Straight ahead is Omni's *Star*, smaller and older than the *Anna*. Omni is all the crew the *Star* has. He is too stingy to divide catches with a partner. Toivo wonders if the old fellow really intends to. . . .

"The ol' walrus is gettin' ready to fish!" Nels roars from the cabin door. He gooses the engine and sends the propeller racing. The *Anna* leaps ahead. The *Star* has suddenly veered and is heading straight across the shallowing water at right angles to the current and the channel. Its slow gait proclaims its purpose, and old Omni is lashing his tiller and lumbering towards his fishing gear.

Nels lets out a bellow and a torrent of profanity, cups his ham-like fists and yells: "Hey! Look out! You're right on top of a snag! You'll foul your net!"

Omni turns his long-whiskered face, sticks a thumb to the end of his nose and wiggles his fingers. Deliberately he throws his buoy overboard and pays out his net with long, leisurely swings of his arms.

Toivo, who has said nothing, touches the tiller once more, and the *Anna* heads straight for the cedar floats on Omni's net rope. Omni, out of a corner of his eye, watches the maneuver. For a moment his arms stop swinging, then he resumes his work. That Toivo should intentionally foul his net is unbelievable. But the *Anna* comes right on at an alarming speed. Toivo looks like grim fate, steering for a point that is bound to cut Omni's net at the gunwale. Omni falters. Another glance at Toivo and he pours out a stream of Finnish to blister the *Anna's* paint. Frantically he begins to haul in his gear. Toivo swings his boat to clear the net. Abreast of the *Star* Nels and Toivo watch Omni clear his net inboard, hasten to his engine and seize his tiller. With a parting curse, he sets course for his customary fishing ground, fearful now lest someone else should preempt that spot while he is trying to steal Nels' and Toivo's.

Now Nels slows down the engine and Toivo turns the boat along the course the *Star* has taken, then lashes the tiller to hold the direction. Both men meet forward, and Nels takes their buoy in his arms, while Toivo eases on the gear. The buoy is new, with cork float and a tube for batteries, and on top is an electric light bulb inclosed in wire netting—for night fishing. He lowers the buoy carefully, then steps aside to let Toivo pay out the net, ready to spell him if he wants it. The *Anna* rolls with the rising waves, and Nels steps aft to steady the tiller, while Toivo with incredible skill and speed, considering that it is some fifteen feet wide, keeps casting out the net. Lead weights at the bottom take the net straight down into the water until it stands like a twine fence, its meshes gaping.

There seems an unending mass of it. More than 200 fathoms. When it is about two-thirds paid out, Toivo signals Nels, who swings the *Anna* around in a circle at right angles to the already floating gear, then the rest of the net is put into the water. The whole looks like a lazy L with the foot pointing towards the current and the ocean to keep the salmon from escaping. The end of the net is fastened to the boat, the engine stopped, and the *Anna* allowed to drift. Both men go below and shut the cabin door against the sprays that the craft is beginning to ship.

Toivo wedges himself into the bottom bunk, completely filling it, and is asleep in a moment. Nels hankers after a cup of coffee, but the idea of holding the pot of water over the diesel burner against the boat's plunging, does not appeal to him. He busies himself with his beloved engine. After a while he goes on top to have a look at things. There's a couple of hours or so to drift—a good hour upstream with the tide, then downstream after the tide has turned. He thinks the weather will hold. He ducks down into the cabin once more, thinks of getting into his bunk, but gives it up. Again he tinkers with the engine. Drifting is the hardest job with him.

Time passes. Suddenly Toivo wakes, yawns prodigiously and literally rolls out. He knows instinctively that it is time to pull net. Also that the weather has held. Had it taken a turn for the worse, he would have known it even in his sleep. He waddles to the cabin door. The engine is idling. Up forward Nels has started the live roller. Toivo takes the tiller and Nels begins to haul in. At first there are no fish, and Nels pulls a long face. Then a chinook appears, its gills flaring from the mesh that has trapped it. It is a beautiful silvery color, with round black spots on back, tail and dorsal fin. The water drips from it and it struggles to get free, but Nels dexterously flings it into the bottom of the hold. He shouts at Toivo. First fish of the season, and a beaut! Must weigh almost 30 pounds. Worth a couple of dollars anyhow.

Hauling in the net with the help of the live roller isn't the work it used to be when Toivo was young and the job had to be done by hand, with the net wet and heavy with a big catch. Nels has the gear inboard in surprisingly short time, with the fish in a pile beside it. A couple of score—but of good size. Average between 20 and 25 pounds apiece, probably. Not a catch to brag about—but not so bad either, all things considered. Anyway, Nels and Toivo are coming out tonight again. . . . Nels goes below and sets the engine going full speed, while Toivo turns its nose towards the Cooperative Cannery. Maybe they'll be the first to dock with the first gill-net catch of the spring run.

Notes

1. The history of fisheries regulation on the Columbia River in the Pacific Northwest is long and complex and most of the techniques referred to in this story have either been banned or have become intensely regulated. For a comprehensive study of legislation and environmental debates in Northwest fishing see Joseph Cone and Sandy Ridlington, eds., *The Northwest Salmon Crisis* (Corvallis, OR: Oregon State University Press, 1996). It's unclear what Olsen means by "net" fishing since both "*gill-net*" and "*seine*" fishing utilize various types of nets, but its likely "net" refers to the practice of *gill-netting*. This method was characterized by a kind of quick and strategic boating technique across migratory fish paths wherein the *gill-netter* would use a fine mesh net to entangle masses of fish. Of all the methods mentioned in this story, *gill-netting* was probably the most adaptable to various fishing environments. *Seine* fishing or "purse seine" methods involved the use of a round net dropped to the water that was hoisted up to the boat deck by the use of some type of winch. The technique was most successful when schools of fish were present. Fish *traps*, like the other methods mentioned by Olsen, were highly dependent on the migratory movement of salmon, and were so "effective" that a few well-placed traps could collect the bulk of

a salmon population in a given fishery. Because of this, the use of fish traps became a major source of legislative and environmental conflict in the Pacific Northwest. They were eventually banned in Puget Sound in 1935 and, with exceptions for a few indigenous populations, were prohibited all over Alaska in 1959. Finally, *trolling* involved the use of four to eight fishing lines set for a specific depth. The lines were studded with lures or baits and dragged through areas where fish were known to be either spawning or congregated before spawning. The method has many critics since it not only captures mature fish, but those below mature size as well. James A. Crutchfield and Giulio Pontecorvo, *The Pacific Salmon Fisheries* (Washington, DC: Johns Hopkins, 1969), 37–42.

2. One who is fluent in "gill-net" fishing techniques. See above description.

WILD BILL

Aida C. Parker (Connecticut)

"*Hillbrook Avenue*—that'd be in Springdale," advised the traffic cop, "Take that bus."

A big blue bus was just pulling into the waiting station across from the Stamford Town Hall, and I climbed aboard.

"Tokens?" inquired the lean-looking individual behind the wheel, noticeable for the brightness of his blue eyes and the independent angle of his handlebar moustache.

I must have worn a blank look, for Moustache explained, with a great show of tolerance for the dim of wit, that straight fare was ten cents—if you "took tokens" it was only eight-and-a-third. Being thrifty I took tokens—three perforated metal discs, dime size, for a quarter. Following Moustache's elaborately patient instructions, I dropped one of the discs into the fare-box.

"Will you let me know when we get to Hillbrook Avenue?"

"End of the line." Moustache's tone indicated plainly that by now his scorn for anyone who knew nothing about the rules of bus-riding and even less about Springdale had gotten the best of his patience. Nursing my sense of inferiority, I settled into a front seat.

Before we had proceeded three blocks I knew Moustache's given name was Bill.

"Hi-ya, Bill—Mornin', Bill—How's tricks Bill?" Everyone who got on the bus hailed him. The most popular greeting of all was, "What d'ye say, Bill?," to which Bill's invariable reply was: "Not a word."

Almost as soon as I learned his name, I made another discovery concerning the owner of the unique lip ornament—he was the Barney Oldfield[1] of the Connecticut Transportation Company. That flat-footed mastodon of a bus responded to his hand on the wheel and his foot on the pedal like a racing car. We snaked through Post Road traffic, if anything so lumbering and inflexible can be compared to a snake. A dozen times I was all keyed up for the inevitable crash, only to discover that what had appeared an opening big enough for a baby-buggy when we headed into it, had miraculously widened just in time to let us go sailing through unscathed.

Bill also seemed especially favored by the law. As we approached an intersection, the policeman's white-gloved hand would go up in warning—a warning which Wild Bill regarded with sublime contempt. Waiting for the screech of the whistle, I saw, instead, a smile of recognition cross the face of the law's representative, while the official hand glided from a stop signal to a wave of greeting, and cross traffic made shift to adjust itself as best it might to the sudden change of plan. But not a driver cussed a protest. As we shot past I read resigned recognition on each one's face. *Everybody* knows Wild Bill.

When we had left the Post Road's traffic problems behind, Bill turned his head, affording me a profile view of his truly remarkable moustache.

"Stranger, ain't ye."

It was a simple statement of fact, but I chose to regard it as an inquiry.

"Yes," I admitted humbly. "I've never been in Springdale in my life."

"Nice town," he offered. "Nice folks. I was born there."

"That so?" My inferiority complex was taking smug satisfaction in the thought that Bill was exactly the type to be satisfied to spend his life in a place like Springdale.

"Yop." Here Bill whirled into a demonstration of startling skill. Without slackening speed, he maneuvered his massive chariot close to the curb and bought it to a dead stop in a space that didn't look much bigger than one of his own tokens. Then, with a sweeping gesture like a cavalier of old doffing his hat, he swung the bus door open to allow a passenger, a pretty but overly plump young woman, to alight.

"Wanta watch out Miz Harrie," Bill called out to her for the benefit of every passenger on the bus. "You're most as fat as your ma already."

The young woman turned, and I waited with considerable anticipation— being definitely on the plump side, myself—to see bumptious Bill get his ears "pinned back." But to my surprise the passenger only smiled and commented, "That's what pa says." Apparently Bill could get away with anything. Still another privilege, I thought, of spending your entire life in one small town.

"Yop." Bill returned to the subject of his birthplace. "I was born in Springdale. Ran away, though, when I was thirteen. Went West. Everybody was wantin' to go West them days."

While I was patching up my smug conception of a typical small town character, Bill brought the bus to a lordly stop in front of an elderly woman with a cane and a shopping bag full of bundles. With the agility of a schoolboy, he slid out from under the wheel and sprang to the curb. With his deft assistance, woman and bundles were aboard in a twinkling of Bill's bright eyes.

"Thanks Bill," the old woman smiled as she dropped her token into the box. "I was hoping it'd be your bus."

The expressive moustache registered its appreciation of the tribute.

By now we were taking on passengers and letting them off with such rapidity there was not time for conversation. On the next corner it was a woman with two small children clinging to her. The woman was pale and carried a baby. Bill leaned down to lift in the two toddlers and then straightened up in time to clap his hand over the fare-box before the mother could drop in her token. I pretended not to see, but I was pleased that Bill had sized me up as being sufficiently human to be taken into his confidence, for when the family had gotten off he explained over his shoulder, "Husband died a few weeks back. Didn't leave her a thing but them three little kids to look out for. She's on her way to cash her food order."

But Bill's humanity, I was to discover, had its limitations. I spied a man sprinting down a side street, waving his hand in wild supplication. I took it on myself to inform Bill of the approach of a potential passenger.

"That's Charlie Peterson," Bill replied, the moustache trembling with dislike as its wearer pushed up the speed of the bus a notch, leaving the gesticulating Charlie breathless and alone. "He only rides the bus when his car's broke down, and then he expects us to turn our whole schedule topsy-turvy to suit him."

I discovered that among the many services Bill renders his regular riders is that of Town Crier.

"Did ye notice if Miz Crosby was home as ye come by?" one woman asked him, and Bill wasn't ruffled by one hair of his beautiful moustache.

"Yop," he answered authoritatively. "Hangin' out her wash just's we passed last trip. Guess she couldn't get to it Monday on account of goin' to George Davis' funeral."

And two young girls wanted to know what was playing at the *State*. That didn't faze Bill either.

"*They Drive By Night*," he reeled off without hesitation! "George Raft and Ann Sheridan. Hear it's excitin'. And *Tom Brown's School Days*. That's one of them old-time pictures. Freddie Bartholomew's in it."

When the girls had stepped off with a gay, "Thanks, Bill," he turned to me to explain, "Ye see folks that live this side o' the theayter got no way o' knowin what's showin'. So I keep an eye out. Never go to the movies myself," he added. "Seems like a silly way to spend an evenin' to me."

I was the only passenger left now, and apparently Bill had sized me up a woman not easily daunted, for he settled down seriously to the business of finishing his run in a blaze of glory and fifteen minutes less than the schedule demanded. But I refused to be deprived of hearing the remainder of Bill's biography.

"You were saying you went West," I leaned forward and raised my voice. "Did you like it out there?"

I could see the protruding ends of Bill's moustache bobbing in regulation with his vigorous nod. "Like it fine," he called back without taking his eye off the road. "Stayed out there forty-five years. Married my wife out there. Took her quite a time gettin' used to livin' in Springdale."

"But she did?"

"Sure." Bill's tone demanded to know how anyone could help liking Springdale, given sufficient acquaintance with the place. "Couldn't hire her to go back now."

"Any place is the right place these days where a man has a good job," I offered tritely, in an effort to appear congenial. Actually, the wide open spaces seemed to me far and away more desirable than what I had been able to see of Springdale from the window of the speeding bus.

Bill's reply showed that he was quite aware of my condescension. "Oh, but I had a good job out there, too." And then with a quick assumption of the professional manner, "Here y'are, miss—end o' the line. Hillbrook Avenue's the second street on your left."

I thanked him and climbed out but suddenly it occurred to me to wonder what had been the nature of Bill's good job out West. I turned back and put the question to him. He was standing up, changing the sign on the front of the bus. He looked down at me over his outstretched arm, his moustache sweeping his coat sleeve as he answered casually, "Oh, I drove one o' them twenty-mule teams you hear so much about—fetchin' the borax out o' the desert. 'Twas on account o' the speed I used to get out o' them mules they named me Wild Bill."

Note

1. For contemporaries of Aida Parker, this reference would have conflated Wild Bill with Berna Eli "Barney" Oldfield (1878–1946), the charismatic and animated figure from the early days of auto racing. With only two weeks of automobile racing experience behind him, Barney Oldfield entered the 1902 Detroit 5-mile Classic and won. Prior to automobile racing, Oldfield had been a competitive bicyclist, but for rea-

sons unknown, Henry Ford chose Oldfield to man his 80-horsepower Ford racecar. In 1903, Oldfield went on to break the American speed record and became the first American to pass 60 miles per hour in an automobile. Later, in 1910, Oldfield would go on to exceed 131 miles per hour. Ralph Hickok, *The Encyclopedia of North American Sports History* (New York: Facts on File, 1992), 327.

THE BOOMER FIREMAN'S
FAST SOONER HOUND

Jack Conroy

A boomer fireman[1] is never long for any one road. Last year he may have worked for the Frisco, and this year he's heaving black diamonds for the Katy or the Wabash. He travels light and travels far and doesn't let any grass grow under his feet when they get to itching for the greener pastures on the next road or the next division or maybe to hell and gone on the other side of the mountains. He doesn't need furniture and he doesn't need many clothes, and God knows he doesn't need a family or a dog.

When the Boomer pulled into the roadmaster's[2] office looking for a job, there was that sooner hound of his loping after him. That hound would sooner run than eat he'd sooner eat than fight or do something useful like catching a rabbit. Not that a rabbit would have any chance if the sooner really wanted to nail him, but that crazy hound dog didn't like to do anything but run and he was the fastest thing on four legs.

"I might use you," said the roadmaster. "Can you get a boarding place for the dog?"

"Oh, he goes along with me," said the Boomer. "I raised him from a pup just like a mother or father and he ain't never spent a night or a day or even an hour far away from me. He'd cry like his poor heart would break and raise such a ruckus nobody couldn't sleep, eat, or hear themselves think for miles about."

"Well, I don't see how that would work out," said the roadmaster. "It's against the rules of the road to allow a passenger in the cab, man or beast, or in the caboose, and I aim to put you on a freight run so you can't ship him by express. Besides, he'd get the idea you wasn't nowhere about and pester folks with his yipping and yowling. You look like a man that could keep a boiler popping off on an uphill grade,

39

but I just don't see how we could work it if the hound won't listen to reason while you're on your runs."

"Why, he ain't no trouble," said the Boomer, "He just runs alongside, and when I'm on a freight run he chases around a little in the fields to pass the time away."

"That may be so, I do not know;

It sounds so awful queer.

I don't dispute your word at all,

But don't spread that bull in here," sang the roadmaster.

"He'll do it without half trying," said the Boomer. "It's a little bit tiresome on him having to travel at such a slow gait, but that sooner would do anything to stay close to me, he loves me that much."

"Go spread that on the grass to make it green," said the roadmaster.

"I'll lay my first paycheck against a fin³ that he'll be fresh as a daisy and his tongue behind his teeth when we pull into the junction. He'll run around the station a hundred times or so to limber up."

"It's a bet," said the roadmaster.

On the first run the sooner moved in what was a slow walk for him. He kept looking up into the cab where the Boomer was shoveling in the coal.

"He looks worried," said the Boomer. "He thinks the hog law⁴ is going to catch us, we're making such bad time."

The roadmaster was so sore at losing the bet that he transferred the Boomer to a local passenger run and doubled the stakes. The sooner speeded up to a slow trot, but he had to kill a lot of time, at that, not to get too far ahead of the engine.

Then the roadmaster got mad enough to bite off a drawbar.⁵ People got to watching the sooner trotting alongside the train and began thinking it must be a might slow road. Passengers might just as well walk; they'd get there as fast. And if you shipped a yearling calf to market, it'd be a bologna bull before it reached the stockyards. Of course, the trains were keeping up their schedules the same as usual, but that's the way it looked to people who saw a no-good mangy sooner hound beating all the trains without his tongue hanging out an inch or letting out the least little pant.

It was giving the road a black eye, all right. The roadmaster would have fired the Boomer and told him to hit the grit with his sooner and never come back again, but he was stubborn from the word go and hated worse than anything to own up he was licked.

"I'll fix that sooner," said the roadmaster. "I'll slap the Boomer into the cab of the Cannon Ball, and if anything on four legs can keep up with the fastest thing on wheels I'd admire to see it. That sooner'll be left so far behind it'll take nine dollars to send him a post card."

The word got around that the sooner was going to try to keep up with the Cannon Ball. Farmers left off plowing, hitched up, and drove to the right of way to see the sight. It was like a circus day or the country fair. The schools all dismissed the pupils, and not a factory could keep enough men to make a wheel turn.

The roadmaster got right in the cab so that the Boomer couldn't soldier on the job to let the sooner keep up. A clear track for a hundred miles was ordered for the Cannon Ball, and all the switches were spiked down till after the streak of lightning has passed. It took three men to see the Cannon Ball on that run: one to say "There she comes," one to say, "There she is," and another to say, "There she goes." And the rails sang like a violin for a half hour after she'd passed into the next county.

Every valve was popping off and the wheels were three feet in the air above the roadbed. The Boomer was so sure the sooner would keep up that he didn't stint the elbow grease; he wore the hinges off the fire door and fifteen pounds of him melted and ran right down into his shoes. He had his shovel whetted to a nub.

The roadmaster stuck his head out of the cab window, and—whosh!—off went his hat and almost his head. The suction like to have jerked his arms from their sockets as he nailed a-hold of the window seat.

It was all he could do to see, and gravel pinged against his goggles like hailstones, but he let out a whoop of joy.

"THE SOONER! THE SOONER! He yelled. "He's gone! He's gone for true! Ain't nowhere in sight!"

"I can't understand that," hollered the Boomer. "He ain't never laid down on me yet. It just ain't like him to lay down on me. Leave me take a peek."

He dropped his shovel and poked out his head. Then he whooped even louder than the roadmaster had.

"He's true blue as they come!" the Boomer yelled. "Got the interests of the company at heart, too. He's still with us."

"Where do you get that stuff?" asked the roadmaster. "I don't see him nowhere. I can't see hide nor hair of him."

"We're going so fast half the journal boxes[6] are on fire and melting the axles like hot butter," said the Boomer. "The sooner's running up and down the train hoisting a leg above the boxes. He's doing his level best to put out some of the fires. That dog is true blue as they come and he's the fastest thing on four legs, but he's only using three of them now."

Notes

1. A "boomer" during the 1930s was a term used for a temporary worker in a number
    of industries such as logging, construction, or, in this case, the railroads. In Conroy's
    story, "boomer fireman" refers to a traveling laborer who worked alongside the loco-
    motive engineer in the cab of the train. His primary responsibilities were to load coal,
    clean the engine's fire-box from debris, and to keep in direct communication with the
    engineer so as to provide enough fuel to maintain the engine's required speed. Calvin
    F. Swingle, *Locomotive Fireman's Boiler Instructor* (Chicago: F. J. Drake, 1909), 1–5;
    Harold Wentworth and Stuart Berg Flexner, *Dictionary of American Slang* (New
    York: Crowell, 1960), 54.
2. Depending on the railroad company he worked for, the roadmaster was charged with
    a number of responsibilities. His primary concern was the condition of the track for
    a given section of a railway, but other duties included oversight of tools, rail materi-
    als, boarding for railway employees, management, maintenance of switching sta-
    tions, and more. Edward R. Tratman, *Railway Track and Track Work* (New York:
    McGraw-Hill, 1908), 287.
3. Conroy's annotation: "five dollar bill."
4. Conroy's annotation: "Rule forbidding excessive overtime."
5. A heavy rod that connected the "tender" to the engine. The tender was a small car
    loaded with coal or firewood that traveled directly behind the locomotive engine.
    The expression would have implied that the roadmaster was angry enough to do
    something so irrational it would've stopped the train. George L. Fowler, *Locomotive
    Dictionary* (New York: Railroad Age Gazette, 1909), 35, 91.
6. Ibid., 53. Bearing assemblies that suspended the train's axles and kept them lubri-
    cated and moving freely.

MULES AIN'T JACKASSES

Grace Winkleman (Utah)

Bare spots were showing on the hillsides, and the run-off water was making min-iature canyons of the truck road. There was a sense of restlessness in the air, and suddenly the office was too small for me. I grabbed an old mackinaw¹ off the hook, and made my way to the hoisthouse. You can't settle down to work when spring is in the air. I slouched over to where One-ear Mike, the hoistman, was leaning against the door looking down over the valley. He moved over to make room, turn-ing his good ear toward me, and yanking his cap over what was left of the other. The remainder of that ear was resting in peace some place behind a saloon in town, where Mike had left it after it had been carved off in a fight.

"Won't be long now," I told him. "I can feel spring coming."

Mike nodded. "Be here pretty quick. Mules is skittish this morning. They know."

"How the hell can they tell? Some of 'em haven't seen daylight for years."

"Don't know," Mike answered, "but they do. Old Bill's having trouble with Mutt, and Katie's playing sick again."

"Guess I'll go down. Old Bill owes me a buck."

"Better get it before Saturday," One-ear called after me as I walked over to the cage. He dropped me to the 1800-foot level where Old Bill was working.

Bill was the prima donna of the mine. No one knew how old he was, but he'd worked under ground so long he blinked like an owl when he hit daylight. All the men respected him even if he did carry a perpetual grouch. Jack Riley stopped his single jack long enough to warn me that Bill was going good. I nodded. Bill usually threw one fit a day, increasing in tempo through the week. On Saturday he really blew his top. Saturday night he'd head for town, drink it off, and be fairly human on Monday. This was Thursday so I knew what to expect.

I walked along the manway² until I heard the roar of Bill's voice coming toward me. I figured he had just about used up that head of steam, because his voice was gradually dropping to a mere rumbling mutter. I saw the flicker of his lamp, and Mutt's disembodied head loomed up out of the darkness, eyes throwing back my lamp's light, ears pricked forward as he heard my step. I slapped him on the neck as he passed and yelled, "Hi, Bill. Understand Mutt's got spring fever and won't work."

Bill's lamp whipped over my way. I smiled.

"Wipe that silly grin off your chip," he snarled. "There ain't nothing funny about mules. Mules ain't jackasses. They're smart, and work a damn sight harder than some people I could name."

"Hell, Bill, I'm not making fun of any mule. They're a lot smarter than the guys that skin them."

That really did set him off. He was smarter than any dad-blasted mule, and could prove it, etc., etc. I let him go ahead until he ran down.

"Sure, I know, Bill. You have to know more than Mutt in order to out-think the son-of-a-bitch." To devil him, I asked if Mutt would pull more than ten cars yet.

He got tough. "Ten cars is enough for any animal to pull! And besides Mutt ain't strong enough to pull more than that."

Well, it wasn't any of my business if he wanted to save his face by making a weakling out of Mutt, but I knew better. Mutt was a real mule—big and powerful and plenty smart. For years Bill had tried to fool him into pulling more than ten cars, but no go. Mutt would tighten up the cars as they were coupled, and apparently he counted the clicks as the chain coupling took hold. When the tenth car was hooked, he was ready to go, but add one more car, and he'd balk. He'd look over his shoulder, lift a lip, and snort. Old Bill translated the snort as meaning, "No son-of-a-bitch can make a fool outta me. Get that car off, or I'll stand here all day."

Bill spat between Mutt's twitching ears. "Hear what happened yesterday?"

"Nope."

"That fancy pants college perfesser they put on for a gaffer (shift boss) was snoopin' around as I was couplin' the last car, and said to stick another on. I tried to tell him Mutt wouldn't haul more'n ten cars, but hell no! He knowed more'n me. Old Mutt learned him, didn't you baby?" Bill slapped Mutt on the rump, and the mule nuzzled him, then started down the track. "He swelled up and got all full of importance, and made some crack about me makin' a family pet outta my mule. The lunkhead was asking for it, so I coupled on an extra car. Mutt he turned around and looked us both over disgusted-like. 'Get goin'!' the gaffer hollered.

Mutt jest laid his ears back and braced his feet. The gaffer got sore and started cus-sin'. I was right shocked, and so was Mutt. You wouldn't have thought he knowed such language. The guy tried everything short of bootin' Mutt in the ass, which was lucky for him cuz I'd a killed him if he had. Finally the guy mumbled some-thin' about he guessed the load was too heavy, and sneaked off down the tunnel. Mutt and me sure had a good laugh. I took the extra off, and Mutt walked to the station as pretty as ever."

We both turned and watched the disappearing train. Mutt was headed for the loading station, his head pumping up and down, his ears like two exclamation points. Now and then a spark flared as his half-pint shoes struck a rock. I felt a sudden affection for the calm, peaceful, easy-going brute. Mutt has that one stub-born idea, but outside of that he is a good mule. Once in a while a mule train gets wrecked, and unless the mule is unusually smart and fast on his feet, he is often seriously, and sometimes fatally, injured when cars tip over. Mutt was too wise to be caught in any wreck. He'd had to scrabble plenty in his life, but he'd learned how to keep his footing and get out of the way of piled up cars and flying rocks. He was valuable in other ways, too. He would breast cars like a circus elephant, placing his collar against the rear car and shoving them wherever they were to go. This saved Bill a lot of steps, because Mutt would breast a train of empties under the chute so Bill could load them without leaving the chute. When one car was loaded, Mutt would push up the next one. This made it unnecessary for Bill to load a car, push it down the tracks, go back, and load the next car, and so on, until the train was complete.

"Mutt sure makes it soft for you. What would you do if you had to load cars like Jerry does? It would kill you in a week."

Bill spat furiously, rolled his eyes upwards, and shouted, "Oh Gawd! Send me down a shotgun and I'll send you up a son-of-a-bitch." He dropped his eyes and glared at me. "You know as well as I do that that hooked-billed hunk of nothin' ain't spent one minute trainin' his mule. That little trick has saved Mutt's life a good many times, and you know it."

I did know it. Sometimes miners, thinking the train has passed, will set a loaded car out on the tracks and leave it, figuring they have time to take care of it before the train returns. If they've guessed wrong and the train comes along, a mule who can't breast cars finds himself trapped between the heavily loaded ore train he is pulling down-grade, and the loaded car ahead. He can get himself pretty badly mashed up, crippled or killed. If he knows how to breast cars, he shoves it along ahead of him until he reaches the station. The skinner,[3] riding in the rear, is cut off from any view of the front by the mule's body which almost fills the tunnel, and by the width of the cars, so he doesn't know about the extra car until he arrives at the station.

A box of grain was always brought to the loading station for Mutt, and he could eat anytime he wished, but he'd wait until Old Bill opened his lunch bucket, and then go over to his box of grain.

Bill told me they were bringing a new mule down to the 2,000-foot level, so I went back to the shaft and rang for the cage. When I got on top, they hoisted the cage clear of the shaft collar—mine cages aren't like elevators, they can be swung free—and the crew slapped a bulkhead over the shaft opening. They brought up a great powerful brute, black as Satan, wild-eyed, and full of fight. It took some time to throw him, and get the specially constructed harness on him. His thrashing pipe-stem legs with their slashing hooves were tied close to his body so he wouldn't kick and get tangled up in the shaft timbers and break a leg. The mule wasn't liking it much, but not being a Houdini, he was out of luck, at least until he got down below. The crew fastened the harness to the big hook attached under the cage, and tied the mule's head close to the bottom so he couldn't stick it out and break his neck against the wall. He was hoisted clear of the bulkhead, which was yanked off the shaft entrance, and the cage was swung over the opening. The mule was on his way down. I rode down in the cage with part of the crew that goes along in case something goes wrong. The men on the 2,000-foot level were ready for him, and placed a bulkhead over the shaft as soon as the cage arrived. Sam, the mule skinner, got a rope on him and yelled, "He's as hot as a forty-five Colt. Watch out for him." The harness was removed, and the mule released. The trip down hadn't improved his disposition any, and as soon as he got to his feet, he went haywire. He chased all the miners into the manway of the shaft, into drifts and any other place they could reach. I shot up the side of a loading chute. Everyone was yelling, "Hold him, Sam!" Sam was fighting him all over the drift, and trying to keep out of the way of his needle-like hooves. Hard-rock Jake looked kind of cheap when the boys on top questioned him. All he could say was, "I ran in by the Chief Consolidated shaft, blew out my candle and hid." He wasn't alone, not by a long shot!

When a mule is brought down he goes to the barn on that level for a few days' vacation to get used to the darkness and to get fattened up. They have to put them on short rations for several days before lowering them—not only to reduce their weight, but to reduce their tempers. Sam told me later, "That big black didn't know what rules and regulations were. He raised all the hell there was, day and night." Sam, who had been a wrangler since childhood, couldn't do anything with him. They tried him out on the cars, but he wrecked them as fast as they'd set them up. Sam got tired of arguing with him, so they hoisted him up and sold him to a farmer. "That no-good-son-of-a-bitch had me as tired as a whore on payday," Sam admitted.

We got to talking about other outlaws we'd had in the mine, and how sometimes one man can handle them, but they are dynamite to anyone else.

"What happened to Missouri?"

"Don't know. Maybe he could tame this bastard. He sure had a way with 'em."

"Yeah, but the damn things were worse after he left. Look what that brown mule did to Lomman. Broke his leg, and damned near crippled him for life, and he was Missouri's pet."

Sam bit off a chew. "Funny how he worked on that mule. I was ready to beat his ears down when Missouri walked over and shoved me aside. He just took hold the rope, talked slow and easy, like he always done, scratched his ears, and the mule was his." Sam spat carefully over my shoulder. "Lookit Nels and that fool Nellie of his. They're just like Missouri and his mule. No one else can handle her."

"No one else wants to," I answered. "The dumb Swede tore Black Jack's bar to pieces night before last when Stud Peterson said Nellie was an outlaw. Nels got out of it with two shiners, a split lip, and a banged-up hand. Stud's taking sick leave. I'm going up on the 1350 and see if Nels looks human yet."

Nels was one of those big, raw-boned Swedes, slow and deliberate and very religious. He was one skinner who never swore. He was a nice fellow but a holy terror when mad. I grabbed a piece of drill steel and parked it on my shoulder like a rifle. This was in self-defense. Nellie, a chunky white mule with a wicked eye, pistons for legs, and razor-edged teeth, never chased anyone if they carried a drill steel or an ax, but if she caught them unarmed, she sure scattered them.

"Why don't you civilize that mule," I hollered at Nels when I caught up with him. Nellie stopped with a clanking of coupling chains, eyed my drill steel and let out a disappointed sigh. Nels turned slowly, and looked at me out of calm, ice-blue eyes completely surrounded by what looked like a purple sunset.

"She bane civilized. Peeples ain't."

"Yeah, I suppose I'm carrying this drill steel because it feels good bouncing around on my collar bone."

"Nellie, she yust playin'."

"She plays too damn rough. You could hide a grapefruit in that hole she bit out of big Red Mulligan."

Nels looked at me. "She yust play."

I dropped the subject. Nellie stomped a hoof and bumped Nels with her nose.

"Who's taking Circus's place since they tied the can to him?"

Nels grinned all over. "Liddle Paddy. That Circus! He sure made 'em yump."

I grinned back. About a week before, the general manager and the superintendent had been walking along the drift when Circus spied them. Circus was a big
gray with a white belly, exaggerated ears, and a perverted sense of humor. People,
as far as he was concerned, were made for him to chase. He took out after the g. m.
and the super, and they took a nose dive behind a pile of timbers. The only way
they could save their dignity was to can Circus.

Nels chuckled deep in his throat. "Dat Liddle Paddy. He is a fine mule, yust
about like my Nellie."

I thought Little Paddy was a heap smarter than Nellie, but the big Swede was
touchy about his mule.

Little Paddy had been on the busy 1800-foot level where a regular train
dispatching system had been set up since they uncovered a vein of high-grade.
Collisions and wrecks were getting too plentiful so the old man put in a train
dispatcher to handle the twelve mule trains. Paddy never stumbled. He managed to side-step all wrecks and keep whole, which it takes a damn smart mule
to do. He was a trim little beast with a neat bobbed tail and a few tricks of his
own. He'd pull along swell with a steady, even jog until near the end of the shift,
then he would slow up to a dragging walk giving a first-class impersonation of
an exhausted, over-worked mule. When he saw the men lined up on the station
at the end of the shift, he knew he was pulling his last loaded train. He'd watch
the loaded cars shoved into the cage, and when the last empty was coupled on
his return train, he was ready to shoot off up the drift. He knew when the brakes
were thrown onto the last car, it was time to go, and the skinners had to jump to
couple the car before Paddy headed for the barn at a brisk trot to deposit the empties for the next shift.

"I thought they'd bring Denver down," I told Nels.

He shook his head, "Ol' Yarge, he like that mule."

"Sure changed his tune since last month," I answered. "You hear what he told
the old man?"

Nels shook his head again.

"Well, George got to figuring he was a privileged character around here
because he grew up with the mine. When they hauled Denver up and put him
to work outside, George had to take care of him along with his night-watching.
George got sore. He busted into the old man's office and yelled, 'Lew, I should get
more money since I have to take care of Denver.' The old man looked him over and
snorted, 'George, there are at least a hundred men downtown who would be glad
to have your job.' 'Sure, I know,' says George, 'but there's a thousand men downtown who'd be glad to have yours.' George got his raise."

Nels laughed and climbed up on his seat, he chirruped at Nellie, and I stepped aside to let her pass. She lunged at her collar, slim legs braced to take the weight until she got the wheels rolling. The cars clicked past one by one as they started, and Nellie settled into a steady swinging stride, her head hanging limp, and her long roached neck bopping up and down as she walked.

I went along the drift to the connecting tunnel. I heard Shorty Murphy's voice, muffled in the distance, raised beyond its normal pitch. I couldn't hear the words, but I didn't need to, the tone was enough. Someone was getting hell. I went back along the tunnel and met Shorty on his way out.

"What's wrong, Shorty?"

"It's that damn Star. She's swiped my lunch bucket again."

"Why don't you hang it up so she can't get it?"

"I did, but she knocks it down. I hung it in the middle of the tunnel where she doesn't stop, and darned if she didn't get the bail in her teeth and carry it to the station with her. She busted it open while Doyle was uncoupling the cars, and by the time he reached the front end, she'd et it all."

"That's what you guys get for feeding her all that stuff. She won't eat hay pretty soon."

"Jimmy Dolan gave her an onion yesterday, thought that would cure her. She et it all down, it didn't faze her. All it did was make tears the size of goose eggs run down her nose. She won't get no more of my sandwiches. I'm going to strap my lunch around my waist in a money belt."

"Why don't you hang five on her?"

Shorty looked at me aghast. "Hit a mule? Have you gone nuts? She ain't down here because she likes it. We brought her down. We can get out and in, but she stays. I'd like to catch anybody taking a swat at her."

"OK, OK, I just thought you wanted to break her of swiping lunches."

"I do, but not that way."

"Seen Gramp Wilson?"

"He's down at the barn cleaning up, and cussin' Katie."

Gramp was as much a fixture around the mine as George. Both were too old for hard work. Gramp worked when he felt like it—which was seldom—and laid off when he felt like it—which was often. When I got up to him he was glaring at Katie.

"She's sick again," he growled at me. "That bloody mule has more sense than I have. She plays sick and stays in the barn and laughs at me pushing cars past her."

"Tough," I told him. "It's sure awful to see an old has-been like you working so hard."

He bristled like a bantam[4] and started cackling at me; he got so mad he really worked, which surprised both of us. I was afraid he'd bust a blood vessel so I started talking to him about mine fires. He leaned against the barn and was off to the races.

"A fire at the Eureka Hill in 1903 gassed up three other mines. Hell's kertoot, it caught a bunch of mules on one level before we could get 'em out. Weren't no chance to save 'em. They all suffocated. They were plenty ripe when we finally got around to 'em. Couldn't load 'em down there, so we hadda carve 'em carcasses up into bits. Phew! It was awful. We got 'em all up though, and buried 'em in the dump. Made us all sick for a week. That drift stunk for weeks."

"Well, Gramp, these electric locomotives will do away with all that."

"Those new fangled contraptions will be the ruination of mining. They jest invented 'em to git a mule skinner's job. Somebody's gotta run 'em all the time, ain't they? Won't go back by 'emselves, will they? Won't stop 'emselves at the loading chutes, will they? They ain't goin' to bring any of those damn things in here, is they?"

I answered, "No," covering all questions with one answer. I knew how he felt. Pesky, stubborn and ornery a mule may be, but sometimes they seemed like one of us. I liked to watch them make their unguided way to the loading stations with their strings of empties, and if the drift was long, see them stop of their own mule-power under the loading chutes. There is a certain companionship between men and these animals that runs deep. They might bite and kick you, but when they made friends with you, they were as loyal as a dog. I couldn't quite picture the mine without mules. Nels wouldn't have anything to love; Old Bill, nothing to boast about; Sam, nothing to fight, and George would get a paycut. I knew it'd be some time before we had electric motors, but I also knew that we'd have them some day. Electric motors would be run more than eight hours; they would pull more than ten cars; they wouldn't be on the sick list all the time like Katie, and they certainly wouldn't swipe lunches, or chase big shots behind piles of timber.

I turned back to the shaft. Maybe it wasn't spring after all. I rang for the cage, and One-ear hauled me up. He wasn't looking down over the valley now. He was hugging the stove. I flipped a hand at him as I passed. I didn't go into the hoist shanty, but went on to the office and hung up the mackinaw.

Notes

1.   A heavy wool overcoat. The origin of the word is in the Ojibway term "mitchimaki-nak," which means "great turtle." Stuart Berg Flexner, *I Hear America Talking* (New York: Van Nostrand Reinhold, 1976), 203.

2. Can refer to any number of corridors in a mine. Manways can be vertical shafts for ladders or equipment, lateral, interconnecting tunnels, or general walkways inside the mine. American Geological Institute, *Dictionary of Mining, Mineral, and Related Terms* (Alexandria, VA: American Geological Institute in Cooperation with the Society for Mining, Metallurgy, and Exploration, Inc., 1997), 331.

3. Mule runner (cf. "teamster," in "The Driller," this volume). Harold Wentworth and Stuart Berg Flexner, *Dictionary of American Slang* (New York: Crowell, 1960), 482.

4. Ibid., 19, 98. Also "chick"; slang for a young girl.

THE DRILLER

Ned DeWitt (Oklahoma)

Drilling today ain't anything like it used to be. Nowadays, they work it all out on paper, right down to where the men're going to stand while they blow their nose. These big companies won't take a chance on anything; it's got to be a cinch before they'll drop a nickel. But twenty-thirty years ago a company'd spend half a million, just taking a chance it'd hit pay sand.

I got my first job in the oil fields in California about 1908. They were paying roustabouts[1] five and six dollars a day, and that was better'n I could get at any other work. I hit it hard for a while, and learned how to drill. Seems like it was easier to learn in those days—like people were more helpful than they are now. Anyway, I got to where I could run a rig with the best of 'em, cable tools or rotary.[2]

I guess I should've explained at the start that there's two kinds of drilling machinery. There's cable tools, which used to be used so much they were called "standard," and the rotary rig. They both make holes in the ground, but they do it in different ways. Let me have a pencil, will you? I'll do a little paper talkin'. . . .

Now, this—this thing here is a cable-tool derrick. It's made out of wood, generally, and it ain't as tall as the rotary because it don't have as much weight to support. It only has one boiler, too, where the rotary has three or even more. This outfit up here at the top is the crown-block;[3] it's on a dead-line, straight up, with the hole you're drilling. If it ain't, you've got a crooked hole. The block has cables running through it connecting up with your bailer and tools at one end and winding up down here in your machinery, around your different reels, at the other. This thing hanging here about halfway between the crown-block and the floor is a casing block.[4]

This overgrown teeter-totter over here is a walking-beam.[5] It's got a turnscrew with a drill-cable running through it and fastening on to the tools at one end. The other end hitches on to a revolving arm that makes the beam move up and down—lets the tools raise and drop, see?

Ordinarily, in drilling, your tools will consist of a bit, a set of jars—to give the tools extra motion—a steam, and a socket for the cable; weigh five or six thousand pounds all together. Of course, there's other tools, too, for fishing things out of the well, for drilling inside the pipe, and a lot of other jobs.

The size of the bit you start drilling with depends on how deep your hole is going to be; on an average you'd probably start in with an eighteen-inch. . . . Well, as the bit rises and falls it keeps turning, striking at a different angle each time. It pounds a hole, it doesn't bore one. It's the driller's job to see that the bit strikes full force, but no more. If there's too much slack in his line the hole will be crooked; if there ain't enough he won't make any progress. As the bit makes a hole, the driller turns this screw I mentioned a minute ago—letting the tools go down farther, see? When he's drilled the length of the screw or as much as he feels is safe without bailing out, he unhitches the screw from the cable, so that it hangs free from the crown-block, and reels the tools out.

I forgot to mention that you drill with water in the hole; the pulverized drill-ings are turned into mud. With the tools pulled out, the bailer is run down, and all this mud is bailed out. Then the drilling tools are let down into the hole again, the turnscrew is screwed back to starting position and hitched on to the cable, and you're ready to drill again.

Ordinarily, you'll put a string of pipe into the hole each time you strike a water sand. If you've started off with an eighteen-inch hole, your first pipe—cas-ing—will be fifteen-inch. That means that when you start to drill again you've got to use a smaller bit. . . . Get the idea? The casing and the hole keep getting smaller the deeper you go. It's kind of like a telescope with the big end at the top.

Well, so that's the way to drill with cable tools, or a simple explanation any-way. A fellow could write a book about it, if he wanted to. A good cable-tool man is just about the most highly skilled worker you'll find. Besides having a feel for the job—knowing what's going on thousands of feet under the ground just from the movement of the cable—he's got to be something of a carpenter, a steamfitter, an electrician, and a damned good mechanic. And rigging—say! A cable-tool driller knows more knots and splices than any six sailors.

Not all cable-tool drilling is done with derricks. They've got portable machines with masts that are put together in sections and take the place of a derrick.

There ain't a whole lot of drilling done with cable tools any more. Most every-thing you see is rotary—they're so much faster, and they can go deeper. They're pretty complicated, though, like a lot of machines that do a hard job the easy way. And they cost plenty money. A good cable-tool outfit'll run you about forty thou-sand dollars, but a rotary comes closer to a hundred thousand.

Look here, now, how much taller the derrick is; it's made out of steel, too. And here's three or four boilers to the standard rig's one. The rotary drills with pipe, see—it rotates it. And when you've got a mile or two of drill pipe to whirl you've really got something.

The first joint of pipe has a bit fastened on to it—what you call a fish-tail. When the pipe is rotated it bores a hole, just like an auger would. As the hole gets deeper the driller just keeps adding pipe. There ain't no pulling out for water sands or to set casing.

Yep, that's about all there is to it. Bailing? You don't have any. These big pumps—mud hogs—force water down inside the pipe and wash mud up the outside. About the only time you have to pull out your tools is to change bits. A lot of people—especially cable-tool men—claim that rotaries ruin the oil sands. But I don't take much stock in it. Sometimes they will run through a sand without knowing it, though. They can't always tell just what they're drilling in, see, like you can with cable tools.

If your hole ain't straight when you're drilling with cable tools you're plumb out of luck—you can't get any motion on the tools, and the casing won't go in. But a crooked hole don't mean anything with a rotary; they're crooked more often than not. They have to take tests and all that to find out just how crooked they really are. Sometimes they drill 'em on a slant to get oil out from under a location where they can't put up a derrick. That's what they call whip-stocking,[6] and it's practiced a lot. When the north Oklahoma City field was being drilled in, near the State Capitol, the governor claimed that the oil companies were whip-stocking their holes and drilling the oil out from under State land. So he leased the State land to the companies, and that's why you see those wells out there all around the Capitol.

I learned all the tricks to drilling that the boys out there in California could teach me, and in 1912 I heard there was a big boom down in Mexico. I jumped my job in California and hit out. Well boy, what I'd seen of oil-field work and tough living wasn't anything with what I seen down there! They used cable tool and rotary, and since I could handle both of 'em I got along fine as far as the actual drilling was concerned. But the things that went with the job! We were down in the Tampico field, the biggest one, and I guess about the only real field in Mexico. There was more money invested in that one field than there is in the whole Mid-Continent field, and Mister, that Mid-Continent stretches a helluva long ways! But in some places in Mexico the companies were wildcatting—drilling test wells in unproved territory—and those places were generally just plain hell. A man'd have to wade through swamps where the mosquitoes were big as mules and twice as mean; chop your way through jungles; and then climb mountains that'd make a goat dizzy! And damned few white men along either. Just a bunch of Mexicans gobbling along and all around you. Drive a man crazy if he didn't shut his ears up and not pay any attention to it.

Why, one day we got orders to move a rig to a location that we could hardly find on a map. I was working for the Aguila Oil Company, British-owned, and we got all our orders from London. Those damned Britishers had already drilled there once, but some smart Limey got the idea that maybe they hadn't gone far enough or that if a well was sunk a few feet away from the first one it'd show samples. They wrote us a long letter, and most of it said, Git the hell away from camp and drill that well. We packed up and hit out.

Of all the plain goddamned misery we had that trip! We moved everything; I don't mean we just picked us up a tent and skillet and some little things like that and set out for a weekend camping trip; no sir! We packed every damned thing we'd need to drill a well—boilers, wrenches, picks and shovels, pipe, casing, rope, steel, timbers for the rig floor, tin for the boiler house and the belt house, everything—and packed 'em on burros. Burros! Little jackasses that didn't look big enough to haul a guinea egg, and about as sociable as a piece of cactus. But that was all there was to haul the stuff with, so we had the Mexicans round us up enough to make the trip.

Away we went one morning. That was something to see, let me tell you! Our camp was on a kind of flat plain between mountains, and when the first part of the bunch was up in the mountains—I was a driller, so of course I was in the lead with the rest of the officers of the camp—well by God, the middle and rear end of that bunch of jackasses was just getting started! We had a string of 'em several miles long, and you could hear them Mexicans singing and cussing up where I was. There was more'n 2,000 Mexicans; teamsters,[7] roughnecks,[8] roustabouts, hands for the picks and shovels, and some of them that was supposed to work but just come along for the hell of it. Those boys knew that with such a big bunch there'd be a swell chance for a fiesta when we made camp.

We finally got to the location. We put up the rig where the geologists in London had said we oughta put it, got the boilers set up, and begin work. The Mexes had to have their fiesta first, of course, and then we went to work. Hell, we didn't get enough oil outta that hole to wet our tools! We all cussed London and the Limey bastards that had sent us out there and then we pulled up and come back. Before we left I asked the general superintendent what he thought it cost the company to make that little pleasure trip. He said it must have cost more'n $40,000! Can you imagine a company now that'd spend that much money to try and get a well down without making somebody else kick in? I can't, and I've been working at this a long time.

Another thing about working down there in Mexico was the food. We didn't get slop like American companies used to put out in the boom days in this country; no sir! We ate just as good as the Limeys did back in London. Those English companies allowed $2.00 a day for each man for food, and we didn't get cheated out of a penny of that allowance either, let me tell you! All the food was shipped over from England, and if what I ate there was any sample, those Britishers eat damned good. Christmas dinner? Man, they fed us meals you couldn't buy for five dollars any place in the world. They put out enough to sink a battleship for each man, and then topped off with big plates full of pickled walnuts and candied fruits, from England, and India, and Persia, and France. When I come back to the United States after working for those Britishers my teeth was just about worn down to the gums; I'd eaten so much and so good!

The only thing I really didn't like about working for those British companies was that you never could get very high with 'em. All the head offices were held down by Englishers, and an American was lucky if he ever got tops with 'em. You take one of those Britishers who'd just come over from the Old Place, and he wouldn't have a thing to do with an American, or anybody else for that matter but another Englishman. If he didn't know something, he'd just stew along till he stumbled on the answer, but he sure as hell wouldn't ask anybody that didn't have a little English blood in him. I worked for the three biggest companies down there, the Aguila, Shell, and Sinclair. The Aguila Oil Company used Englishmen for all their head offices; the Shell used Hollanders and English; and Sinclair didn't give a damn what country a man come from or if he had his afternoon tiffin[9]—Sinclair wanted the job done, and they'd hire anybody and pay him a good wage if he could do it. That's one thing I liked about Sinclair, and any other American company.

Most of the companies paid about the same—$250 a month when you first went down there, and then on up. When I quit I was making $350, and could have got more I guess if I'd hit 'em up about it. We always got paid in United States' bank drafts, drawn on the Chase National Bank in New York City, and they were as good as gold down there too. Drillers got the best pay, like they do anywhere. If we'd got paid in Mex money, we'd of been working for nothing most of the time. When I was down in Mexico there was three bandit chiefs that had the country split up between 'em. Old Zapata had the country 'round Mexico City; Pancho Villa had Monterey and the country south of there; and Carranza had Tampico and what was around the oil fields.

We had to carry three kinds of Mex money with us all the time; just went around loaded down with Mexican bills 'bout as big as soap-wrappers. When we'd get up in the morning Zapata might own the town and his money would pass for good. By the time we'd eat breakfast and went out to buy a pack of cigarettes Villa might have taken the town and his money would be all that was good. And by the time we knocked off at noon, Carranza might have licked Villa and his money had to pass. When any of 'em got beat, his money wasn't any good, then or any other time. If he got back in power, by licking the other two, he just printed some more soap-wrappers. Nobody ever thought of taking up the money that'd already been printed. You can see what a helluva shape we'd been in if we'd been paid in Mex: United States money was worth about 200 to 1, on an average. One time I was in Tampico, staying at the hotel. Next morning I ate breakfast and went up to the clerk to pay my bill. The breakfast, just an ordinary one, was worth $4 Mex, and my hotel bill was a little more'n $1,200! Boom times, huh?

Most of them Mexicans didn't care 'bout their money, or anything else. All they wanted to do was make enough to have a good time at the next fiesta, and they was satisfied. And the fiestas usually come 'bout once a week, sometimes two or three a week. That was the Mexicans that worked as hands, of course; but there was a helluva lot of Mexicans that had a pretty good education and knew what they was doing. Some of 'em had been to the United States and learned about how to drill and how to run a refinery and all, and of course most of those kind of guys had good jobs in Mexico City or some place. We didn't run into a helluva lot like that, though. Most of what we had were peons, Mexican workmen. Most of them didn't know a drill-bit from a tamale shuck. We had a hard time with some of 'em when I was first down there.

The Mexican government had a law that there had to be three Mexes to every foreigner on the rig, and there wasn't a thing we could do about it except put 'em to work. Well, some of those Mexes didn't know what we were talking about half the time. We'd say we're going to change towers—change shifts you know—and those damned fools'd begin tearing down the rig.

The country was running over with bandits. You see a bunch of men lathering their horses along the road, and you better get to cover; more 'n likely it was some bandit gang coming from a raid and feeling frisky enough to shoot hell outa anything they saw moving. Many a time I've seen a bunch of bandits come riding hell-for-leather past the camp, the Regulars—the soldiers—pounding along right behind. The bandits'd run into the jungle; in a few minutes here they'd come again, only this time the bandits'd be chasing the Regulars. Sometimes, if they was outnumbered, the Regulars'd go over to the bandits, and then they'd all come hellin' into town to shoot it up.

The United States come in and took us all out in '14, and brought us up into Texas. We stayed there several months. When it quieted down we went back down into Mexico, and started back to work like nothing had happened. We were drilling a well about nine miles outside a little town just north of Tampico; it was a wildcat and we were going to try to prove up the country. Everything looked pretty peaceful, and we began working like hell to complete the well so we could get another job. We had four drilling crews and were working two towers—one from noon till midnight, and the other from midnight till noon. We were really balling the jack.[10]

'Long about 11:30 one night, when we was just getting ready to go relieve the other tower, we heard a noise coming towards us that sounded like a whole army. We waited; we couldn't of done anything less we had a couple of cannons. About 80 or 90 bandits come roaring into camp, shooting and yelling. Half of 'em run through the mess-hall, where we ate—the pushers,[11] drillers, workmen, and all— and scared hell outa the fellows there. The rest of 'em went for the bunkhouses. I was in the bunkhouse, just getting my shirt on to go to work. In they come like a pack of mad dogs. I hollered, "Let 'em go, men; we can't do nuthin'!"

They frisked us for money, took all we had, and then begin tearing up our bed-ticks to see if we had any saved. The company had had those bed-ticks made especially for our camp cots, and shipped 'em all the way from England, and by God I almost yanked one of them bandits by the scruff of his neck when I saw him take his machete and rip hell outa my tick. They dumped the stuffing out of 'em and kicked it around, and then folded up the ticks—they were a pretty bright-color, and Mexes like colors—and took 'em with them.

There was a boy we'd picked up in Texas, a fellow named Lonnie something-or-other, I can't remember his last name. I remember that he came from Waxahachie, Texas, though. He was a good-looking kid, kind of tall, and looked exactly like he ought to be a boss or something, even if he wasn't. He could speak damned good Spanish too. Well, one of the bandits hollered out, "Who's the boss here?" I was kind of translating it in my mind when this Lonnie speaks up and says, "I am; what the hell do you want?" He wasn't, you see, but I was. But that kid knew if they took me the work'd be slowed up, because I was general superintendent for the company. So before I could say anything, just after I kinda figgered out what the hell all that Spick meant, this bandit says, "All right, Gringo; we'll just take you along." He turns to me and says, "We want 5,000 pesos for this Gringo; you don't send 'em to us in 24 hours we'll send you his ears. Then his legs, and then his arms. Savvy?" And before I could say yes or no, they hustled him outside and lit out.

The others had already run through the mess-hall and taken everything there that they thought they could use—including all the whisky and gin that the English company had brought to us—and they all hit it off down the trail. They put

Lonnie on a horse, tied his legs together and then passed the rope underneath the horse, and they led his horse with 'em. The other tower had heard the ruckus and hid out just over the hill near the rigs. The bandits must've known there wouldn't be anything worth stealing, to them, up there at the rigs and they didn't even go up there. Well, this other tower heard all the noise and laid low. The Chinese cooks we had was squealing like stuck pigs; you could of heard 'em a mile, because the Mexes had grabbed 'em by their pigtails and was swinging them around and making them dance by shooting at their feet.

I run up to the telegrapher's office after they left and sent word to the company office in Tampico what had happened and told them we had to have the 5,000 pesos before morning. They told me to get the company boat—we had a big motor boat up there on the river by the camp—and beat it down to Tampico and they'd have the 5,000 pesos waiting for me. I got in the boat and went down there, got the reward money, and beat it back. I got back in camp 'bout noon the next day, with the 5,000 pesos in a big sack, weighing me down. But I didn't need the money after all.

Lonnie knew the jungles pretty well—that is, he didn't get lost very easy wherever he was, and he could always find his direction by the stars or the sun or something—and he beat me back to camp. He said that the bandits rode fast for three-four hours, and then they begin to get tired. They stopped off beside the trail—there was just a big trail there where all the horses and tractors and burros and everybody had to travel, because the jungle was on each side—and they all piled off and spread their ponchos and covered themselves with our bed-ticks. They put five Mexes to guard Lonnie. He said they untied him because he told 'em his arms was numb and his legs, but they put him in the center of the guards.

The rest of the Mexes was all drunk on our whisky and was pretty tired anyway, and Lonnie said it wasn't more'n ten minutes till the whole gang was snoring. The guards weren't any wider awake than the rest; they watched Lonnie for a few minutes, then they begin dropping their heads and nodding off. 'Bout half-an-hour of this and Lonnie wormed along on his belly about a hundred feet; then he got up on his hands and knees and made another hundred. When he was a good ways from the Mexicans he jumped up off his hands and knees and headed for the timber. All that night he fought through the jungle, and come daylight he wasn't more'n 15 miles from our camp. He hoofed it on in, and beat me back from Tampico.

A "missionary," a fellow who was half-French, and half-something-else, I don't know what, acted as a kind of referee in these things. I'd got in touch with him before I left for Tampico, and he set out after the bandits. He knew where most of them holed up and all. He made a deal with them, but of course they didn't say anything 'bout Lonnie already being gone; they thought they'd put a good one over on us. Well, that damned "missionary" was one surprised human when he come back, and told us what had happened; how he's sacrificed his time and all and got them to promise to turn Lonnie loose for the 5,000 pesos. I let him tell his story, and then I sent for Lonnie. There wasn't anything for him to do but beat it, and I helped him a little with my boot, because I figgered he was in cahoots with 'em.

The bandits come by a couple of more times after that, but they didn't stop long enough to kidnap anybody. They just took all we had—whisky and clothes and food and all; even made us trade boots with 'em, and it got so we wouldn't wear anything but the oldest clothes and boots we had. But that kind of stuff got to be too much. The company was losing money on their stuff, even if they did have some pretty good producing wells, and they sent us orders from London to abandon those particular wells.

We went out on other locations, some of them not quite as good as those we'd had to leave to the bandits, but still they were all right. But I'd had just about enough. Besides I was getting kind of homesick for the United States. So I left Mexico in '17. I went to Mineral Wells, Texas, where there was a little boom on, and worked there for two months. I got a splinter in my thumb while I was splicing a wire cable on a standard rig, and got blood poisoning. I had to lay off a while, and then I came up to Duncan, Oklahoma.

There was a little excitement 'round Duncan, and I stayed there a while. I had a friend on the Corporation Commission here in Oklahoma and he wanted me to go up in northern Oklahoma and drill. I rode around with him for several weeks and finally landed in Garber. I went to work on a rotary rig there for the Sinclair Company. Rotaries were taking over everything, and there wasn't any place for a cable-tool driller. Sinclair shipped in ten rotary rigs from California to the Garber field, and I really caught hell that next winter, '18 it was.

That was the year most everybody got the flu, remember? Me'n another fellow were just about the only drillers in that whole field that didn't come down with it. There we were, by God, trying to run every rig in that whole field by ourselves, and working farm hands and clerks from the towns and anybody else that had strength enough to lift his hand. And it snowed so much that year that lots of times me and this fellow, Johnnie Williams, had to hitch six horses on one little light farm wagon to go into town for groceries. When we got off work nights, we'd go to the bunkhouses and act as nursemaids for those who had the flu. We emptied so damned many slopjars I smelled like a sewer, and I cooked so many eggs and flapjacks and stuff I could've got a job in a hash-house when I got through. There wasn't but two doctors in the whole county and those poor devils was on the jump day and night. They'd come and prescribe some nasty-tasting stuff, and they was so tired and worn out—more'n likely they had the flu themselves—that half the time I bet they didn't know what the hell they'd given a man.

Most of the boys pulled through all right, but that was one helluva winter for me. I kind of roamed around after that, like most drillers do, following the booms. I drilled in Drumright, Cushing, Kiefer, and all around. And those fields I didn't drill in I knew all about because I worked with so many fellows that had drilled in 'em. From '23 to '25 I was in Wyoming, drilling for Carter Oil Company. I was working north of Casper, in a new field. They had a gasser there that was about the biggest I ever saw, or heard. You could hear that thing blowing off—letting the gas blow free—clear up to Buffalo, twenty miles or so away. All the horses and cats and dogs 'round there went deaf from hearing it; the horses'd have to look back over their shoulders to get their orders. No lie; that's what they did. That was pretty good production up there, too, but it wasn't drilled as heavy as it has been since then.

When I came back from Wyoming I went to Stroud and Ingalls and Ripley; I made $20 a day in those fields, and that was tops then. First part of '26 I went down to Seminole and drilled some wells, then I got a job down at Sasakwa, south of Seminole, drilling a well in the middle of the Canadian River. That was a real job, drilling in that damned treacherous river. Liable to lose everything we had in a sudden rise. We had the feet of our rig pierced up on concrete footings, and the roughnecks built a long runway from the bank to the rig, about fourteen feet above the riverbed. One day the pusher looked around and told the head teamster that he'd better move all the loose stuff up on the rig floor or on the bank. We'd left lumber and pipes and stuff like that down in the rig cellar and around on the riverbed below. The teamster snaked the stuff up, and by God, before my tower went off there came a rise in the river that damned near washed up over the rig floor. I don't see how that can happen; there won't be a cloud in the sky, and yet there'll come a rise that'll wash away houses and everything else that isn't bolted down. I've seen the same thing happen down near Newcastle and Blanchard and up on the Cimarron River, where I drilled some more riverbed wells.

But seems like there's always some good production in those kind of wells. I don't believe I ever drilled in a "duster"—one that doesn't make a showing of oil—in a river. Most of those river wells come in good. In February '26 I went to Seminole again and worked there that winter and summer, then I moved up north and drilled a well in the Cimarron River. Drilled a couple over near Cushing, too, that winter. By that time I had a lot of experience. I'd worked in between times at Burkburnette and Breckenridge, Texas; in Carter County, Oklahoma, near Ardmore and Healdton; and down around Walters and Waurika and Duncan, Oklahoma. Most of the time I'd been drawing around $15 a day, and I'd managed to save some of it.

I came to Oklahoma City in the last few days of '29 and waited around to see what was going to happen. Most geologists said there wouldn't be a thing in the Oklahoma City field, and when the discovery well came in there was a helluva scramble for leases, and for drillers and hands to drill the wells. I drilled the second well in the Oklahoma City field; it made a good showing of oil, but there was so much gas pressure that the company decided to make a gas well out of it. They sold gas to the rest of the drilling companies and the next couple of dozen wells that were brought in used the gas from my well to drill with. Doesn't seem like any time since this field was drilled in here at Oklahoma City. I guess that when a man gets older, times goes a lot faster for him.

In '32 I was working on a steam line, trying to get it hooked up, and it broke and threw me off. There must've been about 500 pounds pressure on that line, because when the line broke it threw me about 75 feet away. It broke my ribs and bruised me up a lot, and ruptured my appendix. I had to have two operations in the next eleven months, and course I wasn't worth a damn when the sawbones got through with me. I couldn't do anything; I was too weak to get out on a rig floor and get the job done, and drilling was the only things I knew.

Funny thing about those operations, too. I'd been around gas so much the doc couldn't knock me out with that weak gas stuff they used in the hospital. He tried about an hour; he emptied up a drum or two and he says to the one that was helping him that I was about one case in ten thousand that couldn't be put under with gas. I raised up and said, "You mean, ten-thousand-and-one don't you, Doc?" Well, you oughta seen that old man's face when I raised up and said that! I'd insisted on having gas instead of ether, because I don't like that stuff, but after that happened he made me take ether. When I got out of the hospital that damned ether had turned my hair white, like it is now. Hell, if I was to go out now and strike up some contractor I didn't know, which ain't very likely, he'd take one look at my gray hair and say nuthing doing.

Notes

1.   The lowest man in the drilling crew pecking order, the roustabout was an unskilled laborer responsible for moving equipment, supplies, and for various menial tasks. Leo

Crook, *Oil Terms* (London: Wilton House, 1975), 60–61; Eric Partrige, *A Concise Dictionary of Slang and Unconventional English* (New York: Macmillan, 1990), 549.

2. See "'Snake' Magee and the Rotary Boiler" in this volume.

3. A pulley or set of pulleys mounted at the top of an oil derrick from which the drilling instruments are raised and lowered. Crook, *Oil Terms*, 48–49; R. D. Langenkamp, *The Illustrated Petroleum Reference Dictionary* (Tulsa, OK: PennWell Books, 1994), 94.

4. Given the narrator's description of the location of this apparatus, halfway between the crown-block and the floor, it seems that he is referring to what is more commonly called the *traveling block*. The traveling block is a part of the drilling assembly that moves the weighty drill pipe and casing equipment. A massive hook is attached to the traveling block that connects the pipe and casing to the rest of the moving assembly. Crook, *Oil Terms*, 115; Langenkamp, *Illustrated Petroleum Reference Dictionary*, 474.

5. See "'Snake' Magee and the Rotary Boiler."

6. The term derives from the angled steel block placed in a borehole in order to redirect the drill bit at an angle. The wedge would have allowed a driller to extend underground into a neighboring well property without being visible from the well surface. Crook, *Oil Terms*, 121; Langenkamp, *Illustrated Petroleum Reference Dictionary*, 514.

7. Persons in charge of driving mules in a wagon train. Stuart Berg Flexner, *I Hear America Talking* (New York: Van Nostrand Reinhold, 1976), 107–8.

8. These laborers were slightly above the level of *roustabout* on the drilling crew. Roughnecks worked in the derrick and replaced parts of the drilling assembly as needed. Crook, *Oil Terms,* 60–61.

9. A British colonial expression for afternoon tea. Sarah Murray, *Moveable Feasts* (New York: St. Martin's, 2007), 88.

10. A colloquialism from the logging industry. The meaning is to labor very intensely or quickly at something. Harold Wentworth and Stuart Berg Flexner, *Dictionary of American Slang* (New York: Crowell, 1960), 17.

11. Oil field supervisors, also *gang pushers*. Langenkamp, *Illustrated Petroleum Reference Dictionary*, 174.

"SNAKE" MAGEE
AND THE ROTARY BOILER

Jim Thompson (Oklahoma)

I hear it spread around in some fields that the reason a rotary rig[1] uses four boilers while cable tools[2] only use one is because a rotary got so much more work to do, all of which is a fundamental lie. It taken four boilers for a rotary, because none of them is any good, as to which no man in the country is in better shape to testify than I am.

I only work with one rotary boiler in my time. It was not a rotary rig otherwise—just good old cable-tools—and I would not have been working with it if I'd known what it was. The first I knew that anything was wrong was with the safety valve. You take a good cable-tool boiler and hang a six-inch bit on the safety valve, and you got a head a steam that pulls a mile of hole right up on top of the ground and pulls the derrick right down where the hole used to be. But this rotary boiler—I didn't know that was what it was—didn't react properly. I hang a six-inch bit on the safety, and she goes to jumping up and down, like a walking-beam[3] on soft structure. And I hang a Stillson wrench[4], a sledge hammer, and a short piece of fifteen-inch pipe on the safety, and the results was alarming. The pressure gauge only showed three hundred and eighty pounds to the square inch, but them boiler plates begin to wiggle and squirm like mustard plasters[5] on a itchy back, and the whole thing begin to jiggle like a little boy when the teacher can't see his hand.

We only making about fourteen hundred feet of hole a day, so my tool dresser[6] been staying in town until I need him. But I work with tricky boilers before and need no help. I do not even need to put the fire out. It was a secret of mine, but I will tell it to you in case you should need to fix a boiler when the fire is going.

Take and jump into the slush-pit[7] where the mud is fresh and damp. Then, before the mud getting hard, think of something that throws you into a cold sweat. The cold cause your body to contract, and the first thing you know there is a wall of perspiration between your body and the mud. This keeps the mud pliable and easy to work in, like a big glove, and the sweat keeps you from scorching, when you step into the fire-box.[8] How do you keep from breathing the flame? Well, I will tell you another secret. Most people taken breath from the outside and breathe in; when you are working in the fire, you taken a breath from the inside and breathe out. You can do this, when you know how, because the body is ninety-nine per cent water, and water is nothing but h-two-o. Besides, water purifies itself every fifteen feet and all you got to do is keep moving and you always got a fresh supply of air.

I leave the rig to run itself because we are not making more than nineteen hundred feet of hole a day, and there is really not nah-thing to do. Then, I take a Stillson, a ball-peen hammer, a acetelyne torch, and a new set of flues and go out and climb into the fire-box.

Right away, I says to myself, "Magee," I says, "this boiler is uncommonly frail. I would almost suspect it of being a rotary boiler. We have only four hundred and thirty-six pounds of steam and the heat indicator only shown eleven hundred and ninety-nine degrees Fahrenheit, but there is every evidence of inferior materials. Something must be done with expediency."

I see there is no use putting new flues in the old can, because the plates have begin to melt and will not hold a flue, so I think rapidly. If I have had my sky-hooks[9] there, I would have flipped the boiler over so the pressure is against the bottom instead of the top, but I loan them out that very morning. I finally see the boiler will have to be reversed, so that the outside of the plates, which is cool, will be turned in. This is just like turning a coat wrongside out, and I have done it many times. But just as I am pulling the smokestack down through the fire-box this rotary boiler explodes.

When I wake up I think I am in jail, like I have sometimes seen pictures of men, because there is bars all around me. But then there is a nah-thing beneath my feet or over my head and I am sailing through the air at a terrific speed, and I remember what happen. "Magee," I says, "these are the grates that are wrapped around you, and you are in the air because the boiler blown up." I worry some-what because I am a law-abiding citizen and do not have a license to fly, but then I begin to see that I am slightly hurt. The mud protecting me some, but I have six broken ribs, a fractured back, concussion of the brain, a ruptured appendix, a busted nose, both arms and legs broken in from three to twelve places, and a slight headache.

"Magee," I says, "you have excellent grounds for a damage suit against the rotary manufacturing company. When you are through collecting there will be no more rotaries and wells will be drilt with cable-tools as God originally intended."

I do not think anything very long, of course, because I am traveling somewhat faster than light which is forty-four thousand foot pounds per second, and before I know it I am back in town sixteen miles away and dropping down in front of our boarding house.

I holler for my tool-dresser, Haywire Haynes, who is still sleeping, to come out, and he does so swiftly.

"Are you hurt, Magee?" he asks.

"Only slightly," I says. "I doubt if I will be incapacitated for more than thirty or forty years. But I am going to sue the rotary manufacturing company for every cent they are worth. When I am through there will not be a rotary left on the face of the earth."

He shaken his head. "You can't do that, Magee. You been blown back here so fast you arrived before you got started. You can't sue for being injured because you ain't been to work yet this morning."

I thought a moment and seen he was right. "If that's the case," I says, "I may as well get well, right now."

Notes

1. Categorized by the circulating, boring movement of a drill bit into the earth, aspects of this technology are still in use today. There are a number of mechanical differences between rotary- and cable-tool drilling practices, but the most salient is that rotary drilling is a steady boring into the ground rather than a "percussive" technique. The history and development of rotary drilling runs concurrently with that of cable tools and sometimes the two techniques are used together. From a broader economic perspective, the narrator's skeptical tone toward rotary-drilling equipment is significant. The era of the Great Depression was a period of major technological transition in the oil industry and the years 1934–1937 saw the most dramatic increase in the integration of rotary method drilling equipment than any other period in drilling history. Though the conversion had been taking place for years before the mid-thirties, the substantial waning in the prevalence of cable-tool drilling rigs around this time, and the ensuing decrease in demand for the skills needed to operate them, created industry wide anxieties among oil workers about the security of their jobs. American Petroleum Institute, *History of Petroleum Engineering* (Dallas: American Petroleum Institute, 1961), 138–39, 274–75.

2.   A method of percussion drilling, cable-tool rigs use the inertia of a falling drill bit, attached to a cable, to strike into the earth in order to create downward expansion of a borehole. Though "derricks" (the large, wooden structures rising over the oil well) are present in both cable-tool and rotary rigs, the major visual characteristic of cable tools is the presence of the see-sawing "walking beam." Cable and rotary rigs often shared the same steam-power technologies, and even the exact same boilers, during this time, hence the narrators confusion about the type of rig he was working with. American Petroleum Institute, *History*, 138–41, 274–75, 305; Leo Crook, *Oil Terms* (London: Wilton House, 1975), 57–60, 117.

3.   This steam-powered lever moves up and down to raise and lower the cable-tool bit into the well cavity. Crook, *Oil Terms*, 117.

4.   Known to contemporary Americans as a pipe wrench, the Stillson wrench was patented by Daniel C. Stillson in 1870. It bears a resemblance to the monkey wrench but holds a different patent claim. The primary difference between the two wrenches is that the Stillson uses torsional friction to grip a pipe or bolt, whereas the monkey wrench has flat, parallel jaws that won't hold a rounded surface. Daniel C. Stillson, *Improvement in Wrenches*, (US Patent 107,304, issued September 13, 1870); Roger Jones, *What's Who: A Dictionary of Things Named After People and the People They Are Named After*, (Leicester, UK: Troubador, 2008), 245; Ralph Treves, "The Tools You Need for Pipe Jobs," *Popular Science*, August, 1963: 164.

5.   As a home remedy, mustard has been used as a rubefacient, or topical poultice, for relieving chest congestion. In certain forms, mustard is highly toxic and a severe irritant to human tissue and mucous membranes. It would have caused severe discomfort if left on the skin for any significant period of time. Charles W. Fetrow, *Professional's Handbook of Complementary & Alternative Medicines*, Edited by Juan R. Avila, (Springhouse, PA: Springhouse, 1999), 446–47.

6.   The person on the drilling crew whose job is to replace and rehone the worn cutting surface of cable-tool bits. R. D. Langenkamp, *The Illustrated Petroleum Reference Dictionary* (Tulsa, OK: PennWell Books, 1994), 468.

7.   The area on a drill site where the slurry of mud and particulates displaced by the drilling process is kept. Also called a "mud hole" or "mud pond." Norman J. Hyne, *Dictionary of Petroleum Exploration, Drilling & Production* (Tulsa, OK: PennWell, 1991), 329.

8.   The section of the oil-rig boiler where the fuel source was loaded. American Petroleum Institute, *History*, 304–5.

9.   The name derived from a prank seasoned workers would play on newer workers where the initiate would be sent looking for an imaginary tool. Confusingly, the moniker eventually came to mean a real pipe-gripping tool used on the rig. Also shortened to just "hooks," these tongs were used for gripping round objects such as pipe or boiler surfaces. Eric Partridge, *A Concise Dictionary of Slang and Unconventional English* (New York: Macmillan, 1990), 589; Langenkamp, *Illustrated Petroleum Reference Dictionary*, 208.

SADE DUGGETT

Ned DeWitt

Lots of people act like they think I'm off my nut when I tell 'em I'm in the oil game, kind of. They got the idea that the only thing there is to oil is a bunch of guys drilling a well, cussing hollering and getting drunk payday, but it ain't. One of the most important things 'bout oil or anything else, far as that goes, is eating, and I kind of made it my job to see that all the guys 'round the oil field get enough to eat. These smart punks that think eating ain't connected with the oil game and that the field ain't no place for a woman can go to hell far's I'm concerned; I'll back what I say by the guys that's eat with old Sadie Duggett—that's my full name, but ever' body calls me "Sade"—all these years.

You oughta been here when this Oklahoma City field was wide open, and I'd just started up this eating house. Why, I've seen the time when this place wouldn't hold the men that wanted to eat with me, and this is big enough to feed a hunnerd. They'd drive for miles to get here, and come crowding in, shoving and pushing, and all of 'em hollering at Lovie and me to give 'em personal attention, and that kind of stuff would keep up for hours, with the cash register dinging like a patrol wagon bell. Me and Lovie would be wore out by the time the noon rush was over, and before we could get the place cleaned up and new plates put on and roust the cooks up to get the food cooked, why it'd be evening again, and time for 'em to come back. But that was when there was a boom on; now it's so quiet you can hear the cockroaches walking 'round. Not that I get a lot of cockroaches, but it's just that quiet sometimes.

When I first started in this cafe business, it was good. There was boom oil towns and camps all over the country, and all I had to do was figger just which one I was going to light in and set out. The men that was working in them towns was just a-honing to set their teeth in some homecooked meals, and they didn't mind paying for them neither. They all made good money then too. Many's the time I've set out a platter of bacon-and-eggs, or maybe ham—and, and rung up a dollar on the cash register. But most of the time, until I got Dan to watch the register for me, I used a cigar box or whatever was handy to keep my money in. I didn't trust nobody then, or any other time either, and I always keep my money in something I can carry 'round with me. And I'd get a buck-and-a-half or maybe two for a dinner and supper, and didn't any of the boys mind paying out their hard-earned for it either. They liked my cooking so much that lots of 'em told me they'd give five dollars a platter if they had to—my cooking was worth it.

But eat! Godamighty! I never saw anything could eat like those men could then! They could set down and eat a half-dozen eggs, a side of bacon apiece, four cups of coffee, and push all of that down with a loaf of bread and a couple of pieces of pie. I run lots of family-style eating places—where all the food's on the table, and everybody helps themselves—and lots of times I had to jack my prices up to come out even. But they don't eat enough no more, not like they used to. I don't see how some of these guys can go out and work all day on what they get to eat nowadays. Most of them get married; and their wives think they can work on the same kind of food that they eat, but they can't. No man a-living can do a real day's work on the same things a woman'll fix for herself; there just ain't enough to it. But if they ain't get enough sense but to get theirselves tied down to some little fly-by-night hussy that don't know anything but toast and coffee and orange juice, then it ain't nobody's fault but their own.

You might say I was brought up on food, practically altogether. I always had plenty of it around me when I was growing up, and so it come kind of natural for me to go into running a cafe. My folks lived on a farm down in Georgia, and even if we didn't have much money we always had plenty to eat. You had to have lots when there's nine kids, and all of 'em working from can see to can't see—like the niggers usually say. I'd had to turn my hand to the cooking ever since I was a little bit of a thing, and I like it, so I didn't mind at all. I was as fat as a pig from working in the kitchen and eating so much, but I wasn't bad looking by a long sight. They marry 'em off young down there, and I had a bunch of those country boys hanging 'round the house before I was more'n twelve or thirteen. But I couldn't see 'em for the hay in their ears; I didn't like the looks of the women that had spent their lives on a farm, and I didn't want none of it.

We went to the county seat one Saturday, like all farmers do, just to see the sights and get in the week's buying, and so forth. I had a little money I'd make picking peanuts for a neighbor, and while the rest of the family was going around to the stores I decided to try some city cooking. I went into a cafe there and ordered a plate lunch. Well sir, that was as poor a meal as I ever tried to eat. There wasn't much meat to it, and what there was wasn't half-cooked, and the vegetables looked like they had the hookworm or pellagra, or both. The manager waited on me, and he saw me looking at the food and kind of turning it over with my fork. He ast me if there was anything wrong with it, and I said, No, nothing in particular but a lot in general. I told him that if that was a sample of the best food he could put out, it was a wonder he had any business at all. He got kind of worked up about it, and asked me how I'd fix the book, if I knew so much about it. I was mad, too, because I was hungry, and so I said I'd bet him a dollar to a piece of his pie that I could take the same kind of food and fix it so somebody could eat it without puking. He said he'd just take me up; for me to get behind the counter and get to work. I thought he was joking at first, and then I got mad and hopped around there and pushed the cook out of the way. He was a dried-up old man that looked like he stayed drunk all the time, so I shoved him out of my way and ast this guy what he wanted me to cook for him.

When he saw how I took hold of things he kind of laughed and said he'd give me a dollar and a half a day and my board. I thought it over a minute, just a minute, and I said all right, wait till I told my folks I wasn't going home with 'em. I went out and found my sister Laviny and told her to tell the folks for me, and for her to send other dresses in the next week. Then I went back to the cafe and started work.

I worked for that guy about six or eight months, and then I quit because he was always trying to get his hands on me. I learned a lot about cooking, though, and I worked in another cafe in that town. I got tired of that one and went to Atlanta and worked for a while, and then over to Louisiana. There was a little boom town over in Texas, and one day a feller was eating there in a cafe where I was and he said anybody that could cook like me ought to be in that boom town; I could make a million dollars. I was already tired of the place I was in, and I had some money saved up, not much of course, what with cooking in little towns, and I ast this guy all about the oilfields. Well, by the end of that week I was in that boom town, and had put me up a tent and started a cafe of my own.

I had to pay so much down for my tent and to rent enough ground to throw it on I didn't have a whole lot of money left for groceries. I specialized on pancakes, and those oilfield workers ate 'em up. 'Fore long I hired three girls to wait table and I did all the cooking. I worked about sixteen hours a day most of the time, sometimes all night if the boys needed lunches put up for 'em or something like that, but I cleaned up all right. Before long I had enough money to build me a shack out of sawed lumber and put in a better line of food. I still did all the cooking, but I hired men waiters; the girls weren't worth a damn in a boom town because they don't want to have to work for a living. And when I got better groceries in the boys didn't mind paying six-bits' for a stack of cakes and a buck-and-a-half for supper. The food was good, and there was lots of it, so they didn't mind at all.

I saw the boom was going to die out there, and I sold the cafe for three thousand, and followed the oil to another town. I put in a pretty good place there, and went to making money hand over fist. When that boom started to die I went to another one, but I thought at first I was going to get sunk on that one. The oil companies were putting in camps for their men; they served lots of beans and rice and potatoes, filling things, but not very tasty. I had to compete with them, so I put in a family-style cafe. I did all my own cooking and buying groceries and things like that, but I still had a pretty hard time of it. But it wasn't long till the guys working there got to know me and passed the word along, and then business started on the up. I got six-bits for breakfast here too, and a dollar-and-a-half for dinner and supper, like the other towns I'd been in, but I had to pay my waiters thirty a week to keep 'em. I had a hard time getting any waiters at all, 'cause most of those guys wanted to be out in the field knocking off some big money, they thought, and the birds I did get drank all my lemon extract and vanilla till I couldn't make a pie or anything half the time. Couldn't get girls, and I didn't want 'em anyway after the time I'd had with the first batch of 'em.

One afternoon I just sat down on a stool, so damned tired I didn't know which end was up. We'd had a big noon rush and right in the middle of it I had to put up forty lunches for some guys working on a lease quite a ways out of town. I was hot and sweaty and feeling mad and all when in come a girl and sat down close to me on a stool. The minute I saw her I knew what she was, or thought I did. I'd seen so many women 'round these booms, but it was all right with me if she wanted to eat in my place and had the price. I never barred nobody if they had the cash. This girl sat down and ordered a cup of coffee, and kept looking at me. Finally I said, Been in town long? She shook her head but didn't say anything. That made me kind of mad, her not saying anything, and I said, Where you holing up? She just looked at me, kind of tired. Then she takes a sip of coffee and says, You need a girl? I laughed like hell. Me need a girl; what the hell do you think I am, a queer? I ast her.

She just kept on looking at me till I got through laughing, and then she ast me again, if I wanted a waitress. I said, No; because I didn't want any women hanging 'round my place egging the men on. She said, I'll work for my room and board if you'll just give me a job. That kind of knocked my props out from under me. I looked her over again, and she didn't look quite so bad as she did at first. She looked tired, like she'd been out on a week drunk, and kind of dirty and draggled, but not a bad sort after all. I ast her if she knew anything 'bout hashing, and she shook her head and said, No, but she could learn easy.

Well, I gave in and put her to work at ten a week and room and board. I was saving 'bout twenty a week on her, so I couldn't lose much. That was how I met

Lovie—she's the kind of thin girl back there with the short red hair, filling the salt shakers. I didn't know much about her, of course, but I thought I'd giver her a chance and see if she really wanted to get away from the hotels. I ast her her name, and she said it was Dove something-or-other, one of those foreign names. I couldn't keep from laughing again, tired as I was; a name like that, Dove, and she looked more like a sparrow that'd fell in a slush pit and had just come up. But she turned out to be a good worker and all, and it wasn't long till I got to calling her Dovie, and then after a while Lovie, when I found out how she was with the men.

She wasn't what you'd call a bad girl, you understand, not a regular oilfield whore, but she just couldn't say no to any guy that kept in after her. She didn't want money or anything like that, but they always give her something, but that was just about the only way she knew how to get any fun out of living. That's the way I figgered it anyway, but it wasn't any of my business. All right for her, I guess, but I couldn't see it that way. But she drummed up business, not really meaning to I don't suppose, for the cafe, and I didn't care what the hell she did after she got off work anyway, just so she worked all right. And she did, I'll say that, and I just kept her on.

Well, we made just about all the oil booms there was in Texas. When I closed up a place Lovie would ast me where we was going next, and she'd pile right in the train or in the truck, if we'd got some truck driver to haul us, which we usually did to save paying money for train fare, and she'd go right along with me. There wasn't any use trying to shake her, and since she was a good worker and since I'd used all girls after I hired her, and didn't want to have to up with just any kind of girls I could find 'round a boom town, I let her come with me. She got married several times down in Texas, too; she had a husband in damned near every town we stopped in, I guess. She was kind of like a cat; she wouldn't of knowed her husband that she married three years ago if she was to serve him a lunch right now.

She never did ast 'em to marry her or even hint at it, I never heard her lead 'em on to it anyway, but I guess they just kind of took to that red hair of hers and blue eyes and the way she kind of switches when she walks. The first thing I'd know about a new one she'd come to work one morning all pale and big bags under her eyes and say she'd gone off and got married, and more'n likely, just got in from celebrating it to go to work. The guy'd come 'round and eat at the cafe and all, but Lovie always made 'em pay cash; she didn't let her night work mix in with what she had to do, which is something you can't say 'bout a lot of people. And when we'd leave, she'd just pack up her grip² and light out with me, and never say a word to her husband or anybody else.

She got caught once. I had a bean joint down in Longview, Texas, when it was booming, and she got a knockdown³ to a roustabout there. He was a good-looking kid, 'bout six or eight years younger than she was, but she fell for him and they was out together every minute they was off work. God knows when she got time to sleep, but there never was no complaint 'bout her work; she did that all right, all the time. And somehow 'r 'nother she never did get 'round to marrying this guy, or maybe it was the other way, and it wasn't long till she said she was going to domino.[4] She never had thought nuthin 'bout knocking a kid before, but this time she kind of waited 'round and didn't do anything when she was supposed to. Maybe she liked this guy better'n the rest of 'em, I don't know, but pretty soon it was too late. She up and had the kid, a boy, and 'course she had to lay off a couple of months.

This guy had already shoved off so there wasn't any use looking for money from him. She never did get real acquainted with him; I mean, she didn't know a whole lot about him, so it didn't make much difference anyway where he was. She didn't know anybody else and nobody else give a damn about her, just like an old cat, you see? It was up to me. I did what I could for her, paid her bills and so forth, and when it was all over she showed up one day and put on her apron like nothing had happened and went to work. I said, Where's the kid? She looked at me and said, He's gone. Well, and you know that was about the last time she ever said anything about it. And it was about the only time we got sore at each other. I kept on at her about it for a couple of days, but she wouldn't say anything. Come to find out she'd left the kid on a hospital step, and they'd had to take it in, naturally.

I give her hell about; I said I'd of took care of the kid if she'd let me know she was intending to dump it, but she got plain red-headed about the whole deal. I got mad, too, when she started talking back to me, and I told her to go chase a rabbit— I'd got along damned good 'fore I met her and I could still do it. So she left that night, and I didn't see her for quite a while.

I kind of forgot about her after while; I hired another girl, but I had to pay her more, and got busy stuffing everything I could get my hands on in my sock. I had a pretty good wad, too. You 'member long in '29 and '30 there wasn't a whole lot doing in the oil game; well, when the Oklahoma City field come in most of the boys left from Texas and around and hit out for the new field. I'd wanted to get shet of that place I had in Texas for a long time and when I heard the good news, 'bout the new field, I made up my mind I was going to hit it. Business was poor down in Texas there, and I was kind of stumped how to sell for a while. But a guy came in one night and got to talking with me. He'd heard about the town there and was looking 'round for something to put his money in that wouldn't take a whole lot of his time. He was an old buzzard, and there was just him and his wife. They thought if they could get hold of some kind of business all they'd have to do would be to sit down and in a year or two they'd be millionaires. They was from some place in Colorado; don't remember just what town it was now.

Well, this old bird came by one night and stopped and give me the chin.[5] I told him business was on the boom, but it was a lie. I had 30 tables and 26 stools, and when he was in there, it was on Friday night about eight o'clock, there wasn't but two people in there beside me and him. And one of them was the dishwasher, who'd just got off and was reading the paper on the last stool. But I saw what an old codger he was, and that he didn't know 'bout anything in an oilfield, so I acted like I had a gold mine. I finally broke down and told him my husband was waiting for me in Oklahoma City, and that if I could get a good price I'd sell out and go with him.

The old man bit on it, but he didn't like the looks of all the empty stools. I seen him looking around, just like he was getting ready to make me out a liar about all the business I had, and I said, You come 'round here 'bout nine o'clock, when the shows let out, and I'll show you what a rush there is. You can't hardly get in the door, people crowd in here so. He says, Yes? Just like he didn't believe me, but he wanted to awful bad. And I said, Sure, you just come 'round 'bout nine or a little after and you'll see. 'Course I made my pile at breakfast and at noon and night, but he didn't have to know. I only kept open at night to kind of keep my hand in.

So he moseyed on, after promising he'd be back. I knew he would, because he just had to see for himself. You know how people are; they'll believe something if they can just see it. And he wanted the place pretty bad, too. I served plate lunches and short orders and had an ice cream fountain and all that and it looked pretty good to anybody that didn't know their way 'round. So when he went out the door I went to the cash register and got all the money out of it. I took about fifteen dollars in ones and halves and quarters and told the dishwasher to watch the place a while. I went out and rounded up all the ginks[6] I could and told 'em to come in and drink on me, and I'd give those that I knew eat with me some money, so they could act like they was paying me for what they got.

Well, you know there's always a helluva lot of guys out of work in a boom town, and there was plenty of 'em in town that night, just loafing 'round on the streets. It was bad enough 'bout them not working before, but it worse when the boom died. A lot of 'em had come in off the farms or maybe quit a pretty good job someplace else after they heard about how the guys in the oilfields was getting rich, and maybe they got in a few days or a few weeks work, and then it was all over for them. That's one thing I don't like about the game; it drags in a lot of people that ain't got no business being there in the first place, and they just clutter up things till a guy can't move 'round.

Anyway, when this old feller come back in, right around nine o'clock, he couldn't hardly get in the door; there was roughnecks, and roustabouts, and drillers, and pumpers,⁷ and bums, and women, and kids, and everybody that'd been out on the streets. Looked like half the town was there. And they was all talking at the top of their voices, and some of 'em running out and bringing their friends back with 'em, and so much noise that this old guy got so excited he couldn't hardly talk. And I'm a liar if he didn't grab hold of me and holler at me and want to close the deal right then! He just couldn't stand it when he saw all those people guzzling, and when he thought about all the money that'd roll in my register. I told him I'd think it over, and for him to back in the morning if he was still interested, but I had to wait on my trade. I knew I had him hooked, good and proper.

Well, next morning he was there, bright and early, with his checkbook out and his fountain pen ready. I'd kind of thought about getting somebody else to act like he wanted to buy the place too, only there wasn't anybody 'round that I'd trust with my roll; he'd of had to have a roll to flash around in front of the old guy. Lovie was as honest as the day's long, but she wasn't there and I didn't want a woman acting like that anyway, so I just let it go. I fidgeted 'round with this old guy like I didn't really want to sell, and finally I let him think he'd talked me into selling for four thousand, which was about twice what it was worth, with business like it was. I made him go up to the bank and get his check cashed into bills—I always like my money that way, or maybe in a cashier's check—and then I pitched off my apron and turned it over to him. I showed the old woman how to mix ice cream drinks and stuff like that, and then I left out on the next train for Oklahoma City. I rode the cushions that time, because I'd drew out all my money from the bank and had it on me. I had a little over thirteen thousand in my kick right then, and I was going to try to run it to a million.

But I ain't much closer to that million now then I was then, when I was just thinking about it. 'Course, I've gone ahead a little bit, but I ain't rich yet by a helluva lot. They'd already dealt out the hands when I got up here in Oklahoma City, in the spring of '30. The town looked like a regular boom, but it wasn't. There was the usual number of leg-joints, where you could get anything from a drink of bad whiskey to a swat in the puss, and whore houses, and cafes, and supply houses for the oil companies, and all the rest of the boom-town stuff. But it was run some better. What I mean was the places wasn't showy like you'd expect in a town as big as Oklahoma City is, and people acted like the boom wasn't anything so much after all; like a bunch of farmers, you know. And there wasn't so much hellraising either.

But I knew if there was any money here I'd get my share of it or know the reason why, so I went out right on the edge of the oilfield, on the southeast part of town, and staked me out a lot and put up a big eating house. Prices was higher'n a cat's back for land and lumber and anything else; person'd think there never had been a stock market or a depression the way they charged for things here. And the people that'd been on the ground had first pickings, too; I'd horsed around so long down in Texas I'd almost let this boom get away from me.

I had a lot of friends working here, though, fellers that'd eat with me in other towns, and soon's they heard I was here they come in and brought their friends with 'em. I got along all right after a while, right up till times got too hard for me 'r anybody else to make anything, and I kind of began to look around for something else to put my money in. I didn't know anything but cafes, but I reckoned that if I could make money off them I could make it off something else. I looked around town, and finally I decided to give hotels a go. I got a real estate agent and we walked around the whole damned town. And you can mark me down for a liar if I didn't meet Lovie in one of 'em! Yessir, she'd followed the oil right up here to Oklahoma City, and since she didn't know nothing else either, she went to work in a hotel. She was the same old Lovie, but she didn't look quite so young as she had when she was working for me.

She ast me where I was located, and like a damn fool I told her. It wasn't more 'n two days later she turned up out to my place and said she wanted to go to work. Well, I started to ask her about the kid again, the one she'd gone off and left down in Texas, and then I thought what the hell, it ain't none of my business anyway and let bygones be bygones. So I put her to work, and she's been with me ever since. She's a little bit quieter than she was, but she hasn't changed so much that she don't size up the boys when they come in. Guess it's got to be kind of a habit with her.

I didn't buy the hotel after all. I ast around and found out what I'd have to pay for protection and all, and I decided I didn't want any of it. Lovie told me some about how they run 'em, too. I put my money in real estate instead. Like to have lost every penny I had, too, but now there's a boom on in real estate I'm going to come out in the clear with a pretty good profit. I got married, too, during the depression. Times got pretty tough in '32 and '33, and I wasn't making everything I thought I ought to in the cafe, so I put up some beaverboards[8] in the rooms upstairs in my place and rented 'em out to the roustabouts and workers in the supply houses. That helped out considerable. Had one feller that lived with me ever since I first rented out rooms; he was drilling out here in the field and he got hurt. He didn't have any money saved or anything, and when they brought him there to his room I had to let him stay.

There's some kind of a damfool law says you can't move anybody that's sick out of their rooms, even if they can't pay. Made me pretty mad for a while to think how I was getting stuck, but there wasn't anything to do so I hadda let him stay. I got so durned used to him I didn't even notice him, except that he was crippled pretty bad. Lots of fellows always getting bunged up some way out in the fields; it's probably as hard a work and as dangerous as any kind of man can get, and there don't a day pass that somebody don't get hurt. Some of 'em pretty bad, too, like my old man. He got his tools stuck in the hole and was trying to knock 'em out with the power and pulled the whole rig down 'round his ears. Like to've killed him.

He wore a plaster cast for a year or so, and then when he got out of it he was kind of pulled towards the front; he'd got his back broken, and it never did set straight or something. Well, he got all his hospital and doctor's bills paid by the company, and then, just about the time he got to where he could get around all right and was helping around the place here, he got the check for his compensation. He'd had to turn his case over to the state to collect for him, and it'd taken all that time. But he got it, and showed it to me. I ast him what he was going to do with all that money; it was five thousand and some-odd dollars. He said, What would you do with it, Miss Purley: Purley was my name 'fore I was married, Sarah Purley. I said I'd use it to buy some real estate. I had my eye on a piece of ground that I just felt in my bones was going to be worth something some day. He said, All right; you think you can make something out of it, go ahead. But there's one condition; we'll have to do it together.

I laughed, and said how would we do that; he was an oilman and didn't know nothing 'bout real estate. He said, No, he didn't, but I did, and would I marry him? If I was his wife, maybe he could learn too. That kind of floored me for a while. I'd had lots of guys try to make me, lots of times; I'm not so bad-looking, I mean I wasn't when I was a little bit younger, and there was always somebody hanging 'round trying to put his arms around me or something like that, only usually they wanted more'n that. But I always figgered they was after my wad, and I never did warm up to any of 'em much. Course I ain't no old maid, nothing of the kind, but you understand I ain't like, well, say, Lovie. I kind of pick my own man to sleep with, instead of him me. And that ain't been very often neither.

So when this old Dan Duggett ast me to marry him, I was kind of knocked off, because I seen he wanted a home and all and not just a woman. H was stove up pretty bad, but I figgered it out and finally said, Yes. He was a nice dependable sort of a guy, and I liked him; he was easy on my nerves and all. When we got married—we run off to a little town south of here, like a couple of kids—he had his compensation check all endorsed to me, and handed it over to me before we started. That kind of got me, too, him trusting me like that. Damned few people I'd trust, not even him for very much, and I had all my property made out in my new name the day after we was married. But he knew he didn't have so very long to live anyway, what with being crippled and all, and he knew I knew he didn't, so he just let me take care of my money and his too. That's the way we've handled it ever since; he kind of takes care of the roomers, all of 'em's men, and sees that they pay off prompt and all, and I handle the money.

I got kind of used to Lovie being around, too, and I guess I'll look after her long as she stays with me. I always kind of looked out after people. I guess I always will. Lovie's a good worker, too, and I couldn't get another girl that'd do all the work she does for her ten a week and room and board. 'Course her room don't cost me anything, 'cause this property's all clear and in my name, and if she wasn't using it, it might be empty anyway. But I wouldn't think of charging Lovie rent anyway; it's kind of nice to have a woman around that you know and feel comfortable with, like Lovie, even if she ain't so smart of anything. But she doesn't want much, and I'm willing to put up with her tom-catting around, so long's it ain't with my roomers, so neither one of us has got any complaint.

Notes

1.　Or 75¢. Harold Wentworth and Stuart Berg Flexner, *Dictionary of American Slang* (New York: Crowell, 1960), 479.
2.　A nineteenth-century euphemism for a suitcase or a small travel bag. Eric Partrige, *A Concise Dictionary of Slang and Unconventional English* (New York: Macmillan, 1990), 308.
3.　An introduction to another person. Wentworth and Flexner, *Dictionary*, 308.
4.　To abandon or cease something. In this context, the meaning would be that she was going to quit working. Partrige, *Concise Dictionary*, 210.
5.　To have a casual, shallow or time-wasting conversation. Partrige, *Concise Dictionary*, 135; Wentworth and Flexner, *Dictionary*, 100.
6.　Expression for old, disheveled men. The term can also implicate someone as being smelly and ungroomed. Partrige, *Concise Dictionary*, 289; Wentworth and Flexner, *Dictionary*, 215.
7.　Freeloading persons, or those living on handouts, borrowed money, or credit. Partrige, *Concise Dictionary*, 518; Wentworth and Flexner, *Dictionary*, 410.
8.　Cheap, wooden, wallboard material used to make room dividers or walls. The name comes from a trademark of the Beaver Products Company, Inc., in Buffalo, NY. "Beaver Board," *Factory: The Magazine of Management* Vol. 29, December, 1922: 654.

DISCONTINUED MODEL

Francis Donovan (Connecticut)

"The fact is, Martin," said Fielding, the assembly room foreman, "you're here to take the place of Old Pop Johnson. He don't know it yet, and I hate like the devil to tell him."

"They're letting him go?"

"We call it 'retired on pension,'" Fielding said. "He's been here nearly sixty years. You'd think a man'd be glad to sit back and take it easy at his age, wouldn't you? You'd think those old birds would appreciate a little pension and a chance to rest their bones of a morning instead of hustling down to the shop at seven o'clock."

"You'd think so," Martin agreed.

"Well, they don't," Fielding said glumly. "None of them. Old Pop's down here six o'clock every morning waiting for the gates to open. An hour early, mind you. Winter and summer. I been here ten years and he ain't been late or absent one working day, far's I can remember."

"Some record," Martin said.

"Ain't it? Trouble with a lot of the old timers, they got the idea the company can't function without 'em. That's the way Pop figures. As a matter of fact, methods of clock manufacture have changed so fast the past few years, most of these old boys have been left way behind. Take that movement Pop works on—the hundred and twelve A—they're gonna discontinue it. We couldn't put him on the smaller stuff because his eyes ain't what they used to be."

Fielding took out a plug of tobacco and a jackknife, cut a small slice, and inserted it under his upper lip. He offered the plug to Martin, who declined hastily.

"I got to have tobacco in some form," Fielding said. "You smoke? Don't try it here, in the toilet, or anywhere else. They'll fire you just like that." He snapped expressive fingers.

"Well, come on, I'll show you your bench and get you started."

The room was immense, slightly longer than it was wide, with huge windows of opaque glass. Martin, nervous and suffering from pangs of uncertainty that always assailed him at the beginning of a new venture, got a confused picture of innumerable rows of busy workers, seated closely together at the long benches; heard the whirring of belts overhead and the buzz of small machinery. Over most of the benches were green-shaded electric bulbs and Martin noticed that some of these were in use. He followed Fielding down the outside aisle, and, as they passed, the men and women at the benches looked up, but their busy fingers never faltered. Chairs scraped the floor here and there as men got up with boxes of clock movements in various stages of development, or sat down again after completing an errand.

Fielding stopped at the end of the bench nearest the window. There was a vacant chair here, and tools had been laid out neatly on the bench on a smooth iron plate. At one side, was a shallow, rectangular wooden box, containing tidy rows of shining brass clock movements. Fielding put his foot up on the chair and rested his elbow on his knee.

"This is the famous Pop Johnson," he said, indicating the old man in the next chair. Pop turned, looking up over a pair of gold-rimmed glasses, which hung in a precarious manner half way down the bridge of his nose. Their hooks were poised delicately on the tips of Pop's generous ears, and they were kept from falling apparently by a miracle of balance which precluded any ill-advised motion of the wearer's hand. Behind, or rather above them, Pop's frost blue eyes appraised the newcomer thoroughly.

"Pop, this here lad is John Martin," Fielding said. "We're gonna try and make an escaper out of him. He's a college man, so I don't think he'll have any trouble with this job."

"Oh, sure, sure," said Pop, his voice fairly prickled with sarcasm; "you got to go to college to be a good escaper. I'm a Vassar graduate, myself."

Fielding laughed.

"Don't mind him," he said. "He's the meanest old bugger we got around here. We used to have to muzzle him till he lost all his teeth. Now he can't bite no more."

Pop grunted and turned back to his work. Fielding sat down in the chair and took up a clock movement. To Martin's untrained eye it appeared a vastly complicated array of wheels and pinions, held firmly together by shining brass plates. But he drew comfort from the thought that he'd never yet failed to get the hang of a machine.

"It really isn't so hard," Fielding said. "This here," he tapped with a small screw-driver, "is the escape pinion and wheel; and this is the pallet and fork. In the completed movement, this is where the balance and hairspring go. Now the escape pinion gets its push from the train—that is to say, all the other wheels and mainspring which have been put in before—and delivers it to the escapement through the interaction of escape wheel teeth and pallet. See what I mean? Now, here, look close."

Martin bent to peer over Fielding's shoulder.

"The main thing is to get these teeth to strike far enough up—get 'em a little too low and they skip, and that throws your whole operation out of whack, see? Now you watch me do a couple, you'll get on to it easy enough."

Martin obeyed, watching intently. Old Pop was also watching. Presently he said:

"Seems to me a college man shoulda caught on to that by this time, Fielding."

"Oh, shut up, Pop," said Fielding mildly.

"Sit down, Martin, and try a couple. You think you get the idea? We don't expect you to pick it up in five minutes, of course."

Martin sat down and extracted a movement from the box. He was awkward and self-conscious, and painfully aware of Old Pop's malicious interest. He picked up a pinion from the small cardboard container and inserted one end in the little hole in the plate, and then his fingers were all thumbs and he couldn't get the other end properly in place.

"I guess that operation wa'n't in the college course," Pop observed. Fielding, standing directly behind Martin's chair, said nothing. Martin's struggle with the recalcitrant verge was suddenly successful. It was in place, and he held up the movement as Fielding had done to watch the teeth action of the escape-wheel. Fielding gave him an encouraging pat on the shoulder.

"Take your time now, and don't let Pop get you down," he said. "I'll come around and see how you're doing from time to time."

He left, and some of Martin's tension eased a bit. But Pop was apparently determined to continue his heckling. He turned to the man on his left.

"Look, Dietrich, we got a new escaper."

"You dink I am blind?" said Dietrich. "I seed him pefore." He was a heavy-set man, middle-aged, phlegmatic.

"But he's a college boy, Dietrich," persisted Pop. "They're gonna put college boys in all these jobs, I hear. Then you and me will be out."

"You, maybe," said Dietrich. "You are oldt. Me, nod for many years yet."

Pop's tobacco stained gray moustache, of the type best described as "walrus," bristled fiercely, and his blue eyes flashed indignantly behind the glasses.

"Whatta you mean I'm old? I'm only seventy-eight. My dad lived till ninety-four, and worked for this company till he was ninety."

"T'ings is different now," said Dietrich inexorably. "You know yourself, Bop, t'ings is different. The vork is not the same like it vas tventy, even ten years ago. It dakes young plood, Bop. Pesides, I dell you someding." Dietrich leaned toward Pop and spoke in a stage whisper.

"I hear dot movement you vork on no more vill be made."

"The hundred and twelve A?" Pop's old voice broke in an incredulous squeak. "You're crazy, man, Why, they got orders fer thousands of 'em."

Dietrich shrugged a heavy shoulder.

"I shust dell you vot I hear."

Pop, who had been looking for acquiescence, was discomfited by the rebuffs and turned somewhat uncertainly to the recent object of his scorn.

"Dietrich is always hearin' somethin'," he said. Martin, busy with his work, said nothing. Pop cleared his throat and tried again.

"How you makin' out, young feller."

Martin looked up and smiled.

"Pretty good, I guess," he said. "Tell you better after Fielding inspects some of these movements."

"Uh—Fielding say anything to you about discontinuin' hundred an' twelve A's?"

"No," said Martin hastily. Pop was so reassured that he felt he could afford to be generous.

"You have any trouble with them things, just let me know. I only been doin' this work about forty-five years, so it's just possible I know as much about it as Fielding."

"Fielding said you've worked for the company nearly sixty years," Martin said. The old man was instantly on the defensive again.

"He did, did he? What else did he say?"

"Why, nothing," said Martin, shifting uneasily in his chair. "Just told me I was going to work next to one of the company's oldest employees."

"The oldest employee," Pop corrected. "Yessir, they let a lot of them go last year, but they kept me. The super said there wa'n't no reason to retire the best escaper in the shop, less'n I wanted it. Says, 'Pop,' he says, 'do you want to git out and live a life of sinful ease, er do you want to stick with us fer a while?'"

"I says, 'Jim'—I always call him Jim—'Jim' I says, 'when I'm ready to quit, I'll notify you to that effect.' And then, I says, 'you kin take me out an' shoot me.'"

"'Shooting's too good fer you, you sinful old rascal,' he says, 'we'll make you work till you drop.'"

Pop chuckled contentedly at the recollection of this passage at arms. He was obviously proud to have spoken so familiarly to the "super." His wrinkled old fingers, surprisingly nimble, moved busily at his work; but he used an eyeglass in addition to his spectacles, Martin noticed, though the movement on which he worked was relatively large.

"Yessir, the oldest employee," Pop continued. "Started sixty years ago, lackin' just four months. Started poundin' scrap, down in the press room. And I worked at pretty near every branch of the business. Used to do ear trimin', once. You got to be good to do that. Done adjusin', too, best job in this room at one time."

The thin wire attached to his eyeglass circled his thick white hair. Pop fumbled with it for an instant, then pulled the eyeglass down over the right lens of his spectacles and looked closely at his work. Satisfied with the escapement, he placed the movement on one side and took up another. Martin, too, had quite a number of movements to his credit, and was reasonably sure they were well done.

"You've had plenty of experience around here," he replied.

"You might say so," said Pop dryly. "Why, when I was your age, I used to make my own tools, if I needed any. Think we'd send for a toolmaker in them days? Not on your life, son. I got some here in the drawer I been usin' fer fifty years. Yessir, we learned the business from the ground up."

"That's what I'm trying to do, in a way," Martin said. "I'd like to get in the sales department eventually. If I know something about the way they're made, I'll be a better salesman, don't you think?"

Pop brightened noticeably.

"You ain't gonna stay on this job, then?"

"No longer than I can help," said Martin.

"You hear that, Dietrich?" Pop cried triumphantly. "They're just training this feller for an office job."

"Yah," said the stolid Dietrich. "But I dell you shust the zame, Bop, dey discontinue hunned und twelf A."

The old man flushed angrily.

"Dietrich, in your own language, you're a dumbkopf,"[1] he said.

"Maybe yes, maybe no," Dietrich retorted.

Dietrich's calmness under fire had a bad effect on Pop's morale. He turned again to Martin.

"Why should they discontinue 'em? They sell 'em by the thousands."

Martin pretended deep interest in his work. The situation was making him distinctly uncomfortable.

Fielding came down the aisle and laid a hand on his shoulder.

"Well, how's it going?" he asked.

Before Martin could answer, old Pop spoke up.

"Fielding, I got something I want to ask you man to man."

"Fair enough, Pop," Fielding said gravely. "I got something I want to tell you man to man."

The old man had started to rise from his chair, but there was something so foreboding in Fielding's tone that it gave him a shock and he sat down again. Fielding looked at him compassionately.

"You better come over here, Pop," he said. "Over here by the sink, where we can talk it over in private."

Pop got up, a trifle unsteadily, and followed the foreman over to the corner he had indicated. Across the old man's vacant chair, Dietrich looked at Martin and nodded his head significantly. Bent over his work, Martin could see nothing more of either Pop or Fielding, nor was their conversation audible, but presently he heard the door of the men's room slam, and he became aware that the foreman was standing behind him again.

"I finally told him," Fielding said.

"How'd he take it?" Martin asked, conscious of the absurdity of the question.

"He didn't say anything," Fielding said. "Just walked into the lavatory. He didn't want to break down in front of me, I suppose, the poor old coot."

"It's pretty tough," said Martin.

Fielding nodded. "He has no wife," he said slowly, "no family, only some distant relatives out West somewheres. All his friends are here, his life is here. He's as proud of this company, as proud of the clocks we make as if he was president. His old man worked here before him—knew old Hoadley, the founder of the business, 'way back before the Civil War. I tell you, Martin, it's like pullin' a tree up by the roots."

There was a moment's pause.

"Well, let's have a look at what you've done, young fella."

Fielding picked up a movement, and then put it down again.

"It won't be that he'll have nothing to live *on*, he'll have nothing to live *for*. I seen it happen before. Mark my words, he won't live a year."

"I feel pretty bad, taking his job," Martin said.

"You're not taking his job," said Fielding. It just can't be helped, that's all. His eyes are bad, he can't do his work. And he won't take a sweeping job, or anything like that. What can you do? He'll come out of there in a few minutes and you won't know anything happened. But take my advice, Martin, don't sympathize with him. Old as he is, he'd swing one right at you. Well, this ain't gettin' the work out, is it? Let's have another look at these movements."

Note

1. German for a stupid person. Eric Partrige, *A Concise Dictionary of Slang and Unconventional English* (New York: Macmillan, 1990), 226.

THE TYPE LOUSE

Jack Conroy

Times have changed since the old days when a good typesetter could walk in any shop in the country, hang up his coat, and get to work. Green hands, such as a new devil, would always be asked to look at the type louse at the bottom of a type case, and there was always some water or even ink in the bottom of the case. When the greenhorn[1] leaned over, he'd get his face full, all right.

I never did actually believe there was such a thing as a type louse until quite recently, any more than I did in Santa Claus, though I'd talked about them a lot, joshing around with greenhorns and all that.

But now I know different. I'm fired in my old age,[2] after taking all the trouble to learn to use the line, too. Back in the old days we used to hear tales about a steam typesetter they were inventing. It was like some of the mechanical men they have nowadays, the kind that can answer questions and do all sorts of things by an electric ray or something of the kind. This steam typesetter never did pan out, but it scared a lot of us, just like the men are being scared and put out of their jobs by labor-saving machinery the last twenty years.

I always maintained that the linotype[3] like anything else that takes away the work of a man's hands is the creation of the devil. God gave a man hands that can pick up type better than any machine that was ever invented. You just look at a handset job and then at a lino-set job if you want to know what I mean. There's as much difference as night from day.

We had our hardships in the old days. I've worked in shops where it was that dark you could hardly see your hand before you, leave alone set the smaller fonts of type. There would be dust and trash and mice dirt in the type cases and nobody would ever think of sweeping up the place. Most of the smaller shops never had enough leads, quads or spaces,[4] so we'd be told to "plug the Dutchman"[5] when we complained. That meant you simply had to make out with pasteboard, toothpicks, slivers, tin or anything else to be found.

When you were working piecework, so much per thousand ems,[6] all this cut right in on the pay envelope. Whether you set solid or leaded[7] you had to work fast to make anything.

Green men, too, were taken advantage of. All the fat takes[8] were off the copy hook before you could get at them, and when you went to the copy hook for a take and didn't watch out whatever quads you might have by you would disappear, nobody knew where. I used to take a pocketfull of leads and quads with me when I went to the toilet or to the hook for a take.

In some of the shops we had to punctuate the matter ourselves. It was just written out in a continuous stream, and the typesetter had to use his own judgment. The rule I learned as an apprentice was: "Set up as long as you can hold your breath without getting blue in the face, then put in a comma. When you gape, put in a semi-colon, and when you want to sneeze, that's the time to make a paragraph."

I started to tell you how the type louse got me; how I found out there really is such a creature and he's capable of causing a man all sorts of troubles.

I was working for a firm that specializes in church magazines and the like, all religious stuff, and very dull. A typesetter can get a good education because he has to comprehend at least something of the stuff he's putting into type. That's the way I first read Shakespeare, setting up a one-volume edition of his plays. I still know a lot of the best lines by heart.

I don't blame the type louse for one of the mistakes in my copy, but it had got spread around the shop that I was an agnostic and my job was none too safe anyhow.

This boner was in the Church magazine *Good Tidings*. It was about a B.Y.P.U. convention,[9] and it gets past the proofreaders and everything with this sentence: After the meeting, we brayed and sang together." Of course, "brayed" should have been "prayed," but I had a devil of a time convincing them that I hadn't made it that way on purpose. The proofreaders were all God-fearing folks and they were equally to blame, in a way, so the firm gave me another chance.

But I couldn't get out of the Foreign Missionary job so slick. We'd printed ten thousand copies of the booklet reporting on the year's activities, and I set it up. The boss comes back shaking a copy and swearing like no boss in a religious press should swear.

"Look at that!" he says, and shows me a sentence in the preface:

"Your president is pained to report that the work of the Society during the past year has not been blessed, by God."

The whole thing had to be reset at the expense of the company, of course. The proofreader got the gate, and so did I, though I'm an innocent man. I've done some investigating, and I can put my finger right on the cause.

It's the type louse.

I can prove it, if they'll let me. Just back of where I worked there was a stack of old type cases, and the top one reached a height of about a foot above my shoulder. I'd been bothered by dust and dirt falling down from these cases, but I didn't pay much attention to it since the floor vibrates quite a bit from the heavy presses.

Everybody had been telling me that the type louse eats nothing but metal, and sometimes he holes away in old type cases for years. Just like a bedbug, he can live a long time just on the expectation of getting a good meal. He lives mostly in the ffl and ffi compartments,[10] because they're about the least used. The type louse is smart as a wharf rat when it comes to hiding away, and he's so tiny you have to have a magnifying glass to see him at all. I didn't exactly believe the stories about the type louse, but I could have sworn that when I went to lunch I had just left the line this way:

"year has not been blessed"

without any comma at all.

So I thought to myself: "Supposing a type louse had somehow got a belly-full of lino metal and had been using the top of that type case for a promenade, he might have lost his balance and fell kerplunk on that comma key. He'd be heavy enough to depress the key. I might have overlooked the comma matrix altogether and just set "by God" after coming back from lunch.

So I get me a magnifying glass and I take a squint on the ffl and ffi compartment in the top type case, and, sure enough, there are a number of queer looking insects lazing around like they were too gorged to walk.

When I see one of them coming out of the hell box[11] where there's a lot of dross lino metal, I know I was right. I guess a diet of kerns[12] and fifty-year-old ten pt. italic foundry type like he had been having in the top case had got too tiresome for him. The smell of that fresh-cast metal just got the best of his native caution and he, and probably several of his brethren, had been making the trip up and down. One of them was too full, lost his balance and fell on the comma key. His bellyful of lead did the trick, and caused two people to lose their jobs, one of them—me—as innocent as an unborn babe. But try to tell the boss that; that's the trouble.

Notes

1.   A new, untrained employee. Like, "rube," "hick," or "hayseed," this term has the
      implication of a person being freshly "in from the country" or being "new to the city."

Harold Wentworth and Stuart Berg Flexner, *Dictionary of American Slang* (New York: Crowell, 1960), 229; Eric Partrige, *A Concise Dictionary of Slang and Unconventional English* (New York: Macmillan, 1990), 306.

2. Being agitated, angry, or impatient as a result of getting old. Wentworth and Flexner, *Dictionary*, 184; Partrige, *Concise Dictionary*, 252.

3. The trademark name for a composing machine designed for quickly setting copy. Linotype machines used a keyboard to select characters from a "matrix," and molten metal to create a metal bar, or "slug," of characters from that matrix. The device still required the use of a skilled operator, but dramatically cut down on the time it took to lay in "hand-set type." However, with the increase in speed, there were aesthetic tradeoffs as described by the narrator. Ralph W. Polk and Edwin W. Polk, *The Practice of Printing* (Peoria, IL: Charles A. Bennett Co., 1971), 142; John R. Biggs, *Basic Typography* (New York: Watson-Guptil, 1968), 104, 173.

4. All forms of vertical and horizontal spacing material used for arranging and aligning type. Charles L. Allen, *The Journalist's Manual of Printing* (New York: Thomas Nelson and Sons, 1929), 257–58.

5. To use an improvised method for hiding a mistake, or to use a substitute to do the job. Jeffrey Kacirk, *Informal English: Puncture Ladies, Egg Harbors, Mississippi Marbles, and other Curious Words and Phrases of North America* (New York: Touchstone, 2005), 156.

6. The width of an "em-dash" in any given font; a standard measurement of typesetting which equals the square of the type body, usually 12 picas. Biggs, *Basic Typography*, 173; Polk and Polk, *Practice of Printing*, 71.

7. Lines of type set "solid" were those not requiring the use of spacing "leads" between lines. A "solid" line might, depending on complexity, take less time to set than a "leaded" assignment. Biggs, *Basic Typography*, 175; Allen, *Journalist's Manual*, 257.

8. Conroy's annotation: "Copy quickly and easily set in short lines, such as poetry or short conversations."

9. Acronym for Baptist Young People's Union. *New York Times*, "Baptist Young People's Union: Large Attendance at First Annual Convention in Detroit," July 15, 1892.

10. Also called "ligatures," these are the portions of the type case where pre-cast combinations of letters are stored. Joining the letters on the same type body avoids smudging or bleeding of the inked impression and lends to clarity. Biggs, *Basic Typography*, 173; Allen, *Journalist's Manual*, 257.

11. A box or can in a composing shop where typesetters discarded broken fonts, leads, and other movable type metal. *Oxford English Dictionary Online*, s.v. "hellbox," accessed November 8, 2011, www.oxforddictionaries.com.

12. Letters that were forged on a type body so that portions would hang over, often italics. The overhanging portion of these characters would break easily so they quickly found their way to the aforementioned "hell box" of unusable type. Biggs, *Basic Typography*, 173; Allen, *Journalist's Manual*, 257.

TIME STANDS STILL

BASÍLICO GARDUÑO, NEW MEXICAN SHEEPHERDER

Lorin W. Brown (New Mexico)

It was late afternoon when I approached the camp site in the shadow of El Cerro Redondo (Round Peak), near Jemez Hot Spring. The sheep were still grazing, although all had their heads turned toward the wooded base of the peak, which dominated this upland pasture. The meadow, stretching as far as I could see, encircled the peak. I knew enough of sheep habits to go in the direction in which they grazed, for there would be their *majada* (bedding ground), and close by would be the camp of the *pastor* (shepherd).

A curling blue column rising from a cluster of fir and spruce indicated the spot I sought, and three nondescript dogs gave warning of my approach. Then Basílico's squat, broad figure emerged from the patched and weather-beaten, one-pole tent. He was clad in bib overalls of denim, with an ill-fitting jacket of the same material buttoned over his shirts (the weather determined the number), and a battered black felt hat and home-made shoes.

A low, muttered command to the dogs quieted them, and a circling motion of his arm sent them racing around the edge of the flock to urge on lagging members toward the *majada* and make the group more compact.

"*Buenas tardes*," I said, and added praise for the well-trained dogs. My greeting was returned in a muffled tone, strange and hesitant, the reluctant, inhibited speech of one used to living alone. "*Llegue, amigo*" (Come in, friend), said Basílico, his wind-reddened, bloodshot eyes glaring into mine as if he were angry. Years of squatting over a campfire had given him this baleful look.

I seated myself on a block of pine, while he poured a cup of coffee, the *pastor's* first act of hospitality. A blackened pot is always present on the edge of the campfire. Ground coffee and water are added as needed. Some of the essence of the first potful made in each camp remains until the camp itself is removed.

The beat of many hooves accompanied by the throaty bleating of the sheep and the quicker blats of goats announced the arrival of the flock at the salt troughs scattered near the bedding ground. I looked up to see the sheep clustered in shoving, butting groups along the length of the slightly hollowed logs that held the coarse rock salt—brought from the deposits of the Estancia valley, several miles south of the sheep camp.

A ten-pound lard pail huddled in the coals near the coffee pot, its lid punctured with a nail, emitting jets of vapor which I hoped might come from beans and fat mutton cooking together. Without saying anything more, my host set an iron spider on a bed of coals and put in two spoonfuls of lard to melt. From the tent he took a sack of flour and rolled down the edges, until a mound was formed of the exposed flour. Into this he poured a cup of water, then added the melted grease. Stirring the mixture in the sack, he soon lifted out a ball of dough, which he placed in a small pan. All the flour that had touched the water and grease had become incorporated in the ball of dough, the rest remaining dry. Evidently, baking powder and salt had been added beforehand, making the mixing a quick and simple process.

Pinching off small portions of the dough, Basílico rolled them into balls, then flattened them into round flat cakes, a little thicker than tortillas. These were *gordas* (fat ones), the bread commonly made by the New Mexican sheepherder. Soon six browned *gordas* were taken from the skillet and stacked on a cloth spread across a water keg. The pail of beans was dragged out of the fire and its lid pried off. Just as Basílico was about to seat himself on a log close to the bean pail, one of the two goats that had approached quite familiarly to the fireside bleated softly. Taking down a small pail that hung from a tree branch overhead, Basílico approached the goats, seized them one at a time by a hind leg, and milked them. Tossing the two a piece of old bread, he set a cupful of milk down on the keg holding the *gordas*, first straining it though a piece of thin cloth, part of an old salt sack. The goats' milk was almost as thick as cream.

Basílico needed no spoon. Each mouthful was picked up with a split *gorda*, bent between thumb and forefinger. Meat was enfolded in a piece of the *gorda*, and eaten with it.

A muffled drum of hooves caused me to look up from our meal, and I was aware for the first time that it had grown darker. Four burros stood beyond the light of the fire. Their feet were hobbled, and the two leaders were belled. One of the *almanaques* (almanacs), as Basílico called them, was obviously a pet. He asked for a tidbit in the intimate, soft, demanding tone that pampered animals use. The herder rose and fed them the remnants of our meal, and while they ate he removed their hobbles.

"Aren't you afraid they will stray away, if you loose them?" I asked.

"No, not at night, and scarcely ever in the daytime, either. At night they stick very close to where I sleep, as you shall see." I realized that I was going to spend the night at camp. It was just as well, since I had not yet even mentioned the purchase of the *cabrito* (kid) for which I had come.

I picked up the hobbles that were thrown in a heap close to where I sat. They were home made, and their construction interested me. They were about three feet long and as many inches wide, the inner side lined with cowhide on which the hair had been left to give more protection from chafing. The wide straps fitted closely around a forefoot, just below the fetlock. After several twists, which took up slack between the two front feet, one end fitted into a slot cut in the other. A neat and efficient fastening, which, since the leather was soft, would not be difficult to fasten or unfasten even with benumbed fingers on a cold damp morning. I appreciated this feature, because of my experience with store-bought hobbles of thick leather straps linked with chains and secured with heavy buckles. There is no agony equal to that of trying to unbuckle one of these factory-made hobbles, wet and stiff from snow. Awkward, unmanageable, and perverse, they inevitably produce torn finger nails and bad tempers. These seemingly crude hobbles of Basílico's were a vast improvement. Later, I saw Basílico use them as a tie strap to secure a pack and for other purposes, by linking five pairs together.

The burros did stay close to the fire, except when Basílico slaughtered a lamb and they moved over to look on. The lamb had been seized from the bedding ground and carried to a convenient tree, where Basílico suspended it by a hind leg from a lower branch just high enough to be within easy reach. The shepherd grasped the lamb's muzzle in his left hand and bore the animal's head back and down against the bole of the tree, as his right drew a sharp butcher's knife across the taut throat. This stroke was followed by a sharp cut down the under side from tail to severed throat, while the carcass still jerked and quivered. Incisions up the length of each leg connected with the central belly cut. From this point on, Basílico had no more use for the knife. Tossing it aside, he started ripping off the skin with his hands. One held the carcass away against the pull of the other. Along the sides and back, he used his fist in a knuckling, rolling fashion, neatly separating the pelt from the carcass while rending the paper-thin tissue which held the two together.

The pelt, flesh side up, was stretched out on the ground, and the smaller portions were laid on it, the quarters being hung on branches to cool. The dogs sat around with lolling tongues and cocked ears deftly catching each offering that Basílico tossed them. They did not fight over each other's share but gulped their own and resumed their eager, expectant attitude.

"Hey, don't throw them all of that," I called out excitedly, as I saw Basílico start to apportion the liver around the circle. "I should like some of it for breakfast."

"Here's something else we will have for breakfast," said Basílico, as he held out the lamb's head for my inspection; and from the way he kept his eyes fixed on my face, I knew he was trying to get my reaction to this novel breakfast dish. He had not neglected to save a piece of liver as well.

"*La cabeza es del matador*," I said. My saying that the head belonged to him who killed the animal evoked a pleased smile. I had given him to understand that I knew what a delicacy roast head was considered, especially that of a lamb or *cabrito*.

Digging a hole in the spot from which he had cleared the coals of the camp-fire, Basílico deposited the head therein, after first dampening it and the sides and bottom of the hole with a little water. Directly over the head he placed a tin lid and covered the whole with hot ashes and glowing coals.

"In the morning it will be done to a hair," he said. But for now I will make some *burraniates*. Do you know what they are?" I pretended not to know, in order to allow him the pleasure of introducing a new dish. Taking a chunk of leaf lard from around the kidneys, he worked it into the shape of a wiener; around this he wrapped a good length of the milk intestines, which had first been stripped of their contents. With greedy eyes I watched to see how many of these delectable bundles he would make.

Six—three apiece—I thought to myself, as he handed them to me saying, "You roast these while I make three or four more *gordas*, and don't forget to salt them when they are just about done."

"Leave them to me," I answered, pleased that he thought I could be useful.

When the *burraniates* were finished, I placed my share inside a folded *gorda* sandwich fashion. The filling had just the desired crispness, with plenty of body, but without the greasy taste that might have been expected. The forest round about was quiet, its silence unbroken except for the occasional sound of the cow-bells as the burros cropped the grass nearby.

"And why do you call your burros *almanaques*?" I asked, as Basílico was fixing a pallet for me near the fire. "Oh, they are the almanac of the *pastor*. I can tell of sudden changes in the weather by watching their actions and hearing their bray-ing at unusual hours of the day or night." That was new to me. I had heard burros called many things, some of them unprintable, but never almanacs.

My bed consisted of three woolly sheepskins next to the ground, a blanket over these, and another with which to cover myself. Additional warmth, if needed, would have to be supplied by the "poor man's blanket," the fire, wood for which stood neatly stacked close enough so that I could throw an occasional stick on it without getting up.

My friend, as I thought of him after those *burraniates*, lay on a pallet similar to mine on the opposite side of the fire. Both of us had lighted cigarettes, and I talked to him about the stars. He had interesting names for some of the more familiar constellations. The Pleiades, he called *Las Cabrillas* (herd of little goats), the Great Dipper was *La Carreta* (the cart), and he pointed out to me what seemed to be one star, but which were, he said, in reality two, if your eyesight was good enough. He said the Indians used this phenomenon to test the eyes of their young men. I had to take his word for this; all I could see was one star. *La Estrella del Pastor*, as the morning star was called, received its name, according to him, from the fact that the shepherd is supposed to be up when it appears. He added drily that all the stars might also be called Shepherd's Stars since a *pastor* sees them all nearly every night, sleeping as he does with one eye open, especially when on the summer range in the high mountains.

The moon appeared over the top of El Cerro Redondo. Basílico said it promised wet weather because its points were tilted so that it would not hold water. He told me he could figure in advance the different phases of the moon for months ahead. This knowledge he found very useful in caring for his flock. For instance, a full moon was of great advantage at lambing time. He therefore figured out the exact day to turn the rams (*carneros mesos*) in with the ewes so that the lambs would begin to drop while there was a full moon to light the *pastor's* labors. A full moon was also to be desired when the sheep were driven from summer to winter range or back again.

Basílico claimed, too, to have a method of predicting the weather for a year ahead, by means of *las cabanuelas*. "And how do you do that?" "It is very simple," he replied, then launched into a very complex account.

I was lost in a maze of *primeros, segundos* (firsts and seconds), and *cuarto dias* (quarter days). Boiled down, the method was based on an average of the weather for the first 24 days of January, called *las cabanuelas*. These 24 days were paired to make 12 units, using the first and last together, each pair determining the weather for one month. For instance, the second and twenty-third days of January represent February; the third and twenty-second days, March, and so on. Then there are *los pastores*, the succeeding 6 days of January, which do not enter into the calculation of *las cabanuelas*. These are divided into quarter day units, 24 in all; and, as in *las cabanuelas*, are paired, the second and twenty-third entering into the calculations for February—and so on.

"*Y el ultimo dia de enero*" (and the last day of January)—I was very drowsy by this time, and gathered that the last day of January also entered into this complicated system. Vaguely I heard Basílico explaining that the twenty-four hours of the last day were paired in the same manner as had been the two-day units of *las cabanuelas* and the quarter-day units of *los pastores*, and that they entered into and figured in the calculations for the weather for the months of the year in the same sequence. I recall dreaming something about Einstein and pairs of sheep darting off in different directions, and the next I knew Basílico's voice was urging me to breakfast.

The coffee pot was hissing and the table was laid, my cup and saucer on one keg, his on another. The baked head of lamb lay on a pie tin, skinned, and broken into convenient pieces. The brain pan had been opened, exposing its steaming contents. Basílico had baked several loaves of *pan de pastor* (shepherd's bread), round loaves made of the same dough as the *gordas*, but baked in a dutch oven. This bread keeps, and sheepherders bake supplies of it when time cannot be spared to prepare *gordas* at every meal. The dutch oven sat close to the fire with hot grease smoking inside. "I left that for you to fix your liver to your own taste; I know nothing about that," said Basílico, as he handed me the chunk of liver and a sharp knife. Like most of the rural people of New Mexico he would not eat liver, professing not to know even how to prepare it. (Some think this prejudice is based on the fact that sheep liver is very susceptible to disease.) I sliced the liver, which was soon fried, and heaping my saucer, joined Basílico. The meat of the jaw-bones of the sheep's head had a sweet, nutty flavor, and I also sampled the brains.

The sheep were beginning to move slowly out of the *majada*, the vigilant dogs posting themselves on the outskirts of the flock on higher points where they could catch the warmth of the sun. Basílico had already prepared his lunch. It was wrapped in a white flour sack and fastened around his waist with the long straps of the sling he carried, fitting close to the small of his back.

"I am going to graze the sheep toward El Rito de San Antonio (St. Anthony's Creek), where they will water, and where I can get water for the camp also. Do you want to come along?"

Two burros, already saddled and with water kegs hanging on each side, grazed close by. Basílico handed me a flour sack which bulged with a quarter of lamb. "Here is something for you." I could not refuse the gift, nor could I now say that I had originally come for a *cabrito*.

Since the small stream lay for a distance along my own route back to the stream, I followed the slowly moving flock. I noticed that the ewes were heavy, and mentioned this fact to Basílico. "Yes, we'll be lambing about San Domingo Day. Come and visit my camp at that time, if you wish to see us then. We will be on the north slope of El Rito de los Indios (Indians' Creek), where there is better shelter."

The dogs kept the sheep moving in the desired direction. I commented on the training they must have received.

"Do you remember that *melada* (goat) I milked last night? Well she is the foster-mother of my two youngest dogs. I take young puppies, newly born—before their eyes are opened, and suckle them to a nanny goat. In this way I get dogs that think they are part goat, I guess, because they soon learn to love these animals and take care of them. They take care of the sheep also, but treat them with contempt, just like these *mocosas* (snot-noses) deserve, for they are a very foolish animal."

We came to a saddle in the low ridge along which we had been walking. Here Basílico and his flock would cross and go down the left-hand slope, while I continued along its length for some miles more. As the dogs turned the flock, pressing in on its right flank, its leader, a patriarchal billy goat, swung the first of the woolly wave over and down the slope. We stood to the left and a little higher, like commanders of an army watching it pass in review. Basílico scanned the flock closely, seeming to take note of each individual mutton. "*'Sta bien*," he said to himself as the last sheep passed over. "You didn't count them, did you?" I asked. "*Si y no*," (yes and no), he replied. "I counted my *marcadoras* (markers); they were all there, so the rest must be." These *marcadoras*, he explained, were the black sheep in the flock—about one of these for every hundred of the others. Any *corta* (stray bunch) would be almost certain to include one of the black sheep. So if all the black sheep were accounted for, he could assume the whole flock was intact.

Many *pastores* cannot count beyond the number of fingers on both hands and must use counters. The old Spanish saying, "*Carnero entregado, peso contado*" (whether sold and handed over, a dollar counted out), means that the price is paid for each animal as it is sold because of the seller's inability to reckon the total. A full tally of the sheep is usually made by the owner, or *patron*, on one of his periodical visits to the sheep camp. At that time the *pastor* may hand his *patron* a tobacco sack full of pebbles. Some of these will be larger than the rest and are usually black. The *pastor* has made a count of his *rebano* (flock) some time prior to his *patron's* visit, and his count is recorded in these pebbles. The black pebbles show how many hundreds there were; the white ones, how many tens; the remainder are either committed to memory or shown by notches cut into the shepherd's staff. To account for sheep killed by wild animals, or dying from any other cause, the *pas-*

tor skins and saves the pelt, ears and all, against the day when his *patron* comes to count his sheep, because he is responsible for every one.

"Why don't you come over to the Springs to visit me?" I asked. "I shall be there for a week or ten days more."

"I will if the *patron* sends me a *remuda* soon. But, *amiguito*, I have known those springs for many years. In fact, that was where I first started to herd sheep. My father and I both worked for Don Mariano, who first owned those springs—that is, the grant on which they are located. He was *muy rico*, a man of many sheep and much land. We used to lamb in the grassy valley just above the springs and dip the sheep in troughs built just below the main sulphur spring; and we used nothing else except the very water from the spring to rid the sheep of scab and ticks. It was much better than this stuff we have to use nowadays. Don Mariano was a great *patron*, a great fighter and eater, but of good heart. When he came to visit our camp to count the sheep, my father would always kill the fattest lamb, then open it while it was still warm, even before skinning it, and remove the paunch. This he would place to roast on the *rescoldo*, a big bed of coals prepared beforehand. There was nothing Don Mariano liked better than paunch roasted thus; when it had been roasted sufficiently, he would cut it open with his *daga*, empty the half-digested contents, and cut up the paunch and eat it. He said that besides liking it very much, it was very good for a stomach trouble from which he suffered. *Quien sabe?*"

By *remuda*, Basílico meant a herder sent up to relieve him. On such holidays, Basílico usually took all his burros and stopped at his *patron's* house, where he left them. He then went about his own affairs. On such occasions, his attire varied from that of every day only by being newer and perhaps a little cleaner, and by a new black hat carefully brushed. This hat was kept at the patron's home, and constituted the latter's annual bonus to his faithful servitor, a gift added to his wages. Each year the holiday hat was taken over for workday use, and soon became the battered affair, which Basílico doffed as we parted there on the ridge.

With many *pastores*, leaves meant drinking sprees or women, until, funds exhausted, they were rounded up by the *patron* and set upon the sobering trail which led back to camp. For the married ones, while there might also be a spree, in most cases the arrival of the *remuda* was the occasion for a reunion with wife and children. So far as I knew, Basílico had never been married, and he was very reticent about what he did on his leaves. His *patron* confided that Basílico would go to Santa Fe and return on the appointed day, with never a word as to his activities.

I shook hands with Basílico, assuring him I would be present at lambing time, if possible. He promised to have ready for me upon my return a pair of *teguas* (moccassins), which he would make for me. I had seen *teguas* worn by other *pastores*; they were, however, hybrid affairs, with handmade soles but with uppers salvaged from some pair of store shoes or boots. Basílico's, made of cowhide, with the neatest of stitching, close fitting, and undoubtedly very comfortable, were his own handiwork throughout. He was a master in working leather. He could braid quirts,[1] belts, hat bands, *reatas* (ropes), and those long tapering whips known as blacksnakes. Next to the *teguas*, his neatest accomplishments were the *hondas* (slings) he made, like the one he now carried. They were shorter than those I had when a boy. The egg-shaped piece that carried the stone was larger, and on the end of each swinging string was a lash that cracked like a pistol shot after each throw. Basílico was amazingly accurate with it; he never hit a sheep or goat, but would fling a stone near a straggler to startle it back to the flock.

I returned to Basílico's camp the day before San Domingo Day. True to his prediction, a full moon appeared in the sky that night, and soon afterwards the thin bleats of newborn lambs sounded. Basílico, with three extra men who had been in camp since the first of the month, worked until morning. He or one of his helpers would appear at the campfire to drink a cup of coffee, then return to his labors.

I wandered over to the corral that had been built a few days before for *el ganado prenado* (the pregnant ewes). The bobbing lanterns revealed the whereabouts of the men. I spotted Basílico skinning a still-born lamb. Its mother stood close by baaing incessantly in that stupid manner characteristic of sheep. I said, "Surely you don't have to save the skins of such as those for accounting to the *patron?*"

"No, no, I am fixing it so this *tonta* (fool) may have a foster son, tomorrow perhaps. There will be some ewes that will die tonight, leaving *pencos* (orphan lambs), and others that will have twins. I will take either a *penco* or a twin lamb away from its mother, tie this skin to his back, and fool the *vieja* (old woman) into adopting him. The ewes recognize their lambs by scent at first, and through this trick we save many lambs that would die otherwise." Several diminutive pelts hung around the corral, separated from each other so the scents would not get mixed.

In the midst of the confusion and noise and the constant blatting and bleating, the herder and his helpers moved from one birth to another. I asked one man how he could pair up the right ewe with each lamb pelt; they all looked exactly alike to me. He said there were differences of appearance, and besides, each ewe had a different note to her bleating, by which he could fix her in his mind. Listening to the bleat of one particular ewe, I was able, finally, to distinguish her baaing from the medley that arose from the corral. There were not many of these adoptions to be arranged. Basílico's flock had wintered well, and the ewes had reached the lambing season in very good condition.

It was close to four in the morning when I returned to the campfire. Above the commotion from the corral, the shrill yapping of coyotes could be heard. They seemed to know what the sounds issuing from the corral meant. I could imagine their slavering jaws and burning eyes as they pointed their slender noses to the sky.

In the morning, I accompanied Basílico in a round of inspections of the corral and the *chiceros* (small brush pens). At the corral, we picked up the carcasses of the lambs that had been skinned the night before and tossed them over the side of a near-by bluff. At the *chiceros*, in which the lambs born the night before were kept while the flock grazed, Basílico paused to count again the lambs huddling together for warmth. He seemed satisfied with their number and general sturdiness. As we stood there, one of the extra men appeared with four more lambs; from time to time throughout the day others were added.

One of the men drove a small group of nervously bleating ewes close to the *chicero* where the orphans and twins were segregated. With a lamb clothed in one of the pelts removed the night before, Basílico would head for a particular ewe. Sometimes a good deal of persuasion was necessary before it would allow the lamb to suckle. It would be held and forced to smell this odd-looking lamb with the legs of its strange covering dangling from its sides. The lamb on its wobbling legs would be butted and shoved aside, but would persist in satisfying its hunger, bringing its mouth again and again to the ewe's side, in spite of all rebuffs. When, after many attempts, accompanied by strong language on the part of Basílico and his helper, the lamb was accepted by the ewe, it would kneel to receive the milk, while its tail wriggled ecstatically just below the lifeless one of the lamb whose place it was taking. When it was finished, the ewe would move off to graze, still eyeing dubiously this mysterious creature that had the scent of Esau but the voice of Jacob.

That evening I left the camp after negotiating for a kid, which I held on the saddle before me. Also tied to my saddle were the *teguas* Basílico had promised me. Somehow during the busy days of preparation for the lambing rush, he had found time to make them. Basílico's helpers would depart in a few days, leaving him to the solitude that he seemed to prefer. I said I would try to get back again in a few days. "Yes, come back after these other ones have gone. Then we can talk." As I rode away, my cargo awakened the echoes of hillside and canyon along my back trail.

The next time I saw him was by chance. I was out riding around the hills below the lambing camp and on the slopes of the mountain that led toward the settlement on the Rio Grande. Entering an open park, I happened onto a flock of sheep, obviously on the move from one camp to another. Four burros loaded with camp equipment grazed at the edge of the flock. I recognized the animals as Basílico's, and rode to the rear of the flock in search of him. I met him carrying a lamb in his arms; it had played out some time back. Its excited mother alternately grazed in erratic pauses close on Basílico's footsteps, then dashed towards him, baaing in a stupidly inquiring manner, evoking plaintive responses from the lamb.

"Where are you going with your *ganado*, is it that your *patron* has sold it and you are taking it down for delivery?" I asked, for a movement of a flock from the summer range to winter range country at this time of year was unusual. "*No, nada de eso* (no, nothing like that). The *patron* has a shearing shed down here a little way, and I am driving the sheep there to be sheared."

As we crossed a small stream, Basílico stopped to pluck a green feathery plant which grew under the overhanging bank, close by some violets. "What is that?" I asked, as he thrust the fernlike wisps into his mouth. "It is *plumajillo*, very good for the stomach. Try some?" It was bitter to the taste and should have rated very high in the locality, where the efficacy of any medicine is measured by the strength of its flavor. Basílico asked if I would bring him some *hediondilla* from the vicinity of Socorro the next time I was down there. I confessed that I did not know what that was, but from the name, which means "stinking," it could not be anything pleasant. I learned later that it was the creosote bush, a popular remedy for kidney ailments.

"You know much about herbs, no?"

"Yes, every *pastor* knows about *yerbas del campo* (wild herbs). It is well that he does, he is so much alone. Only a broken leg holds any terror for a sheepherder. I can name you a great number of herbs, and the particular benefits of each, but that would take a long time. Some other time I will give you some of each and directions for using them."

After the sheep had bedded down, as we sat smoking our after-supper cigarette, Basílico talked about herbs. He recited a list that would put an herbalist's catalogue to shame. The most prominent was *osha*, which is so highly regarded by native New Mexicans that it is considered virtually a cure-all. Others were *altamisa, chimaja, chamiso, orteguilla, poleo, yerba buena, amole, canaigra.* The only way one could fix this list of names in mind would be, he suggested, to get a sample of each and record its properties in detail. While on the subject, Basílico also mentioned *pingue* (Colorado rubber plant) and loco weed from which the *pastor* must guard his sheep. *Pingue* is especially destructive in the month of October, or after the first frosts. It is more resistant to frost than grass, and stays green and tender after the latter has begun to dry up. For this reason the sheep turn to the *pingue* and great losses result, unless the *pastor* is careful to keep his flock away from infested regions during that critical period. Loco weed causes losses in the months of February and March. Stock that feed on it go "crazy"; it affects them like a drug; having once tasted it they cannot leave it alone. Eating nothing else, they stagger along, their actions extremely erratic, and finally die from lack of nourishment.

In the morning the shearing crew arrived amid a cloud of dust in a small truck piled high with bedding rolls and other equipment. They were a noisy band of itinerants, shearing sheep on a commission basis all over the State and into Colorado. Basílico would have nothing to do with them, except for handling his sheep so as to keep the shearers constantly supplied. To prepare the sheep for shearing, he would drive about a hundred of them at a time into a small adobe room with but one opening. Here, closely confined, the warmth of their bodies caused "sweating," which makes shearing easier. To get them into the room, he used the patriarch of the small herd of goats he kept with his sheep. It was amusing to see how well the bearded old rogue knew his business. He no sooner entered the door with the sheep close on his heels, than he stepped aside near the exit. He knew that he must get out again and be ready for the next bunch. His whole demeanor showed his supreme contempt for the victims of his guile and his wish to escape close confinement with such idiots.

The sheared sheep, looking more foolish than ever in their nakedness, were held by the dogs in a corner of the hills, while Basílico took care of doling out the others to the shed, as required. I watched the shearers deftly turn their victims, the wool clip rolling off in a soft mat. As each was finished, a cry of *"Uno!"* (one) brought the boss, who acted as inspector. His *"Bueno!"*(good) permitted the shearer to release the animal as properly sheared. A metal disk was handed the worker, to be used at the end of the day in computing his pay.

The crew of shearers would be in the neighborhood for several days, since other owners had requested the use of the sheds for shearing their flocks. I knew Basílico hated to remain in their company any longer than was necessary. He would lose his temper under the bantering of the shearers, who treated all *pastores* with contempt. The crowning insult was that they persisted in calling him Basil Loco. I left that evening, atop a load of the huge sacks into which the wool was packed after shearing.

Basílico and his flock were at the shearing sheds again when I next saw them. The flock now seemed much larger. I thought at first more sheep had been bought, but I soon discovered that it was the spring lambs that made the increase. They were large now, sturdy, fat fellows weighing 70 to 75 pounds, a good average for this type of sheep.

Basílico's *patron* had ridden in with a helper to aid in castrating and docking the lambs. In the first process the lamb was up-ended and held with his head away from his captor. Sometimes, in the case of a particularly vigorous lamb, the forefeet were tied. Both hind legs were held in encircling arms, with hooves caught in the sheepman's armpits. An opened clasp-knife held in the right hand severed the tip of the lamb's bag, held in the left hand. The ends of the testicles showing were seized in strong teeth and withdrawn with a jerk of the head, to be deposited in a pan or pail close by. The men worked singly, as a rule, scarcely making a sound—perhaps because of their blood-smeared faces. The stain spread down the fronts of their overalls. An element of rivalry entered into this task, each worker trying to outdo the other in the number of lambs altered.

At this time, too, the ears of the lambs were marked with the *patron*'s distinctive crop or slit, or combination of both, and its tail was docked to within an inch of its base. The poor creatures, after undergoing this three-way treatment, stood dripping blood from many parts of their bodies, bleating disconsolately and shaking their heads vigorously, sending thin sprays of blood through the air.

At supper that evening I received my introduction to the so-called "Rocky Mountain Oysters," a big dutch oven full that had been fried, and a pile on a lard can lid that had been roasted over the coals. Both ways, I found, they deserved their fame as a seasonal delicacy.

"Yes, we had a very good *hijadero* (lambing season): about half and half ewes and males, and about 90 lambs for every 100 ewes, and very little loss. We will sell nearly 800 lambs, and the *patron* has had me cut out very nearly 300 old and toothless ewes. These he is going to pasture on his home meadows, selling them to the Indians of the pueblos and his poorer neighbors. They are good for nothing else but meat now."

"I will stay here until time to turn the rams in with the sheep," Basílico went on. "This we will do the first of the Month of the Dead (November). I will winter with my sheep on the chamiso-covered flats between here and the Rio Grande. During the month of December I have for many years taken the part of *El Diablo* in *Los Pastores*, that old play that deals with us shepherds, our life in camp, our language. It is directed by my *compadre*, Higinio Costales. I make a very good *Diablo*, wouldn't you think so?"

"Wonderful," I said, smiling, taking in his great dark head, wild hair, and angry-looking eyes under heavy brows.

"Come down to see me do it in the month of *Noche Buena* (Christmas Eve)."

I resolved to do so. *Noche Buena* was the month of *luminarias*, those small fires still lighted in New Mexico on Christmas Eve in commemoration of the shepherd campfires long ago outside the town of Bethlehem. In *Los Pastores*, the Christmas play, with its scene laid near the town of Bethlehem, I would see this solitary Basílico, who lived all year with sheep, among his brothers.

Note

1.   An artfully-crafted, braided whip made from leather, buckskin, or goatskin. Franciscan Fathers, *An Ethnologic Dictionary of the Navaho Language* (Leipzig, DE: Breslauer, 1929), 314.

A TABAQUERO TALKS

Edmond Sharrock (Florida)

"Señor" said Alfonso Fernandez, of Ybor City[1] in Tampa, "I do not like that name cigar maker. I am a *tabaquero*. I make cigars, yes, but I do not call it work. It is an art, as you shall see. I do not nail boards together like a carpenter. I do not watch a great, noisy, oily machine grind and crush loads of cheap tobacco and turn out poor cigars by the hundreds of thousands. It is my privilege to combine the fine clear Havana tobacco with my own skilled craftsmanship in a way that only Latins can do. You shall see how a real *tabaquero* makes cigars."

On the way to the factory Alfonso told me that he had learned the art of cigar making from his father, who was born in Cuba, and from his grandfather, born in Spain. He, himself, is Tampa-born and is far more proud of his American nativity and citizenship than of his Cuban and Spanish descent. Far surpassing all this, however, is his pride in his skill, his ego of the artist.

The cigar factory was typical of others in Ybor City, known as "Little Havana": a rectangular brick building with a flat roof. It contains three floors and a basement, the latter being almost entirely above ground. Even outside the building the odor of tobacco was strong, and it increased as we passed through the lobby and climbed the two flights of boxed-in stairs to the *tabaqueros'* room.

The huge room covered the entire floor. Its ceiling was very high, and on all four sides were unusually tall windows spaced no more than eight feet apart. In a smaller room or one not so well aired, the fumes of tobacco would have been overpowering. There were literally tons of tobacco here, and more tons on the floor above, the floor below, and in the basement. No wonder that those who work in this building day after day find it impossible to rid their bodies and clothing of the all-pervading odor; for in such quantities even the finest Cuban tobacco gives off an odor rather than a fragrance.

Alfonso led the way through aisles between row after row of tables, some occupied and some vacant, until he reached his own *vapor*. A *vapor*, Spanish for ship, consists of six tables in two rows of three each and with broad aisles between them. In this room 120 *vapors* accommodate 720 *tabaqueros*. Each table, approximately four feet long and thirty inches wide, is encircled by a low rail on three sides, leaving the front open. The wood top of the rear rail is known as the dust guard, or *guardo polvo*; Alfonso tossed his hat on it. He wore no coat but was dressed in a soft blue shirt open at the throat, well-creased dark trousers, supported by a leather belt, and tan shoes. Exchanging greetings with others on his *vapor*, he donned a white crash apron[2] that covered him from shoulder to knees and which bore the name of the company stitched in red on the upper part.

At a series of bins in charge of a clerk, or *dependiente*,[3] Alfonso received a supply of filler tobacco, known as *tripa*.[4] This had been carefully selected for the grade of cigar Alfonso is working on. It had been sorted and cured on the floor above and had come down to the *dependiente's* bins through a series of wooden chutes or canals. In northern cigar factories *tripa* is carefully weighed and the cigar makers' output checked against the weight. Not so in Tampa. Alfonso and his fellow-workers would resent such surveillance.

Alfonso carried the *tripa* back to his *vapor* in his apron and placed it on the right hand upper corner of his table within easy reach. He then went to a railed-in enclosure in the center of the room where at *barrils*, half-barrels sat with open end up, the selectors, or *regagadores*, pick the wrappers for the several grades of cigars. Seated upon backless stools that do not impede the movements of their arms, they hold the wrapper leaves in their aprons. Swiftly they finger each leaf and drape it over the edge of the *barril* in its proper group. They make thirty to thirty-five separate groups, according to quality, texture, and color. So well do their sensitive fingers know tobacco that the slightest differences in quality or texture are instantly detected. These wrapper leaves have been previously stripped by girls working in a basement room adjoining the warehouse. The entire center stem is removed so that each wrapper leaf makes two leaves or two wrappers.

Alfonso called out the names of the cigars he was about to roll and was given a pad of wrappers. These were charged to him and he had to turn in a cigar for each wrapper, except those he was permitted to make for himself. Returning to his *vapor* he remarked to me, "Now, *Señor*, you will see us make cigars, and you will learn where Americans who build boats and automobiles and airplanes got their idea of streamlining. We who fashion handmade cigars were the first to use streamlining. Is it not so?"

Just then the coffee man appeared arousing a Babel of talk in English, Spanish, and Italian. Every *tabaquero* bought coffee and rolls or cakes. Alfonso explained that cigar makers seldom ate breakfast at home, preferring to start the day with coffee at their *vapores*. So he drew his chair, called a *taborette*,[5] from under his table, and drew up one for me. I found it a most comfortable seat, slightly higher than an ordinary chair and with seat and back of tightly stretched cowhide, but without arms.

Coffee and rolls having been consumed, Alfonso was at last ready to begin his day's work. His table was furnished with a cutting board about twelve by eighteen inches, a small gauge and trimmer for measuring the thickness of the cigars and trimming them to the proper length, and a cigar maker's knife—a *chaveta*. No common knife, no *cuchillo* or *navajo*, may fashion a handmade cigar. It must be trimmed and shaped with a *chaveta*, which in Spanish means key but also carries the sense of judgment or reason—priceless ingredients in handmade cigars. The *chaveta* is like no other knife. It is an ovoid piece of metal about four inches long and one-half as wide. It has no corners but is rounded on all sides and every part of the edge is equally sharp; hence there is no lost motion in trimming either filler or wrapper.

Now for his after-breakfast cigar. It is an inviolate custom in Tampa handmade cigar factories that no real *tabaquero* would ever dream of making a cigar for his employer before he has made one for himself. Seated at his board, Alfonso selects the largest leaf in his pad of wrappers and with a few swift, deft movements of his *chaveta* quickly trims it to the proper size and shape. His long, slender fingers, slightly widened and flattened at the ends, reach into the pile of *tripa* and unerringly pick up the correct amount of filler for a good big cigar. The leaves are carefully placed with the veins upward and toward the left in such a way as to create a draft for the smoke, and each is trimmed to the same length. While he keeps up a running fire of talk, it is easy to see that Alfonso is vastly proud of his ability to arrange the filler by the "feel of the hand."

The cigar is bunched, then, slipping a small rubber band over one end, he inserts it in the gauge. Both ends are trimmed, and starting at the "tuck," the end to be lighted, he rolls the wrapper on quickly and smoothly. As he gets to the "head," which is the end held in the smoker's mouth, he slips off the rubber band and fastens the wrapper with a tiny drop of tragacanth,[6] a tasteless, vegetable adhesive gum brought from Asia.

The cigar is completed—an unusually large one—and he hands it to me. "Smoke it, *Señor*" he says. "There is a cigar fit for a king or for an American gentleman."

Again he selects a very large wrapper and almost before my cigar is burning he has rolled another for himself. By this time nearly every cigar maker is smoking, but their fingers have lost none of their speed. Slowly Alfonso's pile of finished cigars fills the hexagon-shaped holder on the upper left corner of his table, and each cigar seems as perfect as its mate.

In a continuous rhythm, Alfonso selects, rejects or accepts, and bunches the tobacco he needs. He presses and smoothes and seemingly caresses the bunch until his fingers tell him it is just right. Then he swiftly rolls it in the trimmed wrapper, and after a careful scrutiny places it on his pile. The foreman who comes through about noon will examine one or two cigars on each table. No more than that, or the *tabaquero* would take it as a personal affront and resent it deeply.

I asked Alfonso how long he had been making cigars.

"Fifteen years I have been in this factory. I came as *mochilla*. You know what *mochilla* is? In cigar making *mochilla* is a beginner. The Spanish word for apprentice is *apprendíz*, but in the cigar factories we say *mochilla*, which means knapsack for carrying supplies. When a young man starts in a cigar factory we say, 'Hacer la mochilla'— make the knapsack—that is, provide food for a journey, but in this case, provide for a career, for a journey through life.

"Yes, fifteen years since I was *mochilla*. Then we did not talk so much among ourselves, nor sing to while away the time. We had *lectores*[7] to entertain us." He glanced at the other five *tabaqueros*, all of whom were listening. "Remember *lectores*?" All nodded, their faces lighted with the memory.

"I will tell you about *lectores*," Alfonso said. "They were smart men. Actors. Readers. Elocutionists. Singers. The bosses did not pay them. We paid them ourselves. Each man chipped in at pay day and a good *lector* in a factory like this would make as much as $75 a week. He was worth it, too. He sat on a platform in the middle of the room and read to us while we rolled cigars. Yes, we got all the news then and we were smarter than we are now, because we knew what was going on outside. The *lector* would read Spanish language newspapers and American newspapers. He would read history and stories and pieces from the magazines. He would read plays and often act them out. He had a strong, rich voice that never seemed to tire. He didn't need a loud speaker. Everyone in the room could hear him well. Sometimes he told us stories of his own or would sing an old Cuban or Spanish song. I remember one song that we always liked. Come on, fellows, let us give the *Senor* 'A Lady from Tassa.'"

In low tones, then, all six started singing. Soon the song was taken up at other *vapores*, until the whole room swam with its soft cadence and the peculiar mixture of Spanish and "pidgin" English. Here is a very free translation:

The boat from Cuba hardly tie
The cable at Key West
Before a Tassan maiden win
By heart—and this no jest.
"No savvy Cubano," says this girl,
So softly in her ear,
I try Castillian; still she stand
As if she no can hear.

That night she met me at the gate,
And I, in much despair,
Try English. "Likee me?" I say.
"Come in and have a chair,"
She tell me, so take one seat
And every effort bent
To speaky English so this girl
Could savvy what I meant.

"Well, what you want to tell me?"
Says the girl, "A Cuban swain
Rates high, but an American
Gives me an awful pain.
The dirty double-crossers..." "Wait!"
I interrupt her. "Stop!"
Don't class me American...
I Cuban, feet to top.

"No please don't think I try to shoot
This—what you call it—bull;
I want to marry—I not joke,
No try to pull the wool.
Don't think I 'take you for a ride.'
For at your door I knock
Tomorrow, and you see me here
At seven by the clock.

"I speaky English not so good,
But I am here to say,

The fire I have here for you
Will burn until that day
When I shall kiss that little mouth
And press you to my heart,
For those red lips were made for me,
And we must never part.

"I make seegars here, my dear,
And closely hit the ball.
I makee only very best
Or makee none at all.
The strike is on, but I have cash
In bank and pocket, too.
And I no have to work today,
So speaky here with you."

This was quickly followed by a Cuban folksong, sung in voices of deep pathos and to a haunting, plaintive melody. Alfonso announced it under its Spanish name "*A La Orilla de un Palmer,*" freely translated as "At the Edge of a Palm Grove."

At the edge of a palm grove
A fair maiden sighs;
Her lips are like coral,
Like stars are her eyes.

In passing I ask her
Who lives in her home;
She tearfully answers:
"I live there alone."

"For I am an orphan,
No parents have I,
Not even a friend
To console when I cry.

"At the edge of this forest
There's no one but me.
And I go and return
Like the waves of the sea."

As the impromptu concert ended I asked Alfonso what had happened to the *lectores*. "We don't have them now for seven or eight years," he said. "The bosses said they were making trouble about strikes and labor and trying to make cigar workers discontent and unhappy. So they had to go. We tried radio for a little while but it is not the same. So now we talk and laugh and sometimes sing. It is not too bad."

By this time it was almost noon. Alfonso made two more extra large cigars, one for himself and one for me.

"We must light these before we go out, or they will be charged against my day's allowance."

"Are you permitted so many each day?" I asked.

"Oh, yes," he said. We can smoke all we want in the shop, but seldom do, except the after-breakfast smoke. Then we can smoke one going to lunch and have one for after lunch, too. At night we can take three for smoking in the evening. But these must not be hidden. They must be carried out in plain sight."

I thanked him for a most interesting morning and we shook hands.

"You know now how to make cigars, yes?" Alfonso queried. "Maybe you like to come into factory and *hacer la mochilla*," he added, laughing.

Notes

1. Originally a 40-acre parcel of land east of Tampa, Florida, purchased in the mid 1880's by Martínez Ybor, the city was established in 1886 and soon became known primarily for its population of Cuban émigrés and cigar-making factories. Eric Arnesen, ed., *Encyclopedia of U.S. Labor and Working-Class History*, 3 vols. (New York: Routledge, 2007), 333.
2. Protective apron made of a rugged linen fiber known as "crash." Ellyn Anne Geisel, *The Kitchen Linens Book* (Kansas City: Andrews McMeel, 2009), 25.
3. An assistant, or lower-ranking shop laborer. Margaret H. Raventós and David L. Gold, *Random House Spanish-English English-Spanish Dictionary* (New York: Ballantine, 1996), 113.
4. Ibid., 516. The usage is metonymic for the innards of an animal; tripe.
5. Ibid., 343. Possible misspelling of "taburete" which, as the context indicates, means "stool."
6. Originates from the Greek words τράγος (goat) and ἄκανθα (thorn). "Tragos," is also ancient Greek for "tragedy," and is translated literally as "goat song." The term may or may not have this connotation here. Henry George Liddell and Robert Scott, *An Intermediate Greek-English Lexicon* (Oxford, UK: Oxford UP, 1972) 814, 25.
7. The text explains the cultural and entertainment functions of this unique figure in

Cuban work life and, further in the story, the narrator remarks on the disappearance of the *lector* from his factory. For the tabaqueros, it's a significant event for highlighting the importance of *lectores* to the organization of Cuban labor movements. Often the *lector* helped spur and mobilize the workers to demand renegotiation of labor conditions, therefore it was significant that the workers both hired and paid the *lector* out of their own salaries. Arnesen, *Encyclopedia*, 333–34.

NAVAHO TRADER

Sanford L. Hassell (New Mexico)

Tooth Gone, a white man, one of the 173 licensed traders on the Navaho Reservation, was about to buy a rug from Mrs. Many Goats, a prosperous matron.

It would have been obvious to anyone acquainted with Navahos that Mrs. Many Goats and her husband, Hosteen[1] Many Goats,[2] occupied an important social position. Both wore close fitting reddish-brown buckskin moccasins with silver buttons the size of a dollar decorating the sides. Their necklaces of shell beads were spaced with turquoise of the finest grade. The ten buttons on the front of Mrs. Many Goats' silk plush blouse were half dollars with a small copper loop brazed on the back of each. On the cuffs of her blouse were rows of five dimes. Each of her three skirts contained sixteen full yards of the best quality brown sateen, and each was trimmed with yards and yards of ric-rac.[3]

Hosteen wore a double-breasted blue serge suit. The buttons on the front of his coat were made of quarters and the two ornamental buttons on each sleeve were dimes. His trousers were wrinkled and looked as if he had been sleeping in them, which he had, for most Navahos do not remove their trousers when they go to bed. The price tag and the size tag were still on the suit—they were on it when he bought it six months before, and there had been no reason for removing them. His wide brimmed hat, set squarely on his head, was banded by a strip of silver, one half inch wide and set with turquoise. Around his left wrist he wore as an ornament a silver-mounted leather bow guard also set with turquoise. A heavy silver belt with seven ornamental pieces called conchas, two inches in diameter, encircled his waist.

When Mr. and Mrs. Many Goats, after first peering in, entered the trading post and made a careful survey of the inside, Tooth Gone gave no sign of recognition, for he was an experienced trader familiar with Navaho etiquette. The proper time having elapsed, Mr. and Mrs. Many Goats went to the counter and offered a hand in greeting. Hosteen led the way—like other Navaho men, he liked to make it appear that he was the boss. Tooth Gone responded with a gentle handclasp and a low murmur in Navaho. Then he placed two bottles of red soda pop and a handful of cookies on the counter. Hosteen accepted these without thanks or comment, just the faint shadow of a smile. One bottle he took for himself, the other he handed to his wife. Food and drink were not consumed together. First the pop was drunk, and the cookies eaten afterwards.

Mrs. Many Goats was now ready to trade her rug. From underneath her shawl she produced an oblong bundle wrapped in a clean flour sack and placed it on the counter. Tooth Gone accepted the bundle and placed it on the scales. With hardly a glance at the scales he laid the bundle back on the counter and unwrapped it. Tooth Gone did not buy Navaho rugs by the pound, but the Indians like to see them weighed, and he was accommodating. The rug spread before him wasn't large and it wasn't small, just about the size most used for scatter rugs, three by five feet. It was well designed, with red, gray, brown, black, and white harmoniously combined, and well woven, with plenty of body. Tooth Gone knew that this rug with reasonable care would last a generation and could be passed on to the next.

"Fifteen dollars, my mother," offered Tooth Gone. Mrs. Many Goats wasn't as old as he was, but it was customary to address all Navaho women with children that way.

"All right, my friend," said Mrs. Many Goats accepting with only slight hesitation. She knew this was a better price than she could get from any of the surrounding traders, none of them closer than fifteen miles away—though she would have taken it that far without hesitation if she thought that one of them would pay a dollar more.

Tooth Gone was aware that he was paying a big price for the rug, and that he would be lucky if the wholesale house allowed him this amount for it on his account; he did not, however, expect to lose money, for he was trading goods for the rug and was getting a good price for his merchandise. There was, of course, the possibility that the wholesale house would get overstocked and not buy rugs at any price, and then he would have to keep it for a long time. But there were other reasons for Tooth Gone's liberality. In three months he expected to buy the wool from Mrs. Many Goats' sheep, and in the fall her lambs—that is, if some other trader didn't outbid him. Wool and lambs were the big part of his business. True, he had to pay out some cash for these, but there was always a ready market, and the turnover was rapid. There was, too, the prestige of having well-to-do Indians trading at the store, even if they did demand the highest prices for their products. Poor Indians—and there were plenty of these in this district—liked to follow the rich; and with Indians, like whites, the poor are the reckless spenders.

Tooth Gone tied a tag to the rug and marked it $15.00—nothing more—then carried it to a side room and laid it on a stack of rugs that was almost as high as his head. These had been bought in the last thirty days.

Tooth Gone now took a paper sack and wrote $15.00 at the top and on the bottom scribbled his initials. This was Mrs. Many Goats' trade slip and could be spent or saved for a later date, but Tooth Gone knew that every nickel would be used up before she went. Not that she was a spendthrift—in many ways Mrs. Many Goats was as thrifty as a French housewife—but she had her own way of doing business.

Mrs. Many Goats had brought the rug to trade for supplies, mostly groceries, of which she stood in immediate need. A woman of her means could well afford to keep a large supply of provisions in her home, though this would encourage all of the poor relatives to come and stay with her until the larder was bare.

Mrs. Many Goats had credit at the post and could spend as much as she pleased, and Tooth Gone gave her plenty of encouragement; but she was very conservative. The more she owed him the less cash Tooth Gone would have to pay when he bought her wool and lambs. If she sold to a rival trader she would bring him cash to settle her account.

She also had much of her surplus jewelry in pawn, and could have used it as security for merchandise; but she had it here solely for safe keeping.

Tooth Gone placed the trade slip on the counter and stood at attention. He knew Mrs. Many Goats was ready to do some buying, for her eyes were roaming over the canned goods on the shelves.

"*Acon du que?* (flour, how much)," she asked. The price in trade for a sack of flour had not changed in ten years, but Mrs. Many Goats, like all other Navahos, always asked. Of course, if they were buying in large quantities for a big dance and paying cash, Tooth Gone would sell it much cheaper.

"*Nez nah yawl* (ten bits)," replied Tooth Gone. A sack of flour and a can of K. C. baking powder were placed on the counter. Baking powders are usually included with the purchase of flour. Tooth Gone wrote $1.25 under the $15.00 and subtracted, then drew a line through the $1.25 and $15.00.

"*Du que se* (how much is left)?" she asked.

"*Tah zata doby ah hastah yawl eat za* (thirteen and six bits is left)." Tooth Gone anticipated her wants and placed another sack of flour and a can of baking powder on the counter. So regular were Mrs. Many Goats' purchases that Tooth Gone could have easily guessed the articles she was going to buy, as well as the sequence in which they would be bought.

After the flour came four packages of Arbuckle's coffee, a five-pound sack of sugar, and a four-pound bucket of shortening. Mrs. Many Goats was prosperous and could afford to have all her bread fried in deep fat. Poorer Indians usually made their bread with flour, water, and baking powder and cooked it on a flat rock or a piece of flat iron.

Next came two bits' worth of spuds. Spuds were generally for the poor and not a regular part of their diet, but a change. Tooth Gone threw in a couple of onions.

After each purchase Tooth Gone deducted the amount spent, and Mrs. Many Goats wanted to know how much was left.

When Tooth Gone asked, "What next?" the answer in Navaho was, "After a while." Mrs. Many Goats might decide to buy something else in a few minutes, or it might be an hour. Tooth Gone handed Mrs. Many Goats the paper sack with the row of figures on it. A line was drawn through each number but the last. This was the amount due her.

Two Salt's oldest wife was now demanding Tooth Gone's attention at the counter. She wanted five dollars more credit on a string of white shell and turquoise beads on which she had already borrowed fifteen. He remembered when she had pawned this same string of beads for sixty dollars and he had thought nothing of it; but times were different now. Indians did not prize their old jewelry as much as in years gone by, and if he allowed them too much on their pawn they would probably forget to take it out. Also Mrs. Two Salt could no longer be considered a good risk. Only a few years back she had owned several hundred sheep. The office of Indian Affairs had made a survey of range conditions and said there must be a reduction in livestock. Mrs. Two Salt sold some of her sheep to the Government and a hard winter further reduced her flock, but there were still enough sheep left so that she and her family could live without distress. The real cause of her present impoverishment was the sickness of a daughter, the only one of her five children who had not been sent away to school. This daughter had developed a bad cough, which for two years had continued to grow worse. The best medicine men in the district had attended her, and once Mrs. Two Salt had engaged a medicine man from a distant part of the reservation, one renowned for his curative powers, to come and make a sand painting and sing over her daughter. These visits had cost a large part of her flock. Payments were usually made in sheep; and if a cure was to be expected, a medicine man had to be paid. The white doctor and the nurse from the Indian hospital also had been called many times and had given medicine and advice, but after two years of sickness the daughter had died. Now Mrs. Two Salt's flock had dwindled near to the vanishing point, and almost the only way she had of securing the barest necessities was by weaving rugs. Several times during the past winter the Government had given her provisions, but these were not enough and there was always the possibility that when she needed them most there would be none to give.

Trader Tooth Gone knew most of the ups and downs of the Indian families in his trade district. He was sympathetic, and helped when he could; but there was a limit to what he could give if he expected to stay in business.

He decided in favor of an additional loan and went into the pawn room which adjoined the store to add that amount to the pawn ticket. Mrs. Two Salt had other possessions in pawn and wanted to see them, so she followed Tooth Gone into the pawn room. She had no intention of redeeming anything, but she always liked to look at her pawn and feel reassured that Tooth Gone was holding it for her.

The trader stood for a few minutes looking over his pawn room and then drew a long breath. "Four thousand dollars worth of credit here, and this is my security," he thought. "There is no turnover on it and I am drawing no interest."

He knew other traders who carried more pawn than this, and some who carried less. Twenty-five years ago the investment he had here would not have worried him, for then the wholesale houses expected accounts to be settled twice each year, when wool and lambs were sold. Now he had to pay every sixty days or be charged interest.

The room contained an astonishing variety of articles. A big safe protected most of his valuable items against fire and theft. There were many pieces of Indian jewelry made of silver, some plain, others set with turquoise. There were necklaces of coral, turquoise, and shell, which the Navahos valued highly. Some of this jewelry had been in pawn for a long time, but Tooth Gone had refused to sell it years after the debt was overdue, for he knew that many were heirlooms held in high regard by their owners. Next month all the jewelry would be put on display each day in the store as a reminder that since it was wool season each Navaho should redeem his pawn.

On shelves and racks around the pawn room were objects of less value and more bulk—saddles, bridles, chaps, spurs, rifles, robes, shawls, buckskins for ceremonial uses, and a medicine bag, made from the skin of a mountain lion, that belonged to Big Singer and contained all his magic paraphernalia. There were also several saddle blankets pawned by men with the understanding that if they were not redeemed in a couple of months they would be sold—and they usually were. These were extra fine blankets that some of their women folks had made and given them for presents. It would have been bad form for an Indian to sell one of the blankets, but it was entirely ethical for him to put it in pawn and forget to redeem it.

After marking an extra five dollars on her string of beads, Tooth Gone showed Mrs. Two Salt the rest of her pawn. From the safe he took a flour sack that contained a silver mounted bridle and a string of large silver beads. Each had a pawn tag marked twenty-five dollars and a date more than three years old. Ten years ago Tooth Gone could easily have sold either for fifty dollars. Now he wondered if there were any collectors who would pay twenty-five dollars for one of these rare old pieces.

Tooth Gone hefted the bridle and guessed that at least thirty-five American silver dollars had gone into the making of it. He was sure it was made from American money, for it had a brighter sheen than jewelry made from the Mexican peso. He had heard old traders tell about the times in early days when all Indians' products were purchased with silver dollars. When a Navaho sold his sheep or wool and had any money left after paying his debts and buying supplies, he took it home. The next time the trader saw this money it had been made into jewelry. If a Navaho wanted to pawn this jewelry or sell it, the trader accepted it, ounce for ounce. If dimes, quarters or half dollars had been made into buttons they were accepted at face value. Yes, a Navaho could have his cake and eat it too.

After Mrs. Two Salt had looked at her pawn, she and the trader returned to the store, where Tooth Gone wrote a trade slip for her. He guessed it would take at least an hour for her to make up her mind about what she wanted to buy. Four dollars would probably go for groceries, the last dollar for dye, candy, thread, and novelties. Other Indians were coming in, and it looked as if he were going to have a busy day.

The store had been built thirty-five years before, and few changes had been made in it since, either inside or outside. It was a square stone building with high windows that had iron bars across them like a jail. The west side was flanked by a long warehouse, and Tooth Gone's home joined the store on the north; he could pass from his living quarters to the store without going outside. The front door of the store faced to the east, like a Navaho's *hogan*.[4] It may have been that the original builder had absorbed some of the Navaho religion, or he may have set the door in that position to please the Indians. Actually, the best place for the door was on the south side.

The original counters, wide and breast high, still extended on three sides of the room. The enclosure thus formed was called the bull pen. Here was the customary big, oblong cast-iron heating stove that would take a chunk of wood almost the size of a man's body. Here, too, stood a cheap cook stove and a second-hand sewing machine. Only a few families in this district used cook stoves; most of them preferred to cook on the open fire; but a sewing machine was a household necessity. Stitching endless yards of ric-rac and bias tape[5] trimming around a skirt that contained sixteen yards of material was no small task, especially if done by hand.

Navahos liked to gather in the bull pen and talk over old times or coming events. They liked to talk about the prices of sheep and wool, even those who didn't own any sheep, and which traders were paying the highest prices.

Here in this bull pen many a young Navaho couple had met and sedately talked over marriage while seated on the floor with a bottle of pop between them. It would have been considered immoral and scandalous to have been seen together outside the trading post. Afterwards their parents would get together and arrange the wedding ceremony. Tooth Gone had seen many a courtship which to one unfamiliar with Navahos would have passed unobserved.

Between the store and wareroom was a partition made of boards from Arbuckle coffee cases. Some day Tooth Gone was going to remodel his store and make it really modern. But why hurry? Twelve years ago he had remodeled his home and installed conveniences—electric light plant, running water, and compressed gas for a gas range. That was the year after the big pinon crop[6] when he had made four thousand dollars clear.

The trading post was well stocked. From nails driven into the logs that supported the ceiling hung saddles, bridles, lariat ropes, harnesses, buckets, tubs, cooking pots, and other articles. Tooth Gone smiled when his eyes rested on half a dozen dust-covered brown crock chamber-pots suspended by strings. Years ago these had been good sellers. The Navahos had used them as mixing bowls when making bread, until somebody mentioned what the white people did with them; then they immediately went out of style.

The shelves behind the counters were divided into departments: groceries—including canned goods, consisting mostly of tomatoes and fruit—hardware, and dry goods. (Flour, sugar, coffee, and lard were kept underneath the counter.) The dry goods section was largest. Shelf after shelf was stacked with piece goods, and there were shelves for shirts, trousers, and shoes. Shoes were not much of a problem, for the trader carried only a couple of styles, and the foot sizes for both men and women were so uniform that he rarely had any trouble with the fit. A five or five and one-half would fit most of the women and a six and one-half or a seven most of the men. If the children didn't get a good fit it didn't make much difference. Often a mother would come to the store and, with nothing to guide her but her eyes, pick out a pair of shoes for the little boy or girl who was left at home herding sheep. Rarely did she return a pair of shoes because they did not fit.

Tooth Gone kept a large stock of robes for men and shawls for the women. The only difference between the robes and shawls is that shawls have fringes and robes do not. He also had robes and shawls for children. The dress of Navaho children is the same as that of their elders.

On each end of the counter in front of the dry goods were two old-fashioned, round-topped glass show cases. These were packed with notions, novelties, and Indian jewelry. A little box in one corner of the showcase contained sleigh bells. In years past unmarried Indian girls often wore these tied to the fringes of their belts.

On the counter near the groceries stood another showcase. This one was flat-topped and of a more recent style than the others; even so, it had rested in the same place for more than twenty years. It contained tobacco, candy, and chewing gum. In other years traders sold only two kinds of candy, the long and the round (stick and cheap mixed). The harder the mixed candy was, the better. Now an enterprising trader keeps at least a dozen varieties of candy bars.

Behind the counter and near the door that led to the living quarters was a big mechanical refrigerator, serving both the trader's home and the store. White people and a few young Indians who had been away to school wanted their soda pop cold, but most of the trade liked it as it came.

Mrs. Lean Horse and Mrs. Slow Talker were holding something under their shawls. Tooth Gone was sure that both had rugs to trade and that each rug would be wrapped in a clean flour sack; but he had no idea about their size or design. Tall Cane had a goat hide rolled up and tucked under his arm; for this he would receive thirty or thirty-five cents. Gray Water laid a sheep pelt, from which all of the wool had been clipped, on the counter. A pelt like this was of no value, but still Gray Water expected something for it. Tooth Gone would give him a small sack of candy.

In the trading post, both men and women used the "complimentary makings" freely. Tobacco, cigarette papers, and matches were kept in a one-pound coffee can nailed to the counter. Seldom did an Indian come into the post and go directly to the tobacco can. This would have shown an unbecoming lack of restraint. Usually he would wait fifteen minutes or longer before taking a smoke. After the first smoke he felt free to visit the tobacco can as often as he liked.

There was much talking and laughter among the Navahos in the store, but none of it was loud. The belief that an Indian is silent and doesn't show his emotions is certainly not true of the Navaho. As usual, a spirit of good fellowship prevailed. Navahos believe it is very wrong to lose one's temper.

This time of the year was always hardest for the Indians. The worst part of the winter had passed, but it would be two months or more before it would be warm enough to shear the sheep, and several months before the sheep or goats would be fat enough to kill. It was taboo to kill a poor animal, and this was done only in the face of actual starvation. Many of the Indians had exhausted their credit and had everything in hock for all they could get. The poor made a practice of visiting those, especially relatives, who had something to eat. Navahos are duty bound to share food with their kin, and often they will share it with many who are not. There was no Government work going on at this time of the year, and there was no other employment to be found on the reservation. Yet, with nothing in their stomachs, the Indians laughed and seemed as happy as usual.

Tooth Gone bought two rugs and wrote trade slips for them before Mrs. Many Goats decided to do some more buying. This time she wanted candy, dyes, a small sack of salt, and a five-cent cut of chewing tobacco. Navaho women did not chew the tobacco, but used it for medicine. A very small piece was placed in the mouth, allowed to dissolve, and was then swallowed.

Business became brisk, and several women demanded attention at the same time. This was because Tooth Gone's wife had called that dinner was ready, and all knew that the trading post would be closed for an hour. Tooth Gone waited on a few who he knew really wanted something now; then he good-naturedly shooed everyone outside and locked the door.

Since the weather was disagreeable, Tooth Gone cut his noon hour short so the Indians could have a comfortable place to stay. The first to enter the store were Mr. and Mrs. Left Hand from Smoky Mountain. Mrs. Left Hand had an unusually large bundle under her arm. These Indians were not regular customers of Tooth Gone's, and in order to get to his place they had to pass the trading post in Black Canyon. Tooth Gone was certain that Mrs. Left Hand had a large rug to trade, and that she had already gotten an offer at Black Canyon. Tooth Gone had a reputation for paying high prices for good rugs. Well-made rugs were a good investment, while the shoddy ones were undesirable no matter how little he paid for them. A big can of tomatoes and a loaf of bread were given to Mr. and Mrs. Left Hand, for they had come from a long distance and were doubtlessly hungry.

Tooth Gone bid sixty dollars for Mrs. Left Hand's rug, but it was two hours before she accepted his offer. She had been working on this rug all winter, so why be in a hurry about selling it? When the deal was made, she bought a few groceries and asked Tooth Gone to lend her a coffee pot. From under the counter he produced a box that contained a few tin dishes and an assortment of cooking utensils. These he kept for just such occasions, and for Indians who came from a long distance to trade and stayed in his guest *hogan* overnight. Several times Tooth Gone's wife had scolded him about these dishes being so dirty, and once or twice she had cleaned them, but the next time she saw them they were just as dirty. Tooth Gone tried to explain to her that the time to wash dishes was before you used them, not after.

The guest *hogan* was across the road from the trading post and built in the same manner as most Navaho homes. It was a dome-shaped structure made of logs and covered with dirt. It had one door that faced east, no windows, and a hole in the top to give light and permit the smoke to escape. An open fire in the center served for both heating and cooking. Tooth Gone usually provided a couple of sheep pelts for his guests to sleep on. He believed in giving them all the comforts they had at home.

Tooth Gone's other customers now required attention. They wanted to finish their trading and get home. Navahos do not like to travel after dark. Mrs. Left Hand had practically all of her sixty-dollar trade slip to spend, but he was certain that she would wait until morning before making more purchases.

When Tooth Gone offered Mrs. Left Hand sixty dollars for her rug he made a mental calculation of the amount she would spend for groceries, the amount she would spend for dry goods and notions, and the profit he would make from each. His guess was that not over thirty dollars would be spent for groceries; and the more she spent for dry goods and notions the greater would be his profit.

Tooth Gone looked outside at the shadows and knew that his day's work was nearly done. Most of his customers had left, but there were still two piles of dry goods and groceries stacked on the counter. These belonged to families who lived near by. They had asked for boxes to put their merchandise in, but he had none to give. Recently, since the Indians had begun going to the railroad towns, they had been requesting this service. But lack of boxes didn't bother Tooth Gone; he knew the Indians would pack off their merchandise in the manner in which they had always done. They would spread a shawl on the floor; stack what they had bought in the center, and tie the four corners together.

There was another reminder that it was time to close the store. Jim, the handy man, had just come in from the wood pile and wanted some groceries to take home. It made no difference to Jim how much he owed at the trading post; he was always willing to go a little deeper into debt. Tooth Gone couldn't remember a day Jim had worked for him that he hadn't wanted to spend at least as much as he had earned. Tooth Gone had sworn a thousand times that if he ever got even with Jim he would fire him, but Jim had been working for him for ten years.

Jim was a long-haired Navaho who couldn't speak English. Unless there was a dance in the neighborhood he was sure to be at the store at sunrise. Jim's personal wants were few and simple; it was his relatives, his wife, and his wife's relatives who kept him continually in debt. It was not unusual for Jim to take home a good supply of provisions at night and learn in twenty-four hours that it was all gone. Neither Jim nor his wife was a big eater but their numerous kinfolks were frequent visitors. Tooth Gone remembered the time when Jim had taken home four twenty-four-pound sacks of flour in one week. Jim's wife was a good saver, but as long as he had a job she hesitated to exert herself. The few rugs she made were traded for clothes for herself or for jewelry, never for groceries.

Tooth Gone gave a sigh of relief as he barred and locked the door. Jim had talked him out of a dollar more than he had earned that day. Lucky it wasn't more. Indians and Indian trading hadn't changed much since he had first come to the Navaho reservation thirty-five years before, and he sincerely hoped that as long as he was a trader it would stay the same. But conditions had changed if Indians and Indian trading hadn't.

Before the coming of trucks and good roads to the reservation—and that wasn't many years ago—all winter supplies had to be freighted in by teams before the coming of bad weather. Great quantities of flour, sugar, and coffee were kept in the storeroom. Now it was different: good roads led to nearly every part of the reservation and trucks delivered supplies the year round. Seldom did Tooth Gone keep more than two weeks' stock.

He sighed again as he took the money out of the till to put it in the safe for the night. Yes, he was still an Indian trader. He had had a busy day and there had been an exchange of much merchandise, but he knew that if he counted his cash it would show that he had added no more than ten cents to it. That dime had a copper loop brazed on one side and had been the last silver button on Mrs. Many Children's blouse. She had cut it off and spent it for a package of dye.

Notes

1. Hassell's annotation: "A form of address, equivalent to Mr."
2. Hassell's annotation: "Names like Many Goats are clan names."
3. A form of colorful and highly decorative braided ribbon interwoven into the fabric of Navaho clothing. Andrew Hunter Whiteford and Owen Vernon Shaffer, *North American Indian Arts* (New York: St. Martin's, 2001), 94–96.
4. As the center of domestic and ceremonial life, the hogan was a key structure in the daily life of many Navahos. A number of cultural proscriptions governed the proper construction and uses of the hogan. Primarily, as mentioned in the story, the door to the mud-plaster structure always faced east. Typically, the hut was a conical structure with no windows and a smoke hole in the ceiling. Franciscan Fathers, *An Ethnologic Dictionary of the Navaho Language,* (Leipzig, DE: Breslauer, 1929), 56, 333, 455.
5. A fabric tape used to weave seams, piping, and other decorative elements together. Elizabeth C. Hegemann, *Navaho Trading Days* (Albuquerque, NM: University of New Mexico Press, 1963), 273.
6. Also spelled "piñon," these nuts were a principal food source for several Native American cultures. Robert L. Bettinger, *Hunter-Gatherers* (New York: Plenum, 1991), 68, 70, 72.

AN ORGAN BUILDER'S SOLILOQUY

Carroll Whaley (Illinois)

My earliest recollections are not visual, but auditory. The deep bourdons,[1] rich diapasons,[2] and silvery overtones of the organ, impressive and inspiring but not overpowering, had, to my childish mind, a better chance than the voice of the clergyman to gain the ear of Omnipotence. The two manuals were the result of an accident, I reasoned; the original keyboard, presumably longer than that of a piano, had obviously been broken in two. The organist, poor soul, did the best he could with the mutilated instrument.

Childhood and adolescence brought piano lessons, but to the inner eye I was presiding at a mighty organ. The perusal of the catalogues of every organ builder advertised in *The Etude*[3] had stopped me from wasting further sympathy on broken keyboards. I became familiar with organ principles and with the builders' vocabulary. A complimentary copy of *The Diapason*, an organ builders' trade journal, opened more delightful vistas.

My first earnings went for organ practice in an old church. The organ was fairly well in tune, considering its age, with the exception of the reeds, which I did not have to use, and the low E-Flat on the pedal bourdon. This note was about a quarter of a tone off. I could not get a tuner to look at the organ for less than ten dollars, so I took a chance on tuning the pipe myself. I sought an assistant, or rather an accomplice, for I felt guilty tampering with the instrument. With my helper at the keyboard pressing the right key, I cautiously invaded the forest of pipes, my candle fighting the battle with the darkness. The interior was a cross between the insides of a vacuum cleaner and of a well filled pencil box standing on end, both magnified to grotesque proportions. Guided by the deep "Boo" of the offending pipe, I ascended a vertical ladder toward the tuner's platform, keenly enjoying the solemnity of the sounds.

Forgetting for a moment the object of my search, I viewed the organ's interior from the precarious heights of the platform, gazing down the throats of dozens of pipes below, arranged in double rows and graded by size, varying from the equivalent of a small tube to that of a smokestack seven or eight feet in length. From here the seamy sides of the longer pipes were evident; for the sake of economy about two dozen of the shafts had gold leaf spread only on the outer half of their circumference. Within the organ, the "dummies," too, are mercilessly exposed. The congregation, however, always accepts all the pipes at face value.

It was harder to get down from the platform than one might think. A glance at my clothing convinced me that I could not get much dirtier than I was, so I sought a toe-hold on the edge of the windchest between the smallest pipes, and supported most of my weight on my elbows. The descent was safer than it was graceful. Still seeking the offending pipe, I reached backward to a row of wooden ones, each provided with a bung stopper in the end. One of these was so situated that anyone stepping down would instinctively grasp it for support. A second glance showed that someone had done this, as the bung was depressed an inch or two. Trembling with the delight experienced only by those who have made a great discovery, I reached my hand to the mouth of the pipe and felt a rush of air. Of the eleven hundred pipes in the organ, I had found the one I sought.

I called to my accomplice at the console to manipulate the stops and keys in such a manner that another pipe, an octave higher in pitch, would sound. Then, by moving the bung I altered the pitch of the pipe, and my ear decided when a perfect octave had been attained. The sound of those two pipes speaking in harmony gave a thrill of real accomplishment.

My assistant thereupon undertook to play the organ while I was yet within it. Only one who has been inside the great division of an organ of classic design when it is being played can have any conception of the result—powerful steam whistles blasting right, left, front, and back. The tones of some of the big trumpet pipes were like those of a half-slaughtered boar.

"Push in the trumpet!"

He was incredibly slow in finding the trumpet stop, but when he did, the tone was much improved. Until he tired of playing, I gloated over the hundreds of pipes of geometrically increasing proportions, and wondered which were responsible for the flood of powerful tone. Strangely lacking was any visible evidence of the exhalation of sound. There was nothing comparable to the swinging of a bell, the steam from a whistle, or the action of piano hammers. One might well think that the eleven hundred pipes were sounding at once. Heard from within, the harmony has an effect analogous to an heroic billboard figure viewed at arm's length. And from this position even the most inspired playing sounds mechanical.

Not yet satisfied with my explorations, I detached a dozen or more pipes, one at a time, for closer examination. The smaller and medium-sized pipes can be blown by lung power. The wooden ones seemed the most satisfactory to handle, fine white sugar pine shellacked to a glossy finish. One pipe had a bung, and to my surprise, two mouths, one on each side. So that's what a dopple flute looks like! I blew upon it, and found the tone clear and traveling. Then I sought for a member of the harmonic flute family; these are all double length, that is to say a pipe whose "speaking" length is two feet is actually four feet long, and a small hole is the two-foot mark. Such a pipe vibrates in segments, and may be compared to a vibrating violin string lightly touched in the center node.

I emerged from the interior of the organ looking like a chimney sweep, climbed into the cockpit—an affectionate term for the console—and immediately tested the results of my tuning. I was elated with my success.

The reed pipes, the tones of which are suggestive of the trumpet, oboe, and so on, are usually the worst offenders in any organ, especially in old, low-pressure instruments, or those not frequently serviced. One day during the hard times of the early thirties I found an elderly, unemployed organ builder who consented to help me smooth out some of the rougher spots of the oboe of the swell organ. On his first visit he had drunk too much to be trusted with the delicate mechanism, for I was undertaking the repairs on my own hook without the knowledge of the church trustees. The second time he forgot his tools, so I went for them. The tool case was unusually heavy, and I suspected that he had forgotten it deliberately. I had found the entrance to the swell organ to be a narrow door behind the display pipes a few feet to the left of the center. Prior to the tuner's arrival, I had taken down three or four of these pipes (they proved to be dummies), and had provided a step ladder and an electric extension cord for his use in the chamber. The corpulent veteran made a valiant but vain attempt to get in. Had he weighed some 50 or 60 pounds less, he might have squeezed by. Much less embarrassed at this state of affairs than I was, he promptly suggested that I do the work under his direction from the keyboard. Eagerly I entered the swell-organ chamber. Being enclosed, it was much cleaner than the great division. The longest pipes were mitered, reminding one of the elbowed smoke stacks on section gangs' shanties along the rip track. What I learned in the stuffy, dusty chamber under the direction of that intemperate, old-country tuner came in very useful at my first organ-playing position.

This was in a church, once wealthy and prominent, but in a neighborhood which was on the down grade. The organ was an excellent example of Victorian design, originally pumped by man-power. An hydraulic engine, installed about the turn of the century, had given faithful service for nearly thirty years. It closely resembled a wind mill without the mill, the shaft being moved by a four-inch piston in a cylinder. The amount of water consumed was enormous, but this caused the trustees small concern, as there was no meter. Sweating and leaking had caused the underlying joists of the building to rot, and the engine had been jacked up and placed on a heavy concrete caisson. This readjustment interfered with the orbit of the shaft, and each thrust of the piston had the effect of an earthquake in the organ loft.

I well remember the installation of the electric blower. The caisson afforded excellent support for the two-horse-power electric motor and turbine blower. A fourteen-inch galvanized pipe conducted the wind to the organ chests. The installation of this blower solved one problem, but created another. The old hydraulic system had taken air from the immediate environs of the organ, which was of room temperature. The electric blower drew air from the floor of the basement, and in cold weather the difference in temperature between the auditorium and the air forced through the organ was sometimes as high as 65 degrees. The expansion and contraction of the pipes caused by this change of temperature produced dismaying tonal results.

The janitor and I enclosed the new blowing equipment in a little house about six feet high. An open wooden chimney or air duct about two feet square was erected upon it which reached within eighteen inches of the ceiling, which was unusually high. As the furnace smoke-pipe crossed the room, the air under the ceiling was always warm, regardless of how cold it might be on the floor. Thus, warm air was drawn down from the ceiling and immediately forced up to the organ. A few minutes' fortissimo[4] playing before the arrival of early worshippers had the effect of an organ tuning.

In recent years I have collected, restored, and electrified reed organs, similar to the one my grandparents used to have, dating from the early eighties.

The reed organ is capable of genuine harmony and expression, provided the player does not despise this humble instrument. Most of the old organs were the result of fine craftsmanship patiently expended on excellent materials. The assembly line and mass production as we see them today were unknown. The one organ builder's staple which is an improvement over those of decades ago is the rubber pneumatic cloth which covers the bellows—thanks to the research and experimentation of tire makers. Consequently, an old organ painstakingly restored is probably better than it was originally, and superior to many of those made today.

In my home I have a large collection of organs and melodeons. The living rooms are crowded with restorations of all periods; the basement, from coal bin to laundry, is a workshop. Bellows, chests, stops, and reeds are scattered about on all sides, and the place seems as if seventeen organs had exploded there.

Look at this beautiful white oak. It is from an organ that stood outdoors all last winter. I was on an organ hunt in northwest Illinois, speeding through a town no bigger than a wide spot in the road when I spied this organ standing in a churchyard.

I located the caretaker of the church, a middle-aged Yankee matron.

"You have charge of the church property?"

"Yes."

"I'm interested in that old organ. Do you suppose I could arrange to buy it?"

"I reckon you could."

"What will I have to pay? I could take it along in the car, but don't know when I'll be back this way."

"What'll you give me?"

"Fifty cents?"

"Will you take all of it?"

I found out later that she had made several unsuccessful attempts to give the thing away. In half an hour it was in the back seat of the car, completely dismembered. I salvaged the action and reeds for spare parts.

When the case of a good organ has been abused, there is a temptation to enamel it. That's what I'm doing to a Kimball. When I bought the instrument, it was half buried under a lot of rusty sewing machines. All that gingerbread work over there by the laundry stove came off it. The front posts were broken, so I put in these walnut spindles. A simplified case finished in bone white carefully shaded is very attractive. The work must be done by loving hands, however, for it is long and tedious. The case must be carefully aligned, and the wood thoroughly prepared with varnish remover and sandpaper. Then several coats of flat white underbody are necessary. If the stains of the original finish "bleeds" through the first coat, an application of aluminum paint is recommended. These processes should take place with the action removed.

It would be a sin to paint or enamel over the American walnut of this Mason and Hamlin, or the white oak of that Hinners. These excellent old woods invite the sophisticated caress of a cabinet maker. Many are the opportunities for the simplification of ornate cases by cutting off some of the upper decks, and, perhaps, evolving a new music rack from discarded grille work. If the organ lacks a stool, a bench which matches the case may be made from the discarded top. If this does not yield enough lumber, the seat board may be made of scrap wood and upholstered with the same fabric used in the grille work. . . .

Notes

1. Can either refer to the lower pitches of a pipe organ generated by a complex system of stops and pipe configurations, or the actual pipes themselves. The tones that the narrator refers to are typically generated by the eight-, sixteen-, and thirty-two-foot vertical pipes. Richard Kassel, *The Organ: An Encyclopedia* (New York: Routledge, 2006), 76, 229; Theodore Baker, *A Dictionary of Musical Terms, Containing Upwards of 9,000 English, French, German, Italian, Latin and Greek Words* (New York: Schirmer, 1901), 30.

2. The "principals" in the tonal groups of pipe-organ flue pipes. Air is either allowed or restricted from passing through various combinations of these columns so as to generate the characteristic timbre of the pipe organ. Kassel, *The Organ*, 143, 206.

3. A music magazine covering a wide variety of subjects of interest to musicians. The monthly publication included musical instruction, advertisements for instruments and equipment, sheet music, reviews, and other articles about the music industry. The magazine was launched by Theodore Presser in October of 1883 and continued through 1957. D. E. Bomberger, *An Index to Music Published in The Etude Magazine, 1883–1957* (Lanham, MD: Scarecrow Press, 2004), xiii–xiv.

4. A musical term for forceful and loud performance of a section of music; the opposite of "pianissimo." Michael Kennedy and Joyce Bourne Kennedy, *The Concise Oxford Dictionary of Music* (New York: Oxford University Press, 1996), 249, 262.

SECTION III

MODERN
TIMES

PART ONE: The Producers

ANACONDA

Edward B. Reynolds (*Montana*)

He shoved the white card into the timekeeper's window and growled a greeting. While he waited for the clerk to go through the familiar routine of making out a time card, he continued grumbling to himself. He had been grumbling on the street car all the way up the Hill to the works. Grumbling ever since the clerk in the employment office downtown had given him a work card for the Stack.

The Stack! Rappin' treaters or dumping flue dust. That was a job for sodbusters¹ and greenhorns.² Not for a guy that had been born and raised right here on the ground, here in Anaconda, whose residents do not look at the morning sky to see how the weather is, but whose first glance is at the Big Stack to see how the smoke's coming out. They don't ask one another's health, they ask, "What shift you on?" "How's she going?" is hello; "Tap her light" is good-by. Why, his parents had been there when Old Marcus himself, the Copper King, had bellied up to the bar he'd had built as an exact reproduction of the Hoffman House in New York. The Stack! Jeez, you'd think there was enough Okies and Arkies laying around to take those jobs. You wouldn't think they'd put a guy in a hell hole who'd worked every place from the high line, dumping ore, to the hot metal. If times hadn't been so tough with him, he'd have told that employment clerk where he could stick his card. But . . . Well . . . Hell!

The card hustler handed him the pink pasteboard and said, "Give this to McClelly at the Stack. You'll have to walk. You're the only rustler and there's no sense in sending a bus for just one man. Besides, you should worry; you're getting paid from now on. If walking's the hardest work you have to do, you'll be lucky."

"Okay, okay. Let's have her."

He took the card and started up the road to the Stack. It was a hot July day and the exertion of climbing soon made him remove his jacket. A couple of flies buzzed around his head with soothing sounds. They reminded him of fishing—of luxuriously stretching his legs on the bank of a stream and baking in the sunlight. Far up, on top of the mountain, the Big Stack reared upward to the height of 585 feet. A silvery-grey mass drifted from its top and lazily blended into the deep blue of the sky. Its soft cloud-like formations looked deceptively gentle against the background made hard by the glaring sun. He almost forgot his grumbling.

As he kept mounting upward the Big Stack began to grow and became formidable. It lost its beauty, and its size became overpowering. He began to think again of his job. He was certain he wouldn't get one of the better jobs. A rustler was always put to either rappin' treaters or dumping flue dust.

When you rapped treaters you took a bamboo pole and rapped the dust from plates inside chambers that are built right into the stack. These plates are sheets of corrugated roofing steel, twenty-one feet wide and twenty-four feet high. They are hung vertically, twelve inches apart, in box-like chambers that form the treaters. Between them are rows of small chains, suspended at five-inch intervals. The chains carry a static charge of electricity at a tension of 62,000 volts. When the smoke and gases rise between the plates, the electricity charges the fine particles of dust and repels them from the chains to the plates. The plates are grounded so that the dust particles lose their electrical charge and cling to the plates until they collect in masses large enough to fall through the rising gas to hoppers in the bottom of the chamber. . . . Dumping flue dust is when you get into the tunnel underneath the treaters and pull the lever that opens these hoppers so the dust runs into ore cars to be hauled away to the arsenic plant.

It all sounds fine when you explain it that way, but the new man wasn't thinking of technical processes. He wasn't concerned with the fact that arsenic recovered as a by-product from the smoke and gases that formerly passed off into the air as waste matter now form the basis of a huge industry in itself. He wasn't concerned with farmers who dusted their fields and fought insect plagues with that same arsenic. He was thinking of the 62,000 volts in the chains and the burning and poisonous qualities of arsenic.

It was true that precautions had been taken to eliminate the danger of electrocution and that men were rarely killed. But he remembered cases when something had gone wrong. He remembered stories of the smell of burning flesh, of the blue hole where the juice had passed through a man's feet on out of his body, of rigid forms toppling from the cat walk. He realized that these stories were told by men whose constant companionship with death causes them to exaggerate tragedy in order to relish it the more. He realized all this, but the stories were there in his mind. And, somehow, death by electrocution seemed tawdry after the violent, threatening spectacle of the hot metal.

It was the same with dumping flue dust. That didn't bring violent death, but there was always the chance of getting burned. Here, too, you took precautions, to keep the dust away from your skin. When you sweat and the dust touches your skin it turns to arsenious acid that eats into the body and leaves nasty sores. There is something unpleasant and humiliating about these sores—under the arms, between the legs, around the waist. You look at them and treat them in the privacy of your room. You're ashamed of them. No, it's not like the hot metal, where the leaping, roaring flames and the fiery glow of molten metal places danger on a high level.

As he reached the high line where they dump the great cars of copper ore from the Butte mines, he stopped on a landing of the stairway to "take five" and look back. Below him stretched the reduction works—immense and spreading, like the reptile the plant was named for. The great buildings seemed to flow down the mountainside, wrapping themselves around rocky ledges with snakelike purpose. They were built that way to take advantage of gravity. Raw ore was dumped in at the top and wandered down through the buildings, everywhere undergoing different processes, to the smelters[3] at the bottom of the hill. Here the treated ore was fused and turned into molten copper.

Because he had worked in almost every department on the Hill, his eye, as it roved from building to building, visualized what was happening in each. He watched an automatic dumper grasp in its iron claws a big ore car, fresh from the mines of Butte. He saw it pick it up and turn it upside down, spilling the rock into a huge bin.

He imagined the scene inside the great building built right onto the bin. He could see the doors open and the ore come tumbling down onto the iron bars called grizzlies. He could hear the crashing of rocks, too big to pass through the bars. He could see and hear them moving toward the crushers—in whose jaws they were crunched and chewed until they were at last spewed out, small enough to drop between the bars to conveyor belts below.

In another building farther down the Hill he could sense the ore being crushed still further until it was sand. He could hear the chattering and throbbing of the Hardinge mills with their iron balls pounding the sand. He could see the Anaconda and the Dorr classifiers[4] letting the finely ground ore through and rejecting the coarser stuff. He could hear the bubbling and murmuring of muddy water rushing through little flumes called launders as it washed the finely ground ore toward the flotation machines.

The flotation machines in another building mixed the ore with pine oil and chemicals and blew air into it, until the mixture became a slimy foam. In this process the copper sticks to the oily bubbles and rises to the top; the waste material at the bottom is washed away. The slime goes to great Dorr thickening tanks[5] where it is brought to the consistency of pancake batter. Then it is passed over Oliver filters,[6] shaped like barrels and the water is drawn out. He could see these giant mud pies, rich in copper, zinc, lead, gold, silver, and other metals, being scraped off and loaded in cars for a trip to the roasters.

As his eye moved toward the roaster building, he saw one of the little trains of cars dart out and puff its way up the track. Alongside the big railroad cars these trains looked like toys, but they were big enough if you had to work on them. Little sputtering engines, charged with compressed air, rushed the cars along like a crotchety old spinster herding a crowd of children. The train mounted to the top of the roasters and dumped its load of concentrates.

Inside the roasters the furnaces were built with several floors, and on each floor revolving arms shaped like wide garden rakes pushed and stirred the concentrated ore which dropped from one floor to another. The ore glows a deep orange-red as the sulphur commences to burn. Finally it comes out at the bottom red hot and is dumped into trains of iron cars that carry the smoking material called calcine[7] to the smelting departments at the bottom of the mountain.

His eyes dwelt on the smelters with a mixture of respect and hatred. The blackened buildings with their giant stacks looked like the charred remains of a forest fire. Down there was the hot metal; with its menace that fascinated him. He could see the calcine being dumped into the reverberatory furnaces[8] along with charges of dust and unroasted concentrates. He could hear the roar of the gas used for fuel. From the door of each furnace came a wild red glow like the blood-shot eye of a Cyclops.

He could see the converter furnaces, huge truncated cones that spouted flames, changing from yellow through orange and red to blue. Then there were the fiery rivers of molten copper when they tapped the furnaces, and the darker slag[9] or waste material that was discarded. There were anodes, 630-pound slabs of copper—the finished product as far as the smelters were concerned. These would be further refined and made into wire and cables, but that was someone else's concern.

The rustler on the stairway finished his mental tour as his eyes lit upon the main flue. Sixty feet wide and extending twenty feet above and seventeen feet below the ground, it ran from the smelters on up the Hill towards the Big Stack. Nearly a mile of smaller flues from the various furnaces were connected with it. As it neared the Stack it widened out to one hundred and twenty feet. This is the flue that carries the smoke and gases, rich in metals, that must be recovered by the treaters. The rustler swung his jacket over his shoulder and started climbing upward once again, his grumbling mood returning as he toiled up the steps.

When he reached the top the Stack no longer had form. It was too big—a huge mass of bricks that went up and up and up, overpoweringly. He found the office and gave his time card to the boss.

"Go over to that white shack. You'll find a man there who will tell you what to do."

He entered the door of the shack, a tiny one-room affair, and found a fellow stretched on a bench, reading a copy of *Western Story*. It was Mickey O'Brien, an old friend. He laughed.

"So they finally got you, too."

"Yeah. I guess it's better than nothin'!"

"Yeah, that's right. Is that all you got to do?"

"This is plenty," Mickey tossed the magazine to one side. "You know as well as I do, any time you get a chance to read there's a catch in it."

"That's a fact."

"Remember that guy we saw down town that looked as if the side of his face was eaten off by cancer?"

"Yeah?"

"He had this job before I did. He got some arsenic in his tear duct."

Mickey went to a cupboard from where he took a big roll of cheesecloth, clothes and other gear. "We're dumping flue dust," he said. "I'll show you how to wrap up."

He tore off a large hunk of cheesecloth and wrapped it around the rustler's head, tying two ends behind so that it fitted like a cap, with part hanging down over his neck and shoulders like the riggings Arabs and members of the Foreign Legion wear on the desert. He took another piece of cloth and wrapped it around the rustler's face like a bandit's mask. Another cloth went around the neck and a smaller piece was placed over the bridge of the nose, connecting the mask and cap so that only the eyes peered out.

The rustler now pulled on a pair of rubber boots that reached his knees. Then he got into a pair of woolen coveralls that hung to his ankles, and buttoned them up around his neck and wrists. Fur trimmed goggles went over the cheesecloth on his face, fitting tightly around his eyes. A large dust mask covered his nose and mouth so that the air he breathed would be filtered. Over everything went a woolen hood with an opening for the eyes, nose and mouth.

Lastly, he drew on a pair of gauntlet gloves[10] and over them a pair of canvas sleeves that reached from his wrists to a point above his elbows. When he had finished dressing no part of him was exposed. Mickey, while dressing likewise, told the rustler to follow him and to copy his actions.

The two men made their way to the tunnel under the treaters. As they walked the hot July sun beating down on the rustler's heavy woolen clothes started him sweating. He remembered what would happen if the arsenic dust reached his skin with all that sweat, and he tried hard to stop, but the thought caused him to sweat even more. At the tunnel they found a couple of huge ore cars spotted on the tracks.

Mickey gathered some gunny sacks and started cutting them into small strips with a knife. With these they began to chink the cracks in the bottom of the cars, which could be opened like hoppers in order to dump their contents. It seemed to the rustler as if they'd never get those holes and cracks filled up. Every time he thought he was through he'd take a look and see daylight. At last Mickey tapped him on the shoulder and started toward the door.

When they got out into the sunlight again, Mickey led him to an air hose and started to blow the dust from his clothes. Carefully, he went over every section of cloth; satisfied at last, he removed his hood and muzzle.

"You want to be real careful to blow off good," Mickey told him. "Then wash good in cold water. If you don't you might get some dust on you and get burned. I've been here two weeks now, and I haven't gotten burned yet. Some guys'll get burned the first day."

They went inside and stripped down. It was 11:30 so they started to eat their lunches. After lunch Mickey returned to his western stories, while the rustler found himself an old newspaper. About one o'clock they dressed again to get ready for the actual dumping of the dust.

"When you pull the lever," Mickey said, "pull it slow. This flue dust is finer than water. It'll shoot down into the car if it's going too fast and boil up and splash all over the place. Take it easy."

The rustler nodded.

"I ain't given you no baloney," Mickey added. "I seen cars standing half full of water when it's been rainin'. And I seen that flue dust shoot right through that water and run out cracks that weren't big enough to let that water out. That's why we got to chink it careful."

They went back into the tunnel and Mickey showed him how to pull the lever. In no time at all a thick dust fog had settled like a pall over the place. Mickey became a ghostly shape flitting around cars that seemed like things from another world. The silence interspersed with the soft phut-phut of the dropping dust was frightening. He wished it would hurry. He wondered if his clothes and that dust mask could really keep the arsenic out. His thoughts caused him to sweat and his glasses began to steam. Unconsciously he reached up to wipe them off. When he touched them he remembered the man with his eye eaten out by arsenic. He became panicky and opened the lever a little wider to hurry it. There came a soft sound like the rustling of silk and a flood of dust slapped him in the face and trickled down over his clothes. The car was boiling over. He was almost ready to run when he felt Mickey's hand gently but firmly pushing the lever closed. When the dust once more resumed flowing in a slow steady stream, Mickey passed on, giving him a slap on the back. It seemed like ages before he saw Mickey signaling him from the top of the car that it was full and he could close the hopper tight.

When they got out in the sunlight again it was like coming into a new world. Blowing the dust off his clothes, he was even more careful than Mickey had been in the morning. At last they were finished, and removed their work togs.[11] In the shower room, he blew off his town clothes, too, with an air hose.

Notes

1. A derisive term for farmers. Harold Wentworth and Stuart Berg Flexner, *Dictionary of American Slang* (New York: Crowell, 1960), 501.

2. See "The Type Louse" in this volume.

3. A furnace for melting the partially fused ore. Paul W. Thrush, *A Dictionary of Mining, Mineral, and Related Terms* (Chicago: Maclean Hunter, 1990), 1033.

4. Also "Dorr rake classifier," the name refers to a kind of mechanical separator that, like the "Oliver filter," helps to further purify the copper ore. Thrush, *Dictionary*, 340.

5. As with the "Dorr classifiers" and "Oliver filters," Dorr thickening tanks are used to begin the extraction of copper from its rough, mined ore form. The tank functions by agitating and "raking" the liquid and suspended particles in order to begin separating them. Thrush, *Dictionary*, 340.

6. A further stage in the copper-smelting process in which a cylinder-shaped canister is used to separate particulate matter out of liquid. "Oliver filtering" is a "continuous" filtering process that utilizes a cloth suspended over a barrel. American Geological Institute, *Dictionary of Mining, Mineral, and Related Terms* (Alexandria, VA: American Geological Institute in Cooperation with the Society for Mining, Metallurgy, and Exploration, Inc., 1997), 375.

7. A concentrated ore which is the by-product of either calcination or roasting processes. Thrush, *Dictionary*, 162.

8. A furnace which uses coal or some other fuel source to "fire" the ore and deflect, or "reverberate" material off the walls of the furnace and into a shallow "hearth." The hot gas generated by this process, along with that of the smelters, would have

been reasons for the plant's characteristically large smokestacks or single "stack" as referred to here. American Geological Institute, *Dictionary*, 457.

9.   Ibid., 512. A by-product of the smelting process.

10. Fireproof gloves (sometimes insulated) that cover the hands and forearm. M. H. Fulekar, *Industrial Hygiene and Chemical Safety* (New Delhi, IN: I. K. International Publishing, 2006), 48.

11. Work-specific apparel. Wentworth and Flexner, *Dictionary*, 548.

CANNERY ROW

Gail Hazard (California)

I fill my tray. I pull a gate up and sardines pour out of the flume that carries them from storage tank to me. I pick up the fish and put them into jerking conveyor slots, two by two, heads consonant to cutting knives, bodies dovetailed in. I put the fish into slots, the conveyor jerks ahead under cutting knives (sharp knives! watch your fingers!), and the fish, trimmed and gutted, plop out to be weighed and then dumped into the long water-filled trough that swims them to the packing table.

I open the gate and let more fish flow onto my table. My hands are never still, my cap is pulled down over my eyes, my mouth is tightly shut. Water pours down over rubber apron; I am standing in a pool of brine faintly red-colored with the blood of fish. A deafening rattle, of tin against tin and iron against iron, huddles down around me, and my checker, walking up and down the line of cutting machines, must scream against the rattle or else I cannot hear him. "Watch the heads, boys. Watch the guts!" He carries a long, sharp hook in his hand and he tosses off, and out of the weighing box, fish too bad for packing, fish badly cut.

I do not look up from my work. I want to trim and gut my fish and that is all I want. I am wet with brine, my arms are scale covered, my face is sprayed with fish-gut. I fill my tray again. Into the machines they go, two by two, into the cutting machine and out to be weighed and swum to packing table.

What was that? Did some tiny thought sneak into my brain to distract my hands from measured hustle? I've missed a slot! Save thought for tomorrow. "Watch the heads, boys! Watch the guts!"

Monterey is the largest
sardine canning port in the world.
—Packing Company Pamphlet

There are many canneries on the Monterey shore, all of them ramshackle, hollow wooden sheds built over rocky strips of wet tideland and stuck into the sea. Their roofs speckled by gulls, they squat by the warm sunlit bay, cold and stale; a special kind of cold and staleness is in them: the kind of cold that rinses out of unlighted, sunless, brackish tideland, the kind of staleness that roots itself in rubbish lying under ancient piling, covered with death and rotting barnacles.

But from high up on the hill, where workers live and wait for whistles to blow and machines to move, these sheds look clean and bright and weather-wise, the reminders of past seasons of fish-heavy boats, the heralds of furious work to come. Canneries are tight-shut and dismantled during summer; they have swallowed up their last year's catch and they squat on the shore, vacant and starved. But when the season starts and boats come in with new cargoes of plump firm sardines, cold sneaks out of opened doorways and fish-slots, refuse staleness is replaced by the heat of men and women working, workers furious with the energy of piece-work. Fish pour in from a sardine-bountiful sea and gulls again come to roost in long rows on rooftops or to gloat harsh-voiced over unloading boats.

I stuff my hands into the pockets of my jeans to keep them from shaking with the fatigue that comes from dim-lit cutting tables, and go out into the street. The sun is warm and bright and I squint my eyes against the pavement glare. Other men come out of half-opened doorways and flop down on running board and curb, or walk away hurriedly, saying "Ain't made my minimum" or "They burned better fish yesterday."[1]

Cannery Row is long and drab, now filled with workers—wet and trailing fish-smell, going to home or restaurant or shed or perhaps to car where women wait, listlessly looking seaward. The street cuts sharply between shed after shed, warehouse after warehouse, and ends up smack against another cannery and warehouse. Across this street, high up, are narrow, closed bridges holding endless conveyor belts that catch and bounce back to pavement, back against cannery and warehouse, back and forth like echoing tennis balls of tin.

I meet Ed. His eyes are bright but there are deep circles under them. Fish scale hangs to his sweater and spots his clean-shaven face. Walking, we pass small groups of men hunching over the ground or leaning against sunlit walls, talking fish or food or rent or pay: everyday talk.

"Man alive," they say, desperation in their voices, "are they going to burn all the fish?" Are they going to pour the catch continually into reduction tank and oil press and leave none for us to pack? Will the boats go out tonight? And if so will the catch be burned? Their voices rise an octave. Will the fish be fed into presses that suck out the oil? Poured into drying, chewing, crushing, mangling machines that grind the fish-flesh up into mash and meal and fertilizer? They argue it out. Fish are food and rent and clothing: the canning of fish is work to be done. When fish are turned into oil and meal and fertilizer, there is no pack. Burn the catch and it's as if the fleet hadn't gone out at all.

Will the boats go out tonight? The never ending question: "Will they burn the catch?" Will we haunt the Row tomorrow, useless and work-hungry, or stand bunched in doorways like refugees, or lounge upon the beach, hands in pockets, knowing that the fish will not be our fish? We spit onto the beachmuck. "Look at her," we say, as a ship goes by, "loaded to the ass!" and turn away to sniff the stink of burning fish that sticks in our throats and penetrates coat and sweater and shirt and jeans to drench our skins.

Today, we hurry down the street looking seaward through openings in cannery walls. Off shore boats are drifting or standing anchored to square floating hoppers, their nets piled aft or hauled aloft and fastened to mast. "Now ain't that a sight for sore eyes?" Ed asks and stops. "Look at that boat with its fish-net sail drying in the sun." We stand a moment and breathe deeply of sea-smell, strong and fresh with the odor of swimming things caught and made useful. Sudden sparkles of silver flash like sun-filled mirrors as sardines fall into hoppers. We turn away. "Let's eat. Next shift will be long."

Sitting in Wong's, we bolt our food like hungry scavenger birds. "You hear about that girl over in West Coast? She wasn't watching and she stuck her whole damn hand in the cutting machine." The grapevine is working this morning! "Choke it off, it's time." Time to go back. Time to dive again into fish-gut and slime.

No better fish is canned
anywhere in the world.

We go back to the packing shed. The watchman eyes us suspiciously as we file through the door; an old fool, this man, playing up to the boss for fear of his job, telling nasty stories to older women who listen with great pity and then laugh when he has gone. We slide past this belligerent, pretentious lick-spittle who wants to make us feel guilty as if caught in an act of trespass, strangers uncommendable, weighed in the balance and found wanting, undesirable to the company, and hurry to our machines.

I am anxious. Will the fish be solid and firm? Big? Or will they be soft, broken, and small? I look at my card to see what tonnage I've cut; 115 checks: good. That means I'm cutting 80 cents an hour. If this keeps up I'll get a paycheck: I'm paid 6½ cents for 60 pounds of fish cut—a minimum of 60 cents an hour for which I'm supposed to trim a profitable tonnage. They set this high: It takes a good man with good fish cutting fast to make a living wage. I break my back trying.

I squeeze into place beside the cutting machine and go sliding through an oily puddle. I skid in the muck of fishy, bloody water and smack my head into the fish-gate. The checker looks at me sourly. I make a mental note to watch out for him: he's the kind to heave a fish off the belt—smack into my face.

A fast, cheerful Chinese works with me. His father was a Monterey fisherman in the old days when there were fish. In those days everything was made by hand, even the tin cans, and fish were cut, not with machines but with bitterly sharp knives that whacked deep and sure through scale and gut, and finger and bone too. Men in those days worked until they had cut off all the fingers of the holding hand and then they sat by the sea until they either fell into the water or starved to death because there was nothing else for them to do. I don't believe this story but my Chinese friend does; last year he lost two fingers in the cutting machine.

An Okie, green and California-new, grins over my friend's shoulder, his face quite plainly saying: watch me tease this Chink. "Hey, Charlie, you better cut fast today 'cause I got a pal lookin' for your job." Lee keeps his eyes on the fish and goes on slapping sardines into the machines.

Two by two. Open the gate and let more fish slide into the table. I hunch down to give my arms easy swing, pull my cap down, set my mouth more tightly shut. Four hours to go: Four hours until I get into the street and see the sun again and get a breath of good, gut-free air.

On days when they put the catch into the reduction plant, I mope in the street and bitterly curse my luck and sniff the air, full of acid, oily stink, and wish I was in there, standing in the bloody brine, pushing them into the cutting machine, two by two.

It has been difficult to say whether the business of manufacturing sardine products was essentially one of canning or that of manufacturing commercially valuable goods of a non-edible type.

Large numbers of sardines swim together in schools inside and outside of Monterey Bay. Oldtimers say fish used to be so plentiful that a man could walk across to Santa Cruz and never get his feet wet. Well, there aren't that many nowadays. Or, if there are, they aren't putting cans around them.

My friend is a fish-kicker. He works in the reduction plant. When women come from the packing house, sweater doused, cap limp, dress reeking with the smell of sardines, and board the homegoing bus, tired and frumpy, noses go up in horror. What a stink! But, wait! You think they smell bad?

Pete works in the fish-pit. One day Bill, the foreman, comes slouching up to him and taps him threateningly on the chest: "Into it, your mortified son of a sardine. Climb down into it." And Pete replies "Okay! Okay!" and goes off to the pit.

Pete is a man of some versatility and he sacks and jigs and sews and stacks and loosens up rotten dry fish with equal skill. He grabs a sack and shapes it up and makes an ear; he throws half-hitches 'round and sews across like a half-demented seamstress making shrouds. He goes into the pit, hopping to the bottom like an overgrown monkey. "Fire it to me," he yells and the T-shaped prod sails down.

The tank is full of slippery, oily, pulpy, rotten, week-old fish—100 tons it holds—solidly filling the tank, wasting away, while passing men stop breathing as they pass.

"Loosen away," the foreman yells and Pete, looking up from the bottom, holds his nose; the foreman spits and pulls his ear and turns away.

Pete is standing by the endless screw that moves across the bottom of the tank rolling fish down its length, scooping the catch into oil presses. Great walls tower on both sides of him; 18 feet straight up and down they are, stiff walls of hard-caked sardines that stand like thin concrete dams holding back soft oozing muck that pushes hard like volcano-mud.

He pulls in his breath and gives a poke. Fish chip away from the half-hard mass and are caught up by the endless screw. He pokes again. He rakes. He pulls. He pushes savagely. Sweat flows in little lines down his cheeks. He pulls his cap down around his ears and buttons his shirt collar tight. Looking skyward, high up, he sees a gull and shouts a curse. Slime trickles down and mires him.

The screw moves down the length of the valley it has scooped through the mountainous mass and fish crumble onto it, chipped by vibration from the cliffs. He works beside the screw and feeds it slowly. Careful, Pete, he thinks and probes a cliff. He's like a man walking under a great dam in a deep valley with dynamite in his arms and matches already lit. A jab! That's one stick placed. A jab! That's another. Fingers are itchy to light the fuse! Push hard! A piece chips off to be grabbed up and whisked off and out of sight. Careful: you're prodding too hard! Don't blow dynamite against these walls and expect them to hold safely.

The foreman comes again and looks into the pit. "Kick 'em loose," he yells and a blast of steam whirls 'round his head. "Man, you stink! What's holding you still?" Pete looks up and blinks his eyes. I ain't afraid, he thinks.

A thin slide comes down the cliff and trickles into the screw. He watches it as it comes slowly down to fill the bottom. Drop load and scramble fast! Call out to men above! The foreman flicks his eyes away: "She's caving in," he cried. "Grab the beam."

Pete leaps high and grabs the beam on top of the outlet door; as he gets hold he feels the fish swish around his legs; above his knees he feels the mass grow tight. I'm going down, he thinks, I'm going under! And he sends his nails into the beam, his fingers tight like screws. Fish pour down: they slide and fall with soft little plops like handfuls of mud hitting mud; his thighs are under. His mouth grows foul and he retches, his stomach quivering, his eyes full of burning tears. He looks up at the foreman standing high above him and cries out. The fish now reach his armpits.

He moves his legs to keep the fish packed down. He fights against the mad desire to let loose his hands and push the muck away. He tries to pull himself upward on the beam: his legs are mired and his chest pressed down so that he can hardly breathe. Fish glide past his ear, his nose. "Six inches more and I'll be done."

Done? Oh, dead Manuel: How did you feel that day, Manuel, when you went sliding head first into the tank of lye? How did it seem to you, slipping across the oily muck, skidding falling toppling? Did you cry out? Did you scream when lye filled your eyes and mouth? What were you thinking, Manuel, as the stuff ate into your muscles and dissolved your bones? You struggled, you flailed your arms about but did that help? They fished you out of the tank, bit by bit. They'll fish me out. What good did struggle do, Manuel? It's the same with me. I'm just like you. My muscles strain. I cannot breathe.

The foreman smiles and holds his nose. "Go home and take a bath. You stink!"

Work over! It's late and the moon is bright over the bay. The hill is dark with tall pines but the sea is light, too light, I think, for fishing. "I don't think we'll work tomorrow."

Gertie does not answer me; she's tired. She stops from time to time to rest and to look back for Pete trailing behind us. "We ought to make them put showers and lockers in the plant," she says. "It's bad not to be able to walk with a man just because he smells so bad."

All day long Gertie stands by a three-part conveyor belt popping fish into tin cans. Headless, gutless fish crawl up out of the trough to pile up ten-deep on packing shelf. Overhead long lines of rattling tin cans pound down, can knocking can, tin cans to be filled with six fish, three this way and three that way, and when filled, to slide from her hand down to be pre-cooked, doused with mustard sauce, capped, and then cooked again.

We call to Pete; he seems so all-alone. He comes up grinning. "You think I smell bad? You ought to smell Karl. He had his face right over the lidder when the can squished up. Splap! It went. Splap! Right in his face. You should have seen him dancing around on one leg with fish-glue and mustard sauce all over. Splap! Right in his face and down his front and up his pantsleg."

"That's nothing. That ain't half as bad as what happens with tomato sauce." "I ain't seen the tomato." "They put the sauce in first. Then they dunk the fish in. You ever squeezed tomato juice over your face?" "Hell," Pete says, "you ever sit in a tank with fish-gut up to your neck? Tomato sauce!"

Gertie sits down. "Take fifteen cans off the top conveyor belt," she says, imitating a forelady. "Like this, girls. Then turn one over, bottomside up. Fill the rest with fish, three this way and three that way. Put fourteen filled cans on the middle conveyor belt and keep the fifteenth for the checker. Work fast now and don't stay too long in the restrooms."

Gertie gets up and we go on up the hill, frequently turning back to look at the moonlit bay. "Getting too late for fish." "They went out tonight." "Sure they went out but does that mean they'll get any?" "If they do, they'll burn it." Pete's clothes foul the clean night air. "Well, the more fish they burn the more I stink, and the more I stink the more I work."

Gertie takes Pete's arm and begins to talk. It's easy for Gertie to talk when she gets a little rested. She hates the canneries.

"Look, Pete," she says "it's like this: you fill a can with fish and they pay you for your work. One seventh of a cent. You fill a can and then you fill another. Another and another and another. If you're lucky you get a good spot and then you make money. But if you get badly placed, you get nothing but small and broken fish and you might as well have stayed home. You turn a can bottomside up, every fifteenth can, and the checker gives you a mark for it. Two cents. Two cents. Two cents. They come around and say, 'Don't you dare turn up two cans instead of one, now. That's cheating and we'll catch you.' Over at West Bay they've got an automatic checker. You grab a can from the top conveyor belt but watch out! A can cuts deep sometimes! Fill it with fish, three this way and three that way; reach up and push it through the slot. Pick up your paddle and haul fish onto your table; slap them into cans—for this work you've earned your beans. Slap and push, slap and push. 'Come on, girls,' they say, 'what's holding up the parade?'"

"'Push the can through the slot only once,' they say. 'You'll be fired for cheating.' Grab for another can. Hurry! Make your hands work fast. Oh, faster, faster! Fourteen cans pushed through the slot adds two cents to the paycheck. 'Don't try to cheat! We're watching you!'"

"Work four hours. Rest. Work four hours. Rest. Work some more. 'Fast girls, Faster. Make those fingers work!'"

"Well"—Pete grins—"you're a cannery worker. What do you think you are, a housewife?"

"I'm a sardine choker, and I'll always be a sardine choker. When I get to be just a housewife, I'll grow me fins and scales and swim out to sea."

Home again, we check the fleet over the shortwave.

"...just made a good set and got 70 ton ... off Point Lobos ... Made two sets ... got 90 ton ... good fishing. ..."

Fish tomorrow! Call up Bill: Hey Bill, they're getting fish tonight. We'll get the hours tomorrow.

" ... Fred's had some pretty bad luck ... poor fellow ... caught a shark in his net ... he's all cut up ... poor fellow ... no fish ... no, it don't look so good ... Where are you? ... just cruising around now ... ain't made one set ... nothing in sight ... going in. ... "

Only some of the boats are getting fish. Hey Bill, might as well get drunk. They'll probably burn it!

I shut off the radio and go to bed.

As soon as a boat comes in with
a load we have our help ready and
waiting to handle it ... there
is no victory without a battle!

The phone rings. "Going to cut," they say and hang up. I'm lucky today. That was Dick, the cutting boss, and it means that they won't burn the catch and that I'll work and the men who are waiting outside the plant door won't. There are men always waiting for my job.

I dash cold water into my eyes, swallow a cup of coffee, and beat it for the Row.

This morning Cannery Row is not unlike yesterday morning: the same acid, oily odor, the same long street, the hollow wooden packing sheds, the warehouse, the echoing bouncing noises, the quiet-by-day brothels. I meet Joe coming up as I go down. "You're early," I say. "I'm going home early too." Joe is sore. "I could make more in the cotton." He's stockily built, a can catcher and twentieth-of-a-cent-a-bunch carrot puller—white cap down over one eye, clean blue jeans, brown necktie knotted carefully in army shirt. Joe came out from Missouri, a free and independent man—or so he says. "That is, I'm free part of the time. When I ain't working."

I don't talk long with Joe. "Take it easy. You can't stop them from burning fish."

Joe starts me thinking. Have I earned my social security this season? How much have I earned? I try to remember and while I am remembering I suddenly see the Row as it really is: a drab street filled with bouncing machine noises, with job-hungry men. How many men work here? How many women? I do not know. They come and go, season in and season out, like migratory seagulls.

My shed is not yet ready and I go out back, on the seaside, to watch the boats come in. Friends are there watching the unloading fleet; strangers too. Here we all are: cutters, packers, seamers, casers, boilermen, warehousemen, fish-kickers, pressmen, sack sewers (fish butchers, can-catchers all)—all the rank-and-file of the Row watching the boats come in and unload.

"Hey, Bill, any mail for me?" (Hell, no. What do you want, a check?)

" . . . and so I got me a job from my old lady scrubbing the kitchen floor. My old lady sure knows how to push a man. . . . "

"You ain't eaten this morning? Well, hell, where's that ten bucks you earned last week."

Laughs.

"So I got me a haircut instead. A man feels better with his ears lowered."

"I'm no damn bum. I always wear a necktie to work."

"Hi there, Charlie. How much you earn yesterday?" (He, he, he, he, he)

" . . . and boy, has she got a system. She comes down and collects his check and he ain't got a comeback. . . . "

Laughs.

These are my brothers, I think, and hunch down into a crap game. Thought makes me sick! Why do men say silly things? Overhead, gulls are flying high, over the fishing fleet, lazy, living for sun and sky just now, living in sensation and forgetting fish and food and quarrels. (Have I made my social security?)

Women go past. I look up and smile at friendly faces. Pete comes up grinning. "Seen you. You look worried." "I'm all right." "It ain't good to worry." "I ain't worrying."

When the game peters out we sit back on our heels and talk. Johnnie starts a story and we listen with half-interest. The early sun is warm and sea blue-bright and we listen more to the sound of the sea than to each other. I have a lively interest in the sea, in the resting, fish-packed boats; I am alive and eager for the pack. " . . . and this fellow says to me 'Have you seen my wife?'. . . . " What kind of a story is this! Walk to the edge of the water and squat down and let shore-muck filter through you fingers!

It's time. No one need blow a whistle. We just get up and drift away, each man to his own shed. All at once our fists slowly close and open again.

These men are strangers; these women are not mine. These brothers of mine: who are these men? What do they want? Where do they live? These job-hungry men here to take my job from me, some of them, to deprive me of my living. Pete shakes my arm. "Stop worrying," he says and smiles.

We stand there watching the unloading boats, but not for long. How can we stand together for long when we are cannery workers, warehousemen, and reduction men—divided, one against the other? One gang of cutters against another gang, maintenance men who would be maintenance men, workers against workers. I almost run to my plant because men will be waiting outside ready to jump my job if I am not there. I scowl as I pass a warehouseman, all slick and cocky, going to his post. "What gravy,"[2] I think and sneer at his clean jeans.

Notes

Published a few years after Hazard's account, the first two sentences of John Steinbeck's 1945 novel of the same name artfully describe the declining canning industry in Monterey: "Cannery Row in Monterey in California is a poem, a stink, a grating noise, a quality of light, a tone, a habit, a nostalgia, a dream. Cannery Row is the gathered and scattered, tin and iron and rust and splintered wood, chipped pavement and weedy lots and junk heaps, sardine canneries of corrugate iron, honky tonks, restaurants and whore houses, and little crowded groceries, and laboratories and flophouses." John Steinbeck, *Cannery Row* (New York: Penguin, 1994), 5.

1.   Prior to the writing of this story, around the time of World War I, canning plants began to increase their production of nonedible fish products such as fish meal and fish oils. Extraction of the waste by reduction tank and oil press was found to be more profitable than producing packaged fish for human consumption. Therefore, the fish bodies, after they were gutted and pressed, were incinerated. H. D. Severance, "Control of Cannery Odors at Monterey," *Sewage Works Journal* Vol. 4, No. 1 (Jan., 1932): 152–55.

2.   An expression decrying some effortless task generating income with very little effort. Harold Wentworth and Stuart Berg Flexner, *Dictionary of American Slang* (New York: Crowell, 1960), 228.

THE FRUIT PACKERS

John Delgado (California)

I swing the heavily loaded car off the public road onto an unpaved, rutted lane bordered on each side by the ranch-owner's "family orchard"—pomegranates and peaches, apricots and quince, cherries and plums—two or three trees of every variety that will grow on this soil. I drive a few hundred yards, past the owner's house, a white, rambling, two-story building surrounded by a flower garden and shaded by gigantic oak trees.

Behind this building—far enough away that the horde of pickers' children will not molest him with their noisy games, but near enough for Old Man Blake to see it clearly from his home—is the "white camp." Lost somewhere in the vast 400-acre forest of tall, spreading pear trees are the Japanese and Hindu camps, but I have never seen them, although I have worked on the Blake Ranch two seasons. Neither has my father, who has worked almost every inch of the ranch.

The "white camp" is the melting pot of all Caucasian nationalities, Spanish like ourselves, Portuguese, Germans, Americans—peoples of all nations who annually descend upon California's vast orchards and leave behind them stripped, bare trees.

We clamber out of the car, my father and I, to select a site for our tent. My mother and sister remain behind until the tent poles and other equipment can be taken from the running boards and the doors can be opened. Workers who have preceded us have already erected a miniature tent city.

Carefully my father examines the soil to determine if it can easily be tromped flat. He judges the distance to the community pump from which my mother must draw water for cooking and washing clothes. Small details must be considered, for this is to be our home for three months and, once the season starts, there will be neither time nor energy to move to a better location.

Friends made during past seasons greet us, and my father accepts a glass of wine from a *paisano*, a countryman from Andalusia. They cannot take time, now, to exchange news or curse the heat of the mid-afternoon June sun. My father clears the site he has selected of twigs and large clods while I bring the car as near to him as I can through the soft, plowed earth.

We take the load off the fenders and drive in the tent poles and stakes. My mother and sister, free at last of the furnace-like car, empty boxes of pots and pans, dishes, knives, and forks. Swiftly, with the deftness developed by repetition, the tent is set up. A large double mattress is spread on the ground along one side of the tent for my parents. My sister sleeps on a cot.

The tent is divided into two rooms simply by throwing a blanket over a rope extending the length of the canvas dwelling. The bedding is brought in and a couple of suitcases filled with clothes take up all the rest of the space in the tent. Into an up-ended lug box, with boards nailed crosswise for shelves, go the knives, forks, and dishes. The oil cook stove is put on a box outdoors and other boxes support rough boards for a table under a tree. There is no fear of rainy weather. We are all drenched with perspiration and it will be even hotter the rest of the season. A coal-oil lamp is cleaned off and put inside the tent. It will not be much used, for even its feeble light silhouettes the actions of everyone in the tent.

The tent is too small for another bed and I must sleep in the bunkhouse. My father and I walk off together to the timekeeper's shack. Arrangements were made a week ago, and now we merely check in: my father will work as a picker, my sister as a sorter in the shed, and I will feed the machine.

We men—I am just eighteen—are paid thirty-five cents an hour this year and my sister thirty cents an hour. We work nine hours a day, from seven a.m. until noon, from one p.m. until five. Fifty cents a day is deducted from my wages for my bed. Board and room, "found" in the language of farm workers, would cost me $1.25 daily.

Technically a "white collar" man, the timekeeper dresses like the rest of us—a blue work shirt open at the throat and a pair of black jeans. He writes down our names and gives my father the tools of his job: a galvanized bucket, with a hook on the handle to hang it from limbs of trees while he picks with both hands, and a "ring" that looks like an oversized bottle opener. The thirteen-foot ladder which he must climb a thousand times a day will be taken to the field by wagon.

The bunkhouse is a long, barn-like building, lined on each side with some fifty narrow, hard beds. Some of the men have decorated the walls with pictures of nude women or movie stars; others have placed lug boxes beside their beds for reading tables. I will spend all but my sleeping hours with my family or at work, so I leave my place untouched. I tell the bull cook which bunk I want—since they are identical, the selection is not difficult—then go back to our tent.

My mother has begun a stew and my sister has made the beds. She has hung a tiny mirror on one of the tent poles and pinned a picture of her sweetheart on a wall. My father has put the five one-gallon jugs of home-made wine near his bed—later he will wrap them in wet burlap to protect them from the torrid sun—and is impatient for his dinner. In two or three weeks he will drive the thirty-five miles to our house in Rocklin to renew our wine supply and see that no one has broken in.

Thus without fuss or emotion, we have established our new home. In three months it will be torn up completely. We have gone through this process too often to think of it now. We are eager to have our dinner over. There is much to be done.

My father must join the other men to speculate about the crop and the heat. He must learn where the best prices will be paid grape pickers, and what conditions will be on the various ranches. He must reminisce of other ranches and other years.

My mother will be told of the new babies born and of the girls who have been married during the winter. She will listen with horror when she is told of the shameless behavior of Miguel Torres' daughter.

Other girls of my sister's age will seek her out. They will tell her exaggerated stories of winter romances; when they are finished she will tell them of her sweetheart. Reveling in the others' jealousy, she will add that next year, if she comes to the Blake ranch at all, it will be as a wife.

I can scarcely wait to see if Carmen's folks are back this year. It is not fitting that I should openly ask for her, since the Spanish are very rigid in such matters, but I shall soon find out. I will talk with Tony and Joe and very casually I shall ask, Is so-and-so here? What about the Guerreros? And then, as if in afterthought, has anyone seen Carmen's family?

The great bell rings promptly at five-thirty in the morning. Its peal permeates the bunkhouse and shatters my dreamless sleep. Without protest I rise and dress quickly. I wash in cold water and walk briskly the two hundred yards to our tent. My family is already up and breakfast is ready. My father has never overcome the habits of old Spain and has been up for an hour. I well know his unvarying routine: a large glass of wine (in winter it is *aguardiente*[1]) to be taken at one gulp and a bulging cigarette rolled in brown paper. Then he dresses and, although he knows it's going to be hot and dry, habit forces him to cast a quick look at the sky to forecast the weather. Satisfied it will be a scorcher, he bangs the pots and pans so noisily that my mother must of necessity get up. Always he begins making breakfast, but never once has he finished it.

Each of us who are to work eats two fried eggs and generous portions of fried tomatoes and peppers, washed down with several cups of steaming coffee. My mother dashes from stove to table, anticipating our wants. She will eat at her leisure later, when we are at work. There is little conversation, for time is short and breakfast large.

My sister and I must walk about a quarter of a mile to the packing shed, so we leave before my father, who will meet the foreman of his crew at the timekeeper's shack. There he will be told which field he will work, and he will cram the "ring" disdainfully into his pocket, where it will remain until he loses it or throws it away. The ring is to measure the pears, to make certain that fruit too small—and therefore under-ripe—will not be picked, but my father has been too long at this work not to be able to judge the size of the fruit at sight.

The packing shed is a large, almost square building constructed of rough one-by-twelve boards with large cracks between them. The floor is smooth so that the hand trucks can be rolled easily over it, and the roof is made of tin, which serves to increase the heat. It has only two walls: one side is open for unloading wagons from the orchard; the other side opens onto a spur track where freight cars are loaded with packed pears.

Old Man Blake's son, the packing shed foreman, knows I have worked here before, and gives me no orders. The Japanese or Hindu crews started work yesterday, so the shed is partially filled with lug boxes of green pears in piles of six boxes each, placed on the right side of the machine. Young Blake turns on the power, and the machine begins the humming, whirring sound that will be dinned into the brain of every man and woman there. The machine takes the place of a whistle or a time-clock. When it starts, everybody goes to work. When it stops, everybody quits working.

It is the heart and nerve center of the fifty-man plant. It is an uncomplicated mechanism, so simple as to be almost childish, yet were it to falter, some four hundred men and women—packers and pickers, sorters and truckers, teamsters,[2] waterboys and foremen—would be idle. It consists of an endless canvas belt which carries the pears under three sets of brushes. The brushes turn counter-wise to the movement of the belt, so that the fruit is twirled about. As the pears pass under the brushes, they are cleansed of the poisonous spray covering which protects them from parasitic growths.

There are about two hundred pickers on the ranch—white, Japanese and Hindu. Countless times each day they climb their ladders with empty buckets, which they fill as they work down the trees, and sink ankle-deep into the soft soil as they empty the buckets into lug boxes. They must be careful to pull the pear against the grain of the limb to break the whole stem cleanly; they must not drop the fruit too hard or it will be bruised. Sometimes it is so hot they cannot work in the middle of the afternoon and must put in their nine hours early in the morning and late in the evening. They are given two ten-minute "smoke times" during which they can relax in the shade of a tree and enjoy a cigarette.

A score of teamsters scatter throughout the ranch to gather the lug boxes from the field. They rise at daybreak and, before breakfast, prepare the horses for the hard day's work. In the field they have to load the wagons alone. Through the day, from all corners of the ranch, they converge upon the packing shed, man and animal covered with perspiration and dust. At the shed a swamper helps unload the forty boxes carried each trip. Truckers carry the fruit to the machines.

A half-dozen young men—holding the coveted "waterboy" jobs—race around the ranch in light two-wheel sulkies, carrying five-gallon cans of water to the pickers. Foremen walk from row to row behind the pickers, scanning the trees to see that no desirable fruit is left behind, for by the next picking it will be too ripe.

At the other end of the machine from me are eight girls—the sorters—lined four on each side of the endless canvas belt. The cleaned fruit passes before them on review; they pick from the moving belt fruit that is too bruised or too small. They work steadily, keeping up with the flow of fruit, their eyes intent upon the belt, their fingers flitting here and there to remove the spoiled pears.

Beyond them are two lines of packers—Japanese of both sexes. Endless cables carry the fruit to them. The cables are narrow at first but widen gradually, so that the small fruit drops through into the first bin and the largest into the last bin. Thus the pears are graded so that those dropping into each bin are of nearly uniform size.

The packers face the machine, with their right hands nearest the bins. Directly in front of them is a packing box. To their left is a sheaf of tissue-thin paper with the Blake brand. Their movements are so fast they can scarcely be followed. Both hands move at the same time. The right grabs a pear, the left a single sheet of paper. With lightning speed they wrap the pear and slap it into the box, tier on tier to get the maximum number into each box. Rapidly the box fills, even with the side at each end but forming a heap in the center. Packers are paid on a piecework basis and are the fastest and highest-paid workers on the ranch.

As each box is filled, the packer lifts it to a set of rollers inclined downward. A slight push moves them to the "topper," who nails the lids on. The topper slides the box under a machine with a concave steel hood. A lever operated by foot forces the hood neatly down over the heaping box, leaving only the ends of the lids exposed so that the nails can be driven in. The topper piles the boxes in shaky stacks beside him and they are quickly trucked away to the waiting box cars. As soon as the cars are filled, an engine hooks onto them and rolls them to Marysville, where they will become part of a 99-car refrigerated train for the East.

The machine is the outstanding unit in this inter-dependent series of operations that takes a green, dusty, spray-covered pear from the Sacramento Valley and transforms it into a delicacy for the best New York hotels. Here in this rural area it is the symbol of the mechanization of work done by human hands for centuries.

The machine is my responsibility. I must keep it satisfied, but I must not demand too much of it. I must judge its capacity; I must keep it exactly at this level. Too much or too little and the whole scheme of operation is upset.

At first it's easy. I take the top box off the pile and empty it so that the pears cover the whole belt but do not pile on each other. The second box, the third, and the whole stack of six. I take the full boxes from my right and put the empties on my left. Truckers constantly keep a pile of full boxes near me and carry away the empty ones.

I am engrossed in my work until long unused muscles begin to ache in protest. I concentrate on that pain; I console myself with the thought that soon I shall become used to the bending, when a new sensation forces itself upon me.

I am hungry. Maddeningly, unreasonably hungry. There is a persistent gnawing at my stomach. I feel faint; I think I shall collapse. It must be nearly noon. With one hand I feed the machine; with the other I work my watch out of my pocket. Eleven o'clock. Without breaking the rhythm of my work, I wipe the spray off a pear and take a mouth-filling bite. The sweet juice drips down the side of my mouth unheeded; the snow-white pulp gives me nourishment.

The hour passes slowly but at last young Blake turns off the switch. My sister and I fall into step and hurry to the camp. The sun blazes down upon us and the perspiration mixes with the dust we kick up from the road. When we get to camp our father is waiting. His crew is working nearby now but later he will be too far away to come home for lunch.

We eat in the shade of a tree, but it is stifling hot. Not a breath of wind can penetrate the solid rows of trees twenty feet high. Heat waves radiate and shimmer above the sandy, river-bottom land at the edge of the camp. We eat no hot food during the noon meal. Cold meats and bread and perhaps a *sopa fresca*—cold well water enriched with olive oil, vinegar, raw onions, garlic and green peppers.

There is no time for conversation because we must be back before one o'clock. The machine resumes its whine and the gigantic plant becomes animated. At mid-afternoon the sun reaches its zenith. We swelter beneath the corrugated tin roof and the thermometer climbs steadily until it touches the 116-degree mark. I take off my shirt and my exposed body glistens with sweat.

I am "in the groove" already and feeding the machine is a mechanical task that employs only my arms, back and legs. My mind is completely free. My thoughts turn to Carmen—her family hasn't come this year. I look about for a substitute. Only young girls are hired as sorters, and to me all of them are attractive.

The girl working next to my sister is a pert little blonde. The two girls are already friendly and this is a boon for me—my sister can break the ice. In a futile attempt to keep cool, she wears little beneath her dress; it clings to her with perspiration, accentuates her upright breasts and the flat lines of her stomach. In my imagination I picture myself holding her close in the cool of the evening. It is a fine thing when the stars are out and the night is still to lie on the warm sand. . . . The heat and the work are forgotten and I am relaxed in mind and body. I can close my eyes and dream—the same dream always—of a little ranch of my own where I can plant the crops and nurse them along and harvest them myself. The dream never varies, even though my father urges me to go to college and become a professional man.

"Get away from this life, my son," he says. "Farms mean back-breaking work and belly-robbing poverty. You will curse when it rains and you will curse when it doesn't rain. You will blaspheme against the heat and you will pray for heat. Get away from it, my son," he finishes sadly. Yet he always stays as near the good, life-giving soil as he can. He has had jobs with the railroad and in factories, but he always goes back to the land. He has his dreams, too.

The little blonde becomes aware of my intent stare and her embarrassed glance brings me back to reality. I become conscious of my surroundings. My mind heeds the aching of my muscles, weary now, and consuming my reserve strength. The machine becomes an invention of seventeen devils. It keeps me rooted in this oven when my whole body craves a cold, clean bath and starched white clothes.

The machine seems to have conquered me, yet I know that I am its master. I can dump four or five boxes into it at once and choke its gloating roar; I can stop feeding it and laugh at its pleas for fruit, I can. . . .

Suddenly the belt stops, as young Blake turns off the switch. The first day's work is done. A heavy weight seems to lift from my shoulders and my heart beats faster with relief. A few moments ago my feet were heavy, but now I run to catch up with my sister and her new girl friend. They, too, feel the stimulation of the hour. The talk is halting and self-conscious today because we are not well-acquainted, but on other days it will be quick and we will laugh.

I get to the bunkhouse before the men from the fields and have the shower room to myself. I take off my socks and shoes, dripping with sweat, and even my trousers are wet through. I turn on the water, hot at first but gradually turning cold, and exult under its cleansing flow.

I dress in clean, white clothes and set off for the camp, hungry and tired but alive in every pore. Tonight I have a date with the little blonde.

Notes

1. An extremely potent distilled spirit. In Spain and Portugal it referred to a liquor made from sugar cane, but, in the American West, it become a kind of catch-all term for any brandy-like spirit. Aguardiente translates literally to "fire-water." Winfred Blevins, *Dictionary of the American West* (Fort Worth, TX: Texas Christian University Press, 2008), 3; Nicholas P. Cushner, *Lords of the Land: Sugar, Wine, and Jesuit Estates of Coastal Peru, 1600–1767* (Albany: State University of New York Press, 1980), 71.
2. See "The Driller" in this volume.

STILL OPERATOR

James Phelan (Illinois)

I remember when I drove into the town ten years ago, looking for work. It was at sunset, late in the spring, and the acrid scent of crude oil was a taint on the April air ten miles before the town came into sight. A month later I stopped smelling it, and I didn't smell it again for six years. I lived in the middle of it, and the smell of crude became as much a part of the air as oxygen itself.

You saw the refinery before you saw the town, whether you came in by day or night. From miles across the prairie the aluminum-painted tanks, drenched with a continual stream of water to hold down their temperature, glistened in the sun, and over the whole plant floated a great slow rope of smoke. At night you could see the refinery fifteen miles away, a smudge of yellow and red on the horizon. As you came closer the smudge broke down into ten thousand electric bulbs outlining each still and charting each catwalk, with the low-hanging cloud of smoke giving back the cherry glow of the furnaces like a man-made aurora borealis. The crude thickened in the air, the hum of the plant deepened, and then suddenly you came upon the town.

It seemed incidental. The refinery hemmed it in on the north and east with a ten-foot wire fence, and the town huddled in the angle between the strands of barbed wire as if it were blown there by the wind. Beyond the fence rose row and endless row of squat tanks, black stills, and box-like warehouses and powerplants, dwarfing the town's buildings into triviality.

Life in the town was geared to the refinery, as though an unseen power-belt ran from the plant and turned the daily wheel of existence within the angle of the fences. At seven in the morning, three in the afternoon, and eleven at night a huge whistle hooted twice. At this signal men began to emerge from the rows of houses and flow together through the streets towards the big gate where the north and east fences met. At the far edge of town a dinky suburban street car disgorged hundreds more from near-by towns. Traffic on the main state road quick-ened, and more men poured in by auto and bus, all funneling into the gate where the fences met.

At ten minutes to the hour the whistle spoke again, once. By then the move-ment into the plant would almost have ceased, save for now and then a late driver screeching around corners in a race with the time-clock at the gate. At five min-utes after the hour the movement was reversed as the relieved shift poured out. Men sought their homes, the roads became clogged with out-going traffic, the bus-ses thinned away, the last dinky rocked off over the uneven tracks. It was as if the refinery took three deep breaths a day, at eight, four, and midnight; inhale and exhale, a thousand men at a breath.

Even the sounds of the town were smothered in the unceasing thrum of the plant. The noises that the refinery made were of two kinds. From around dawn, all day, and late into the night it emitted a deep-pitched, steady hum that was the composite of a thousand well-oiled pumps stroking almost silently, the hiss of oil coursing through a buried network of pipes, the subdued roar of oil-and-steam-spray burners in a hundred furnaces. After a few days you scarcely heard it unless you listened for it. The other noise was something else. You got used to that, too, but you never got so that you had to listen for it. It came late at night, usually around two, a quavering, anguished scream, as of some pre-historic beast in pain. For four or five hours it continued, monstrous in volume, ranging through a con-vulsive and unbearable octave, and then it would cease, as suddenly as death. For perhaps thirty seconds it would leave a vacuum of silence, and then the regular hum of the plant would re-emerge to the surface of hearing.

The first night in town I had been asleep for hours when the roar smashed into my room and wiped away sleep with a brutal hand. From the window the refinery was a red inferno and the quavering scream came from the heart of it. The walls of the room flickered with reflected light and the scream filled the room and beat upon my eardrums. I grabbed the phone and asked the desk clerk what the hell was happening.

"Nothing," he answered sleepily. "Just cleaning the pressure stills.[1] They use an air-drill to knock the coke[2] out of the tubes. Do it every night about this time."

I went back to bed but I didn't go to sleep until the scream shut down at dawn. That afternoon I got a job at the refinery sampling tanks for the pressure stills. Ten months later they started training me to operate a still, and after three months I was put on as a full-fledged stillman. I kept the job five years and then quit.

* * *

There was a uniform: oil-soaked overalls, a sweatshirt tucked in them, heavy safety shoes with steel caps over the toes, yellow-lensed goggles around your neck, a safety cap like the crash helmets daredevils wear, asbestos-palmed gloves, and a sixteen-inch Stillson wrench.[3] With this equipment, and intimate knowledge of the complicated guts of the still, you ran a pressure still that made 4,000 gallons of synthetic crude an hour. The still took the heavy residue oil left when the gasoline was skimmed from the crude oil, subjected it to high heat and pressure, and "cracked"[4] it into a light distillate[5] and coke.

The still ran in a cycle. You "brought it up," ran it for three days, and then shut it down for the cleanout, when the pressure chamber had become filled with coke and there was no longer room for the cracking process to occur. Almost anyone could learn to operate the still in a week's time; the bring-up and the shut-down took skill and a delicate hand. It was the ability to jockey the huge still into running order and then ease it back down again that accounted for the top wages we got. We made $1.10 an hour while the base pay was $.65, but nobody begrudged it to us. There was a reason for that.

A bring-up took from five to ten hours, and a shut-down about the same time. You took over after the coke-knockers were through, when the guts of the still were clean, and all the lines, return-bends, and chamber-heads had been bolted into place again. You opened a line, started a pump, and filled the entire still with oil. When every inch of the still was full you kept the pump pushing the oil until the pressure went up to 350 pounds per square inch, and held it there. Then you went over the still like a Mayo doctor[6] examining a multi-millionaire. If it was leaking anywhere you'd better find it then and get it fixed, or something would break loose when the still was up and going, and then you probably wouldn't be in any condition to give a damn.

Okay, no leaks. Set the pop valve, which keeps the whole thing from blowing sky-high if the pressure goes haywire. Open the draw-off valve to drag the charge of oil down to operating level. Line up the flow, opening a dozen valves here, closing another dozen here. Call the pumping station. Light the fires in the furnaces, squinting through yellow lenses at the flame, juggling the flow of oil-spray and steam until the burners roar with a steady *whoooooooo*. Start the centrifugal hot oil pump that thrusts the oil through the network of tubes in the furnace. Dash for the control room to check the rise of temperature on the battery of electric recording machines. Too fast, too fast. Sprint for the furnaces again, dodging a sample-carrier at the door. Cut down the oil-spray on the burner a sixteenth of an inch with a nudge of your wrench handle. Then the steam is too strong and the burner begins a broken *whoomp-whoomp-whoomp* as the steam blows it out and the incandescent walls immediately relight it. Nudge the steam valve. Easy. Too much, the flame licks out in a long smoky tongue. Tap the valve back, until the flame shortens again. Back to the control room to hunch over the temperature recorder, watch the swing of the needle as it dips every thirty seconds to leave an irradicable record of your control over the still.

Fires okay, you jerk out your watch and time the pumps, counting the strokes for thirty seconds, multiplying by two for the rate per minute, mentally converting the result into a gallons per hour. (There's a chart on the wall but you haven't used it since the first three months. You can call off the figures in your sleep.) Almost two hundred gallons low per hour. Insert the key, give it a quarter turn, listen briefly while the pump speeds up and levels off at a slightly increased rate. Okay, don't bother to check it again; you can hit two hundred gallons on the nose, or within ten gallons, by instinct.

It's been an hour now since you've tested the level in the chamber. Out of the control room around the furnace, up the ladder that mounts the sixty-foot reinforced cylinder. Eight try-lines stud the side of the chamber at regular intervals. You take a guess, try the second from the bottom, get a hiss of hot vapor into the waste funnel. You loosen your grip on the ladder and drop the eight feet to the newest platform, spin the valve on the bottom try-line frantically, and hear a welcome *swoosh* of hot oil. Caught it on the head! You drop beneath the chamber, spin the two-foot wheel on the draw-off line until it's closed, then crack it open a half turn to keep the level constant at the bottom.

You're spattered with oil now, the wrench is beginning to slip in your greasy gloves, and when you glimpse your face half-reflected by the glass front of a pressure gauge the right half of it is brown with residue oil from somewhere. Two and a half hours gone, five and a half to go.

You've got it coming up now, and you can slow down a little. The first couple of hours pass as a dead run, just getting the essential things done. More time now, but you have to be more careful. The pressure is coming up, the temperature is over six hundred degrees Fahrenheit. Anything can happen now, the whole works can go to hell in three or four minutes. Nurse it along, check the pumps every few minutes, keep an eye on the fires, watch the level in the chamber.

You get hungry, eye your lunch-bucket covetously, decide to risk one sandwich. You get the box open and stop as an undertone in the roar of sounds around you suddenly shifts a half-note. You slam your box closed, flip your goggles on, and run for the furnace. Both of the fires are out. Back to the control room, cursing every step of the way, to dial the pumping station. Some damn fool has let the fuel oil tank pump dry. You shout obscenities into the phone, bang the receiver in the pumper's ear, and stamp back to the furnaces. Two minutes later the burners roar on again, but without looking at the indicator you know you've lost at least a hundred degrees. You boost the fires to catch up what you've lost, and after forty-five minutes and seven trips between the burners and the indicator, you get lined out again.

After six hours the pressure reaches three hundred pounds, and you tell the pressure-man to start releasing gas on still four. He stands before a battery of gauges, eyeing them constantly, regulating a valve for each of the four stills in the control room. As the pressure goes up too high he opens up and lets vapor off, when it falls, he pinches off.

An hour later the temperature hits 945 degrees, the level of your run. You ease off the burners to check the heat where it now stands. Twenty minutes later the pressure man yells, "Here she comes!" as the yellow distillate begins to rise in a glass gauge in the small run-down tank in front of him. You leg it for the storage tank, clamp your Stillson on the big valve, and throw your weight to the right. The valve creaks and breaks loose. Under your feet the distillate begins to rumble through the pipe into the tank.

You go back, take off your gloves, and write in the report book, "On stream at 11:25 p.m." You check your pumps for the shift total, take another turn around the still, and then it's quarter to twelve and your relief man comes in, clean-faced and heavy-lidded. You stand by silently while he looks over the battery of recording instruments.

He turns and grins. "Nice bring-up."

"Yeah. Came up without a hitch. 'Night."

"Take it easy."

Standing dog-tired in the shower, scrubbing the oil off you with Lava soap, you suddenly realize that you forgot to eat your dinner. What the hell, you can eat it when you get home.

*   *   *

Running the still was comparatively easy, but it wasn't a cinch. A pressure still is as unpredictable as a woman. The essential task of running it once it was "on stream" consisted of keeping the temperature constant at 945 degrees. With some stills you'd get the recorder leveled out and the rate of feed set, and the still would run for three days without being touched more than a dozen times. Another, right alongside of it, would make hen-tracks[7] all over the chart and keep the operator chasing back and forth and cursing the whole eight-hour trick.[8]

But even with a good steady still you couldn't relax. If something went wrong you had to grab it when it happened. If the hot oil pump lost suction you could coke up the tubes solid in six minutes at the outside. Then you had an emergency shutdown on your hands, and after that a session on the carpet with the head of the pressure-still division. Unless you had a damn good explanation you'd probably be out sending wires around to other refineries the next day. So even when the still was running as smooth as silk you had to hover over it continually for eight hours. Turn your back for ten minutes and you'd find yourself wrapping bundles in a department store, longing for those good old days of $1.10 an hour.

* * *

I liked the work. There was a certain pride and satisfaction in it. The whole thing was in your hands; when you brought up one of the monsters you could look at it and say, "I did that. I lined it up, nursed it along, held it in check, brought it to this precise balance of production." And when you filled one of the bulky storage tanks and switched to its companion, you could climb the ladder, remove the cap from the gauge hole, and hear the subdued slosh of the thousands of gallons of distillate that you had shepherded through intricate processes and unexpected crises into a product that would serve a thousand motorists well. It was a tough job, but it was better than clamping bolts in a production line, because you had to use your head, exercise your judgment, and the end-product had something of you in it.

* * *

I saw two men get killed on this job.

The first was a young still-cleaner named Red. I came to work and the still was down for the cleanout, and I just lazed around, keeping an eye on things. This kid Red had been on the cleanout gang on a dozen other shutdowns, and I had got to know him by sight. The operators and the cleanout men didn't mix much, but you got to know some of them although you wouldn't always get the same gang.

We were shooting the bull at the foot of the still's dephlegmator[9] tower when one of the cleaners yelled down for Red to give a hand up in the tower, eighty feet above us. "Be down in a minute," the kid said, and started climbing the ladder.

Five minutes later one of the cleaners yelled down hoarsely, "Call the ambulance, for Christ's sake." I dialed emergency, and the ambulance was there when they had got Red down. There really wasn't any rush; they could have taken their time, because he was dead minutes before they eased him down the ladder. A pan in the bottom of the dephlegmator had been coked solid, and two of the cleaners hooked a block and tackle to it while Red got down in the chamber and tried to kick it loose. The two cleaners were hefty guys, both over two hundred pounds, and when the pan wouldn't break loose they started chinning themselves on the tackle's chain. Between them they straightened out the steel hook that held the block. The forty-pound steel block dropped twenty feet and caught Red on the side of his head. It crushed his crash helmet like an egg-shell and bashed in the side of his skull.

It was too damn bad. There wasn't anyone really to blame, the safety inspectors decided. After that, they said, they'd specify thicker hooks on their blocks.

The other guy was named Pauley Ufert, and he operated the still next to mine. One afternoon he went out to light his fires on a bring-up. His was one of the few plants that operated on gas; the rest of them burned oil and steam. About two minutes after he'd left the control room we heard a dull *whoom*. We all rushed out, and there was the end of Pauley's furnace blown out, and no Pauley. They recovered what was left of him an hour later, under six feet of bricks. A gas burner had been leaking, and when he thrust his torch into the furnace the mixture of gas and air had gone up, blowing out the weak end of the furnace. Unfortunately, that was the end where Pauley was standing, but he probably had little time to contemplate this whim of fate.

* * *

I didn't think much about these things. They happened now and then, but I'd been running a still for five years without any trouble, and they didn't seem related to me. I had begun to feel a mastery over my still, and I figured that if I watched things closely, nothing would happen.

One night I came to work at midnight, about two hours after number four had gone on stream. It was running smoothly and the four-to-twelve man said that everything was okay except that there was a spot on one of the tubes in the furnace. That wasn't anything unusual; it probably meant that the texture of the tube-wall was uneven. It was something to keep your eye on, but you didn't have to worry about it unless it began to leak. Then you'd have to shut the still down, but the blame for that would go to the tube inspector.

Right after I took over I went out, climbed to the peep-hole at the top of the furnace, slipped on my goggles, and squinted into the glare of the hell-room. I saw the spot right away; it was on the top bank, about two inches in diameter and a bright red. It didn't look bad and I forgot about it for a couple of hours.

Sometime after three I went out for another look. I slid up my goggles, swung open the peep-hole, and focused on the glare. The spot had spread, and now made a big circle around the whole top of the tube. It was a brighter shade, almost an incandescent white, and was like nothing I had ever seen before.

I remember the split moment that followed. Something grabbed me deep in my stomach, fear or premonition. I had one complete thought: *Y'd better call the stillman about this.* Then a nightmare exploded on me. There was a roar that filled the universe, and a great upflaring of light brighter than the heart of flame. There was a crash and a shock of pain that pushed consciousness to the edge of oblivion. Flame swept over me and I tried to scream. I scrambled mechanically and blindly from the flame, and when my arms and legs would no longer move I sank into a nothingness whose horizon flared with a great wall of fire.

* * *

Two weeks later I was all right, and ready to report for work. They told me what had happened; with the still running under full pressure a tube had blown out fifteen feet from the peep-hole where I stood. Raw oil had rammed into the incandescent furnace through a foot-long fissure. The explosion had blown me fifty feet, and I had automatically crawled out of danger with only a few second-degree burns. The next day they had fired the tube inspector who had okayed the top bank of tubes without checking it.

I went back to work when they released me from the hospital. I worked for a little better than an hour, and then the temperature began to fall off. I picked up my wrench automatically and headed for the furnace. Three steps out of the control room I stopped. During my convalescence they had repaired the furnace, and the end wall of new brick stood out baldly against the weather-beaten walls on either side. Beyond the wall I could hear the fierce *whoooooooo* of the burners, the hiss of oil through the tubes. I turned, went back in the control room, called the head stillman, and told him to get someone to take over number four.

He didn't understand. When he finally got it through his head he wanted to know why. But I wasn't in any mood for arguments, so I hung up on him and went away, walking very fast down the line of stills to turn in my time.

Notes

1. "Still Operator" centers on the industrial distillation process of crude oil. The technicalities of the process varied, but, speaking broadly, distillation occurred by heating the oil to around 700 degrees Fahrenheit, evaporating the most reactive compounds

under pressure, and then collecting the resulting "distillate" in the purest possible form. The process is fraught with hazards for the worker, the most dangerous periods being start-up and shutdown of the stills. H. S. Bell, *American Petroleum Refining* (New York: Van Nostrand, 1945), 210; British Petroleum, *Hazards of Oil Refining Distillation Units* (Rugby, UK: Institution of Chemical Engineers, 2008), 3–4; Paul W. Thrush, *A Dictionary of Mining, Mineral, and Related Terms* (Chicago: Maclean Hunter, 1990), 1077.

2. The resulting particulate residue left in the stills after the distillation process. Thrush, *Dictionary*, 233.

3. See "'Snake'" Magee and the Rotary Boiler" in this volume.

4. The "cracking" process is less substantial in terms of molecular rearrangement of the compounds involved and stops short of distillation. The remaining fuel by-products, depending on the type of "cracking" performed, can be sold for a number of applications. Thrush, *Dictionary*, 274.

5. Ibid., 334–35. The liquid produced as a result of "cracking."

6. A doctor practicing medicine at the highly regarded Mayo Clinic in Rochester, Minnesota. Annette Atkins, *Creating Minnesota: A History from the Inside Out* (St. Paul, MN: Minnesota Historical Society, 2008), 284.

7. Erratic scribbling; unreadable penmanship. Harold Wentworth and Stuart Berg Flexner, *Dictionary of American Slang* (New York: Crowell, 1960), 99, 253.

8. A period of work. Eric Partrige, *A Concise Dictionary of Slang and Unconventional English* (New York: Macmillan, 1990), 665.

9. A device used to help keep the crude oil from mixing with the purified vapor in the distillation process. Thrush, *Dictionary*, 313.

POGY BOAT

Robert Cornwall (Florida)

We reached the Mayport, Florida, factory at night. The white shell road through mosquito-ridden marshes led to a confusion of lights and noises. One hundred yards, more or less, from the huge pile of wooden and corrugated-iron buildings, a breeze carried to our noses, clothes, and the car's upholstery an unforgettable odor—the menhaden plant in operation. It is an odor that rivals that of the skunk, heavy, encompassing, and inescapable once you are in the neighborhood. Curiously, it is rendered less offensive when you learn that big gangs of men are working in the midst of it.

Leaving the car at a loading platform, we picked our way through the piles of menhaden scrap that grew larger by the instant as an overhead dragline deposited its cargo on the scrap-house floor. Enormous droves of flies buzzed to and from their feeding places on the piles of desiccated fish. In the electric, dusty light, they seemed larger and greener than ordinary flies. I had never before seen these insects so preoccupied, and uninterested in men. In crevices of the floor, maggots devoured rotten leavings.

Deep in noises of men and machines we hurried through a lane that we saw ahead. Menhaden scrap sprinkled upon our heads, steam pipes hissed threateningly in all directions, steel gears protested at the lack of oil. Off to the right was a sight familiar in any industrial plant; the bulky fireman shoveling coal into a furnace door. On all sides were half-naked Negroes, sweeping, pulling, pushing, bending, carrying unidentifiable things through the pungent murk.

The dim, 32-volt pinpoints that we saw as we entered the loading platform doors now came closer and proved to be the running lights of the boat we wanted, *The Boys*. I had pictured a vessel about the size of a shrimper, but here was a ship built for the high seas. She had a length of 109 feet, a 17-foot beam, and the seaworthiness of a freighter. Resembling a tug, *The Boys* had been constructed in World War [I] days for use as a submarine chaser.

It was close on midnight, and the ship was dark but for the tinted skeleton formed by forward, stern, port, and starboard lights. Members of the crew picked their way over the dock's loose planks and felt their way aboard. The pilot had evidently counted them, for when the last man reached the ship he pulled a cord in his invisible bridge that clanged a bell in the engine room, and the motor started. Almost at once the menhaden plant seemed a quarter of a mile away.

Twirling his wheel over and back, back and over, the pilot maneuvered us into the St. Johns River channel. A strong ebb tide caught *The Boys* (named in honor of its three former owners), helping the 180 horsepower Diesel engine drive us toward the inlet at the river's mouth. We could see the towering, evil-smelling plant dropping back on the starboard side, its lights gleaming deceptively like those of a summer hotel. For the first time in an hour we were upwind from the odoriferous menhaden scrap. As the town of Mayport slid past, an inshore breeze freshened. Ahead lay the formidable granite boulders of the jetties that bordered the stream and jutted one mile in parallel lines into the ocean.

Churning along at twelve knots an hour, *The Boys* eased between the treacherous shoals of St. Johns Inlet, and struck a north-by-east course to the Georgia coast. A whistling buoy sounded faintly, and the red and yellow glow in the sky told that Jacksonville Beach was late in going to bed. The Florida July had been hot in town that day, but now the air grew chilly. We were on the Atlantic Ocean with the prospects before us of an all-night run to Sapelo and St. Catherine's Sounds, where another menhaden crew had reported fish playing in large schools.

For the day just past, *The Boys* had returned a catch of 150,000 menhaden, or "pogies," as the Negro sailors call them. The crew was sleeping below, the engineer had retired to the forecastle to take one of his frequent catnaps, and the captain and pilot were working in silence. We were invited to join them on the bridge for conversation and a warming drink.

The menhaden, known to science as *Brevootia tyrannus,*[1] is a handsome fish with a large head, small fins, and silvery scales that have a bluish undertone. It is a member of the herring family. A large black spot marks the menhaden behind the gills, and there are smaller spots on its body. With a deep body nearly oval in shape, it is a comparatively slow swimmer. It lacks teeth, and feeds on tiny marine plants and animals. A single school may cover an acre of ocean, and contain a million or more fish, ranging from six to sixteen inches in length.

The public knows little about menhaden, perhaps because it is not a game or food fish. It is of great commercial value, however, and is the most numerous fish of the Atlantic coast from Maine to Florida. Aside from its industrial importance, fishermen often use the menhaden for bait, and southern Negroes claim that "its roe beats shad when you gets it fresh."

The menhaden bears a great variety of names along the seaboard. "Menhaden" is derived from *munnawhat*, a Narragansett Indian word meaning "the fish used for fertilizer." Some of the more popular names today are pogy, bonyfish, hardhead, mossbunker, oldwife, bugfish, and fatback. Often it is mistakenly called porgy, the name of a species of food fish.

Americans on the Atlantic seaboard have used menhaden as fertilizer for more than three centuries. In 1621, Governor William Bradford of the Plymouth Colony expressed gratitude to an Indian named Squanto for informing the settlers of the need for enriching the soil. The friendly Squanto also taught the *Mayflower* Pilgrims how to catch the fish and place them in the ground with seed corn.

But the big catches did not begin until the nineteenth century. In 1801, a Long Island landowner, Ezra L'Hommedieu, in a report on experiments he had conducted, recommended menhaden to increase the yield of barren soil. This created a great demand for the fish, and small companies began operating haul seines,[2] supplying menhaden to the farmers of Long Island and New England at $1 and $1.50 a thousand. At that time the whole fish was buried in the ground, 6,000 or 8,000 to an acre, and no by-products were derived.

About ten years later the first menhaden oil was produced in Rhode Island. It was obtained by filling large casks with fish, and adding water. Boards were placed on top and weighted with stones. The fish gradually decomposed, and the oil, lighter than water, rose to the surface. The process was wasteful and yielded only an inferior quality of oil. Cooking kettles were soon introduced, large receptacles perforated at the bottom, through which live steam was admitted. After cooking, the oil was skimmed off the top. The bodies of the fish, called "chum," were dumped on the ground and after being dried in the sun were sold as fertilizer.

The next advance in the industry came in 1845, when, to meet the growing demand, large purse seines[3] were perfected. With these, entire schools could be surrounded and scooped out of the sea. The purse seines, in turn, produced a need for larger ships to bring home the heavier catches, and for larger factories and improved processing methods. Following the general trend, machines were invented to speed up production and reduce labor costs.

Menhaden fishing reached its peak in 1877, when seventy-three land factories and two floating factories were operated on the Atlantic coast. The next quarter of a century showed a slight decline. The fish became hard to catch in New England waters, and the industry drifted southward. It centered in Virginia for a number of years; by 1914 the plant at Reedsville, Virginia, was the most important one along the coast.

Like most businesses that depend upon the sea, menhaden fishing is, at its best, filled with uncertainties. The 1911 catch was one of the largest ever known, and the profits brought about the construction of sixteen new factories. In contrast, 1913 was a very bad year. Good years came again, but so did the bad ones; some years the fish are lean, yielding a minimum of oil. Since 1918, the fish seem to have been diminishing. On July 1, 1940, an average day, the catches of the five Mayport boats varied from 50,000 to 150,000—totaling less than one-third of capacity.

The hazards of the trade are reflected in the attitude of the men. A strong *esprit de corps* keeps them looking hopefully into a future of big catches. Also, since most have no experience in other fields, they see no way out but to keep plugging at their jobs. Said the pilot of *The Boys*, his eyes, blue as the sea, wrinkled and close-lidded, "Workin' on boats for forty-nine years, I lost many a wink sittin' to a wheel." The burly captain, stoical as any of his Negro sailors, expressed the belief that the fishing would be good in the morning.

The captain seemed willing to talk all night, but we decided to go to sleep when he mentioned two unoccupied bunks. Fernandina, Florida, has passed astern, and the lights of Brunswick, Georgia, gleamed in the sky ahead of the starboard bow. As we turned in for a four-hour rest, the boat was riding smoothly and the Milky Way stretched over-head. It seemed that but a few minutes had passed when the ship's whistle sounded the breakfast call—one long and two short blasts. The meal was enough to fortify one for a hard day's work: fried country sausage, eggs, hot biscuits, grits, and over-sized cups of strong coffee.

The fishing began at six o'clock. The captain and his Negro mate climbed the rigging of the forty-foot mast into the crow's nest. The crew put the gear in order, while the engineer idled the Diesel. Five other menhaden boats were standing by at half-mile intervals behind us; the rising sun had changed a blur on the western horizon into the thickly wooded coast of Georgia, and a ribbon of water going inland became Sapelo Inlet.

Suddenly from aloft came the shout, "There they play, boys!"

Excitement hit the ship. The mate had sighted a school of menhaden. As though by command, every man on board came to attention momentarily, and all eyes turned in the direction indicated by the mate's outstretched black arm. On the water a few hundred yards to port appeared a small reddish-brown shadow—the school.

The crew of *The Boys* consisted of eighteen men: captain, engineer, pilot, mate, cook and thirteen workmen. The first three were white; the others were Negroes, except for the captain's young brother-in-law who served as a handy man. The engineer went below and silenced the engine; the pilot twisted his wheel to hold *The Boys* in position.

Those who were going into the two thirty-four foot purse-boats shoved their legs into knee-high rubber boots, and many donned rubber aprons. Already the twelve-foot, deep-bellied, cedar striker-boat had cleared the ship and set off for the school. Its single occupant rowed skillfully in a standing position, face forward. The new-laden purse-boats were swiftly lowered from the davits, and hovered astern, bows together, while the men clambered into them. The captain took command of one and the mate the other. Only the pilot, engineer, and cook remained aboard *The Boys*. It was the duty of the pilot, now called the "boat-keeper," to keep the ship in position until the fisherman came alongside with the catch. We climbed into the swaying crow's nest to watch.

The man in the striker-boat shipped his oars about 500 feet from *The Boys* and then waved one oar in a wide arc, as a signal to the purse-boats that he had reached the edge of the school. He gave other signals to indicate the direction in which the fish were swimming and what course the purse-boats should take. Staccato sounds burst from the purse-boats as their Model-A Ford motors were started. With bows roped securely together, they circled widely beyond the striker-boat and halted opposite it on the far side of the school. Then the boats parted and, playing out the seines as they went, described nearly the exact semi-circles around the school, surrounding the menhaden with the seine. The encirclement ended on the spot where the striker-boatman had done his signaling, but he was now rowing straight through the school, occasionally slapping the water with his oars to frighten the menhaden into the sides of the net. He stopped when he had cut a circumference and reached the seine at a point opposite the purse-boats. So swiftly and efficiently had the men done their work that, with brown corks dancing on the surface, it seemed they had created a magical circular pool in the ocean.

The purse seine, or net, is a huge affair woven of linen twine, with large corks on top and brass rings at twenty-foot intervals along its bottom edge. The net is 1,000 strands, or 875 feet. A new net costs about $1,400.

Before settling down to the back-breaking labor of tightening, or pursing, the net around the fish, the purse-boats were lashed together at the bow. Next, the ends of the purse line—a stout cord of Russian hemp running through the rings at the bottom of the net—were passed through a pulley attached to a 300-pound lead weight, called the tom. This weight was heaved overboard and, in falling to the bottom, it puckered together the submerged end of the net, acting much as the string on an old-fashioned pocketbook. The ends of the purse line were fastened to two snatch blocks on an upright iron support about eighteen inches high, called the crane, which stood in the captain's boat about ten feet from the bow. The men then began pursing the net, reeling in the purse line and hauling the net aboard the two boats. The flatter was carefully folded so as to be ready for the next "set," as the menhadenites term a catch of fish. A snarled net is the bane of all fishermen. When it happens, the men may sometimes have to stay in the purse-boats for hours, sweating over the tangle. Such an occasion also means that thousands of fish escape, and the net may be torn or otherwise damaged.

Steadily for nearly an hour the men pulled with their fingers until the big circle had been reduced to an area hardly larger than a room. The boat-keeper and engineer had kept an eye on the proceedings, and, without waiting for a signal, they maneuvered *The Boys* alongside to take the fish into the hold. The tom was pulled into the captain's boat, and the sterns of the purse-boats were made fast to the side, amidship. With their noses pointed away from *The Boys*, the purse-boats formed an almost perfect triangle against the ship's side. Within the triangle an estimated fifty thousand menhaden were futilely seeking an exit. The men were in high good humor: they had captured a big set. The gigantic black cook, who had prepared fluffy little biscuits earlier in the morning, jumped into the center of a purse-boat to lead the process of "hardenin up the fish." This consists of pulling the seine closer to the surface so that the fish will form a relatively hard mass. The set was so good that the men decided to "sing em to the top." Almost to a man they were North Carolinians and proud of their singing. A clear, high tenor picked up the first line of a chantey, *Lord, Lord*, and all the men chorused it after him and added a refrain:

> *Ev'ry mail day I gets a letter,*
> *Ev'ry mail day I gets a letter,*
> *Sinnin son, come home,*
> *Lord, Lord, son, come home.*

At the end of the first verse, the men, needing every ounce of strength to pull the net, saved their breath and hauled in unison. But each time they paused to get a new grip they picked up the chantey:

> *How can I go when I got no ready-made money?*
> *How can I go when I got no ready-made money?*
> *I can't go home,*
> *Lord, Lord, I can't go home.*

> *If I just had me one more dollar and a quarter,*
> *If I just had me one more dollar and a quarter,*
> *I'd go back home,*
> *Lord, Lord, I can't go home.*

I left my baby standin in the back door cryin,
I left my baby standin in the back door cryin,
Daddy don't go,
Lord, Lord, daddy don't go.

Do you see that black cloud risin over yonder?
Do you see that black cloud risin over yonder?
It's sign of rain,
Lord, Lord, it's sign of rain.

Cap'm, have you heard all your men goin leave you?
Cap'm, have you heard all your men goin leave you?
On the next payday,
Lord, Lord on the next payday.

The chantey ended when the fish were corralled near enough to the surface for the dip or bail net to begin its work. The captain directed the men from the deck of *The Boys*. Near the boat several porpoises were currying about the green water—we could hear them breathing the air—and diving for menhaden that had escaped the net. A few seagulls and a lone pelican bickered over some dead pogies.

The engineer took his place beside a gasoline engine used to operate the bail net. This has a capacity of 3,000 fish, and dips from the seine an average of 1,500 each time. It is bowl-shaped when full, and is four feet deep. A steel chain passes through rings that line its bottom. When the fish are alongside, the net is raised and lowered from cables attached to the gaff, a long, wooden arm extending from the mast, behind and below the crow's-nest. Lifting power is supplied by the engine. When the net dropped toward the purse seine, the cook dipped its open top into the struggling fish by means of a sapling pole, resembling the long handle of a pot, wired to the edge. Guy ropes to steady the bailer were controlled by men in the boats. While the cables raised the net and suspended it over the empty hold, another Negro, who had been holding the bottom chain tight, let go, and the fish—sparkling and dancing—fell into the hold. Those on top leaped against one another, until the bail net showered down a thousand or more and covered them and their motions of life.

Perhaps the most fascinating aspect of menhaden fishing is when the bail net goes to work. It dips, time after time, bringing up an unbelievable number of fish. Nearly every dip contains one or more sand sharks, often invisible until dumped into the hold. When first surrounded by the seine they had been peacefully feed-

ing on the menhaden. Now these savages of the offshore shallows are as helpless as
their prey. In the hold they seem to suffer a more inglorious death than the menhaden. Perhaps because the shark's weight is centered in his head and the fore part
of his body, he usually falls nose foremost into the quicksand of menhaden, and is
stuck with his tail waving in the air, until even that is buried.

After each load had been deposited, the captain stood on the far side of the
hold and peered into it, searching for any edible fish that might have been snared.
Using a fishing pole with a bard on the end, he managed to remove two mackerel
and a bluefish from the 50,0000 menhaden. The sharks he left alone. Some criticism has been directed against the menhaden industry by persons who charge that
great numbers of food fish are caught and turned into fertilizer. The captain kept a
close watch and found but three in the first set, and five more later in the day. He
gave them to sailors for cooking ashore.

Scarcely had the last menhaden been scooped out of the seine when the captain and mate were again aloft on the lookout for another school. In less than five
minutes the mate yelled for a second time, "There they play, boys!" The fishermen left the ship once more, but this time they ran into difficulties. The school was
swimming in shoal water, and the seine became snarled in a hundred places. The
sun was riding high when, three hours later, the men returned with a half-lost set.
Everyone was dispirited; the men cursed instead of singing, and the captain was
silent as he and the mate climbed the rigging a third time.

A snarled net or a scarcity of fish means less money on Saturday night. The
crew and officers are paid according to the number of fish caught. The common
workmen, a majority of the crew, receive three cents for a thousand menhaden.
The percentage ranges upward, in proportion to the degree of skill required, with
the captain receiving top wages—seventeen cents a thousand.

Soon the striker and purse-boats had set forth again. Their third and final
catch of the day proved to be a good one. It was early afternoon, fifty thousand silver bodies spilled into the hold, and the weary men went to the galley for a meal
of potato salad, boiled ham, spareribs, field peas, biscuits, and coffee. The Boys had
to be back at the factory early enough to get ready for the next day's run, so the
captain regretfully ordered the engineer to put about and head for Mayport. At a
speed of twelve knots, we would reach there in perhaps eight hours. The hold was
half-filled with less than 125,000 fish.

The return trip was uneventful; the wind freshened at sunset, a light rain
squall passed over the vessel, and the waves grew big enough to form whitecaps
that dashed over the high prow. Before retiring to their bunks for rest or to the galley for conversation and card games, the men spent the afternoon doing chores.

Cleaning the seine was the biggest job. The purse-boats were raised from the water and slung into position under the supporting davits. One-half the seine had been furled in each purse-boat, and the connecting portion reached across the aft deck. The crew divided into two gangs and climbed into the long boats. Foot by foot they fed the net out on deck. Then two 100-pound sacks of raw salt were emptied into each boat. The seine was furled back into the boats, one man sprinkling salt over the folds with a shovel. In an hour or more the unfolding and folding process had been completed. The shoveler took a bucket and sluiced water, from the purse-boat's hand bilge-pump, over the net, again and again. The strong brine, composed of sea water and 200 pounds of salt, served to preserve the net and clean fish slime and sea weed out of its folds. Periodically the nets are spread out ashore for a thorough drying and for repairs. Holes are torn in them by stubborn sharks outside the nets that viciously refuse to end their menhaden meals after the little fish have become the property of man.

Down in the hold the menhaden were turning from silver to red. The bottom fish were being squeezed of their blood and oil by the top fish, and this mixture rose to the surface. The Diesel's vibration settled them more firmly, and the bilge pump steadily evacuated back into the sea hundreds of gallons of liquid refuse from the hold. Many fish had died on deck and the intensely hot sun had cooked their bodies until oil oozed in tiny streams over the planking. All the menhaden were beginning to spoil, and they gave off a nauseating odor quite unlike the factory smell.

Several of the men were busy amidships, bathing and washing clothes with water dipped from the ocean. We climbed to the bridge where the officers were gathered and listened to their talk.

It developed that the captains of all five menhaden boats operating out of Mayport are surnamed Willis, yet only two of them, cousins several times removed, are knowingly related. The captain said, "You walk down the street in Morehead, North Carolina, and say to any man you see, 'Hello, Mr. Willis, nice day, ain't it.' The chances are he'll speak back. If he don't, you just change over and say, 'Hello, Mr. Taljot.' He'll sure speak to you then, nine chances outa ten."

Keeping his squint eyes ahead, the pilot told his favorite tale. It dealt with the local saying, 'old Doc Winter's in town.' "Old Doc was a rich un who lived in Raleigh. He come down and had em build him a pleasure house at Morehead, where the breezes and fishin was good, and they wasn't much activity. Well, they built it, furnished it with high-costin things, and old Doc brought his friends down for a pile-up big house-warmin. Foren they got there, it commenced to blow, they's a big wind, and more rain than need be. They wasn't nothing for them folks to do but go back to Raleigh. Old Doc tried it again in two, three months. The same thing commenced. Specially rain, an no sun in the sky to make them Raleigh folks feel cheerful. Well, he tried it some more, they tell me, with worse things happenin till he had to give it up. Finally, old Doc sold that place and bought another un on a different street, trying to break his bad number. Wasn't no use. It kept happenin. That's why them boys say 'old Doc Winter's in town' ever time a storm's comin up. It don't matter if you movin off the coast of Georgia, like now, or if you at home in Morehead or Mayport."

"Men on the pogy boats ain't got many superstitions," the engineer contributed. "It ain't like when I was sailing for the first time on a windjammer[4] that went round the Horn. Them sailors had signs for ever'thing. Ever bird meant some different sign. Nobody'd let a cat on board. They meant bad luck. Why don't they have em on pogy boats? Yessir, they's nice pets and they's plenty of fish for em to eat. I don't rightly know. Guess we just hate to bother with em, havin em underfoot all the time. We got bad luck withouten cats to make it worse."

Pappy and Fats came up as delegates of the crew and asked did we want to hear some more chanteys. Soon the men were singing in the galley and on deck. They opened with "The Johnson Girls:"

> *Them Johnson girls is mighty fine girls,*
> *Walk around, honey, walk around.*

> *They's neat in the waist and have mighty fine legs,*
> *Walk around, honey, walk around.*

> *Great big legs and teeny-incy feet,*
> *Walk around, honey, walk around.*

> *One on the henhouse, two on the pole,*
> *Walk around, honey, walk around*

> *Beefsteak, beefsteak, make a little gravy*
> *Walk around, honey, walk around.*

> *They got sumpum under yonder called jewmaka jam*
> *Walk around, honey, walk around.*

They sang remembered lines, and with great laughter improvised others on the spot. Some were too lewd for reproduction here. All joined in singing "Rosie Anna:"

> *Bye bye, bye bye, bye bye, bye bye;*
> *Bye bye, sweet Rosie Anna.*
> *I thought I heard my organ say*
> *I won't be home tomorrow.*

> *Steamboat coming around the bend,*
> *Bye bye, sweet Rosie Anna.*
> *Is loaded down with Harvey's beans,*
> *I won't be home tomorrow.*

> *Do do, do do, do do, do do, my darlin child;*
> *Do do, my sweet Rosie Anna.*
> *I thought I heard my organ say*
> *I won't be home tomorrow.*

Always in fine harmony they sang. *They Put John on the Island, When I'm Gone, Hikin Jerry, Lazarus,* and *Evalina.* One of the men boasted, "When it comes to chanteyin, North Carolina wears the bell all over the forty-eight."

Darkness came and everyone lost interest in singing. Three porpoises off the starboard bow escorted the ship for a time. The Georgia coast blurred and then became part of the cloudy night. Ahead we could see the lights of another pogy boat as it changed its course to enter Cumberland Sound, outside its home port of Fernandina. The pilot told us how to remember the color of the lights on each side of a ship: "Say the short words together and the long ones together. Port, left, red; starboard, right, green." In another hour we were docked. After tying up, the men went to the shore messhall for an eleven o'clock meal, while the factory "fish gang" of twelve men came aboard to unload *The Boys.*

***

The long wood-enclosed bucket elevator, turning on an endless chain, was lowered into the hold by means of cables controlled from a gasoline engine on the dock. Almost immediately the fish gang, Negroes stripped to the waist and wearing kneeboots to protect them from the slime of blood and oil, were raking the menhaden into the revolving buckets with straight-pronged pitchforks. All were heavily muscled men, and they worked without pause in the fumes from the putre-fying fish. In an hour *The Boys* was ready to go to sea again.

***

Dead sharks from the hold of *The Boys* and other ships were hauled out and thrown in a pile on the dock. Perhaps twenty or thirty of them, three to six feet in length, had been caught. In the morning a skilled workman would set to work on the stiffened bodies. A cutting knife is used to strip off the sand-papery gray skin. It is first salted, then dried. Shipped to another factory, it is turned into high-grade leather. The Mayport plant throws away the shark's huge liver, but some plants process it and obtain a medicinal oil with a higher vitamin A content than cod liver oil. The fins are sliced off for export to China, where wealthy Chinese gourmets boil them to obtain a tasty, gelatinous soup stock. The backbone, which is really cartilage as the shark has no true bones, goes to talking-stick manufac-turers. The eyes and teeth are used in making watch charms and ornamental jewelry.

The sweating fish gang clambered out of *The Boys'* empty hold with their pitchforks and descended to the messy cargo of the *Southland*, which had just docked. The arm and shoulder muscles of the men were swollen by exertion; the black-skinned bodies seemed to move more slowly than they had an hour before. Our attention shifted to the dripping fish being carried up the sloping elevator. At the top they spilled into the hopper, an upright measuring device, with wooden walls about 20 feet high, and divided into four compartments, each capable of con-taining about 1,000 menhaden. As one compartment became filled with fish the hopper automatically revolved and dumped them into the buckets of a second end-less chain which led to the raw box. . . . Men eye the hopper with great interest for it tells what their earning will be Saturday night.

The raw box, slowly filling with fish, is an immense wooden receptacle that stands between the dock and factory. At least two stories in height, it can hold the cargoes of several vessels. Some nights all five of the Mayport boats will reach the dock within a few minutes. The fish gang can handle two boats, one at each end of the dock. A ship's crew, from captain to cook, considers it an honor to be the first to reach the factory. Sometimes, when the coast is clear, a ship will douse its lights, strain every horsepower out of its Diesel, and attempt to pass another boat leading the homeward race. The crew of the forward boat condemns this as unethical—until it has a chance to take revenge.

From the raw box the fish move continuously forward, in conveyor buckets, to the cookers. At this stage the menhaden begin to lose their identity. In a few hours intricate machines turn them into oil and dark-brown scraps of dried flesh and bone. The horizontal steel cookers are forty feet long, two feet in diameter, and a multitude of pipes lead hot steam into them. The steam cooks the fish in a twinkling, and they are carried forward again on the inevitable conveyor buckets to the curb press. This is a steel tub, more than three feet high and nearly as wide. When it is filled with fish, a large weight, called the head, is mechanically lowered. It presses the fish like a gigantic potato masher. Water and oil are squeezed out of the tub, squirting and flowing downward through small spaces between the tub's steel staves. Shields around the press catch both water and oil, sending them through troughs into tanks. About four pounds of oil, forty-six pounds of water, and fifty pounds of scrap are extracted from each 100 pounds of fish in the press. In the tanks, the oil is cooked again, and a portion of the water is eliminated. The oil gradually rises to the top. It is then skimmed off and piped into storage tanks. Barge-tankers call at the plant and transport the oil to soap factories. The best oil has an amber color and brings the highest price; dark-brown oil is an inferior grade. Market prices fluctuate greatly.

The squeezed mass of fish drops out of the tub's trapdoor bottom and is carried to hot-air dryers. These are iron containers as large as railroad locomotives. As they revolve, hot furnace gases blow through them, thoroughly drying the oily scrap—but creating most of the factory's disagreeable smell. The latter has aroused public protest in some localities, and many factories now mix crude sulphuric acid with the scrap. This, in a proportion of one and one-half gallons to 500 pounds of scrap, takes away the disagreeable scent. It also dissolves the fish bones and makes the scrap unhealthy for flies and other insects.

A final conveyor chain carries the scrap overhead and sifts it into cone-shaped piles on the floor of a huge, barn-like structure, called the scraphouse. Fine particles float in the air and settle as dust; workmen armed with brooms sweep it neatly into the big piles. Twelve to fifteen thousand fish are required to make one ton of scrap. Other employees shovel it into large brown "croker" sacks for shipment to fertilizer factories and to plants that use it in meal for cattle, hogs, and poultry. The scrap's rich ammonia content makes it valuable as a plant food, while the bone and oily flesh provide a nutritious feed for animals.

We stepped from the factory into a soft Florida night. I had attributed several attacks of dizziness to the grinding, hissing, clanking babel within the factory, but another attack came when I touched the ground. I was suffering from the vertigo of land-sickness. Across the road, the wives of ship officers sat in automobiles, waiting for brief meetings with their husbands. Behind the cars, the messhall and Negro quarters were lighted and filled with activity. At midnight, as we drove toward Mayport and Jacksonville over the white shell road with washboard bumps the words of a chantey the Negroes had sung that evening at sunset kept recurring:

When I'm gone, gone, gone,
When I'm gone, to come no more,
I know you're goin to miss me
When I'm gone.

Notes

1. Misspelling of "*Brevoortia tyrannus,*" the scientific name for Atlantic menhaden. "*Brevoortia tyrannus,*" FishBase, accessed 17 August 2010, http://www.fishbase.org.
2. See "The Fish are Running" in this volume.
3. See "The Fish are Running."
4. A large, tall-masted class of sailing vessels. John Harland and Mark Myers, *Seamanship in the Age of Sail* (Annapolis, MD: Naval Institute Press, 1984), 46.

SHINGLETOWN

Verne Bright (Oregon)

Before I was dry behind the ears I was well in the way of becoming a "timber-beast." Left an orphan at the age of ten, I had been spewed from the fifth grade onto the skidroad[1] with my neck fur yet to grow. By the time I was a fuzz-face I had gone through the many stages of water-boy, whistle-punk,[2] bull-cook,[3] and swamper[4] in a logging camp; a mule-twister[5] on a railroad and a gandy-dancer;[6] a bundler[7] and sawyer[8] in a box-shook factory; a lath-saw operator,[9] planerman,[10] lumber-piler;[11] and tackled many another job in and out of the woods. Gradually I had grown from gaycat[12] to timber-kitten. But in all the hullabaloo of jobs I had never worked a shingle mill.

And then one night in Erickson's I met a rounder[13] who said: "In the empire of lumber the shingle-weavers are the untouchables, the aristocrats." He leaned his elbow on the bar and took a long quaff from his schooner of Heidelberg. "Yes, sir," he went on, "the shingle-weavers are the house of lords in this man's parliament. A lumber mill, now, or a logging camp! There's a dog's life. But a shingle mill—ah! by the holy old mackinaw, that's the only place for a real man of the forest." So I decided to become a shingle-weaver.

With this idea in mind one night at dusk I swung off a string of empty log trucks in the little seacoast village of Shingletown. Along the steep shore of the bay sprawled the settlement, and up a street that rose almost perpendicularly into the darkness a neon sign flashed, BAYSIDE HOTEL. I climbed the hill, rented a room, and turned in for the night.

The new sun was gleaming on the distant breakers beyond the sandspit that thrust a long finger of dunes between the bay and the sea as I came out of the gray weather-beaten house that clutched precariously at the steep forested hill-side. The morning breeze from beyond the bay was sharp with the odor of clam flats while the white seagulls, perched on the salt-caked piling at the edge of the water, lifted raucous cries. Below me the village scattered, and beyond it columns of smoke and steam belched from the stacks of the shingle-mill among a cluster of houseboats, barges and drying fish-nets. Curving along the bayside stretched the one paved street, the landward side bordered with rain-silvered wooden buildings, interspersed here and there with modern brick or concrete structures. As I stood looking out over the town and the bay toward the sea I began humming a ballad of the camps:

> Oh they said you are a flunkie and I said, how come?
> If you think I'm just a gaycat you're pretty damn' dumb.
> I'm a timberbeast from Kokomo, I'm leavin' this damn' land,
> I'm gonna be a weaver an' with the weavers stand.

And I grinned like the cat that licked the cream as I started down toward the mill. I had just turned twenty-one and here, I thought, is maybe the kind of job I could stick to and settle down permanent. It was time a fellow was thinking about the future.

Well, I decided to see the whole works before hitting the type for a job. Even before the early shift came on I was walking the booms[14] at the mill pond. I looked the place over. It was new and strange to the eyes of an inland logger. A young squirt of a kid was on the booms, pike-pole[15] in hand, waiting the beginning whistle. He was about eighteen, slender, and tough as a pine knot. But he had the steady eye and the agile foot of an old time river-hog. His dress was that of a typical riverman: "tin" rain-hat of paraffined canvas; gray flannel shirt under a black slicker jacket; tin pants "stagged" or cut off six inches below the knees; and sixteen-inch Chippeway logger boots, with half-inch steel spikes or caulks in the soles.

I walked over to the kid and gave him a bit of chin music, not wishing to appear too inquisitive, but wanting to find out all I could about his job.

"Well," drawled the kid as he nudged a big blue butt with his pike-pole, "these here logs are all cedar. They're gathered at the regular loggin' camps up in the mountains and hauled to the river on trucks where they're dumped in and floated down in rafts. We run this here boom made by timbers chained together around 'em to keep 'em from floating off down the bay. My job is to select the logs and herd 'em down to the slip yonder, and the slip man chases 'em into the jack-ladder, that inclined trough or slip that goes up into the mill. He stands on that little platform at the bottom of the jack-ladder and with his pike hauls 'em in reach of the bull-chain which pulls 'em up into the mill."

The kid jumped lightly from the boom to a floating log. It was small and bobbed beneath him, but in an instant he had leaped to firmer footing on a huge king-cedar that he rode like an expert performer riding a circus stallion. Jauntily he guided his mount toward the log-slip, then leaped to a smaller log about two feet in diameter and began to roll it. The log gained momentum until it was a whirling blur of water and foam. Suddenly the kid brought the log to a quick stop tipped his hat back careless-like and announced: "That's called birling."

I walked to the end of the boom and up the cat-walk beside the bull-chain. As I reached the top of the incline the mill whistle blew. The head sawyer in his cage by the huge circular cut-off gave a signal and a sharp short *toot! toot!* stabbed the morning air. Slowly at first, as if reluctant to rouse from the night's inertia, all the machinery in the mill began to take on life: each wheel and pulley and saw accelerated, the noise rising in a gradual crescendo until the whole mill was enveloped in a consuming roar.

The bull-chain began to move; the pikeman hazed a log into the slip. The hooked cleats on the log-haul caught the timber and pulled it into the trough. Up the jack-ladder it came dripping-wet to the saw platform. As it reached the head-rig the log was brought up sharp by the steel stop which determined the length of the block to be cut; the cutoff sawyer kicked a lever throwing the bull-chain out of gear and settling giant steel clamps that held the log firmly. A great circular saw ten feet in diameter hovered beside the log, buzzing like a huge angry wasp. The hairy hands of the sawyer gripped the levers; he was an old man with lined face and intent eyes. He tugged at a lever and the saw, a whirring blur of chained lightning, swiftly sliced off a block, round and yellow as a mammoth cheese. As the cut fell away the old sawyer calmly kicked the stop lever and the log moved forward— sixteen inches, precisely.

The splitter-man, a "skookum-charlie"[16] with shoulders as wide as a door, grabbed the block and heaved it onto the power splitter. The powerful machine, fed by steam, quartered the block and requartered it ready for the saws. With a flip of his hookaroon the splitter slid the small blocks to the conveyor which bore them to the battery of shingle machines that stretched away into the depths of the mill.

I squeezed back against the wall as the blocks toppled from the head-rig and were shoved into the splitting machine. The sharp whines of the saws crashed on my ears, mingled with the heavy hum of the cyclone-fan blowing the refuse to the fuel house. The air was thick with sawdust and the incense smell of the cedar was heavy as perfume in a rooming-house.

Just then the big tyee[17] came along.

"Hy-ya, bub!" he grunted, "looking for someone?"

After hemming and hawing a bit I got my back up and answered him:

"Yeah! I was sorta looking for the head push. You him!"

"That's right. Need a job?"

"Well, I thought I'd kinda like to work in a shingle mill. I've worked in box-factories, lath-mills, logging camps and sawmills; but I'm a greenhorn about a shingle mill."

"I need a man out on the pond if you'd like the job. Maybe later I could use you in the mill."

"Gee, thanks, mister!"

"I'm Dan Forest, but the men usually speak of me as the Little Bull. What's your moniker?"

"Ernest Breit, but the fellows in the camp always called me Missou because I came from Missouri."

"Alright, Missou! We'll just take a little gander through the mill before you go to work, so you'll know what it's all about. You see how this big saw here cuts off the blocks from the log when it comes up the chute, and how the splitter hosses them onto the splitting machine. They are split up that way to make them easier to handle at the shingle machines. He splits the blocks so they have an edge-grain face. That makes the best shingles, and that's the kind we aim to turn out."

We walked along beside the conveyor belt toward the upright shingle machines that stood regularly spaced and even as a battery of artillery. A steady flow of shingle blocks passed to the block pilers who took them from the conveyor and put on the block tables for the shingle sawyers.

The Little Bull took a big bait of Copenhagen and yelled above the roar of the mill.

"There's two kinds of men work in a shingle mill—huskies to work on the decks and handle blocks, and the speedballs for packers and sawyers. The speedballs make the most money."

Right away inside of me I determined to be a speedball.

"Gahagan, there, is a speedball right," the Little Bull went on. He can turn out more shingles than any buzzard[18] I ever saw."

I watched the star sawyer on the first upright as he dropped a block onto the carriage of the cutting machine between the feed rolls. Seemingly without turning his head to look at the machine or the block he adjusted it to the carriage so that the wood grain was at right angles to the plane of the saw. He threw a small lever and the carriage began a steady shuttle, carrying the block against the thin-gauge, razor-sharp, circular saw. Back and forth. Back and forth. The saw glittered under the electric lights as the whirring blade smoothly sliced off a thin wedge of cedar at each stroke. The sawyer's gaze was intent, his narrowed eyes sharp and practiced. Back and forth. Back and forth. The smooth face of the shingle block flashed before him.

"How come," I shouted in the Little Bull's ear, "the saw knows enough to cut one end of the shingle thick and the other thin?"

"Its kind of complicated to explain, but every time the block comes back some little gadgets on the machine called pawls work with the feed rolls so that first the top part of the block and then the bottom part is cut thicker giving the shingles that wedge-shape."

The sawyer was a little runt of a man with two fingers missing from his right hand. Nearly all the sawyers had fingers missing. I didn't like the looks of that. It made my stomach kind of squeamish to think of those whizzing knives slicing meat as well as wood. The sawyer worked like a mechanical man, his movements swift and precise, rhythmical as music. Maybe because his pay-check depended on the number of shingles he could saw at a shift.

Each time the saw cut into the block a short, sharp "yi-ah!" split the air. Above the deep wave-like roar of the mill these quick cries were hardly distinguishable from those of the seagulls circling above or perched on the pilings of the millpond.

As each shingle dropped from the saw the sawyer picked it up and put it on a "springboard" with the butt end held firmly against the guide to the trimming saw. With a shrill "zing" the trimmer saw clipped off the overhanging edge of the shingle. A quick flip of the wrist and he turned the shingle over, pushed down the springboard, and trimmed the other side smoothly parallel to the first.

As hands and body reacted automatically with the physical movements necessary to control the machine, his mind was busy grading and sorting the wood. Unerring eyes searched out every variation of grain, every knot, every blemish. With a final movement in the rhythmic series he dropped the shingles into the chute that led to the packing bins below.

"How much can you cut in a day?" I yelled at the sawyer.

"A hunnert and twenty-five, thirty bundles," he answered without glancing away from his work.

"Ain't that an awful pile?"

"Not as much." He jetted tobacco juice at a knot-hole in the floor. "Seen a speedball once could turn out a hunnert an' fifty."

He paused long enough to brush the sawdust from his shaggy eyebrows and pull a rusty cap a little lower over his eyes.

The Little Bull laughed as we moved away, the sawdust grinding beneath our shoes: "I've seen it done. But a sawyer that can cut a hundred and fifty bundles in a day ain't exactly human."

"Maybe Paul Bunyan helped him a bit," I ventured.

The machines occupied the upper floor of the mill; the first floor was a dark cavity of shafts and pulleys and belts, except for the long row of shingle bins and packing frames just below the battery of shingle saws. The Little Bull led me down steep stairs into the shingle packing room. A long line of men was standing beside another endless-belt conveyor upon which bundles of shingles moved toward the drying kilns. Before each man was a packing machine consisting of a bench frame and two slotted over-hanging steel rods. The motions of the shingle-weavers were as swift and rhythmic as those of the shingle sawyers above them. Quickly and methodically, hands flashing gracefully, expertly grading as they moved, they packed the wafers of wood into the frame, thin tips overlapping, until the right number was in the bundle. When the frame was filled the weaver put a cleat between the overhanging rods and kicked a foot lever drawing the wooden cleats together while he nailed metal strips to them binding the bundle.

Here in the packing room the noise of the mill was subdued to a whirring hum, stabbed by the ceaseless gull-cries of the shingle-saws. I stopped beside the first packer, a middling-oldish man with a few streaks of gray in his dusky red hair. The light from the electric bulb poured down, high-lighting his forehead, nose, and chin, darkening the hollows of his eyes and the long furrows in his cheeks.

The Little Bull broke in: "If the packer ain't quick as a cat, with a knack for an easy even gait he don't pack many shingles. Ain't that right Casey?"

Casey answered without looking up and without a break in his rhythm. "They have to be done just so," he said with a touch of the old sod in his speech. "As the spieler says at the country fair, the hand has to be quicker than the eye. Not only that but the eye has to be quicker than anything else this side a streak of lightnin' to pick out the right size and grade of shingle to put in the bundle."

I put in my two bits worth.

"How long you been packing shingles?" I asked the weaver.

"Ever since I was a fuzz-face. I'm fifty now."

Yi-ah! yi-ah! yi-ah! The saws upstairs and the gulls outside kept up their antiphonal chorus.

"I been in damned near every mill on the coast."

Yi-ah! yi-ah! yi-ah!

"A boomer, that's me. Hell, my feet itch. But I like shingles."

When I was watching the sawyers I was sure that I would be a top sawyer some day, and now as I watched the packers I was just as sure that I would make a top-hand weaver.

I stood in the open door of the packing room, looking out toward the drying kilns and the loading freight cars on the siding and along shore to the docked ship taking cargo. The booms and the mill and the whirring, shrieking saws; the odorous dust of the packing bins; the sunlight pouring down between the mill and the drying kilns and glancing from the polished rails of the mill siding; all thrilled me. Everything that I heard, felt and saw seemed to say that this would be my life. A shingle-weaver, Wagh!

The voice of the Little Bull broke into my dream.

"Well, I reckon that's about all, Mizzou. Come on to the pond, I'll show you your job."

I followed him to the tool-room where he selected a seven-foot cross-cut saw, an axe, a maul, and a wedge. I carried the other tools while he carried the lithe whipping saw down the cat-walk and out onto the booms. At the upper end of the pond were logs forty to sixty feet in length. My job was to cut these logs into shorter lengths as they floated in the water. My short training as a bucker in the logging woods helped me in this new job. I started at once on a huge cedar.

No matter how competent a man may be at a certain type of labor changing his job often places him on the level of the veriest "greenhorn," even though the job is similar to the ones to which he is accustomed. The first day on my new job proved to be my last.

The boom was filled with all shapes and sizes of cedar logs; big ones, little ones, rough barked ones, and some slipperier than hell. I didn't have any calked boots, either, but figured on getting them come pay-day. I thought I knew as much about bucking logs as the next one, but this job was different. I had to stand on the log I was bucking and saw straight up and down with the other end of my saw under the log in the water. When the tide was running as it was that day the pressure of the water against the saw made it buckle and bind and run plenty hard. But I was bound to make good so I sawed away with a will, pausing now and then to get my breath and smell the tang of salt-water and cedar. I had my first log about half sawed through when along came a tug-boat raising swells six feet high that rolled out behind her and spread from shore to shore of the bay.

I straightened up from my bucking and just stood there watching the tug-boat coming up the bay and enjoying the scenery and the tangy smells. The tug was moving in close to the boom where I was standing. As she came closer she tooted her whistle and it echoed back and forth among the hills along the bay. She was whistling to warn me but I didn't know it at the time. I only stood there gawking. Just then I glanced toward the mill and saw the pond man waving friendly-like at me, so I waved back and went on staring at the tug-boat.

When the tug had passed, the big swells she had churned up began to roll out toward the boom, and before I knew it, they hit the boom and things began to happen. Those sixty-foot cedar logs began jumping around like corks in a wash tub, and me standing right in the midst of them. There I was with slick-soled shoes; if I lost my footing and fell between those milling logs I would be ground to hamburger. I knew then what the boom man had been yelling and waving to me about. However, I didn't have much time to think things out. I had to do something pretty damned quick or I was a goner. About twenty feet away was a piling thrust ten or twelve feet in the air. With my heart in my mouth and my soul in the hands of the Lord I started for that piling, hopping from log to log, timing each jump so I wouldn't lose my balance. My timing must have been good. In a second or two that seemed like a year or two, I reached the piling. I couldn't climb it because it was slimy and spray-washed and slick as a peeled onion. From the top of it though, there was a piece of old cable dangling. My luck was good; just as I got on the blue butt that was scratching his side on the piling a big swell, a four-foot roller, lifted the log and me on top of it within reach of the rusty cable. I grabbed it and hung on, pulling my legs up under me.

When the logs quieted down again, I slid from the pole and walked shakily across the boom to where my saw still stuck half way through the log, the slippery handle waiting for me to grab a-hold and finish the cut. But as far as I know the saw is still waiting. I didn't have stomach for any more of that kind of logging. I pulled stakes and went away from there.

As I scrambled along the booms toward shore the boom man hollered: "Next time watch out for them tugs; this ain't no-summer picnic!"

"There ain't going to be any next time," I yelled back. He grinned and watched me climb the bank. I looked back at the shingle mill belching smoke and steam. . . .

"Yi-ah! yi-ah! yi-ah!" screamed the gulls.

Notes

1. In literal logging terminology, the "skid road" was the roadway created by dragging large timber through the forest to a nearby river or cargo road. Of course, the term also has the connotation of being that area of a town where the "seedier" activities take place—the province where not incidentally, loggers often spent their down time. Harold Wentworth and Stuart Berg Flexner, *Dictionary of American Slang* (New York: Crowell, 1960), 481.
2. See "Logging in the Rain" in this volume.
3. Can refer to the male cook at a logging camp, or to someone who assists in the kitchen or with other assorted tasks as needed. Wentworth and Flexner, *Dictionary*, 72.
4. One who works, either in mining or logging, to load transports with timber or ore. Paul W. Thrush, *A Dictionary of Mining, Mineral, and Related Terms* (Chicago: Maclean Hunter, 1990), 1109.
5. Presumably a synonym for "mule-skinner," or one who drives mules. Also truck driver. (cf. "teamster"). Wentworth and Flexner, *Dictionary*, 349.
6. A repairman or railway track installer. The Gandy Manufacturing Company made much of the equipment used by these workers, thus the origin of "gandy." More specifically, however, the term denotes the "section gangs" who would encircle a spike and take turns striking it into the railroad tie with their sledge hammers. From a distance, the small crew looked like a freakish, multi-armed monster, or a "gandy-dancer." Wentworth and Flexner, *Dictionary*, 207; Eric Partrige, *A Concise Dictionary of Slang and Unconventional English* (New York: Macmillan, 1990), 279.
7. A laborer who assists in constructing mine-shaft support structures. The term could have a number of other meanings as well, but given the close connection between mining and logging this seems like a likely meaning. Thrush, *Dictionary*, 151, 1093.
8. Ibid., 64. Stone cutter. But used later in "Shingletown" as the operator of a shingle saw.
9. Ibid., 627, 1080–81. A wet saw used for cutting and shaping various types of rock.
10. Ibid., 830–31. Someone who works and carves stone.
11. Ibid., 1143. Likely a "lumber packer." A worker who brings lumber to a working area in a mine.
12. Can have various meanings, but the general meaning is of a young, itinerant, inexperienced person—either in worklife, in associating with women, or even criminal activity. Wentworth and Flexner, *Dictionary*, 210.
13. Ibid., 434. A bar patron.
14. The series of connected, floating timbers that have been prepped for floating down river to the mill. George Stenzel, Thomas A. Walbridge Jr., and J. Kenneth Pearce, *Logging and Pulpwood Production* (New York: John Wiley and Sons, 1985), 340.
15. Likely a "cant-hook" or a "peavey." See "Logging in the Rain".
16. A formidable or courageous person. Wentworth and Flexner, *Dictionary*, 483.
17. Ibid., 559. Boss.
18. Ibid., 82. An experienced, somewhat shabby, older worker.

MINE TIMEKEEPER

Clair C. Anderson (Utah)

This morning, as usual, I went to the crusher house[1] first, and stood in the door to avoid the choking dust. Pushing back my hard hat, I marked Don's name in my time book and watched him work through the grizzly screen.[2] As ore fell through the steel bars, it was instantly chomped to pieces by the steel jaws of the crusher, and then dropped on a conveyer belt which carried it between fine-grinding rollers.

Don was a swell boy, a young Mormon boy who had returned from a mission and married a girl from Sand Wash a year before. The going must have been tough to force him to take a job away from home with a little outfit like ours. Our mine was like a hundred others in Utah, able to produce about fifty tons of low grade ore a day. And, because it was low grade, we had to mill it to cut down transportation costs.

When Don saw me standing there, he shut the crusher down, much to my surprise, and came quickly to the door. The air was still filled with dust, and when the grinding, clanking noise stopped it made you ache with the silence.

"Andy, I got to get a couple days off, I've just got to, and the old man says there hasn't been any men rustling for jobs for three days. There isn't time to get a man out of Salt Lake, and I've got to be in Sand Wash no later than day after tomorrow."

"What's so important?" I asked. "You've never been in such a hurry before."

"Well, you know, our baby is coming, and I've just got to be there; she expects me to be with her, and I can't disappoint her."

He pulled his respirator down off his face, and it left a clean white streak on each cheek, where the elastic bands had been. On a couple of days growth of beard the dust had settled thickly. It made a little flower on the end of each whisker, gathered like steel particles sticking to a magnet.

"How much ore is there in the crushed ore bin?" I asked him.

"Over two hundred tons, it's really enough to run the mill for four days. The tire is over the top of the upper cross beam in the bin—you can look for yourself." He was almost trembling with eagerness now.

He had me stumped. I was carrying twenty-seven men on my time book now, with the old man—the Super—and the cook and myself, all on salaries; it meant we couldn't hire another man. But the kid was right, he had crushed enough ore to run the mill for four days. So I told him to finish this shift and keep the ore up in the bin. Then if we ran out, I would stand his shift myself for a day or two. I could get away with it because the mine foreman could keep time for me underground, where most of the men were working.

His gratitude made me feel silly, and brought a lump to my throat. Hell, I've got a couple of kids myself, so I turned quickly and headed for the mill.

I didn't get near that roaring, clanking ball mill, but checked the helper's name in my book. Here the crushed ore was mixed with water and whirled around and around to be reduced to powdery fineness between steel balls.

On the floatation platform[3] everything was running smoothly, the motors making a quiet, lulling hum. Rodney was titrating and I watched him. First, he would pick up a test tube containing the solution taken from the floatation cells. Then to this unknown chemical solution he would add a drop of this, and a drop of that, and the solution would change color; the drops, of known strength, told him whether or not his chemical circuit was all right. It was this careful control of the chemicals that gave Rodney such perfect results. Turning, I watched the bubbles that were floating or carrying the concentrated ore up and over the launders and into the troughs—just right. Rodney looked up.

"Hi there, pencil pusher. Put me down for two shifts."

"I will when you work them. How can you eat your lunch with such dirty hands and arms? Even the muckers[4] don't get as dirty as you and they play in raw muck."

"Takes a good man to get this dirty. The boss is going to see how he likes it. Promised to give me three days off next week and work my shift himself, yes he did. Said he had been wanting to see how things were going anyway, and I wanted to run home for a couple of days. I'm worried about my oldest boy; he hasn't been well and if he isn't any better I am going to have his tonsils taken out."

I told Rodney I hoped the boy would be better, solemnly promised to pay the boss with no more than a millman's wages when he was working at it, and started towards the mine buildings.

The blacksmith hardly looked up. He was finishing a chisel point on a piece of drill steel. Giving the point a few more light taps he gauged it and then dipped the dull, cherry-red steel tentatively into the big tub of water. He removed it. Now it was all peacock colors. The purples and blues chased each other and played along the steel towards the tip, scale began to form, and he plunged it into the tub to the bottom and moved it like he was stirring a huge pot of soup. I've always liked to watch a blacksmith work, and I didn't mind Mac not speaking to me. He is like that. Never said a word, except maybe, "Pass the Hash." As the length of steel joined its fellows on the ground, I turned towards the hoist house.

The big compressor was idling, but about every fourth cycle, it would give a hell of a bang and belch unburned fuel and black smoke out of the stove pipe above the roof. Old Dan, the hoist man, had his foot on the brake and was leaning on the handle. I nearly scared him off the platform when I poked him.

He set the brake and took me over to a shelf. There was just about the prettiest piece of machinery you could imagine. It was a dry washer[5]—and no bigger than a typewriter. He had made it himself, and there was a tiny hopper about the size of a tea kettle. As I turned the crank a little eccentric operated the heavy canvas bellows and puffed air through the tiny riffle board.

"Think she'll blow the sand out and leave the gold?" asked Dan.

"Bet your life," I answered, cranking enthusiastically. It had little legs about a foot high and that would keep it from being buried too quick when you started to use it. Why, the whole thing didn't weigh ten pounds.

We had often discussed what we considered placer ground[6] across the valley and wished we could try panning some of it. Course, it wasn't the kind of placer ground they tell me is up in the High Uintas—so big the grains of sand are the size of your head. There wasn't any water across the valley, but now, with this little dry washer, we could try it. So, I accepted Dan's invitation to go with him next Sunday.

In the shack, just outside the collar of the shaft,[7] I took my lamp off the hook, filled it with carbide and water and lighted it. Putting it on my hat, I started down the shaft. This was not a vertical shaft, but an inclined shaft, about twenty-eight degrees. It had a manway[8] with steps, and we brought the skip up from the lowest level, the 400, on rails.

Seeing a light on the manway I backed up and stood just outside the portal as Scotty came out with an armful of starter steel.[9] Scotty had been battling in a drift that had some of the hardest rock he had ever seen. And if that doesn't mean anything, Scotty said it was the hardest he had ever seen, and he has worked all over the United States and Mexico.

"Didn't you take any starters down this morning, Scotty?"

"Sure, but that damn rock is so hard I've dulled all these this morning."

I didn't believe him but he was the miner and shouldn't have left his machine; so instead of arguing I thought I'd bawl him out.

"Well, why didn't you send your helper up instead of coming yourself?"

"Send my helper up? Why good God man, he couldn't come up; he's down there at the face, with his finger marking the spot we started on."

This hole had grown on me. I had got to enjoy the dank, muggy smells coming from the drifts, and sometimes the sharp odor of burned powder that would sting your nostrils and tickle your throat. Often I thought I could tell where I was in the dark, just by the different smells that came from the drifts, each one had its own—the type of rock, I guess.

In the "A" drift on the 200 I saw Johnson and Maguire with their machine shut down. A steel, with no shank, lay on the floor, so I knew they were trying to get the broken-off shank out of the chuck.

"Look out. Here comes the boss's stool pigeon,"[10] shouted Maguire.

"Wouldn't it be nice to have an education and nothing to do but push a pencil?" asked Johnson, apparently talking to Maguire.

"Yeah," answered Maguire. "I went to school twelve years and still didn't get an education. I had to stay in the third grade nine years. Not my fault either, but Pa would have whipped hell out of me if I'd passed him."

"Mine was the same, only different," sighed Johnson. "I only had one brother, but he was the laziest Swede in Minnesota. It was his fault I didn't get any education, but I had to leave home when I was twelve years old, because I couldn't stand to see my poor old mother cut wood."

"Say, listen you damned monkeys," I grinned. "If you think I've got a snap around here, remember that at this hole I'm a timekeeper, bookkeeper, office manager, trouble shooter, first aideman, storekeeper and bull cook. And just yesterday the boss asked me if I couldn't learn to assay so I could help the assayer[11] in my spare time."

Those two screwballs would get along all right, so I went back to the shaft and down the "B" drift. Half way to the face I stopped and stood motionless, holding my breath. There was the crash and rumble of falling rock where no rock should have been falling. Some of it seemed to strike against metal with a strange muffled sound, and the light that had been coming towards me went out: That meant a man down.

I started to run as fast as I could along the track. The echoes were still rolling back and forth in the narrow, low tunnel. My light didn't tell me I had headed into a thick cloud of dust—going too fast—but my nose did: If I hadn't shoved out my hands I would have hit that mine car at full speed. No telling what it would have done to me, any place from my ankles to my chest, I thought, as I tried to get over a pile of rock on the hanging wall side. I couldn't get by, but I crawled between the car and the footwall, sneezing from the dust.

Behind the car, shoved against the wall, was Czernac, the Pole. Rock covered him to his waist, his hat was off, and blood was spreading from a dozen cuts on his head and face. One arm was doubled behind him awkwardly, and the other was shoved out, resting stiffly on top of the pile of rock, just like he had been playing football and tried to straight-arm somebody. His mouth was open and his head cocked to one side as if her were listening for something.

I didn't touch him, but ran along the track to the face for help. Neal and the other mucker were there, and they came on the jump.

Exactly above Czernac was the chute from an old mined-out stope.[12] The gate was only wood and I supposed that the rocks had been falling from the old stope, perhaps for years, and gathered at the gate, which broke just as the trammer[13] was under it.

Czernac wasn't hard to get out of the rock, but we handled him carefully and carried him to the tunnel station where we laid him down flat, I jerked the ball wire viciously nine times—the most dreaded signal in a mine; after a pause I gave him the level signal. Some luck anyhow. The skip had been empty and it got there right away.

We loaded the Pole into it. I was afraid to ride with him; if he should regain consciousness and force my head or arm up it would be just too bad for me. The low roof would not clear anything stuck over the side. I rang three and one—man on, take her up. Good Old Dan! That skip started without a jerk and went up so slowly that I kept up with it, running up the manway steps, Neal and the mucker behind me. Dan stopped the skip just outside the portal and came hurrying from the hoist house to help.

Where in the hell was the boss with his car? Well, Supers don't have to report to the timekeeper, but we certainly needed some transportation now. Just then one of the trucks pulled up, and I stopped him before he backed under the big ore bin. We threw a couple of camp cot mattresses in the truck and piled up some ties to stand on. Just as we started to put that Pole over the high sides of the dump truck he came to, groaning loudly, so we laid him back on the ground for a minute. In a small mine we had no opiates; I wouldn't have known how to use them, anyway. Running to the office, I got a bottle of aspirin and forced half a dozen into his mouth, and held his head while he drank a tin cup of water. When I put another flock of aspirins in his hand and told him to chew on them if he wanted, his hand closed on them so tightly the knuckles showed white under the dirt. He was biting his lower lip so hard a trickle of blood started to run down the side of his chin.

We got him into the truck all right. Just as we took him over the side, he screamed, just once. A woman's scream is not so bad, maybe because you are used to it. But when a man screams, it simply drills your guts. It was a relief to have him pass out again.

The driver got away. I hadn't wanted to waste time on an accident report, so I told him to tell the Doctor that the boss would be in with it later. By rights I should have ridden in with the Pole. But he couldn't fall out of the dump truck, and there wasn't much I could do for him, as long as he was passed out. The driver said he would keep looking back to see if he came to again. Then there was no Super around today, so I thought I had done the right thing.

Sticking a cigarette in my mouth, I tried to light it. The match burned my nose and singed my chin; my hand was holding it everyplace but against that cigarette. Trying to hide my jitters from the men I told them to go back to work and keep their mouths shut. Men can't finish a shift after hearing there has been an accident, and not knowing how badly the man was hurt.

Taking a drink of water I went back down into the hole and paused near the face of the "B" cross-cut. Hansen, the miner, was yelling his head off, but I couldn't hear a word from his helper.

"You dirty little son of a bitch! I'll take that steel away from you and bend it around your neck. You young whelp! I'll pull you limb from branch, you little bastard. I'll pull one of your arms out by the roots and beat you to death with it!"

Where in the hell was the shifter?[14] This was a mine foreman's job, not mine. First, an accident, and now a fight between a miner and his helper. God damn it! Why couldn't Supers and shifters stay on the job? Was I running this hole? If I was, they weren't paying me for being the brains.

Drawing closer, I saw Hansen backed up to the drill and the helper, just a kid, holding him off with a five foot piece of drill steel. My beef melted into a grin as I saw the way that kid was doing it. He was holding the steel bayonet style. Hansen knew it was deadly, but he couldn't figure out how to get around it. Where the kid learned that trick, I can't imagine. When a miner wants to use steel for a weapon, he uses it like a club.

They wouldn't tell me who started the fight, but I got it stopped by sending the kid on top. Then I left Hansen alone and went down to the 300 foot level.

There was a lot of pyrites[15] in this drift and my lamp brought glittering lights from the crystals. It was like magic, so black you could almost feel it except where the light struck, then as though the iron was a thousand diamonds, rainbow lights would leap and glow, and then suddenly go out as you passed.

When I got close to Nevada Red and his helper, they saw my light, shut off the air and sat down to roll cigarettes.

"Say, bookkeeper," asked Red, "do you know where the deepest mine in the world is?"

"In Spain or Mexico, I don't know which."

"No, sir," he asserted, "It's right in the United States, in Arizona. One time another fellow and me got passes to go down and see it. We came to the hoist house, and it was a big one, bigger that the Homestake. Inside the hoist house the cage was coming up, and believe it or not, on a cot lay the engineer—asleep. I looked at the signal board and jumped six feet to shake him 'your hoist is coming up, and there are men on the cage.' Well, he kind of rubbed his eyes, and said, 'What day is it?' and I said, 'Why it's Wednesday.' He kind of sat up and said, 'You don't need to get so excited, they won't be up until Friday.'"

Red kept a serious face in spite of my grin. As I left, they turned on the air, and the hammer took up its throbbing, ear-splitting chatter again. In the "D" crosscut I found Shorty and his helper all excited. The last round has brought in some high-grade[16] and they were sorting it all out and talking like a couple of old women.

"Look at that, timekeeper," jabbered Shorty. "Why that stuff is so heavy a strong man couldn't lift fifty pounds of it."

It *was* heavier than the average run of the mine, pretty, galena crystals[17] shining like diamonds, but it didn't look too unusual.

"Yeah," I said, "that ought to be pretty good stuff. Don't hand pick a sample of that high-grade and run to the assayer tonight. Just let the shifter pick the samples off the cars, and we won't have an assay of four or five hundred dollars to the ton. It won't go very much over two thousand pound to the ton, anyway."

As I left them they were setting up to go to work. When I got to Slim I was going to curl his hair pretty and pin his ears back. He had been going down a canyon a lot to see a prospector who had a nice little hole up on the hill and called it his mine. He lived in a little shack near a spring with his wife and kid. The Old Man wanted to buy a motor the prospector wasn't using, and thought that if he sent Slim he could get it cheaper. So he let Slim take the pick-up to town last night—on condition that he would see the prospector and get the motor cheap. Slim hadn't brought back the motor.

"Say, Slim," I asked, "why didn't you get the motor?"

"Oh, I don't know."

"Did you stop and see him?"

"Well, I stopped, but I didn't see him," hesitated Slim.

"Well, what in the hell happened? I got to explain to the boss, you know."

"Well," said Slim, evidently with effort, "just between the two of us here is what happened. I stopped at the gate and there was the kid swinging on it. I said, 'Hello there, is your ma in the house?' And the kid said, 'uh-huh,' and I said, 'Is your pa up at the mine?' And the kid said, 'Huh-uh, he's in the house too.'"

Slim adjusted his lamp, taking his hat off of his head to do it, and found several things that needed his immediate attention.

"That can't be all that happened. Go on, did you go in and see him?"

"It's just about all that happened," sighed Slim. "All I said then was, 'Well, tell your folks I said hello.'"

I turned away and hid my smile until I got back down the tunnel a ways. This was a great bunch; seemed like every one of them was screwball as hell; but it was the kind of screwball I liked. Swell guys.

In the stope where the Finn was working I almost had to crawl on my hands and knees. It was one of those veins that lay down on you instead of being vertical. The Finn was working alone, drilling on the roof. You couldn't set up a stoper in a place like that, and after the shot it was so steep the ore just slid down the chute. Powder fumes stung my throat and bit at my nostrils; they never got out of this stope, it was too steep and the fumes rise.

His hammer made so much noise in the small space that it pounded on my ear drums, actually seemed to make my brain throb. There he was all right, stripped to the waist. Sweat was running down his back in little streams that cut clean places through the dirt, following the creases between the huge muscles, exactly like a creek goes through the lowest land. He was holding that sixty-five pound hammer almost above his head, the handles against his chest. The merciless pound of the thing was making all of his muscles dance and jump, sort of individually. His great back showed every muscle, jerking in rhythm to the recoil of the hammer, and each set of muscles in his heavy arms were dancing. The steel was boring in and, as it ate its way into that rock, a little stream of water, carrying slate colored mud, trickled down from the hole.

When he saw my light he shut off the air, but just stood there, one hand on the hammer to hold it and the steel in the hole. He looked at me, gasping for breath, and wiped some of the sweat off his face which was plastered and smeared with dirt and sweat.

"Are you going to get your round in?" I asked.

He spat, thickly, and said, "Yah," and turned on the air.

Exactly a month before he had drawn his pay check and gone to town. Reports had come in that he was drinking heavily, from a quart to two quarts a day. Running out of money is what must have sobered him up and he came back. Because he was such a good man the boss had hired him back. At breakfast I watched him curiously. He had eaten nothing, simply drank about eight cups of coffee. Yet here he was, sick, nothing on his stomach, the first day after a month's bad drunk—and taking it.

I was almost afraid to go down and see Cousin Jack,[18] because if he were still having trouble he might quit, and he was another exceptionally good man. He was working in some more of the damnably hard rock and besides that had been trying to repair his hammer which had broken. Yesterday I had got some parts by parcel post and had given them to him this morning.

As I got close, I sort of sneaked up on him; if things were too bad I was going to turn around and not let him see me. There he was, all right. No holes in the face, and I knew his hammer hadn't been working all day. He was on his knees, swearing to himself. Wrenches and extra parts were scattered on the steel muck plate. When he had first come to work, it had been hard for me to understand his ungodly gibberish. It wasn't Welsh and it wasn't Cockney—almost like monkey talk—but I had got used to it. He was doing a first class job of profanity; he was really good at it, and I had learned a lot from him.

Suddenly he picked that hammer up in both hands and held it away from him, then laid it down, almost reverently. Folding his hands and holding them in front of him he bowed his head, and said:

"Oh, God, if there is a God, please come down and help this poor ignorant miner—and don't send your son, Jesus Christ, because this ain't no place for a boy. Amen."

Notes

1. Given the description here, it's likely that the narrator is referring to the building where copper ore is "stamped" or "crushed" to prepare it for the next early phase in extraction which is called "dressing." Also called a "stamp mill" in more recent mining parlance. Paul W. Thrush, *A Dictionary of Mining, Mineral, and Related Terms* (Chicago: Maclean Hunter, 1990), 349, 1066.

2. As explained contextually, this is a mechanical sorter for separating the larger pieces of ore, averaging around six inches, from the powdery material. Powder may or may not have contained copper so it was not discarded. However, the extraction process for the fine material differed from that of the large chunks of ore so it was processed

differently. American Geological Institute, *Dictionary of Mining, Mineral, and Related Terms* (Alexandria, VA: American Geological Institute in Cooperation with the Society for Mining, Metallurgy, and Exploration, Inc., 1997), 513; Thrush, *Dictionary*, 247.

3. The area containing the "floatation cells" where yet another method of material differentiation took place at the mine. The "floatation" process involved the exploitation of differing buoyancies among the various particles via the use of chemical additives that reduced the surface tension of the water in the tank allowing it to foam easily. The foam would then incorporate the desired material and the waste materials would descend. Chemical analysis, or "titrating," would then be employed to measure for the desired chemical outcome. Finally, the froth would be transported via "launders" out of the cells and onto the next stage in refining. American Geological Institute, *Dictionary*, 213, 305; Thrush, *Dictionary*, 444.

4. At the bottom of the subsurface mining crew pecking order, the mucker's task was to shovel "muck," or nonusable mining debris, and also harvestable ore into "mine cars." American Geological Institute, *Dictionary*, 358; Thrush, *Dictionary*, 732.

5. A gold separating apparatus in which pebbles are blown across "riffles" on the "riffle board," via a "bellows," and are simultaneously agitated so as to separate and determine the presence of gold. Thrush, *Dictionary*, 359.

6. A Gold Rush term for property that is thought to contain precious metals. Stuart Berg Flexner, *I Hear America Talking* (New York: Van Nostrand Reinhold, 1976), 174.

7. A wooden support structure at the opening of a mine tunnel. American Geological Institute, *Dictionary*, 112.

8. See "Mules Ain't Jackasses" in this volume.

9. Coarse drilling material used to begin the boring process. American Geological Institute, *Dictionary*, 535.

10. Having the sense of being an annoying surrogate for the mine boss; a minion, or tattletale. Eric Partrige, *A Concise Dictionary of Slang and Unconventional English* (New York: Macmillan, 1990), 623; Harold Wentworth and Stuart Berg Flexner, *Dictionary of American Slang* (New York: Crowell, 1960), 523.

11. A mine worker whose job was to inspect ore and quantify its quality and potential market price. Thrush, *Dictionary*, 57.

12. A working "vein" or sometimes, more generally, the room containing active mining planes. American Geological Institute, *Dictionary*, 541.

13. A miner's helper whose job was to perform various support tasks such as filling and moving mine cars, to carry support lumber, and to put ore onto sorting machines and conveyor belts. Thrush, *Dictionary*, 1157.

14. Mining assistant not involved in actual ore extrication. American Geological Institute, *Dictionary*, 500.

15. Flammable mineral materials. Thrush, *Dictionary*, 880.

16. Ibid., 542. Ore with rich mineral content.

17. Also called "galenite," cube-shaped crystals of the mineral "galena." American Geological Institute, *Dictionary*, 228.

18. A miner from Cornwall, England. American Geological Institute, *Dictionary*, 130; Thrush, *Dictionary*, 273.

GREEDY-GUT GUS, THE CAR TOAD

Jack Conroy

There's nobody better at hogging and cheating than a piece-working[1] car toad[2] when he's cut from a selfish pattern. He'd steal the pennies off his poor old dead grandmother's eyes or acorns from a blind sow[3] if it'd put a deemer[4] extra on his time slip at whistling time. He sashays around the livelong day like a blind dog in a meatshop, hollering for lumber jacks and bolt house boys. And if he leaves his box car for one minute, some creeper may come sneaking up and cabbage[5] onto castings or nails or bolts or siding or flooring or sills or drawbars or coupling springs he needs for his own job.

Car toads have lungs like glassblowers. They come by that bellowing like a bull, natural; they shake the slats over their cradles with their bass voices before their navel cords are clipped loose. It's worth traveling miles and paying a pretty piece to see and hear those leather-lunged rascals standing by their cars and yelling from one end of the yards to the other:

"Lumber jack! Double track!

Oughta been here and half way back!"

***

"That lumber jack wasn't hardly out of his didies when he started out after my roofing, but he'll hava a beard long enough to play Sandy Claus with before he gets back. You have to drive a stake in the ground to see whether he's moving at all or not."

"Every time he takes one step forward he slips back two. I wish to God he'd turn around and start this way so's he'd get there hindside before."

Boys, I'm here to say and state that that piece-working merry-go-round will make a man slap his own dear baby brother square in the mouth and pick his pockets or steal his sugartitty[6] when he ain't looking. It's dog eat dog and the devil take the hindmost. A man had better get him a tin bill and pick horse apples with the chickens. He'd better let somebody punch out his eyes and get him some blue glasses and a cup and a sign "Please Help the Blind" and sit on a corner the rest of his natural days.

"Come on, Sleepin' Jesus! Come and see me! Come and see me! I miss you so and it's been, oh, so long since we said goodbye."

That's the way a piece-working car toad has to holler at the lumber hustlers all day long if he wants to keep sow tits[7] and hominy on the table and the seat in his pants.

Greedy-Gut Gus was born a twin, but he soon rooted the other one away till it died of starvation before it had a chance to cut a tooth. The old man got tired of Gus eating him out of house and home, so he put him out in a pen with the hogs. Gentlemen, ladies, and little children, I'm here to swear on oath that it wasn't a month until Gus was fat as a butterball, but every pig that had the misfortune to be in that pen with him was so gaunt he had to lean twice to make a shadow.

If there ever was a born piece-working car toad, it was Gus. He could holler louder and sneak more than any other man in the yards. It got so the other car toads had to chain down everything loose about their cars when they left at night. They didn't dare go away for lunch, because by the time they came back Gus would have packed off everything but the rails the car had stood on.

Gus learned how to skimp his work, too. This can be done by putting a whole side on a car with only one nail holding all the boards or by not tightening nuts on drawbar bolts or leaving the nuts off altogether. You can leave an old journal brass in the journal box and put fresh dope around it and get paid for putting in a new one. Of course, it may run a hot box and throw the truck off the rails and play glory hallelujah with a whole train and send the crew to Kingdom Come, but Gus never bothered his head about that. Just so he was smart enough to make the inspectors believe he was doing the work right.

A man can't do wrong and get by for always. A dog never run so fast that his tail didn't follow close behind. There came a time when Greedy Gus was in too much of a hurry to go after a good jack, and in too much of a hurry to put tripods under the car after he had jacked it up with a condemned jack that always slipped its cogs. The jack slipped, the car came down—boom!, and splat! went Gus. It was the end of Greedy-Gut Gus's piece-working on this earth.

When the Devil saw Greedy-Gut Gus coming in with his tool box, he said: "You're just the man I need to keep my Central of Hell Railroad rolling stock in tiptop shape. I'll make you king of all the car toads in hell. No piece-work here, though. You may not like that, being born and raised to it, and you won't get retired on a pension, either. You're signed up for me from now on."

Well, friends, it went all right for a few million years. Gus was supposed to keep in good shape all the coal cars on the line running from the coal mines to the fiery furnaces that run three shifts a day to keep the temperature at frying heat.

Then Gus's old piece-working habits got the best of him, and he started to skimping and robbing Peter to pay Paul. He'd take castings and wheels off one car and put them on another. He did his nailing and bolting so slipshod that the cars got to falling to pieces all along the right of way, and the shovelers were leaning on their shovels and the fires smouldering low. The first cool breeze in seventeen hundred and eighty-nine trillion centuries sprang up in the southeast corner of the northeast section of hell and started blowing pretty strong on the graying cinders. It worried the Devil half crazy. You can't have a first-class hell without plenty of heat.

Greedy-Gut Gus got his time. He isn't going to be a car toad for all eternity after all. The Devil just couldn't put up with a man that has been spoiled by the piece-work system. Pretty soon a car toad who had been a day worker turned in his checks on the Baltimore and Ohio, and he was too wicked a man for any place but down below. He's a man that always took his time, being a day worker, and, taking his time, he does a good job of it. He'll hold the job from now on and the fires will roar and burn while Gus shovels in that coal forevermore.

Notes

1. Refers to a compensation system most commonly used in the textile industry, but also other industries such as the railroads. In this arrangement, employees were paid according to the actual number of objects they produced as opposed to receiving an hourly wage. In "Greedy-Gut Gus, the Car Toad," the pay was based on the number of railroad cars maintained or repaired. The practice of paying workers by the "piece" was a major source of labor disputes, especially in the 1930s, because it didn't take into account employee exhaustion or injuries sustained on the job. Adding to the difficulty of working under this approach, employers tended to lower the rates paid per piece if workers became faster at their jobs. Carl E. Van Horn and Herbert A. Schaffner, *Work in America: An Encyclopedia of History, Policy, and Society* (Santa Barbara, CA: ABC-CLIO, 2003), 433–34.
2. Slang for a railway employee whose primary responsibility is to repair or assess train cars. Harold Wentworth and Stuart Berg Flexner, *Dictionary of American Slang* (New York: Crowell, 1960), 89.

3. A metaphor for a person's selfishness and contemptibility. Peter R. Wilkinson, *Thesaurus of Traditional English Metaphors* (New York: Routledge, 2002), 345.

4. Conroy's annotation: "dime."

5. Conroy's annotation: "seize, or take possession of."

6. Or "sugar tit," meaning a dearly prized article; something highly valued by its owner. Eric Partrige, *A Concise Dictionary of Slang and Unconventional English* (New York: Macmillan, 1990), 630.

7. Or "sow-belly," 1920s and '30s readers would have understood this to mean "bacon" or "salt pork." Wentworth and Flexner, *Dictionary*, 505.

SAN FRANCISCO LONGSHORE GANG

Sam Kutnick (California)

Dispatched from the union hall, he strides along the Embarcadero, hands deep in his pockets against the cold, sleep clearing from his eyes. From the Bay hidden by the great gaunt warehouse comes the moaning of the foghorns, and instinctively his ears identify the pitch that denotes the ferry boat, the hoarse cry of the tug, the plaint of the freighter, the imperious call of the luxury liner.

At one moment the asphalt-and-cobblestoned street is silent; the next, the work day has begun, and the area is filled with wharf-bound vehicles—darting automobiles, low-slung heavy-duty trucks whose bellies miraculously escape plowing the cobblestones, curiously constructed lumber-carriers that ride on stilts high above the animated traffic.

The sidewalk, too, has its flowing passage, the tide running in single direction, fanning out to the piers. Longshoremen in their dark Frisco jeans, their cargo hooks arching from back pockets, move quickly to their places of labor. To the rumble and roar of traffic is added the murmur of their voices, the scrape of their heavy shoes. They call, "Hi-ya, Johnny, what's doin'?" And he nods and answers, a smile glinting on his face.

He walks effortlessly, his feet never quite forgetting their past life at sea. They neither fall blankly, as does a farmer's, nor seek for purchase like a mountaineer's. Intuitively they are prepared for the ground to swell and buckle, to heave and fall as though to a restless sea, and they reach for the earth, rather than a drop of their own weight with the delicate unpremeditated caution of a cat, ready to adapt themselves to any circumstance. The ground, however, remains stationary, firm. He is not aware that his feet have been thinking, remembering.

He turns into a warehouse whose farther end is lost in a haze. Naked girders rise to support the roof, and here and there stiff-ribbed steel doors are open, revealing the rusty sides of a berthed ship or a strip of murky water. He moves past neatly stacked piles of cased fruit, sacks of flour pyramided on heavy paper, sleeping jitneys,[1] inanimate hand trucks. On the wharf edge he joins the longshore gangs. The vessel which they are to work, looming above them against a background of gray sky and squat warehouse, is being nosed into the slip by a tugboat. A seaman high in the bows of the ship lets go a heaving line. It snakes through the air, the weighted monkey's fist carrying to Johnny's feet. He scoops it up. His comrades lending a hand, he hauls in the wet heavy mooring line and makes fast to a pier bitt.[2] Deft hands quickly secure the stern lines, and soon, to the groaning of winches and the cries of the ship's officers, the freighter is snubbed to the dock. It is a matter of moments before the tugboat is gone, the ratguards[3] in place, the gangway lashed down. Heavy nets are slung into position, spanning the narrow corridor of water between the sides of the ship and the pier against the possibility of spilled cargo. The gangs, one to each hold, take their places.

They begin with the rigging of the gear. It is a collective effort, each man knowing his part. No orders from the gang boss are necessary. Scrambling over the deck, the longshoremen plunge into a jungle of lines whose number and position would baffle any but the initiated. Each has a name and a purpose, and unerringly the proper ones are selected, slackened away, hauled tight, made fast. Quickly the yardarm[4] is winged out over the dock and the midship boom[5] over the hatch. At the foremast Ross Willoughby, a Negro with bunched muscles and a skin as fine as settled soot, stops off a line and makes it secure to its cleat.

The sixteen men composing the gang find their stations. Johnny takes his "trick"[6] at the winches while Alimony Jones, his relief man, stands by in the role of hatch-tender. Of the remaining thirteen, seven descend to the dock, two working under the hook and five disappearing in the warehouse to prepare the loads. The gang boss, or foreman, and the half-dozen hold men remain aboard. The canvases with which the hatch is battened down are removed, then the wooden hatch covers. There remain only the "strongbacks" to prevent free access to the hold. These steel girders are far too heavy to be lifted by hand, and machinery is utilized.

Johnny is seated between the twin winches overlooking the hatch, a lever at either hand. He tests them gingerly. The released steam, controlled by his touch, sends the winch barrels spinning madly, the wires coiling and uncoiling to the clatter of the engines. Satisfied, he nods. Alimony Jones secures the "blacksmith"—a heavy hook joining the wire falls, or runners, dropping from the booms to one of the strongbacks. With a single motion Johnny presses down on both levers. The girder swings free of its sockets, and guided by quick hands, clears the hatch combings.[7] In rapid succession the strongbacks, steel girders, are lowered to rest against a bulkhead, and soon the hold is ready to receive its cargo: refined sugar for Rio, fabricated steel for B.A.,[8] dried and canned fruit for Bahia and Rosario, bone meal for Santos, rice and beans for the islands of the Caribbean.

The six hold men disappear below decks, lash a cluster light fast to dissipate the brawling shadows, and prepare for the incoming freightage. First they "dunnage the skin"—build a platform of loose boards on the bottom of the hold. The floor of planks, or dunnage, arranged on a base of crosspieces, is so constructed as to allow water seeping into the hold to escape freely to the scuppers[9] without damage to the cargo. Sweat boards lining the bulkheads are adjusted; if here and there is one missing or broken, it is replaced; and at a signal from a man below, relayed by Alimony Jones leaning over the hatch combing, the winches clatter into action.

A steady slanting rain begins to fall as the loading of the one-and-one-half-ton T-beams begins. Because of their cumbersome length and dead weight this calls for delicate judgment, lightning reaction, and superb confidence. A moment's hesitation may result in a crushed skull, a broken back. Poor judgment in the "placing" of a load adds incalculably to the labor of those in the hold, for upon the winch driver depends the distance into the wings the men will have to pack the cargo. Johnny can scarcely distinguish the figures of the men fifty feet beneath him, in the mist raised by the rain. Yet so certain is his technique that with a single unfaltering motion he swings a T-beam aboard and lowers steadily away. Simultaneously the winch levers cut off the steam. The length of steel hovers a few feet above the skin of the hold. The longshoremen push at the dangling weight, the hatch-tender gives the all-clear signal, and the load is dropped into position.

It is noon, and the men "hang the hook" for the lunch hour. Some have brought their food in dinner pails; others, Johnny included, walk slowly through the warehouse to the near-by coffee joint. There is little conversation. They eat with a solid grinding of jaws and take great swallows of steaming coffee. Their appetites at length gratified, they glance at the clock over the pie counter, idly search cavities with toothpicks, or light up cigarettes. They begin to talk. In his role as union gang-steward Johnny listens to one of the men air a grievance and agrees to take it up with the dock superintendent. Ross Willoughby discusses the defense program with Olie Olson, a rugged, fair-haired Swede, and they wonder how it will affect organized labor. Alimony Jones recounts a story about an heiress. It is less humorous than bawdy, but Johnny laughs because in laughter there is relaxation.

"How long you figure it'll take to stuff her?" someone asks, referring to the ship.

"Couple of days, on the nose," Johnny estimates.

Bill Malotti, a young Italian, greets him from across the tables, and the pair walk into the warehouse together. "Riding the winches?" Bill questions, and to

Johnny's nod he grins happily, saying, "I got me a sitting down job, running a jitney."

"How you like?"

"I never got me calluses there before."

By late afternoon a layer of beams covers the bottom of the hold in parallel rows. The winches are silent to allow the men to top the lines of fabricated steel with heavy dunnage. This serves a twofold purpose: it provides steady footing for the longshoremen and a solid roof to prevent the beams from being pressed out of shape, over a long voyage, by the tons of cargo resting upon them.

Inside the warehouse Bill Malotti sends his jitney, a miniature gasoline auto, scurrying to the mountain of sacked goods. Longshoremen are loading small flat trucks with 100-pound gunnysacks of blood meal. Deftly he swings his jitney about, and like a railroad engine backing into a boxcar, maneuvers into place: without leaving his seat he couples the flat truck to the jitney and trundles the load to the side of the ship. The sacks have been pyramided on rope slings, fifteen to a sling, and with the "blacksmith" hovering just overhead, the hookmen make fast. The winches rumble remonstratively, the 1500 pounds are whisked into the air and devoured by the ship, to be digested by the cargo-handlers below. So the loading continues under a steady downpour.

The next morning work is resumed. Now, however, the somber sky is riven. A pale sun gradually goes golden and Johnny smiles with pleasure. He strips off his lumberjacket, and finding his perch between the winches, rolls up the sleeves of his hickory shirt. His bare arms are tattooed with voluptuous figures that squirm and cavort to the play of his muscles. The gang is still loading blood meal. From it rises the stomach twisting exhalation of the slaughter house. A fine heavy dust seeps from the gunnysacks to swirl in clouds that irritate the eyes and burn the throat.

Alimony Jones calls, referring to the Japanese vessels that take on shipment after shipment of bone and blood meal, "Like one of them hoodoo marus, huh?" "Maru" is Japanese for ship.

The thick dust is worse than the previous day's rain. Johnny can scarcely see down to 'tween decks, let alone to the lower hold, and must depend entirely on the signals of the hatch-tender who, roving starboard and port, forward and aft, is in the best position to determine what is taking place below. Though he cannot see them, Johnny visualizes the activities of the men unloading. In his imagination, he watches their powder-sprayed figures, hears their chocked curses as they stow the sacks in the artificial gloom, and he chokes and curses with them.

He is relieved at the winches by Alimony Jones, and takes his place at the hatch-combings. A cigarette dangles from his mouth. He draws a deep breath of clean air as he looks about him. The well deck is littered with debris: broken dunnage, hatch-covers, chains, snarled lines, and ship's muck. The buff paint on the bulkheads contrasts sharply with the black of the steel plates underfoot. On a stage slung over the offshore side of the vessel two sailors chip and scrape the rust blisters, spotting the wounds with red lead. A convoy of mewing gulls rises and falls to the slight swell of the oil-streaked waters just beyond, and high above rears the dirty white of the ship's superstructure. In the distance grows a forest of masts flying the pennants of half the world.

Once again Johnny is at the winches. The sacks of bone and blood meal have been loaded and papered off to keep the smell from fouling the rest of the shipment. Canvas slings are substituted for the rope slings, for sacked sugar and flour are being made ready on the wharf and these need gentler handling. Down in the hold they are stowed in alternate layers, as a mason lays bricks, the sack above binding the one below in such fashion that only the most violent of seas will disturb them. Sling after sling plunges into the depths, and the longshoremen sweat and grunt as they lift the 125-pound sacks over their heads and flip them into position.

Johnny plays on the winch levers like a virtuoso on his piano keys. In his fingers rests the strength of a thousand men. The wire "guys" answering the rush of steam released by his hands become the extension of those hands. With the power now invested in him so he can reach 100 feet onto the dock, snap up with ridiculous ease a load that would break the heart of a giant, plummet that load into the bowels of the vessel at break neck speed, and still deposit it on the bottom as gently as a feather: His face is solemn, intent, the eyes alert, the mouth slightly parted to allow the tongue to moisten the dry lips.

"Slack away on your midship guy!" the gang boss yells, but Johnny has already anticipated the order and the midship boom yawns over the section of the hold yet unoccupied. On the wharf the hookmen replace the canvas slings with chine hooks, metal clamps extending from short steel wires. The chines, utilized in the style of an iceman's tongs, are clamped over the lips of a quarter-ton oil drum, and the iron barrels, four at a time, are hoisted for the journey from shore to ship. In the hold one long row is fitted into the hollows of the other.

The packing of light goods commences. The chine hooks are replaced by a bridle, a steel triangle from which drop four short reins that hook onto a board sling, a wooden platform about the size of the ordinary desk top. On this is loaded a miscellany of dry goods: fiber-board boxes, paper cartoons, wire crates. Swung inboard they are dropped down to the square below the hatch opening, trundled into the wings, and with the longshoremen making use of their cargo hooks, stowed neatly away.

As the last of odds and ends are being bedded, a derrick barge comes alongside the freighter under its own power. An iron framework not unlike the tower of an oil well, but webbed for heavy work, rises from the flat of the massive scow. The enormous booms dwarf those of the ship. The deck is strewn with battered drums, rusty machinery, a lifeboat showing two inches of rainwater and a single oar, and snarled stern lines. The barge is moored to the freighter, and the most exacting of jobs begins. An eight-ton dynamo[10] is to be transferred from the barge to the ship. The ship's officers gather on the deck. The first mate hovers near the hatch combing, while the skipper, in baggy trousers and a visored "high-pressure" cap, looks down from the bridge.

Everything is in readiness. The barge engineer sits at his winches. His signalman climbs nimbly from scow to ship and takes his stand near the hatch, a whistle ready in his mouth. The freighter's engines are silent as the barge winches rumble to life. The dynamo rises with stately grace to a distance of seventy feet above the scow. Slowly it is swung over the ship. The momentum causes the 16,000 pounds to sway perilously. The thin boom trembles and the guy wires sing. All faces are tilted to the sky. It seems an eternity before the pull of gravity steadies the dynamo. The barge engineer cautiously presses his lever, and with infinite care the tremendous load begins its descent.

To save the valuable time it would take to move the ship's booms out of the way, the engineer attempts to lower the dynamo clear of the guy wires. It is a ticklish proposition. The signalman whistles impatiently. But no, the way is barred. The dynamo is raised, once more to be dropped. And yet again. Still the center of the hatch cannot be found. The eight tons of dead weight begin to swing anew and the engineer dares not lower away lest the idle ship's gear be fouled.

The gang boss moves to the hatch, calling to the longshoremen standing by 'tween decks, "Heads Up! Look alive there!" Suddenly the barge wire slips. The cable drops a mere three feet, is jerked up short, its strands groaning to the strain of the rocking dynamo. And the dynamo, brushing the chest of the gang boss, sends him flying across the deck. A couple of men leap to his aid. He has only been touched in passing, grazed, yet when he opens his mouth, gasping for air, bubbles of crimson-flaked foam tremble on his lips. His chest is crushed. Quickly he is handed down the gangway to the warehouse, where a private car is commandeered to rush him to the emergency hospital.

The 16,000 pounds of destruction still dangle malevolently overhead. If the gang boss had been killed outright the men would have knocked off for the rest of the watch. But he is still alive, so work continues. The men curse angrily, their faces grim and vindictive. Not that it is the gang boss's fault; a wire cable fouled on the winch drum is the cause of the accident. But the victim might have been any one of themselves, and thinking of their homes and children, they curse savagely as they turn to their uncompleted task. There is no time for sympathy—the ship must be loaded.

Johnny takes command of the gang. He addresses the signalman with a flow of words. The man's face shrivels with thought. His eyes glance upward to follow the trend of the monologue, and his head shakes dubiously. Johnny's words become a torrent, and under its influence the signalman now reluctantly nods. Several blasts of the whistle direct the dynamo higher aloft. The boom is coaxed farther inshore and once again the tons of metal endeavor the descent. The path now lies through the tangle of wires rather than outside them. With breathless caution the monstrous weight settles. The most delicate of maneuvering is required. A runner is scraped, cleared. Another. At length, to the almost audible sigh of all within sight, the dynamo is devoured by the hatch. No sooner has it found its site than Chips, the ship's carpenter, "shores" it up under the watchful eyes of the mate. This anchoring of the dynamo is imperative; 16,000 pounds on the loose is capable not only of crushing a cargo into kindling, but even, in a choppy sea, of smashing through the side of the vessel.

The holds are full to bursting. Quickly the strongbacks are slipped into their notches, the hatch-covers returned to their original positions, and the hatch itself battened down. The longshoremen retreat to the dock. The cargo nets are retrieved, the gangway lifted and secured, and the lines let go. As the snorting tugboat backs the freighter into the stream the seamen begin cradling the booms.

The men on the wharf disperse. Johnny alone remains, leaning over a salt-blackened piling. A moment's sadness fills him as he watches the vessel pull away. With the suggestion of a sigh he turns toward the dock telephone. He makes two calls, one to the union reporting the accident, and another to his wife, explaining that he will be late. Then he blows himself to a taxi, and lighting a smoke, says, "Emergency hospital, brother. Step on it, huh?"

Notes

1. Transport vehicles. Harold Wentworth and Stuart Berg Flexner, *Dictionary of American Slang* (New York: Crowell, 1960), 292.

2. An upright stanchion or cleat used for securing boats to the pier. Deborah W. Cutler

and Thomas J. Cutler, *Dictionary of Naval Terms* (Annapolis, MD: Naval Institute Press, 2005), 188, 222.

3. Round steel apparatus used to prevent rats from climbing up the ship's "hawsers" (ropes securing the ship to the pier). "Rope Works Ship's Rat Guard," *Popular Science*, February, 1934: 47.

4. The outmost parts of a "yard." These lateral, wooden beams often protrude beyond the span of the ship's hull and bear the sails of a "square-rigged" ship. Cutler and Cutler, *Dictionary*, 208.

5. Ibid., 31. The bottom, wooden "spar" that attaches perpendicular to the "mast" and is maneuvered to control the direction of a sail.

6. See "Still Operator" in this volume.

7. Or "hatch coamings," these raised, rectangular-shaped frames protrude from the deck's lateral surface so as to provide water-tight housings for the hatches. Thomas Walton, *Present-Day Shipbuilding* (Philadelphia, PA: J. B. Lippincott Company, 1907), 138.

8. Abbreviation for Buenos Aires, Argentina.

9. Openings in the ship's hull above the plane of the deck for draining excess water from the surface. Cutler and Cutler, *Dictionary*, 192.

10. A machine that outputs electricity. Charles C. Hawkins and F. Wallis, *The Dynamo: Its Theory, Design, and Manufacture* (New York: Whittaker and Company, 1893), 2.

PART TWO: Selling the Public

TOBACCO AUCTIONEER

Leonard Rapport (North Carolina)

It's five minutes of eleven, the sun is giving the flat roof hell, sunspots are all over the floor under the sky-lights, and here inside the warehouse it's a hundred degrees. The sale is blocked, has been since the market[1] opened last week, and will continue to be for days; as much as you can see of the two acres of floor is covered with baskets of tobacco, and when you came in this morning the trucks and cars, loaded with tobacco, were lined up on the ramp, in the driveways, on the street, bumper to bumper, waiting to get in. Yet here you are, sitting on a pile of tobacco, drinking a Coca-Cola, waiting for five minutes to pass.

In a way you're glad of the stop, though you're not tired yet. But when you've had thirty years of selling tobacco you begin to feel the heat on your head, and the tobacco dust in your eyes and mouth and nose, and the concrete floor under your feet. It's a good thing you run to the skinny and not to the fat (you grin, thinking of Bob selling that South Georgia market and wonder how much he's sweated down; last year he lost thirty pounds); but Eastern Carolina in August is no picnic either, and you've wrung at least a quart of water from the handkerchief tied around your head. Now if this were only the little South Carolina market you were on a couple seasons back, where, after the first week's rush, you were getting through each day by noon and driving twenty miles to Myrtle Beach—

You look at your watch; Al North, the starter, looks at his, almost eleven, and you stand up. The buyers are lining up along the 721st basket of tobacco. Not that it carries that number but selling 360 piles an hour means that promptly at eleven o'clock you're starting on that basket and not the 722nd, for in that case you'd owe the tobacco board of trade a $25 dollar fine for exceeding the selling limit.[2] It's certainly nothing like it was five or six years ago when you'd have had at least a thousand piles sold by this time. There was one day when the house had hired an extra ticket maker, an extra bookman, and an extra clipman for you and you'd said,

219

"Watch my smoke, boys," and sold the house from wall to wall by noon—a house that was supposed to hold a sale until three o'clock. That was six or seven hundred piles an hour, you booked plenty of extra commission, for both yourself and the house, but it was too fast, and it wasn't fair to the farmer or the buyer. It's about right now, three-sixty or four hundred; four hundred's what you're really selling when you get to the three-sixty marker five or ten minutes before the hour like you did on this row.

The buyers are lined up across the baskets of tobacco, pulling out sample hands, turning to get a truer light, feeling, smelling. There's Carroll, Jones, and Mallory for the Big Three, Imperial's buyer, the new buyer for Export, buyers from the four large independents who are on this marker, and seven or eight pin-hookers.[3] "Let's go," says Al. "Nine dollars."

You pick it up. Nine dollahs nine dollah bid nine nine nine (You really make it more "nigh nigh nigh"; no man can sell tobacco fast and get in every syllable.) Some of the old boys, old when you were starting in thirty years ago, sort of talked bids. But that was the way they had started; some as courthouse or backwoods auctioneers, talking bids as if they were selling a piece of land. When the sales began speeding up they either dropped into a chant or dropped out of tobacco; a man can't be expected to sell three or four hundred piles of tobacco an hour and say, "Nine dollars, nine dollars, nine dollars and a quarter, nine dollars and a half, nine dollars and three quarters" and so on, selling a pile every eight or ten seconds. You have to do just what you're doing now—"nigh, nigh nigh anna wahta wahta wahta anna hoff hoff hoff an three ree ree"—which translates into nine dollars, nine dollars and a quarter, nine dollars and a half, nine dollars and three quarters—the starting bid being nine dollars a hundred weight (or nine cents a pound.)

"Three ree ree." Your eyes are going up and down the line, watching every pair of eyes, every pair of hands. You're holding that three-quarters, hunting the ten dollar bid. Eight seconds ago Keeney, one of the speculators, had given a little nod that meant he would take the nine dollar price that Al North had set on the pile as an opener. You'd taken Keeney's bid up the line, back down, and then had caught a wink from Carroll that upped it a notch to nine and a quarter. Then Al had kicked your ankle close to the basket where nobody could see, and you had taken it up another notch, nine and a half. You had gone back to Carroll, got his wink again, had gone to nine and three quarters, had looked at Keeney, nothing there, no more kicks from Al, up the line once and down, all done, and sold at nine and three quarters to Carroll.

That had taken ten seconds, a second or two more than most piles. You'd started moving at the first bid, a kind of sideways, backward shuffle, shifting your

weight from one foot to another in rhythm with the chant; the steps take you just
one basket length each sale. Ahead, a boy is pulling hands out at random from the
basket of tobacco and spreading them on top; but the buyers like to draw their
own samples, so the neat piles are in pretty much of a mess after the line gets by.
Just ahead of you and on the same side of the baskets is Al North, the starter, who
is one of the partners in the warehouse. Now Al gets the starting bid on a second pile. "Twenty. Twenty dollars gentlemen, for this good lemon leaf;[4] dandy
tobacco, gentlemen, dandy tobacco." You slap your hands together like a pistol
shot, a trick picked up years ago to keep the sale alive. "Twenty dollah, bid twenny
wenny wenny wenny" up the line, back down, catch Jones' eye inquiringly, he
was buying this type yesterday; Jones shakes his head a fraction of an inch, still
no bid, so drop it down to nineteen and a half, no bid, nineteen, no bid, eighteen
and a half, eighteen, seventeen and a half, you look at the pile a fraction of a second and see it's good tobacco but poorly graded, seventeen and Al nudges you and
the house takes it at seventeen. They'll regrade it and maybe squeeze it in and get
it resold on the same sale. Out of the corner of your eye you see the farmer whose
pile you just sold and you recognize him; he brings a lot of business to this house
and you figure Al started the bid high because he wanted to show him he was trying to do what he could but they just weren't paying that much today.

The next pile belongs to the same man, about two hundred pounds of trashy
lugs with a few scattered hands of better tobacco. Four dollars and a quarter, half,
three, five dollars, and one of the speculators takes it at five and a quarter. "Sold
to the pinhooker," you kid. He grins but you know he doesn't like that name any
more than the rest of them do; "speculator," "rehandler," "remodeller," anything
but the name everybody calls them. He'll dress that pile up and make a few dollars
on the resale.

This pile looks like fair smoking leaf; Al starts it at fifteen, Carroll touches
himself and takes the bid; Jones looks at you and from fifteen years of facing each
other across millions of pounds of tobacco you know that look and carry the bid to
fifteen and a half (bids from one to fifteen go by quarters; from fifteen to twenty-
five by halves, and from twenty-five up by dollars, you couldn't—or wouldn't—cry
a fifteen and a quarter bid any more than you would say "I are.") You look at Mallory, the third of the Big Three buyers, and he crooks a finger toward himself and
now they are all bidding. Sixteen, and a half, seventeen, and a half, eighteen, and
a half, nineteen—that's Jones' bid. You've got a little problem. Jones, you're sure,
is through. Mallory seems to have a twenty-cent top on this type but Carroll has
been going higher; therefore you want to throw Mallory in the twenty-cent hole.
So you dodge Mallory for the half bid, catch Carroll's eye, he nods, and then you

go to Mallory as you figured he crooks his finger and you've got him in the twenty-cent hole, then back to Jones, but again, as you figured, he's through; so back to Carroll, and sure enough he nods and you've got a twenty and a half bid. You go back to Mallory but he's through. For a split second you consider catching a bid off the ceiling and picking Carroll, who is the youngest and greenest of the company buyers, but he might not bite so you decide against it. But you're pleased with the finesse of that particular sale; thirty years of hunting buyers' weak spots and having them hunt yours have taught you a few things.

Thirty years has meant a lot of buyers faced and a lot of tobacco sold. It has meant at least a dozen bright flue-cured[5] markets in North Carolina and a dozen more in South Carolina, Georgia, and Florida. It has meant flue-cured and dark-fired[6] markets in Virginia and burley and dark-fired in Kentucky and Tennessee. There was a time when you were catching three belts, starting in late July in Georgia, then to North Carolina in September, and ending up in February or March in Kentucky or Tennessee. Now you're satisfied to sell on the Eastern North Carolina belt for three months and finish up in the Kentucky burley. For six or seven months of that you're drawing between three and four thousand dollars.

It's hot, hotter than blazes, but you've got to keep pep in the sale, keep the buyers interested, keep things moving. Maybe in a minute you'll mix in a little talk—kid Jones about that flush he lost seventeen dollars on last night. You're not one of these auctioneers who like to mix in a lot of chatter but maybe it'll liven things up and get a few smiles on some of the faces. You listen to your own voice and it sounds all right, after awhile you'll rest it by changing the pitch a bit. Right now it's carrying forty or fifty feet and that's enough, it doesn't have to be heard all over the floor; you'll save that for four o'clock when you're coming down that last row. What you like is a musical voice, one with some life and clarity in it. You're a baritone like most auctioneers but you still like to hear a good tenor or bass. You remember, as a kid in a Virginia market town, hearing the auctioneers of that day, fine-looking, well-dressed men with authority and dignity. (You wonder how their dignity and starched collars would have held up at four hundred piles an hour under a South Georgia August sun; they never really got started in those days until about October and two hundred piles was fast selling.) You've heard some auctioneers in your time; Bodenheim singing out bids in his splendid tenor, Crenshaw coming down the floor sounding like a brass band, Col. Langhorne whose girl, Nancy, became Lady Astor, Herbert Baker, perhaps the greatest of them all. Even as you remember you've sold another pile of smoking leaf, Carroll and Mallory carrying the bids and Mallory taking it at nineteen. The circuit riders of both their companies were by this morning and you're pretty certain now that they must have left orders to buy heavy of this type.

Al starts another pile. "Twelve dollar bid," you begin. "This is good tobacco, gentlemen," rattles on Al. "Good Pitt County bright, nobody in Pitt raises prettier tobacco or girls than does Dan Jamerson and this is some of Dan's leaf. And here's one of Dan's little girls who's going to take him home the money, so bid up." Across the baskets, behind the buyers, a seventeen-year-old girl smiles and blushes. You remember bolder girls who stood on their tobacco and gave the successful buyer a kiss. That didn't look good to outsiders and you're glad it's about done away with. Some of the buyers turn to smile at the girl. You pop your hands, lean toward the sweating buyers (if you didn't know them personally you could still tell the big Three by the Camel, Chesterfield, and Lucky packs showing through the pockets of their wet shirts), and reach your right hand toward each man as you turn toward him so that it looks like you almost pull that opening bid out of Imperial. "Twelve dollah bid tweh tweh tweh anna wahta (one of the pinhookers raises Imperial) wahta wahta wahta anna hoff (Mallory touches himself) hoff hoff, back to a wahta (Mallory has shaken his head; he was only hitching up his pants) wahta wahta again a hoff (Imperial comes back) hoff hoff ('Good tobacco, gentlemen,' says Al, 'let's help the little girl.') three ree (the pinhooker comes again) ree ree ree thir-teen dollar bid" (both Imperial and Jones look up; and you nod toward Jones and chant inquiringly at Imperial; he closes his eyes as if he is tired and you've got another bid) "anna wahta wahta wahta (up the line, try Jones, but he is already reaching into the next pile, down the line, all done), sold Imperial." You glance toward the girl and see that she's excited by the whole business, but you know that, like most of those whose tobacco you sell, although she heard every sound you have made and has followed your every gesture, to her, as to the rest, it's all gibberish. She won't know until she reads it on her tag that her two hundred and thirty-two pounds of lemon-colored primings sold at thirteen and one-quarter cents a pound.

It's now one minute after eleven o'clock. In this minute you have sold six piles of tobacco. You'll have to sell a little faster if you're to finish this three-sixty and still have a couple minutes for another Coca-Cola.

Notes

1. The narrator of "Tobacco Auctioneer" mentions the various markets he's worked where tobacco was grown and sold. Though the curing and grading of American tobaccos is highly-involved, the most important fact to keep in mind is that the dif-ferent types of "leaf" could only be grown in certain soils and, therefore, the tobacco industry had a distinctly regional demarcation schema. By the 1920s the cigarette had become the most popular tobacco product. Comprising a blend of "fillers" and "Bright Leaf," along with blends of "Burley" ("Kentucky Burley" is a variant men-

tioned here, but "White Burley" was used as well), the cigarette's popularity drove the pricing of these types of tobacco. Robert Heimann, *Tobacco and Americans* (New York: McGraw-Hill, 1960), 148, 220–22, 268.

2. Ibid., 167, 180–83, 227–30. Many of the markets established rules about how many "piles," or "baskets" could be sold in an hour. These were often literally just that— piles of tobacco arranged on the selling floor. According to Heimann, most tobacco auctioneers profited by quickly appraising (in not more than a few seconds), and often undercutting, the fair value of a pile. Therefore, a variety of rules were put in place, depending on the particulars of the regional market and the auction houses involved, about how much crop could be traded in a given period of time. As an example, auction houses were limited to somewhere around 300 piles per hour at the beginning of the twentieth century, By the 1930s, however, cooperative pooling of crops, and curing among farmers, had begun to significantly alter the nature of market rules. Also see W. F. Axton, *Tobacco and Kentucky* (Lexington, KY: University Press of Kentucky, 1975), 145.

3. Smaller tobacco re-sellers who, by keeping a watchful eye on market volume and pricing, bought low and sold high. These were often unscrupulous sorts who went out into the streets during busy market times and spread rumors among farmers about "overproduction" or various other price-lowering factors. The "pinhookers" then, capitalizing on farmers' anxieties and distrust of auction houses, would buy from these farmers at deeply discounted prices. Heimann, *Tobacco and Americans*, 181; Joseph C. Robert, *The Story of Tobacco in America* (New York: Alfred A. Knopf, 1952), 197.

4. Slang for "Bright Leaf" tobacco. The adjective "bright" and the "lemon leaf" moniker, come from the fact that these strains of tobacco become yellow in the fields due to sandy soil conditions. Heimann, *Tobacco and Americans*, 148.

5. Depending on the end product of a given type of tobacco and the desired flavor, whether it be for chewing, pipe-smoking, cigarettes, or otherwise, different methods were used to dry and flavor the leaf. "Flue-curing" became the dominant curing method for American cigarette tastes. As the name implies, "flue-curing" was achieved by heating and drying the leaf in "flues."
    Axton, *Tobacco and Kentucky*, 70; Heimann, *Tobacco and Americans*, 185.

6. Another method of preparing tobacco, "dark-firing" was performed primarily on the tobaccos of Western Kentucky. It imparted a heavy flavor to the "leaf" by means of smoking it over hickory wood. Axton, *Tobacco and Kentucky*, 70.

PAY DIRT

Isaac Schwartz (Ohio)

"*So you write* for a living?" the baker's flour-dusted hand held out the letter of recommendation I had brought.

"Sam's a good egg," he went on before I could reply. "Always helping people. All I said was: 'Sam, our bakers' association is planning one of them weeks—you know, like apple or safety week'—and he says he knows the right man and he sends you. He sure put the sugar on you in this letter. Been long in the writing trade?"

"Twenty years." I held out a sheaf of sample writings and catalogued clippings of publicity campaigns.

"Got you beat," the baker grinned. "Been baking 27 years. Funny thing; the day after I started I swore I'd quit—but here I am. This was my boss's shop."

His huge paw took the papers I offered. That hand impressed me. It had no wrist, the forearm melting evenly into the extremity. He turned the sheets over, reading the last one first.

"Lotta writing you done for the Progress League," he held up some of the clippings.

"They campaigned a new venture—needed new money," I explained, wondering when he'd get down to business.

"Did they?" He picked up the papers from his ample lap, at the same time rubbing the flour from his fingers on the apron.

"Promises," I replied. "The League was selling light and air—educational stuff. Philanthropists like to see substantial stuff for their money. Now your association," I was grateful for the lead he had given me, "you give the customers something they can take home—not a talk on civics."

"And it sticks to the ribs," he cut in. "Listen son," he leaned forward benignly. "You help us put on a big Eat More Bread Week and you'll have this job every year. It's our first week and lemme tell you, you've struck pay dirt."

"When is this week?" I asked.

"A whole month off—lots of time." He thrust my sample writings into my hand. "You'll find our association swell to get along with—"

"I'd like to meet your officers and members." It was plain he knew none of the amenities of the gentle art of public relations.

"Oh, they're leaving it all to me—I been president four times now. Between you and me, they're just a bunch of clucks that know only their own roost. I'm the only one that thinks up any ideas. Anyway, you couldn't meet the whole bunch—there's 150 bakers in the association."

At length we got down to the subject of finance; he said he had hoped to get by with about $100 for all promotional costs. When he heard my fee alone would be at least $150—just $1 per member for a whole month of promotional work—he guessed it might be arranged, but added that their rules did not permit spending more than $100 in any one month for "outside" activity.

"Now, what ideas have you got for me," he asked with finality.

"If you want a permanent annual feature I suggest you establish it as such—a kind of institute in the interest of good health."

He burst into boyish laughter.

"An institute—for dough mixers." The tears ran down his chubby cheeks. "Say my gang would never forgive me. Do you mean it?"

While he wiped the moisture from his face with a corner of his apron I took from my brief case the record of an institutional publicity campaign that involved many related problems. I moved my chair close to his. The selling point of the visit had arrived. The baker would have to be convinced with this assemblage of facts, or not at all.

Carefully I presented the possibilities of a successful demonstration of the indispensable nature of the baker's service. He was not selling bread alone, I pointed out, but contentment within the home. He conserved the health as well as the wealth of the family and the nation.

"Now, if your budget allowed it," I brought out an argument that usually amounted to half of the sale, "we might include some radio features—"

"You mean I'd be on the radio?" he straightened up.

"Just a possibility," I waved aside the welcome interruption. "We'll get the mayor to proclaim Eat More Bread Week. The school kids will compete with essays on baking. Some of the better women's clubs might be persuaded to include you or members of your association as speakers during the week. We'll stretch the program to include things besides bread. How about giving cakes to the editors of all the papers?"

"Great," he responded. "I'll get Bill Watson—he's the best cake baker in town, has the Sunshine Sweet Shoppe—he'll do anything I tell him."

He turned thoughtfully to me.

"Say, the layout you just give me—that's enough to run a whole institute, as you call it."

"It is the institute—the Better Baking Institute," I replied.

So he hired me to establish the Better Baking Institute and my pay was to be $175. I knew it meant a month of unusually strenuous work. At the same time, I thought, if the effort should succeed it might become a permanent enterprise.

Three busy, happy days of intensive research into the origin, development, improvement and mechanization of baking followed. I found the background of the subject fascinating and was in high hopes when things began to happen.

It started innocently enough. The bakers' president called me on the phone.

"Did you say that the women's club would get in on the Week?" He seemed eager for an affirmative reply. I gave it.

"Well, my old lady is treasurer of the Midweek Literary Circle and she wonders if you would help her write something for her to give on Bakers' Week."

I hesitated. Experience had taught me to hold down the campaign to the terms agreed upon. But the boss' wife—

"Happy to help," I lied.

This intrusion into the scheduled program meant more cramming but I managed to churn out a readable and not too erudite piece on the emancipation of woman from the bake-oven into the not too bright light nor very clear air of the whist club. The baker's wife thought it was deep and asked if I would like to meet her club.

"After we finish with Bakers' Week." I bargained, but she accepted it as a pledge.

In a moment of unguarded enterprise I had mentioned radio to the bakers' president. He had not forgotten it, and brought up the subject—with trimmings—at our next conference.

"The executive committee agreed with me it would be swell to have a radio piece about better bread during our week," he began. "They know it will cost something and they're leaving it up to me. What can we cook up for a radio program—something the people would like to hear?"

"You have less than three weeks to make such a program and I would advise against a rush job on the air." My worry was very real, but he refused to understand it.

"You've been hired to do a job for us," he shot back. "Even if we have to cut out something, let's give the boys a play for their money."

"But I'm all set for a big stunt with the mayor getting a cake from your association this week—even got the newspaper photographers lined up," I explained. "It takes a lot of talking to get such things done—and time, too."

"Don't the radio people work up the programs for you?" He was determined.

"They do and they don't," I answered. "They have to get basic material, just as I am doing for you on this week. If it is an entertainment affair, there is music to be arranged. And the writing of the script, rehearsing of players—you run into the time element all along. Most important, I am afraid you can't get a good time interval on such short notice."

"With nearly three weeks yet to go?" He was incredulous. "Now let's call up a station and find out what's what." He handed me the telephone directory.

We got a likely evening spot. A former reporter-associate in the commercial script division of the station assured me he would give his personal attention to the details, but agreed that an interview would be more helpful on such short notice than a play. My baker embroidered the suggestion.

"How about interviewing all the officers?" he asked. "I don't want he boys to think I am hogging the show."

My friend at the other end of the wire groaned.

"Tell him it will be bad enough if one is on the air," he suggested, but added hurriedly, "I'll figure out something—but not for more than five men. It's a ten minute thing and with a recording fore and aft of the program it will leave just about a minute and a quarter of patter for each."

A harrowing four days of advance interviewing with all members of the executive committee followed. Life histories, long, tedious yarns about great events in the "old" days before automatic firing of ovens made baking "kid's work." One member—the secretary—insisted on recalling a story of a live pig that had accidentally gotten into a batch of dough.

"This institute stuff is all o.k. for big shots," he said, "but our kind of people want something they can understand."

The second vice president agreed with him.

"How would this story be?" he suggested, and proceeded with a tale of a baker who paid a master craftsman 100 dollars to teach him the secret of fine bread-baking.

"And what was the secret?" I hurried him along.

"Why, don't forget to salt the dough," he chuckled amid the guffaws of his fellow-bakers.

I turned my notes and sample interviews over to my writer-friend of the radio station's staff.

"Good grief—do those bozos really intend to go on the air with such stuff and pay for it, too?" He was worried even more than I.

When I told him of the headache I had collected arguing them out of more incredible notions, he sympathized and offered to have one full rehearsal for my sake.

"Can they read?" he asked as an afterthought.

The presentation of the cake to the mayor was rendered unexpectedly difficult by the decision of the president to make a formal speech. The weather was bad at the time and this gave me an argument to use.

"If you appear in formal dress, you'll get nicely drenched just when you want to look your best," I pleaded.

"I said nothing about formal."

"But a speech of the kind you have in mind needs an appropriate setting and the mayor is a busy man and is always on the go—you might even embarrass His Honor by such a ceremony. Anyway, speeches are usually made by people dressed for the occasion," I concluded hopefully.

He compromised. If I would write a brief but "educated" little sentence or two to go with the cake, that would be satisfactory.

"Still, with the papers taking pictures of the thing, I should dress up," he sighed regretfully.

In general all my nice forethought, all my hard studying to establish the Better Baking Institute, were being scuttled. They had one argument, and a potent one: "You are being paid for it, so what difference does it make?"

The school superintendent was not cordial to the idea of "exploiting the children for commercial promotion" and told me so in plain Princetonese. I wondered during that interview how my baker would handle him and decided to bring up the boss to sell the idea of an essay contest on the subject of health as related to good bread, or vice versa.

My baker jumped at the chance, and the superintendent jumped when he heard the arguments.

"We've got this institute just to help the kids to be good citizens." The baker indignantly pounded the desk. "We're giving sets of swell books to the kids and to the schools that produce the best write-ups. If there's any charge connected with this—"

"None at all." The superintendent looked at me appealingly. "Our rules are strict on monetary considerations where such matters are concerned. The books will be very nice, I am sure. But on such short notice—I'm afraid the students have not had enough time for any research on the subject."

"Don't let that bother you, mister," the baker's brusqueness shocked even my news-hardened nerves. "We got a publicity man to do all that for you—he's head of the institute." The baker laughed loud and long.

To make the task easier, I carefully selected from the available material such academic morsels as the moppets' might digest on casual mastication. I recall slicing a chunk from the speech I had prepared for the baker's wife; another bit of filler came from the account given me by a member of the executive committee for use on the radio program; the rest was a bundle of odds and ends from government reports, department of labor statistics, and old-fashioned common sense, plus some random guesses. I washed my flour-coated hands of the essay venture then and there, leaving the superintendent and the bakers' president to argue the more intrinsic details.

But I was not to escape so easily. The treasurer's wife called me up.

"My little girl gets the best marks in school for language and history work," she began, and I braced myself for more trouble. "She wants to win this essay contest—you know, it ain't the books and stuff, but the child is proud of her record."

"I understand." I hung on the phone wearily, wondering whether any of my news releases on the Better Baking Institute read as badly in type as my thoughts of the moment.

"Please get me right on this," the treasurer's wife confided sweetly, "I don't want you to write the essay for her—just look it over and take out anything that don't read right. That's fair, isn't it?"

"Fair as Captain Kidd,"[2] I thought, but I mumbled agreement.

Came the big week. The speech at the Midweek Literary Circle, the radio interviews, the awards to the children for miles of essays on household economics ranging from killing bugs to repairing the plumbing with almost nothing about bread or the altruistic services of the baker. The papers printed my learned effusions on the "service" of the newly established "institute," and one editor (he got the biggest cake from the association) wrote a two-paragraph editorial on "The Sweet Things of Life." The mayor's proclamation, with its three "whereases" and concluding "therefore resolved," was impressively framed in the window of the bakers' association so that all might behold the triumph of service—and publicity.

I presented my bill for $175 to the bakers' president.

"Boy, you did swell." He signed the check with a flourish. "I got a surprise for you."

I was ready for anything.

"The association was tickled with all you did for us in starting our institute. They want you to do it for us again next year, just like this one. Now here's something from the boys—a grand cake by Bill Watson himself," and a great flourish indicated a two-foot gaudily decorated cake on a shelf.

It bore a neatly sugared legend:

"With best wishes, from the Better Baking Institute."

The bakers' president beamed.

"Didn't I tell you that you'd struck pay dirt?"

Notes

1. An archaic expression for a small child. Joseph T. Shipley, *The Origins of English Words* (Baltimore: Johns Hopkins, 2001), 258.

2. A fabled figure in maritime history. William Kidd, a Scottish seafarer, was tried and hanged for piracy in 1701. His trial is said to have been wildly unjust thus resulting in Kidd dying an honest man. Therefore, the speaker's tone here would have been sarcastic. Sir Cornelius Neale Dalton, *The Real Captain Kidd* (New York: Duffield, 1911), 195–99.

SLAPPY HOOPER, WORLD'S BIGGEST, FASTEST, AND BESTEST SIGN PAINTER

Jack Conroy

Slappy Hooper wasn't big because he was six-foot-nine and wide between the eyes, no more than because he weighed three hundred pounds without his cap on or his bucket in one hand and his brush in the other. It was just that there wasn't no job any too big for Slappy, and he never wanted a helper to mess around with.

Even when he was painting a high stack, he didn't want any rube[1] staggering and stumbling around the lines to his bosun's chair.[2] He knew too well that lots of times a helper can be more trouble than he's worth. He'll yawn and gape around, or send up the wrong color or the wrong brush, or he'll throw rocks at birds, or he'll make goo-goo eyes at dames passing by. Like as not, he'll foul the lines or pull the wrong one and send you butt over appetite to Kingdom Come.

At any rate, a helper keeps a man uneasy, and when a man's uneasy he ain't doing his best work. They ought to make it a penitentiary act for a helper "gapering, mopering, and attempting to gawk." Slappy said his life was too short to take a helper to raise up. He could let himself up and down as fast as a monkey could skin up a cocoanut tree or a cat lick its hind leg with its leg up and its tongue out. Anything Slappy wanted on the ground he could lasso with his special long and tough rawhide lariat and pull it up to where he was working.

Slappy done some big jobs in his day, and he done them right and fast. He says if there ever was a crime against nature it's this way they got here lately of blowing paint on with a spray gun like you was slaying cockroaches or bedbugs or pacifying a cow to keep the flies off her until she can get milked. Slappy liked to splash it on with a good old eight-inch brush, and he never was known to leave a brush lap or a hair on the surface when the job was finished. Slapping it on up and down or slapping it on crossways or anti-goggling[3] you couldn't tell the difference. It was all of a solid sheet.

With all these new inventions like smoke writing from airplanes and painting signs from a pounce[4] (even pictures they do that way), it's hard to appreciate an old timer like Slappy.

He used to get jobs of lettering advertising on the sky, and it didn't fade away in a minute like smoke that pours out of a plane and gets torn to pieces by the wind before you can hardly spell out what it says. It was all in pretty and fancy colors, too; and it'd stay right there for days if the weather was fair. Of course, birds would fly through it, and when it'd rain the colors would all run together—when the clouds rolled by, there'd be what looked like a rainbow, but it really was nothing but Slappy Hooper's skywriting all jumbled together. No man, woman, child, or beast, alive or dead, was ever able to invent waterproof sky paint. If it could have been done, Slappy would have done it.

His biggest job was for the Union Pacific Railroad, and stretched from one end of the line to the other. The only way you could read it all was to get on a through train and look out of the window and up at the sky all the time. Everybody got stiff necks, of course, so Slappy had the bright idea of getting Sloan's Liniment to pay him for a big sign right at the end of the Union Pacific sign.

Nobody ever did understand how Slappy managed to do the sky painting. The only thing people was sure of was that he used sky hooks[5] to hold up the scaffold. He used a long scaffold instead of the bosun's chair he used when he was painting smokestacks or church steeples. When he started in to fasten his sky-hooks, he'd rent a thousand-acre field and rope it off with barbed wire charged with electricity. He never let a living soul inside, but you could hear booming sounds like war times, and some folks figured he was firing his sky hooks out of a cannon and that they fastened on a cloud or some place too high for eyes to see. Anyways, after a while—if you took a spy glass—you could see Slappy's long scaffold raising up, up, up in the air and Slappy about as big as a spider squatting on it.

But that played out. Somehow, it wasn't that people didn't *like* his sky-painting any more, but the airplanes got to buzzing around as thick as flies around a molasses barrel and they was always fouling or cutting Slappy's lines, and he was always afraid one would run smack into him and dump over his scaffold and spill his paint, if nothing worse. Besides, he said, if advertisers was dumb enough to let a farting airplane take the place of an artist, it wasn't no skin off his behind. He could always wangle three squares a day and a pad at night by putting signs on windows for shopkeepers if he had to. If I can stay off public works,[6] I'll be satisfied, he thought to himself.

So *Slappy* said to hell with the *big* jobs. I'll just start painting smaller signs, but I'll make them so real and true to life that I can still be the fastest and bestest sign painter in the world, if I ain't the biggest any more.

He knew he could do it with one hand tied behind him and both eyes punched out. Some sign painters couldn't dot the letter "i" without a pounce to go by. It was enough to make a dog laugh to see some poor scissorsbill[7] wrastling around with a pounce, covered all over with chalk wet by sweat until he looked like a plaster of paris statue.

Then, like as not, they'd get a pounce too small for the wall or billboard they was working on. When it was all on there was a lot of blank space left over. The boss'd yell: "Well, well, Bright Eyes! Guess the only thing to do is fetch a letter stretcher!" If the pounce happened to be too big, it was every bit as bad. "A fine job, Michael Angelo," the boss'd holler, "except you'll have to mix the paint with alum so's it'll shrink enough to squeeze it in with a crowbar."

One of Slappy's first jobs after he took to billboard painting was a picture of a loaf of bread for a bakery. It would make you hungry just to look at it. That was the trouble. The birds begin to peck at it, and either they'd break their bills and starve to death because they didn't have anything left to peck with, or they'd just sit there perched on the top of the billboard trying to figure out what was the matter until they'd just keel over. Some of them'd break their necks when they dashed against the loaf, and others'd try to light on it and slip and break their necks on the ground. Either way, it was death on birds. The humane societies complained so much and so hard that Slappy had to paint the loaf out, and just leave the lettering.

He didn't like this a bit, though, because, as he often said, any monkey who can stand on his hind legs and hold anything in his fingers can make letters. The loaf of bread business sort of gave Slappy a black eye. People was afraid to hire him.

Finally, the Jimdandy Hot Blast Stove and Range Company hired him to do a sign for their newest model, showing a fire going good inside, the jacket cherry red, and heat pouring off in every which direction. In some ways it was the best job Slappy ever done. Right in middle of January of the coldest winter ever recorded by the Weather bureau, dandelions and weeds popped out of the ground on the little plot between the billboard and the sidewalk.

It was when the bums started making the place a hangout that the citizens and storekeepers of the neighborhood put in a kick. The hoboes drove a nail into the billboard so they could hang kettles and cans against the side of the heater and boiled their shave or boilcup[8] water. They pestered everybody in the neighborhood for meat and vegetables to make mulligan stews.[9] They found it more comfortable on the ground than in any flop house in the city, so they slept there, too. They ganged up on the sidewalk so that you couldn't push through, even to deliver the United States mails.

The company decided to hire a special watchman to shoo hoboes away, but this was a terrible expense. Not only that, but the watchman would get drowsy from the warmth, and no sooner did he let out a snore than the bums would come creeping back like old home week. Finally, the company got the idea of having Slappy make the stove a lot hotter to drive the bums clean away.

So he did. He changed the stove from a cherry red to a white hot, and made the heat waves a lot thicker.

This drove the bums across the street, but it also blistered the paint off all the automobiles parked at the curb. Then one day the frame building across the way began to smoke and then to blaze. The insurance company told the Jimdandy Hot Blast Stove and Range Company to jerk that billboard down and be quick about it, or they'd go to law.

Slappy says now he feels like locking up his keister[10] and throwing away the key. They don't want big sign painting and they don't want true-to-life sign painting, and he has to do one or the other or both or nothing at all.

Notes

1. A jeering term for a new, untrained, unskilled worker. It also implied a sort of hill-billy. See "greenhorn," in "The Type Louse" in this volume; Eric Partrige, *A Concise Dictionary of Slang and Unconventional English* (New York: Macmillan, 1990), 550.
2. Or "bos'n's chair." A seat or plank used in painting, construction, and logging that was suspended from cables or ropes for working on elevated job sites. Construction Confederation, *House Builder's Health and Safety* (Northampton, AU: Construction Industry Publications, 2008), 57; George Stenzel, Thomas A. Walbridge Jr., and J. Kenneth Pearce, *Logging and Pulpwood Production* (New York: John Wiley and Sons, 1985), 340.
3. Conroy's annotation: "Slantwise, or crooked."
4. Conroy's annotation: "A perforated paper outline or stencil for painters unable to do freehand work efficiently. Derived from the bag of chalk, or pounce, used to mark the outline on the billboard or sign."
5. See "'Snake'" Magee and the Rotary Boiler" in this volume.
6. Conroy's annotation: "It is the pride of many independent craftsmen and boomers that they have never been chained to a job on 'public works,' i.e., in a large factory with a time clock and deadening routine. To the freelancing artisans, going on 'public works' is a fate worse than death."

7. A doltish worker; a dupe. Harold Wentworth and Stuart Berg Flexner, *Dictionary of American Slang,* (New York: Crowell, 1960), 448.
8. Conroy's annotation: "Boiling of clothing to kill body lice."
9. An improvised, hobo stew made from readily accessible vegetables and meats. Wentworth and Flexner, *Dictionary,* 349.
10. Conroy's annotation: "Satchel, resembling a rigid suitcase, in which itinerant sign painters keep their work materials and often their clothing."

PART THREE: The Artists

JAZZ MUSIC: CHICAGO STYLE

Sam Ross (Illinois)

I don't think there is much I can tell you. You see, I'm considered an outcast by the boys, because I don't make a fetish out of the business. I quit it a long time ago, and really quit it. For years now I have not thought in terms of notes. I really quit the business and am doing all right now. Guys like Johnny Hammond[1] and so forth, they come up and want to interview me. I tell them point blank, "Listen, you guys are a bunch of phonies, trying to coin in on a form of music as critics which you know nothing about." I'm not interested in giving interviews. From a folk point of view, there are stories I could tell, so many I don't know where to begin. Jazz was played long before this craze about it came to being. Nobody made too big a fuss about it. There is nothing that is being done today that wasn't done by the boys in my band or by the New Orleans Rhythm Kings.[2] If you want to know, that outfit was the real influence on Chicago style. In fact the bands today aren't even playing as good or what my band was playing back in 1923 and up. Because we had Beiderbecke[3] in our band nobody has been able to touch him since. The other day I was down at Nick's in the village and Bobby Hackett, he plays just like Bix, almost a perfect imitator, came up to me and said, "Listen to me, will you, Dick, and tell me if I do anything that Bix didn't do." And I listened to him for some time and he did almost everything Bix did, but he wasn't as good, nor did he have Bix's originality. Bix was really a genius. He came from Davenport, Iowa. His father was some sort of a lumber contractor, pretty well off, and Bix didn't have much education. He was a tense frustrated guy, perhaps with homosexual tendencies which never really became active. You can feel his frustration and tightness many times when he plays. He was the kind of guy who would never send his clothes to a laundry. Never thought of it. He would throw off his stuff into a closet and leave them there and rummage through them for a clothes change and finally some guy in the band would get disgusted and send his clothes to the laundry. But he was a true artist. He had an infallible sense of values. He was the first guy I ever knew in the music business who appreciated the modern novel; his feeling for them was good and the points he would discuss and argue about were poignant. Sometimes we would go down to the art institute and although he knew nothing about painting, that is from books, he would always stop in front of the best paintings and point them out and admire them. If I remember right he was nuts about Picasso, and he liked a modern composer, I forget his name now. He used to play his music a lot on recording. It was colorful music. Bix had a fine feel for color tone on his horn too. He was doing things musically, along with some of the other boys in the band, without even being conscious of it, which Sibelius gets off in his symphonies, certain progressions. That's why I say that we were doing the same things which are being done today by Goodman and Shaw and Crosby, and even better, because the men in the Wolverines were all fine musicians, who didn't play notes, which a lot of these men are doing now, but created them.

I was the worst musician in the band, but was the business head. All the boys knew that I was the worst musician but they also felt they needed me to keep them together and to discipline them. They were this sort of a gang. We would have to make a train at 9:30, say, and I'd be waiting at the station for them, and they'd get off on a drinking spree or a love fest or something, and come running half dressed to the station just when the train was pulling out. Things like that were enough to drive a guy crazy. But going back again, I had a better musical training than all of them. I'd do the skeleton arrangements during rehearsals. But you never had to tell them what to do, even though most of the fellows couldn't read a note. They'd pick up a tune from the melodies I'd knock out on the piano and then in their solos they'd create around that melody so that the music came out like a work of art. In the ensembles they never got lost but stayed in and played in perfect harmony, their musical feeling seldom betraying them.

Although Bix *felt* more when he played, there was a man called Teschmaker, who played clarinet, who was also a genius but who had a calculated manner of playing. He, like the others, could never articulate verbally about what they were doing, but Teschmaker was like an intellectual compared to the others, for he knew the value of each note he hit, and knew why he played them. He had a marvelous musical background, which most of the others didn't have, and it didn't hamper him any, for his feeling for jazz was superb. He might have done greater things if he had lived.

Because of Bix we couldn't stand anything but a cornet in our band. I remember when Bix left the band and we had to get a new cornet player. We were almost driven to distraction trying to get someone who could really fit in. We tried out a few but they didn't do. We even brought up Sharkey Bonono from New Orleans. He walked in with a trumpet and all the fellows shook their heads. He wouldn't do. Sharkey played fine trumpet, but we had got so used to the cornet because of Bix we just couldn't see a trumpet. Finally one of the boys in the band said that he had heard a kid from Chicago play who sounded pretty good. We sent for the kid and he turned out to be Jimmy MacPartland. He had studied all our recordings and especially Bix's parts, and he worked in perfectly. But he could never excel Bix. We were very happy to get him because he filled Bix's place pretty well and because he was so influenced by Bix he worked in fine right off the bat.

It's a peculiar thing the way this swing craze had hit this country. Hell, in those days we were doing all the stuff that is now being done but people just accepted it and didn't go intellectual over it.

Notes

1. Early in his career, around 1931, the point at which he's being referred to in the story, John "Johnny" Hammond wrote about Jazz for *Melody Maker* and *Grammophone.* Later he became a Jazz producer for the English Columbia Company and Parlophone where his career became interwoven with that of Benny Goodman's. Hammond drafted Goodman to be one of his bandleaders and, though Goodman was a well-established session musician prior to this appointment, the move is credited with bringing Goodman to a wide range of Jazz listeners. Alyn Shipton, *A New History of Jazz* (New York: Continuum, 2007), 235; Ted Gioia, *The History of Jazz* (New York: Oxford University Press, 1997), 139–40.

2. The narrator's remark regarding the roots of Jazz being embodied in the Dixieland and Ragtime groups of the early twentieth century, ensembles like the "New Orleans Rhythm Kings," is well documented by Jazz historians. The New Orleans Rhythm Kings were a group of white musicians from Louisiana that based themselves in Chicago, and their early partnership with Jelly Roll Morton is considered an important moment in the desegregation of Jazz. Gioia, *History of Jazz*, 43, 46.

3. A major figure in the history of Jazz, Leon "Bix" Beiderbecke was known for his ability to improvise his cornet playing within solo sections of Jazz arrangements and to tie that improvisation back in to the chorus. He first recorded with the Chicago-based Wolverines and became a major influence on musicians (brass or otherwise) who heard him play. In the summer of 1923, Benny Goodman first heard and played with Beiderbecke in the Austin High Gang—Beiderbecke would have been 19 years old and Goodman in his freshman year of high school. Ironically, Beiderbecke died in 1931 of pneumonia, a complication of his alcoholism, before the end of the prohibition. His death marks the close of the itinerant session musician era in Jazz history, a time before the listening pubic could buy alcohol and listen to Jazz on the radio at home. Gioia, *History of Jazz*, 136, 139; Shipton, *New History*, 110–12.

EVERYTHING'S DANGEROUS

Ralph Powell (Montana)

We were standing by the corral fence watching Curly Vaughn and a couple of the boys cut out the horses which were going to be rode in the night's show. The floodlights were already on although it wasn't dark yet, and the bleachers across the arena were empty except for two or three guys who'd come early to get the pick of the seats. It was the third and last night of the Butte rodeo and those of us who were lucky enough to be riding for the final money were talking over our chances.

"Th' whole damn thing in a final ride, or in any ride, is jest pure luck," says Bill Mack. "There ain't a one of us but what's won first money more times than we got fingers and toes. We can all ride—if we couldn't we wouldn't be in this show—so say I, if th' breaks come right we win and if they don't we don't."

"Yeah, you're right there," Bert Dillon agreed. "We've all made pretty rides on some damn tough hosses, and then again we've all been jerked loose and maybe piled off of plugs what should've been pullin' milk wagons. Hell, I've rode sunfishers,[1] and swappers[2] and straight buckers[3] that hit th' ground so hard you'd think they was goin' right on through, and ... What th' hell you grinnin' about, Ken?"

I says, "I was just thinking about a certain ride you made in Wisdom the other day. Did you ever figure out how that old skate[4] shook you off, Bert?"

"Sure I figured it out," says Bert. "Instead of comin' out buckin' like any respectable hoss would, he comes out runnin. Pretty soon I figures there ain't no buck in 'im so I loosens up, and th' minute I do—what happens? He puts his head down and starts to raise hell right. Naturally I'm caught off balance and off I go."

"One thing I won't do," put in Chuck Walbert, an old-timer who's crawled on more ponies than all of us put together, "and that's to loosen up—even if a cayuse[5] won't buck. I see a fellow one time come out on a horse that loped—loped, mind yuh—'till th' gun went off. Well, th' guy figured, like Bert here did, that th' horse was plumb tame. So instead of pullin' himself off on th' fence or waitin' 'till th' pickup man could git to 'im, what does he do but swing his leg over th' saddle, mind yuh, like he was gittin' offen a cow horse. Well, the minute he swung his leg th' horse went to pitchin'. Th' guy's boot heels was wore down and his left foot went through th' stirrup. I helped pick 'im up after th' cayuse got done draggin' 'im around and kickin' hell out of 'im. It weren't a pretty sight. He died that night. Since then I don't trust no horse that comes out of a chute."

"Well," I says, "if I'm going to ride tonight I've got to rivet the rowell[6] on this spur. Who's got a hammer?"

"I got one in my war sack," says Bert. "Come on, I'll get it for yuh."

"You think you'll need spurs on that chunk of dynamite you drew for tonight?" says Bill Mack, winking at Bert.

"I'll admit he'll buck without 'em," I says, "but I want to get 'em in shape so I can comb his foretop which he's bucking."

Bill says, "Careful th' black don't comb your foretop with all four feet. He ain't a horse, he's a rodeo all by himself."

"There's only one sure thing about ridin' that black hoss," says Bert as we turned away, "and that's a guy knows what to look for."

"Okay," I says, "what do I look for?"

"Well, if it was me," Bert grinned, "I'd look for a soft place to light."

By this time the cash customers were filing in in a steady stream. It looked like another good night. I'll say one thing about Butte—for miners they sure like their rodeo. I'd guess that the bleachers and grandstand full would seat about four thousand people, and on the two nights we'd already showed you couldn't of bought standing room. At a buck four-bits for most seats that's some pickin's. And hell, Butte's a small show compared to Pendleton, Calgary, Cheyenne and some others. If I was smart enough to do anything but ride broncs, I think I'd like to promote rodeos—twenty thousand bucks take in three nights at a small show. Oh man!

Bert found me a hammer and I found a rock to use as an anvil. I'd just started to rivet my spur when I heard a rope swish through the air. I looked up, but too late. Jack Flower had my arms pinned down as pretty as you please. Jack's a fancy rope artist, and when I say fancy I mean just that. He has a special act he puts on every night; he ropes the four feet of a running horse while laying on his back; he stands up in a saddle and jumping through a loop while his horse is going to hell bent for election; and does a dozen other stunts that look impossible. He makes good dough, but he sure earns it. He practices all the time when he isn't sleeping, eating or putting on his act for the show. He has to handle a rope constant to keep from getting rusty.

It was nearly eight o'clock so I went over to lend Curly Vaughn a hand getting the Brahma[7] steers into the chutes. The show always opens with five or six steers coming out at the same time. It gets the crowd in a good humor because the Brahmas can cause plenty of fireworks. Those babies can really buck, and it isn't many boys can stay with them. I'm supposed to be a fair rider, and I never did have any luck on a steer. The rules say you've got to keep one hand above your head, hold the surcingle[8] with the other and scratch them every jump. Sounds easy, don't it? Well, it would be easy if the critters didn't roll their hide underneath the seat of your pants. They move that hide just like they was shaking off flies, and when they do you move right along with it. For instance, if I'm figuring a steer for a jump to the left, I'll lean my body left so that when he hits I catch the jar square. It's a question of outguessing the steer. Maybe I figure right and he does jump to the left. Fine—except that he'll roll his hide, moving me around until I'm off balance, then when he hits the ground my name's mud.

The show finally got under way. I stood around gabbing with the boys and watching the rides, waiting for my turn with the big black. In a way I was glad I drew that particular horse, and in a way I was sorry. I was glad because he was tough enough to make a rider look good. But he was so damned tough I was a little afraid he might make me look bad.

Curly run the big boy into the chute and you'd of thought he was a twenty-year plow horse. He didn't make any fuss at all—just acted gentle as a lamb. But he didn't fool me a damn bit. Jack Connors, the man who furnishes bucking horses for most of the Western shows, brought him down from Canada early last spring, and he's only been out of the chutes six times. But the first time he bucked he got himself a reputation. He was an outlaw, that boy, and only the toughest horses, maybe one in every hundred, ever earn the handle.

Connors showed him first in the Cheyenne show. The fist boy that crawled that big devil was Texas Dunn, and any pony that Tex can't ride has got to be a bucking fool. Well Tex sat him for just three jumps and he was all over the saddle after the black hit the ground for the first time. Then Tex went sailing through the air, wondering what in hell he'd got mixed up with.

But that wasn't all. When the black tossed him, he proved right then that he was a bad cayuse. He whirled like lightning, teeth bared and squealing like a fire engine, and tried his damnedest to pound poor Tex into a pulp. The boys finally fought him off, but not before he'd fixed Texas up for the hospital. The next five boys that come out on him got shook off the same way. He piled them all within ten foot of the chute gates, and he went for them the minute they hit the ground. That baby was a pony to respect, and he was respected. There's no puncher alive that don't admire a good horse, and the black was that, even if he was about as mean as any cayuse that ever tore up the dirt in a corral.

Now that he was in the chutes I took a good look at him. He was big—a lot bigger than I figured. That wide chest of his told me he had plenty of staying power, and the proud crest of his neck, his Roman nose and mean eye told me that he had one hell of a disposition.

Curly Vaughn finished putting the halter on him, then grinned down at me from the top of the chute. "Gittin' acquainted with 'im, huh?"

"We'll be old pals within the next fifteen minutes," I says.

"Toss up your saddle, kid," says Curly.

I hoisted my saddle to the top rail of the chute, and Curly started, in his business-like way, to put it on the black.

Curly was a good man around the chutes. Up until 1934 he'd been riding for the big money in all the shows. Then one day in Miles City a cayuse turned a somerset while he was on deck. Six months later the doctors turned Curly loose, sound as a new dollar except for his left leg which was twisted so bad he could never fork tough broncos again. But he was lucky in one way. As soon as he got out of the hospital Jack Connors gave him a job taking care of the bucking string during the rodeo season. So Curly followed the shows just the same as he did in the old days when he used to screw himself down in the saddle and yell, "Powder River—turn 'im loose!"

"Your luck's running' good tonight, Ken," he says, straddling the chute and easing the saddle down on the big horse's back.

The black shook as the saddle touched him. Then like a flash up he come on his hind legs, cutting the air to beat hell with his fore feet. But as he come up Curly moved, hauling the saddle with him.

"Easy boy—easy," he says from his perch on the top rail.

Bert Dillon, holding the end of the halter rope, took up the slack until he had the black's nose snubbed clear up against the post.

Curly straddled the chute again. "I say your luck's runnin' good tonight." He was watching the horse close.

"Yeah," I says, "it's about time. That was a lousy deal I got in Livingston."

"Tough break," Curly sympathized. "That was a bum pony you drew for a final ride."

If there's anything that makes a rider boil, it's to pick tough ones and ride them pretty until he gets up to the finals, and then draw a horse with no fight. That's what happened to me in Livingston. I'd been clicking swell and I had a good chance for first money, but all I got was third. That last cayuse beat me out of fifty bucks, and the fifty bucks would have bought me the new chaps I'd been wanting. Yes, and there'd of been enough left over for a damned good drunk.

Curly slid down the side of the chute, leaned up against the gate to take the weight off his game leg, and began to straighten out a long piece of wire with a hook on one end.

"Well," he says, "if you can sit this boy, th' money's yours."

He was reaching beneath the black's belly with his wire. He hooked the cinch, pulled it over slow to where he could reach it, and then with smooth, quick motions he tightened it up.

He turned grinning. "He's all yours, kid, and from what I've seen of this baby, you can have 'im. Now let me give you a tip. If he does toss you, for Gawd's sake light a runnin'. He'll kill you if he gits th' chance."

I nodded. To tell the truth, I'd been thinking of that. I wasn't scared. Fear and bronc riding just don't pal around together. It takes a certain amount of guts to climb on a cayuse that you know is going to do his damndest to kill or cripple you, and a rider without guts don't ride very long.

Still, I'll admit I always feel funny before a ride. I get that empty feeling inside. And my belly wasn't feeling any too good while I was sizing up the black. They tell me fighters get that same feeling while they're waiting for the bell. Then when the bell rings and they go into action, the nervousness is all gone. Well, it's that way with me too. As soon as the chute gate swings open and my pony hides his head between his legs I'm as calm as though I'm riding a rocking chair. A lot of friends say it's that way with them too.

Curly and I leaned on the gate and watched Clem Whipple, the clown go through his act with a Brahma bull. Clem's an old-timer in rodeo and between you and me I don't know how he's managed to live long enough to enjoy the title. He takes plenty of long chances. A full-grown Brahma bull isn't the safest kind of play-mate. It's about as mean as any critter that walks on four feet. And there was Clem, thumbing his nose at one of them, teasing the bull into charging. Finally the bull did go for him. Clem stepped aside and that devil's horns just missed him by inches.

About that time the chute gate we were leaning on started to shake, and the damndest thumping and squealing you ever heard broke loose in the chute. We moved pronto. Curly skinned up the side of the chute to quiet the black. He talked in soothing tones to the horse, then he says to me, "He's gittin' anxious."

I didn't say anything. The horse wasn't half as anxious as I was. That's what gets me—that waiting. If I could have crawled on him as soon as he was saddled it wouldn't have been so bad. But rodeo shows are just like any show. There's certain acts that got to go off on schedule night after night, and if a boy happens to have a pony all saddled and ready to come out when one of the acts are on—well, it's just his hard luck. He's got to sit there waiting and worrying until his turn comes.

The black quieted down and I went back to watching Clem and the Brahma. A breeze drifted in from the chute side of the arena and I got a good whiff of the smell that goes with the rodeo. It's not one smell. It's a blend of cattle, horses and sweating men. I wondered how the crowd over in the bleachers like it. Probably they didn't. A guy's got to be raised to it to enjoy that smell.

Clem had the crowd in a swell mood. He was risking his neck to get laughs. He knew it and we knew it, but I doubt if the crowd did. One night about two years ago we were showing in Calgary. Clem was putting on the same crowd thriller, teasing a Brahma. The bull charged him, and for once Clem didn't move fast enough and hit hard. As he went head over heels with the bull after him, I says to myself, "It's curtains." But Clem got to his feet, dodged the bull, and finished the show just as though nothing had happened. When it was all over he asked a couple of us to take a look at his ribs. We did. Then we called a doctor. Three of his ribs were broken.

But Clem isn't the only one who takes chances. Every boy that works the rodeos is on speaking terms with the old man who carries the scythe. Lots of times people have asked us why us rodeo boys make our living the hard way. I usually say, "Do you know of any job that beats riding for a living?" They tell us sure, any job beats that, and that we're a bunch of damn fools, or words to that effect.

Maybe they're right—I don't know. But I do know that if those same people had been raised in a saddle like I was, and like a lot of my friends was, they'd be fighting broncs too. They would if they were like most riders I know. Hell, it's the only thing we can do. We never learned nothing else.

Take my own case for example. I was raised in the cow country—the Big Hole Basin country in Montana. Without a word of a lie, I was a pretty fair rider before I could walk without falling down. But that's only natural. Riding was as much a part of our life up in the Basin as driving cars is a part of city life. We worked on horseback the year around.

They say that kids make up their games by mocking the things their folks do. A sailor's son builds boats and talks the seamen's lingo; a lawyer's son makes jury-men out of his playmates, then stands in front of them and tries to argue them into hanging or freeing the criminal. A cowman's son runs a bunch of yearling calves into a corral and spends hours roping and riding them. He comes by his skill while he's still in rompers.

Sometimes, as in my own case, a boy turns out to be a natural in the saddle. And as long as there are rodeos, why not try for some of the easy money? Because after all, it is easy money. Try and convince any rider that it isn't. If we were punching cows on a ranch we'd be drawing just forty bucks a month and board. On a good night at a rodeo, when our luck's running right, it isn't hard to pick up forty or fifty dollars—a whole month's wages.

But let a rider tell an outsider that we make our dough easy and the first thing the dude says is, "Your work's dangerous. You stand a chance of being killed." And the rider will come back with, "Hell, everything's dangerous." Most cowboys figure that what's going to happen is going to happen in spite of hell or high tide.

Here's the way I got it doped. If I'm going to get it, I'll get it no matter what I'm doing. I could be walking down a street and a building could cave in on me. Or I could be sitting at home and get hit by a bolt of lightning. So why pass up a couple of hours work in a rodeo when I stand a chance of picking up some quick easy money?

Clem finished his clowning and they got the arena cleared. I hitched up my trousers and waited. Pretty soon the announcer's voice came booming through the loud speaker.

"Coming out of chute number three—Ken Davis of Wisdom on the Killer. Climb up there Ken, and do your stuff."

I pulled on my gloves and climbed the chute. As I balanced myself on the top rails, Curly said, "Be sure you're set when th' gate swings, Ken. He don't waste no time gittin' goin'. If you can stay with him th' first three or four jumps you got a damn good chance. And if you get piled, don't forget—git to th' fence poco pronto."

I nodded as I braced both arms on the chute rails and eased myself into the saddle. I could feel the black shake as my weight came down on him, but he kept his four feet planted on the ground. I found the stirrups and then grabbed the halter rope that Bert Dillon was holding out to me. A man's hold on that rope is important and I made sure I grabbed it right.

The announcer was talking again. He was giving the black a build-up, as though the Killer needed any build-up.

I glanced out over the top of the chute and saw Buck Evans, the pick-up man standing by. I felt better. Buck's the best pick-up man in the business and it helps a rider a lot to know he's with you.

"All screwed down?" Curly was hovering over me like a mother hen over her chicks.

"Turn 'im loose!" I yelled.

The gate swung wide and I reached for the black's shoulders with my spurs. He let out a bellow and up he went, twisting like a corkscrew. When he finally hit the ground I knew I was on a horse. My God but he hit hard. My neck snapped back and my spine felt like it went through the saddle. From then on I don't remember much about what happened. I know I had sense enough to scratch him high on the shoulders for the first three jumps before I brought my spurs down to work on his sides. And I know he was pulling every trick I'd ever seen and a lot that I hadn't seen. One second the crowd in the bleachers was a blur in front of my eyes and a roar in my ears, and the next second I'd catch a hazy glimpse of the chutes.

I remember wondering why the gun didn't go off. It seemed like I'd been riding for an hour. And then come the awful feeling that I was going. I couldn't take any more of that terrible pounding. But a man's mind works fast in a pinch. Even as the thought hit me that I was washed up, I thought of what that black would do to me if he bucked me off. Better to pull leather, I figured, and try to stay until Buck could pick me off. My hand started for the horn, but before I could reach it the gun sounded.

I'll never hear a sound as sweet as that again. Nothing mattered now. I could pull leather or get piled higher than a kite. I'd stayed my ten seconds, and the black's reputation was all shot to hell. I'd rode him!

I grabbed the horn—not with one hand but with two. But I still took an awful beating before the pick-up men got there to take me off. The ground felt good under my feet, but I must have had sea legs because I staggered like I'd been hitting a keg of hootch. Then a bunch of the boys was running out toward me. They grabbed me, held me on my pins, shook my hands and pounded my back. One of them dabbled at my nose with a bandanna and brought it away red. That's what a tough horse can do to you—mix up your whole insides.

As soon as I could I slipped over to the fence below the grandstand and layed down. My neck felt like it was broke and my head was splitting.

Up in the grandstand behind me I heard some fellow say, "See that lad there—the one laying down by the fence? He's the guy that just rode The Killer."

Then I heard another voice say, "God, but that boy's a rider!"

And I just grunted to myself, "So what!"

Notes

1. There are several colorful terms used by "bronc-riders" to describe the ways wild horses and steers contort themselves to throw off or "buck" cowboys off their backs. Here the term "sunfisher" denotes a wildly bucking animal, but one that looks like it's attempting to drop down on one shoulder and then to the other, wriggling itself into a half-moon shape. Sunfisher can also refer to a good score at a rodeo. Ramon F. Adams, *Cowboy Lingo* (Boston: Houghton Mifflin, 2000), 96–97; Harold Wentworth

   and Stuart Berg Flexner, *Dictionary of American Slang* (New York: Crowell, 1960), 529.

2. Bulls that turn completely around in the air while bucking; Also called "swap ends." R. G. MacBeth, *Policing the Plains: Being the Real Life Record of the Famous Royal Northwest Mounted Police* (Philadelphia: McKay, 1931), 144, 152.

3. A horse that jumps or bucks in a straight line, usually large, striding leaps forward. Adams, *Cowboy Lingo*, 96–97.

4. A tottering, old horse or bull. Wentworth and Flexner, *Dictionary*, 480.

5. A horse having its lineage in equestrian lines of the American Northwest. Clifford P. Westermeier, *Man, Beast, Dust* (Lincoln, NE: University of Nebraska Press, 2005), 164.

6. Or "rowel"; the spiked, free-moving wheel of a cowboy's spur. Fay E. Ward, *The Cowboy at Work* (Mineola, NY: Dover, 2003), 230.

7. An extremely violent breed of rodeo bull bred from a cross of Texas Longhorn and Indian cattle. The oxen have long, sharp horns and can weigh approximately 900 pounds. Johnie Schneider, "Ace Rodeo Rider Tells How He Tames Vicious Broncos," *Popular Science*, August, 1934: 24–26.

8. In bareback rodeo riding, the horse is girdled with a thick leather strap, or surcingle, around its belly. The rider is only allowed the use of one hand to hold on to the horse and cannot switch hands during the run. Westermeier, *Man, Beast, Dust*, 210–11.

SOUP CIRCUIT

M. B. Moser and Isaac Schwartz (Ohio)

Well Jake—of all people—what brings you to this whistle-stop? Sure you can come back stage—mind your legs, we got in late and things are a little ragged— a wash-out near Grassville Junction. Put yourself on that crate near the switch-board so we can be together. When did I take over as stage-manager? Couple seasons back, and am I sorry! At that it's better than plugging tunes at Coney.

Hey, Sue—watch that punch-line in No. 4—it laid an egg last night. Yes, I know about your arm, but don't let him pinch so hard. It's an act, you know.

What was we saying, Jake? Gotta step on it—nine minutes to the bell so don't mind if I break away. You ought to be glad you took up managing a garage—at least you eat regular. All we hit now is the soup circuit.[1] It's awful strange—there isn't what you can call competition. People have just lost interest in flesh-acts. And it ain't the flicker-shows, either. Them door-prizes and screeno get more laughs than the movies.

There's the opener—you know who wrote that ensemble? Hap Moore— remember his bar-fly routine? He overdid it last season and is on a long lay-off. Hap sure was a hard worker—something the new talent knows nothing about. Hap's through with hoofing, I'm afraid.

Classy number, this. Every kid on her toes, too—even the dumb ones and I got a few. I've had to be a Simon Legree the past month. Got so the wardrobe looked like a rummage sale. The kids know I mean it for the best. Where would the troupe be if someone didn't do all the worrying?

Oh Jimmy—Sue's complaining about her arm; it's risking a good gag and when you go through that clinch with her, remember you're only a stage-cop.

Jake, this next piece convinces me that the public is just one big rube. Remember how you and me did this alley-business when we played the good time? The straight man here is Eddie Green—the line I played to your comic; notice him smelling the cork when the bottle is empty. The dope is George Hall. The house always howls with fun when he wrinkles his nose and Eddie pushes the nose-putty back in place. My old man used to do it almost the same way—only he and ma played it in those days. Remember the time we landed in that Alabama cotton town and the theater manager doubted if we could play because "How can you vodvil without a woman?" Well, we have a skit in which we use that very line—it's coming up now.

It's a black-out[2] with a lot of fast work that brings on a sweat. The customers let it lay four out of five and I'm all for changing it for something else but the troupe loves it and wants to keep on with it anyhow—never saw such a gang of hard workers.

The mechanics on these soup circuits, Jake, will kill me yet. Look how that monkey in the roost shoots that hard white light smacko on the straight man's face—he'll be blind the rest of the night. That piece called for a golden glow that comes up to full, but slow. If we tell the house about such a bloomer like the one he pulled now they yell "union rules" and we have to shut up.

That's our ingénue[3] and crazy about the juvenile parts—all 26 years of her. Small as a bar of soap and that helps with the illusion. She and the soubrette[4] there have been getting in each other's hair—taking out their bad luck on each other. I blame the small dressing rooms on the circuit. The soubrette is an old trouper. Her folks were circus riders and were killed in a train wreck. She sings, patters and kicks high with the best in the line. When she puts on her strip she's a gasp—you know the bit, "bathed in sunlight and innocence." She'll be done in a minute and you can meet her.

Notice this next drop, Jake. Just a set of foliage and rural atmosphere but it set us back $600—and the studio wouldn't take due bills. Seems like everybody gets money out of shows but the people who play them. In this bit we got two real sisters who put on a mother-daughter act—"Experience Counts." It has the melo-drama touch but it's fast going; if it slows by 30 seconds it dies for keeps. The girl brings up a count who thinks he's found some rich Americans. The mother takes him into the country, stops the car at the side of the road. The black-out comes when she gives her daughter the low down that the count is of no account.

Here comes the soubrette—Jake, meet Miss La Roo. She's the best handy-man in the business. Roo, please be nice to Jeanie—she thinks we are cramping her style. No, not you, Roo—believe me. I'm trying to be a mother to you two kids but you won't let me. Next season things'll be different—if we're off the soup circuit.

Well, Jake, the first half's over and we killed about four lengths but these bingo hounds didn't know the difference. If we pulled that many chestnuts[5] on the big time we'd be jailed, not fired. Notice the stage crew sweat with the scene-shift—gee I hate these narrow spots—no room for a poodle's tail. In Beamertown the stage was so small we parked half the scenes in the alley, but the yokels thought our show was so big that the opry house couldn't hold it all. And did we cut the acts, brother.

We open our next half with "Radio Rhythm." I claim it's new. We have a take-off on all the big names around the dial of a radio. We got a riot in one black-out in this piece about a grandma who wants to go with the grandchildren to take in the hot spots and the children get out of it by teaching her the rhumba and turning on the radio and leaving her in the groove.

We had trouble with this piece in Riverdale. Seems like they got a Purity Council or something which takes in all the shows—the rougher the better, from what I saw of some of those blisters on opening night. Well, they see grandma—that's our soubrette—passing the rhumba to a hot down-beat and they objects. "Crude vulgarity" they calls it and the soubrette is all for showing them where they're wrong. So I told her to put her rhumba bumps into second-gear and we sandpapered some of the sharp corners of her bit where grandma makes whoopee with the elevator man and it got by.

Funny thing happened when we played in some town in Indiana. We got a skit of a couple of blacks. One says he's in a hurry, going to a wedding, and the other asks who and he says his own wedding—"cause Ah'm outta woik and gotta do sump'n to live." They kick that around some and they get mixed up explaining a veranda; one says it's something that "runs around de place" and the lead straight says "Oh, you married, too?"

Well, Jake, so help me, the local drama critic tells it to a college professor who takes in the show and writes a long yarn for a highbrow paper on "Survival of The Persian Entendre." The circuit press agent got a copy and told me it meant that double-talk is coming back after 3,000 years. Tie that one.

Still, it don't bring in the trade. We now say "The show must go off" and not on. One hog-wallow in the Midwest had a flash flood the day before we arrived and the show-barn was a wreck so we played in the district school. Looks like stage-managing is getting to be a school-teacher's job. That town had some slickers in it and the superintendent was a guy who sure liked his white meat—the way he went for our ingénue. The way he went for Jeanie's strawberry curls you'd think he was after a fire, but I couldn't blame him. She has that certain thing deep down under the baby stare and it gets 'em coming and going. If she was only a foot taller she'd be in the bright lights in a year.

This Dutch Mill number always gets them for some reason and it isn't over 100 years old. Maybe because it's got some kid-stuff—toward the close we got a scene of the old woman who lived in a shoe. The first comic lays them in the aisles when he starts to saw away the toe of the wooden shoe and the old woman pokes her head out and says be careful or you'll be cuttin into paw's wooden leg. It's a clean number; one of the kids asks, "Why did the old woman have so many children?" and is told, "Because she didn't know what to do?" and the first one says, "You asking or telling me?"

Jake, I wish I could go back to the old times when people worked in show business because they loved it. Most of the kids we get today come in with big notions of how important everybody else is. It if wasn't for the born troupers in this outfit it would all fold in a minute. Three of the girls in the first line took dancing in an academy and when they had to learn show-stepping all over again it broke their hearts to think of the money they threw away learning it in a school run by a bum.

And the new men coming into the business are no prizes either. They do a little road-house patter or song plugging in a record shop and learn a couple of stomps and just because they join some union they call themselves actors. Worse than lazy, too—just can't get them to put much into rehearsals. If they had to go through some of the training you and me had to take—all-night rehearsals and polishing up rusty spots between shows—they'd die of overwork.

We been a little lucky this tour and haven't had any accidents. Last season Billy Edwards who originated the ankle shuffle all these hoofers think they're doing broke his leg when he fell over a trunk. The doctor said his bones are brittle but I know it's old age. Imagine a guy 58 years old doing a fast hoofing act twice a day a whole season—that's one for these newcomers to shoot at. Lucky for Billy his brother got a good farm and can look out for him. I haven't even a brother. But I'm keeping up my insurance.

If we get television, Jake, we'll be in the money—I hope. At least we'll be in one place long enough to press the wrinkles out of our duds. Radio all but killed the show business but radio's baby may bring it all back. Anyway, you did smart when you took up motor cars. Yes, I know you saved your dough and I didn't, but what's dough when everybody thinks in-the-flesh acts are old-fashioned and those in the business think different? We old timers love the business, dough or no dough.

There's the curtain, Jake—watch your step around those wires. Almost lost an ear that way in Saint Looey once. You gotta see the show out front, Jake, and tell me what you think—honestly. Come into the hotel after the show tonight—we're having a little bender for the comic; it's his birthday—53 yesterday, but we had to make such a fast jump to get here in time to put up the scenery we couldn't celebrate with him. You'll like George Hall—"The Dope"—an old trouper, like you and me, Jake.

Notes

1.   Another idiomatic expression for the "borscht belt," or the "borscht circuit." This string of predominately Jewish vacation hotels in the Catskill Mountains was a training ground for many popular comedians, actors, and actresses from the '30s onward. Harold Wentworth and Stuart Berg Flexner, *Dictionary of American Slang* (New York: Crowell, 1960), 56–57.

2.   A comedic sketch in which the punch line is punctuated by an abrupt curtain drop or the house lights turning off. It could also be a series of quick scenes or jokes that end in the same manner. Donald W. Whisenhunt, *Tent Show: Arthur Names and His "Famous" Players* (College Station, TX: Texas A & M University Press, 2000), 129–30.

3.   A role written for a young female; similar to the "soubrette," but tending more toward the dramatic than comedic. Alfred Hennequin, *The Art of Playwriting* (Boston: Houghton Mifflin, 1890), 81.

4.   A part in early twentieth-century theater written for a young, exuberant, fresh, female. The role comes from the French comedic tradition wherein the role was often a chambermaid. Alfred Hennequin, *Playwriting*, 81.

5.   Well-worn jokes or clichéd scenarios. Wentworth and Flexner, *Dictionary*, 97.

SVEN, THE HUNDRED PROOF IRISHMAN

Edward Miller (Tennessee)

Old Gallagher polished his old bald head. "It's too bad," he says to himself, "Every son of the Old Sod[1] I hire turns out to be a booze-histing[2] floater.[3] And what work they do ain't much good. But I can't help liking the lads from the land of my dear old Mother."

Old Gallagher scratched and sighed.

"What I ought to do is hire me a Swede," he says. "They turn out good work and they're steady. But I don't like the daggone lunkheads! They just naturally rub me the wrong way. Still, it's a cinch I got to get somebody. I need another blower bad."

Next morning a floater came in the plant.

"What kin ye blow?" says Old Gallagher.

"Anything you want, from pints to five gallons," says the floater.

"What's your name?" says the old man.

"Shaemas O'Toole," says the floater. "Burprrrp!"

"OK," says the old man, "get on out to the five gallon tank before your breath makes me drunk."

Shaemas staggered on back in the plant. Next morning he drew his day's pay to pay board and never showed up again.

The old man roared.

"Out drunk again, the bottle-busting boozer! He never had got good and sober, even. Two five gallon jugs he made. Two! Two for eleven bucks!"

In a few days in came number two floater. The old man looked at him hard.

"What kin ye blow?" says he.

"Anyshing from pintsh to five gallonsh," says number two.

"Good, ain't you?" says the old man. "How about window glass?"

"Shure, all winnow glash you want," says number two.

"I bet," says the old man. "What's your name?"

"Patrick Michael Shullivan," says number two.

"All right. Get on back and make one gallon if you can walk that far. Say, ye ain't drunk, are ye?"

"Never toush drop shtuff," says Sullivan, reeling out.

He lasted a week and drew full pay. Fifty-five dollars.

"Never see him again," says the old man.

He didn't.

So a few days later Sven Murphy came in. Old Gallagher glared at him fierce.

"What kin ye blow best, boy?"

"Anything from pints to five gallons," says Sven. "Or window glass if you want it."

The old man let out a roar.

"Anything, huh? I bet! How much do ye weigh, boy?"

"Ninety-one pounds and six ounces," says Sven, "with my shoes on."

"Been drinking, ain't you?" says the old man.

"Sure," says Sven, "I just had breakfast."

The old man hit the ceiling.

"Git out!" he howls. "Another dog hair! I just been stung by two in a row and not another one will I hire! No dog hair! No floater! No booze-hister! Git out!"

"I ain't no dog hair at all," says Sven, never batting an eyebrow. "I ain't no floater. My name is Sven Murphy and I just got to this country from Ireland. I ain't no booze-hister. I just drink for my health. Just a few quarts a day to keep my nerves steady. On Saturday maybe a few gallons more so I can sort of feel it."

"From Ireland, huh?" says the old man, very nice now. "Sven Murphy, ye say? What kind of a name is that? Are ye Irish or not?"

"My father was Irish, my mother was Swedish," says Sven.

"Swede, huh?" Old Gallagher frowned. "But your father was Irish? Go on back and make pint bottles boy. I'm afraid ye couldn't handle fifteen pounds of glass and you only weighing ninety. Fifteen ounces is nearer your size."

"Ninety-one pounds and six ounces with my shoes on," says Sven, starting back to the tanks. "But I'll make pint bottles if you say so. Thank you kindly."

The old man took an interest in Sven. That evening when Sven was leaving he stopped him.

"How did they go today, boy?" he says.

"Just so-so," says Sven. "Not so good. But I'll do better tomorrow."

"How many pints did ye make today?"

"Three hundred dozen," says Sven. "But I'll do better tomorrow."

The old man swallowed three times. Then he went back to the tanks. The foreman was there.

"Flaherty," says the old man, "how many pints did the new man make today?"

"Three hundred dozen," says Flaherty. "And he knocked off twice to go out for a drink. The glass-blowingest fool I ever seen."

"Praise the saints!" says Old Gallagher. "Maybe he's the man I've been needing. An Irishman that works like a Swede! Put him on quarts tomorrow."

Next evening he stopped Sven again.

"Well, how many quarts did ye make, me boy?"

"Not many," says Sven. "Two hundred and sixty dozen. But I'll do better tomorrow."

"Put him on gallon jugs tomorrow," Old Gallagher says to the foreman. "He's a glass-blowing fool, all right. Now if he just sticks with me."

Next day Sven made a hundred dozen gallons.

"But I'll do better tomorrow," he says.

"Make five-gallon jugs tomorrow," says the old man.

Next day he went out to watch Sven work.

Sven stood by the five-gallon tank. The gathering boy gathered fifteen pounds of glass on the end of a pipe and gave it to Sven.

Sven took the pipe and blew. He swung it right. He swung it left. He clamped it into the mould and blew.

Sven broke the pipe loose and gave it back to the gathering boy.

The finisher put a rim on the jug.

The gathering boy handed Sven his pipe. Sven swung it right. He swung it left. He clamped it into the mould and blew.

Another five gallon jug.

Old Gallagher's mouth hung open.

"Boy, ye're a glass-blowing fool!" he says. "How do ye do it so easy?"

"My wind is good and my nerves are steady," says Sven. He grabbed the pipe and swung it right. "But I'm not so good today." He swung it left. "I'll do better tomorrow." He clamped it into the mould and blew.

The old man roared. "Ye're a glass-blowing fool!" he says. "Make a window glass tomorrow. I want to see that."

Next day the whole crew stood around to see Sven Murphy blow window glass.

The gathering boy handed Sven his pipe. Ninety pounds of glass on the end. Sven swung it as easy as a mother swings her baby. Ninety pounds of glass on one end and ninety pounds of man on the other. He swung it right and left in the trench. He drew such a breath you could feel the draft, and blew like Hell's own bellows.

Then he swung it up and they caught it and broke it off the pipe. A six-foot cylinder of glass, two feet through and shining like silver. They carted it off to split it and melt it down flat in the oven.

Sven grabbed his pipe and swung it.

"Praise the saints!" says Old Gallagher. "Boy, ye're a glass-blowing fool! No Irish, no Swede, nor no human could blow glass like you can. Ye must be a son of the devil!"

"I'll do better next week," says Sven, breaking the pipe loose again.

That was the end of the week.

Monday morning Old Gallagher went to the plant feeling fine. All his troubles were over. He was humming: "Sure, I love the dear silver that shines de da dum; and de dum da, de dum—"

He opened the door to his office.

Sounded like the roof fell in. Old Gallagher swallowed his upper plate.

Sounded like a riot back in the plant. Glass breaking and people yelling at the top of their voices.

Old Gallagher was fat, but he moved fast. He took the other end of the plant in no time.

He busted in the door to the tank and storage room. The place was a wreck. The floor was covered with broken jugs, bottles, and window glass. Men were lying around in the mess, some bleeding from cuts, some with big lumps on their heads. Gallagher was just in time to see Sven Murphy smash a five-gallon jug to the floor, and Flaherty bend a blower's pipe over young Murphy's head. Murphy went down in a heap.

"Flaherty! Flaherty!" says the old man, running up. "Name of the saints! What's the matter?"

Flaherty was panting and blowing.

"This crazy fool," he says. "When we got here this morning he was here busting all the glassware he had made. Every last piece he had made last week. He just then busted the last jug. We tried to stop him but he couldn't be stopped. He laid out every man in the plant but me and went right on with his busting."

Sven Murphy stirred a little. Old Gallagher bent over and shook him.

"Murphy!" he says. "Murphy! It's old Tom Gallagher, boy. Name of the saints, what's the matter? Have ye gone plumb looney, boy?"

Sven opened his mouth a little.

"Alla men," he mumbles, "alla lil green men."

"What men, boy?" says Old Gallagher, propping him up in his arms. "What men are ye speaking of?"

"Alla lil green men," says Sven, "inna bottlesh I made lash week. Got to worrying 'bout 'em Shaturday night. Been in here all lash night bushting bottlesh to let 'em out."

Notes

1.   A colloquialism for an Irishman or a person of Irish descent. Eric Partrige, *A Concise Dictionary of Slang and Unconventional English* (New York: Macmillan, 1990), 471.
2.   A heavy drinker; a drunk. Harold Wentworth and Stuart Berg Flexner, *Dictionary of American Slang* (New York: Crowell, 1960), 631.
3.   A term for an itinerant worker. In the '30s, the term *floater* could also convey the sense of a lazy or unproductive laborer. Eric Partrige, *Concise Dictionary*, 259; Wentworth and Flexner, *Dictionary*, 191.

PART FOUR: For the Future

SALMON FOR THE COLUMBIA

Howard McKinley Corning (Oregon)

As Lee Norwood swings out the door of his small green-roofed cottage, the cool morning breeze of late September strikes his cheek and rolls his gray hat-brim. The time is just past seven and the sun has not yet topped the gorge wall where the mighty Columbia cuts through the towering Cascade Mountains. Buildings and grounds of the Bonneville Fish Hatchery still lie in shadow. But the sky is cloudless and the fair weather of the past fortnight should hold for another day at least, Norwood, hatchery superintendent, observes. And that's good, for the fall spawning season is at its height.

Coming out of his own small cottage at the west edge of the hatchery grounds is Kurt Monson, Norwood's first assistant. Norwood calls to the heavier man striding easily toward him. "Looks like the big day. The ponds were full of salmon last night and the breeze is holding upriver."

Monson, hatless and sandy-haired, nods. "Yah, and beeg fellas. Maybe feed off a school a whales. Yah." His blue eyes twinkle in his ruddy round face.

Norwood, younger than Monson, who is just past middle age, smiles faintly. "They'll be plenty hard to handle—those big ones." Surely today will be tops, he thinks. Yesterday the two crews of six men each took nearly 800,000 salmon eggs, all Chinook, and last evening, just before dark when he looked at the ponds they were fuller with the returning horde than on any night before. He is glad he told Ed Compo to bring two extra men with him from Cascade Locks when he returns this morning.

Beyond the small office structure, the men approach the 200-foot long hatchery building, center of propagation activity. Peak-roofed, shingles painted green, it faces the channeled streams that interlace the fifty-odd outside ponds, many of them at this season filling up with returning fish that three years earlier were liberated from these same waters, the place of their birth and early growth. The streams chatter softly, and everywhere light is refracted from the ceaseless current—diverted from Tanner Creek which gushes down from the green Cascades. Five hundred feet to the west the creek spills over gravel-bars into the Columbia. Upriver a third of a mile the giant span and powerhouse of Bonneville Dam rear their white walls against the down-rushing waters of the continent.

As Norwood and Monson reach the hatchery door, Lafe Mullens, known as "the Kid," comes out carrying three empty buckets in each hand. Lafe, red-headed and eager, is already in his shirt sleeves, despite the earliness of the hour and the cool air. He passes down among the maples and birches that stand between the ponds where yellow leaves lie scattered over the gravelly earth; others hang to the thinning boughs. The cottonwoods up by the Union Pacific bridge show color, too. The alders and the few oaks will be the last transformed.

"Beat us to it again," Norwood remarks. "Make a good fish man, the Kid. Catches on quick, knows where the hook's bated."

Three men in rubber clothing are swinging down from the entrance drive-way curving in through the arched eyebrow of the railroad overpass. They descend along the winding beaten paths and over the footbridges that span feeder streams and pools, overcast by the morning shadow of the gorge wall. They are members of the spawning crew, and live in the small frame structures that hug the brushy slope on the opposite side of the highway, US 30, the Old Oregon Trail. Norwood tosses them a salute before entering the hatchery door.

Within, the air is even cooler than outside, and heavy with moisture. Here, as elsewhere, the sound of cascading waters is close and pervasive. Water, water! It is the life of the hatchery; it must be kept flowing. Norwood assures himself that the proper volume of water is pouring through every one of the 120 hatching troughs. Should the flow cease for as much as a minute the eggs in their wire baskets or trays must be lifted from the still waters to open air, to prevent smothering, while the fry[1] must be kept from bunching. Oxygen, which both eggs and fish must have, is abundant only in flowing water. For this reason the troughs, which stand equally divided on either side of the center entryway, are arranged in parallel pairs separated into three sections, each on a level about six inches lower than the one above, so that the waters spill downward from section to section, at a rate of from ten to fifteen gallons a minute. Norwood notes the glistening of light on the curving-over streams, and recognizes that all is well.

From the entryway platform, enclosed to restrain visitors (welcome in the balcony above), the superintendent steps through the gate and down to the cement floor, darkly puddled and never wholly dry.

"Creek still running?" asks one of the arriving crew.

"All O.K." Norwood replies. "We'll give it a lot more work to do in a few more days, the way the big ones are coming in."

"Going to keep us busy, eh?" He is thinking about his job.

"Looks like it."

"Let 'em come."

The men swing down to the floor level. Down one aisle Monson is looking at the baskets of eggs set in the troughs the previous day. His face expresses sober thought. Presently he strolls back to the center of the building's one long room. He and Norwood draw rubber trousers over their high boots, and don rubberized coats. Picking up buckets, knives and clubs, the group leaves through the door in the center.

On the way out they meet five of the six men who have been coming each day from Cascade Locks, three miles upriver. "Ed Compo will be along shortly; he's bringing those two new guys you ordered," one of them reports to Norwood, and the entire gang starts down the path toward the two holding pools where the spawning platforms have been set up. "Compo got a coupla fishermen ain't ever worked at anything but seining.[2] From Astoria, he said."

"Let 'em do the seining for me and Monson in our pool," one of the crew suggests.

Another man speaks up quickly. "What's matter with my pullin'—too fast for yuh?"

"Too damn jerky. You make 'em wild. I keep telling you yuh gotta pull steady and hold the net in. Those bucks splash like hell, you know that."

The other scowls and grumbles. "I'm a deep-sea fisherman, I'm used to tuggin' against the swells, nothin' easy 'bout that. I'd be out doin' it right now if the wife didn't have the rheumatism so damn bad. I'm doin' this because we gotta live and I know fish. Hell, it's us fishermen makes the jobs you regular fellas got takin' spawn and hatchin' fry."

"Yeah, so you'll have some fish to catch."

"And pay a license fee to do it, too."

"And ain't you gettin' that all back and more too, right now on this job? You're lucky."

A member of the group, previously silent, begins to chant:

"Round she goes, and round she goes,

And where she stops nobody knows."

A yellow maple leaf slips down from the bough above and lights on his shoulder. The next second the upriver breeze gently lifts it off.

The party, moving for the most part in single file, draws up beside the nearest of the two pools designated for that day's egg-take. Within the shaded shallow waters moves a blue and silver horde of salmon, the females round-bodied and blunt, the males slender, with hook-like jaws and sunken eyes. The males whip into agitation as the men approach, but the lazy, journey-wearied females glide slowly along the silted pool-bottom. A few "ripe" ones, buffeted by their companions in close confinement, have already begun to lose their eggs.

"Plenty ripe lot, eh Monson," Lee Norwood comments. "Looks like the big day."

"Yah, yah."

"Take a million, you think?"

But Monson will not commit himself. Monson will take the next pool down, twenty feet west, aided by Ed Compo when he comes. A big fellow, Charley Meeves, will work this pool with the superintendent. Each unit will have two strippers and several assistants.

The Kid, who first arrived on the scene, after depositing his buckets beside the pools, has gone on down the connecting raceway to peer into the creek proper, where the water is glutted with ascending salmon. Now he makes his way back, bearing something of a look of amazement under his red thatch. He has never seen so many live fish so close up before. And such big ones! He says so as he comes up to Norwood.

Norwood remarks, "Four of the biggest does will fill a bucket. You watch." His two seiners take hold of the net that was left last night to dry on the mending frames. The Kid gives a hand to pulling one end around the 30-foot oval pond. As the men draw the net-ends forward on either side of the pond, the net sinks into the water behind the advancing fish. The underside drags bottom, while the top, supported by wooden floats, rides the surface. At the pool's lower end, Norwood raises the gate just enough to lessen water-depth to around eighteen inches and hold it there.

Foot by foot the lashing horde advances before the constricting mesh. The several hundred trapped bodies are forced gradually closer and closer together. Now and again a salmon, more agile than its companions, leaps the float cord and is temporarily free.

"We'll get you later," a seiner says.

As the mass of fish is drawn toward the upper end of the rock-walled enclosure, Norwood and Meeves step down into the lowered waters. A club man descends with them.

It takes a sharp eye and quick handling to pick the ripe females. Their bodies are full and round and soft to the feel, almost like mush if they are ripe, and the hundreds of eggs inside have loosened hold and are ready to be spawned. With the left hand grabbing a fish by the tail, Norwood expertly reaches down with the right and feels the smooth undersides. This first one is not quite ready and he flings it over the net. But the next one is—a specimen weighing nearly twenty-five pounds. Always, for an instant after capture, a fish is still. The right arm must then be quickly thrust around it, with the salmon's head protruding behind. The club man then hits the fish a bob on the head. Senseless and quivering and easy to handle, it is tossed onto the spawning platform where the two strippers wait. Heavy fish are handled by hooking the fingers of the right hand into one gill, holding to the tail with the left. Sometimes the club man aids, or hoists the fish alone. It is strenuous labor.

As the first female is tossed out, Norwood exclaims, "There's the first five thousand."

"Another fish story in the making," someone remarks in jest.

Meeves, meanwhile, flings up his first ripe female, a rather small specimen. But almost immediately he selects a twenty-pounder that the club man deftly bobs. The two toss it out.

These first fish have been comparatively easy to capture. But now the mass is overcoming some of its initial fright. Those not too exhausted from the two or three months' journey up the Columbia, are still fighters. These are chiefly males. The ripe females are heavy with eggs and near to death.

"Snug the net in a little," Norwood suggests.

The next fish taken is small and flings an enveloping shower of spray over the workers. Its tail catches Norwood on the face, knocking his felt hat into the churning waters. The club man grabs it out and slaps it on Norwood's wet head. The next instant he clubs the fish into insensibility.

"Right down my collar," Norwood grunts, flinging the body over to the rack. But he grins, and goes for another ripe one.

It is now eight o'clock. The sun rolls up over the rim of the gorge wall, the light slanting down through a fringe of Douglas firs. Ed Compo has arrived from Cascade Locks with the two new men and Kurt Monson and his crew commence similar spawning operations below. The long day's work has fully begun.

When a dozen or so females have been taken by Meeves and Norwood, they select and toss out a few males. These gaunt, savage creatures are hard to handle and fight viciously. Now and again their large, white, dog-like teeth snare an unwary hand or finger. Such hurts heal slowly, especially when the worker must keep his hands constantly in water for weeks. Today, no one suffers injury as these first males are taken. They too are bobbed on the head.

On the plank spawning platform alongside the pool, the strippers have, until now, stood idle. Now one of them selects a male, or buck. Tucking the body under the left arm, the stripper passes his right hand under the fish's belly and presses the milt[3] out into two of the waiting buckets—enough to cover the bottom. The live male is then flung aside and the egg-stripping begins.

In this operation the female fish, held by the left hand through the gills, is suspended directly over a milted bucket. With a sharp, short-bladed knife the spawner makes an incision from the vent upwards, through the thin abdominal wall. Beneath the ascending blade the red round eggs each nearly a quarter of an inch through, spill into the bucket, held and guided by the second spawner. The emptied body is thrown aside and another female is caught up, and the process is repeated. This is continued until the two buckets are sufficiently filled—the egg-take of from ten to twelve fish filling a pair of two-and-one-half-gallon buckets each three-fourths full. The spawners work rapidly.

"Now some more buck juice." And the spawn of the two buckets is further fertilized by the milt of from six to seven more males. This done, one of the spawners stirs with his hand the entire mass, thus insuring complete fertilization, which is instantaneous. Lafe Mullens hurries with the filled buckets to the hatchery building.

Within two minutes after taking a "freezing" process begins, during which the eggs adhere to one another; this lasts for half an hour. They then separate and are quite hard and if dropped on a solid surface will make a distinct "ping" and will bounce. They retain this firmness for several days, when they reach a tender stage that calls for care in handling.

It is the hatchery man's task to get the freshly spawned and milted eggs into washing-up baskets and under water as quickly as possible. Usually he pours the contents of two buckets, sometimes as many as thirty thousand eggs, into a single wire container, clamps the lid over it, and submerges it in the clean-up trough. The running water washes off all excess milt, and any fungus spores, blood or grime that may have adhered in handling. When the freezing process is completed or the eggs are sufficiently clean, the hatchery man lifts them out of the bath and counts them. This is done by counting the number of eggs to an ounce, which runs from 65 to 72 in Chinook spawn. The average count will hold for the entire basket, which is then weighed. The computed figure, accurate to within a few dozen eggs, is entered in the record books. Two inside men handle this work.

"Lots of big biddies today," Lafe remarks to Monson's bucket man as the latter comes in on his third trip. Monson's man is tall and silent; the bucket-toting job keeps his long legs stretching from pool to hatchery and back to the pool again. He will get little rest with operations at the full.

But Lafe is ahead of the strippers for a few minutes. He pauses to watch Hendrickson picking over a basket of eggs taken only three days ago. With a blunt metal tweezer, five inches long, he lifts out the empties, or all that do not show eyes. Only the "pin-heads" are fertile, although some of these may later die. Already Lafe has learned that about four per cent of each batch is lost—a small figure. Some succumb to fungus growth. A few hatch freaks—double bodies that mature to the feeding stage, when the stronger side grabs most of the food, leading to starvation for one and consequent death for the other. Two-headed salmon occasionally survive. One bi-sexual specimen, fully-grown, is preserved in a glass container on the visitor's balcony.

But Lafe cannot tarry long indoors, and he hurries back for another pair of filled buckets. This time, upon returning to the hatchery he stops to look at a trough of recently hatched fry, their slender silver bodies, less than an inch long, still attached to the yellow yolk-sacks which feed them until fully absorbed. From thirty to forty days pass, from hatching date, before the fry are completely "buttoned up."[4] Artificial feeding then begins. Soon thereafter the fingerlings,[5] as they are now known, are siphoned off and removed to the outside ponds. These newly-hatched fry, Lafe knows, are a part of the experimental spring take of Chinook. They will be going down the Columbia around Christmas, at the time the last fall-run Chinook female will have ascended for spawning in the waters of Tanner Creek and with an expert flip of her tail will have covered her eggs with the stream gravel.

Lee Norwood, at the upper spawning pool, is pushing his crew and himself to the limit. He wants the station to show its best record this year. The hatchery, rebuilt in 1936, can handle 20 million eggs annually. So far the top production figure stands around 13 million. Not enough. So he works hard and fast. Right now he and his companions are each handling from three to five fish a minute. Two or three of these are thrown out as ripe. But the strippers can manage only little more than two females a minute, so now and again Norwood climbs out to the platform and helps. No female can be allowed to lie around for more than twenty minutes, if her eggs are to retain sufficient life for proper fertilization and hatching.

As the morning advances, the air and the upriver breeze grow warmer. In greater numbers the autumn-drying leaves rustle down. When the rains start they will darken and fall in clouds. On the harsh wet earth they will soon blacken. When the bitter east wind of winter comes down the gorge, snow will ride on its back.

By 10:15 Norwood and Meeves are ahead of the strippers by twenty-odd fish. Norwood climbs out of the pool and strides over to see how Monson is making it to determine if the two new men are any good. They seem to be catching on, he observes. Monson, from the restless live waters, nods in his speechless manner, as if to assure his superior that all is well, or perhaps to indicate that the salmon average larger than on any previous day, just as Norwood had predicted.

The superintendent steps over to a nearby pond of fingerling Chinooks, now almost six inches long. Big enough for dispersal. This noon he will open the gates and let them go. The pool is needed anyway for the advancing horde of three-year-olds.

Moving about the hatchery grounds and peering into the many pools are several dozen visitors. In favorable weather they come in large numbers from early morning until darkfall. Several thousand a day may arrive in summer months. Two men, seeing Norwood for the moment unoccupied, step up and question him about the work. Their inquiries are typical, and Norwood replies:

Yes, the Bonneville station takes only Chinook and silver spawn, but some blueback[6] eggs are brought in and hatched. Salmon eggs hatch in from six to twelve weeks, depending on water-temperature—in sixty days for a fifty degree average. The shad[7] battery you see at the hatching house is operated out of doors, at St. Helens, in April. Two million fry at once. Shad roe hatches in forty-eight hours and the fry mature in a week. Yes, we raise a few trout here, steelhead, but mostly for local color—people like to look at them. Did you see the sturgeon in the pool over there by the driveway? The hatchery never sells fish, no.

Two more tourist cars with Eastern licenses roll into the parking area north of the grounds and their occupants spill out. A girl in red slacks alights and points to the great shute of Table Mountain[8] rearing skyward on the Washington side. A man in brown follows her and they move over to the drinking fountain.

Norwood goes back to his spawn-taking operations.

Another hour passes.

"Get the count when you go up this time," Norwood directs Lafe as he starts away with two more buckets. It is now nearly 11:30. While he is gone the seiners tighten up on the net, pulling the somewhat reduced salmon mass closer in about the legs of the three heavily-garmented pool men, making it difficult to step about and maintain a sure footing. In reaching for a large ripe female, Norwood is forced off balance. He attempts to wrap his arm around the fish and take a step forward at the same time. But the mass will not yield. The fish he clutches flips and he falls with a splash among the plunging salmon. A shout from the lower pool goes up. Norwood shakes his fist at them but he is smiling. Despite his rubber clothing, he is thoroughly soaked.

Such an accident is a part of the task, and happens to all pool workers several times a season. Although the creek waters are chilly, Norwood will remain on the job until noon before changing. Up toward the hatchery, he sees Lafe coming back.

"Just over four hundred thousand," Cardwell says. "That's the best—"

"That's the best yet, but it's not any too good. We'll have to hit it a lick this afternoon and work till six to go over the million mark. We did a million four hundred thousand one day last year. Let's go." And Norwood, his wet hat tossed out on the bank, grabs for another ripe fish.

Between spells at the net, the seiners have been busy filleting the salmon carcasses, stripping the flesh from the bones and putting this meat into 30-pound boxes, which they wheel down to the storage house, for freezing. Later it will be fed to the fingerlings. This year nearly sixty tons will be preserved at small cost. Additional fish and viscera will come from the canneries at Astoria.

The strippers are talking among themselves as the noon hour approaches.

"Fastest stripper I ever saw was Indian Dave. Worked up at the White Salmon station three years ago. He was half-breed Klickitat and when he was going good he could strip three biddies a minute. Went hunting with him once and he gutted and cut up a deer in less'n fifteen minutes. Indian nature, I guess."

"Ever see them fishing from the rocks up at Celilo? Boy, are they quick!"

"Yeah. But salmon, after they get up that far, ain't so good eating. No oil left in 'em. Dry. Why, they've been three months getting up there. And they haven't eaten a mouthful since leaving the ocean. Just look at the fish we take here. No guts left, even." He runs his knife up the underside of a thirty-pound Chinook he is holding; only the round red eggs gush out.

From the time salmon reach fresh water their appetites decrease, and their throats and stomachs gradually shrink, until, at the approach of the spawning season they have become entirely incapacitated for food; the desire and ability to feed has left them entirely. The great reserve of flesh and oil brought with them from the ocean enables them to keep the vital organs active until their mission is accomplished. Under normal circumstances, after they are entirely spawned out they remain in or near the beds, deteriorating rapidly, the flesh shading off to a light, dirty pink, and they become foul, diseased, and much emaciated. Their scales are partly absorbed, and, in the males, wholly enveloped in the skin, which is of a dark olive or blue hue; blotches of fungus appear on their heads and bodies, and in various places long white patches of skin have been partly worn off. Their tails and fins become badly mutilated, and in a short time they die.

Norwood, without slowing his actions, puts in a comment. "Those Indians up the river are still getting plenty of fish. The Dam doesn't stop them, as they said it would. I was asking up at the fish ladders yesterday noon and the boys said the count of the fingerlings coming down stream was going to reach an all time high this month—thought they'd reach the 400,000 mark, almost, for Chinook alone."

"Not to mention Steelheads and Silversides."[9]

"They'll make another 50,000."

"They can't come down if they don't go up," the second stripper comments.

"Besides, that," Norwood continues, "we've released over seven million fingerlings so far this year; and there are still four ponds to go. Make a good round eight million. We'd have had more but we shipped away three million eggs. Some of them went to Finland."

"Are they taking Chum up at Ox Bow this year?"

"Oh, sure, but it's not a very important run. Chum dries well; that's why the packers demand it. The Ox Bow station is important right now for the job it's doing in marking fish. This year they released 100,000 marked Chinooks above Bonneville Dam and the same number just below here. Those that don't get eaten by other fish or caught by fishermen will be back in three years and we'll see then how many get above the dam. Those released three years ago are going up the ladders now. And the count of survivals averages about normal. We rarely pick one up here; that shows they're going on up. Pretty hard to fool a fish, if it's got the strength to get upstream; providing, of course, it eludes the fishermen. . . . Well, that sun says noon, fellows." And Norwood tosses up a twenty-pound female. "That's the last for this morning. Got enough males to finish with? Good."

He clambers out and his companions follow. They fling the water and fish scales from their heavy garments. There is little odor about them, even in the sun-heated air, so fresh are the stream waters. The strippers finish their work and, buckets in hand, the crew moves up toward the hatchery house.

Visitors, in greater numbers, are moving about the grounds. They walk in single file along the pool sides and stop in small groups conversing. Women watch less curiously than men the egg-taking procedure where Monson and his crew are finishing up. Over near the picnicking grounds two children are breaking up parts of a sandwich and tossing it bit by bit to the thousand greedy fingerlings that dart like silver flashes about a square concrete-walled pool. On a near-by table three women in bright clothing are spreading out a lunch. The girl in the red slacks and her escort are studying a marker that says here camped the overland explorers, Lewis and Clark, in the late autumn of 1805. "Why, we studied about that way back in grade school! And here we are—imagine that!" Her companion adds, "I'll bet they had plenty of salmon for dinner that night." He chuckles.

Up by the hatchery door, Norwood glances at the western sky. White clouds are rolling up. He turns and looks eastward; the air of the upper gorge is darkening, growing thick. From the looks of the sky and the atmosphere, this good weather won't last much longer.

As he makes his way along the gravel walk to his cottage and his lunch, he catches up with Monson, going the short way home. "I think we'll make our million, Monson," he declares.

"She rain tomorrow," Monson replies.

Notes

1. Salmon "fry" measure around 30mm depending on the species. Sometimes used interchangeably with "alevin," or "sac fry," the term denotes an early stage in the life cycle of salmon development. Generally, "fry" refers to the period immediately after the eggs hatch, up until the salmon begin to develop their distinguishing markings at which point they are called "Parr." Depending on the source, the "fry" period can be anywhere from 12–15 weeks up until the end of the first year after the eggs hatch. The term is also the origin of the expression "small fry." Dorling Kindersley Publishing, *The Dorling Kindersley Encyclopedia of Fishing* (New York: Dorling Kindersley, 1994), 152–53; Thomas P. Quinn, *The Behavior and Ecology of Pacific Salmon and Trout* (Bethesda, MD: American Fisheries Society, 2005), 3, 15, 165; Harold Wentworth and Stuart Berg Flexner, *Dictionary of American Slang* (New York: Crowell, 1960), 491.
2. See "The Fish are Running" in this volume.
3. Essentially salmon sperm, milt is a fluid released by the male in order to fertilize eggs. When salmon are spawning, this fluid is released in very large quantities. Quinn, *Behavior and Ecology*, 3, 114; Cornelis Groot and L. Margolis, *Pacific Salmon Life Histories* (Vancouver, BC: University of British Columbia Press, 2003), 22.
4. A fisherman's expression for the period in which the young salmon "fry" or "alevin" have filled up their yolk sac and have finished feeding on it. Quinn, *Behavior and Ecology*, 163.
5. A broader, less life-cycle specific, descriptor of young, developing salmon. Especially during the early part of the twentieth century, due to economic implications for commercial fish hatcheries, the distinction between "fry vs. fingerling" was a complex discussion and a source of significant legal wrangling in Columbia River fisheries management. Quinn, *Behavior and Ecology*, 3; Joseph E. Taylor, *Making Salmon: An Environmental History of the Northwest Fisheries Crisis* (Seattle: University of Washington Press, 2001), 204–6.

6. Also "sockeye" salmon, "blueback" are the second most abundant species in the Columbia River. Quinn, *Behavior and Ecology*, 14.

7. A non-salmon species of fish, "*Alosa sapidissima*." Like chinook salmon, the general focus of this story, shad are migratory and also harvested for consumption in the Columbia River. Quinn, *Behavior and Ecology*, 5.

8. A variant of "chute" (also called a "couloir" by climbers), the narrator is possibly referring to a distinguishing, visible gorge on the side of Table Mountain that descended into a series of rapids before the Bonneville Dam was built in 1938. This would likely be on the North side of the river depending on the vantage point of the viewer. R. J. Secor, *The High Sierra: Peaks, Passes and Trails* (Seattle, WA: Mountaineers Books, 2009), 120–21.

9. Species of salmon and trout. Dorling Kindersley Publishing, *Encyclopedia of Fishing*, 152–55.

THE SHIPYARDS GET A WELDER

Chester Himes (Ohio)

He took the last rod from the bench, a number 8 special, and stuck it in the plier-shaped handle of the arc welder,[1] kicking its tail, that garden-hose-sized black cable leading back to the high-voltage generator, out from under his feet. Before he started running off the job, he took a quick look at the job selector and current control to see if his arc was right and his juice full. The dials, as large as plates, always reminded him of the speedometer on his hack.[2] He reached over and adjusted the current control so that it was set as nearly perfect as the slight fluctuations caused by the operation of the other machines in the room, a room of darkness and blue fire, permitted.

Picking up his shield, a shovel-shaped affair of asbestos composition with a short handle and a two-by-four-inch dark glass window, he held it in front of his face, turning the semi-gloom of the welding booth into pitch blackness. Then he pointed the end of the rod into the angle of the metal on the bench before him and began to run a "C" weave up a vertical "T" joint, turning his wrist in steady, regular motions something like a penmanship expert forming a series of "C's," one inside the other.

The white-hot juice jumping from the end of the rod to bite a crater deep into the metal, melting the rod to fill the crater as it moved in its series of "C's," was a live, vicious thing, a concentrate of light and heat so intense that it seemed as if light itself had been captured and dried and powdered and driven through the end of the melting rod with unbelievable force to form a spitting, frying arc. So whitely hot that in ordinary atmosphere it showed blue beyond white, the tiny arc filled the asbestos curtained booth with a blue-white brilliance that splashed on a naked eyeball like a handful of lye. Through his shield, however, the arc was cunningly toned to a tiny stream of lightish green with a pale aurora about it; a flashlight in a green fog.

In the room where he worked there were four rows of booths, separated by narrow aisles, and each booth enclosed with a tattered asbestos curtain. In each a student laboriously practiced the fiery knitting together of the metals. There was little light outside the booths and less inside, for in welding there is no need of lighting. The base metal upon the bench on which he worked was visible enough in the bloom; and when the arc spit its blue heat, filling the booth with agate brilliance, it was all light, solid and hard to the touch and filled with a frying sound that had gotten on his nerves at first. It was the way you thought of the sound of a body burning in the electric chair, and, until you got used to it, the scratchy sputter made you itchy inside. Like a foundation supporting the hard block of light was the sound of the machines, the dry, incessant roar of a hundred million hidden locusts. Blue-white smoke, billowing up from the frying arc, filled his nostrils and his mouth and his palate with a sharp acrid odor, tasting like acid, metal shavings, burned peas, and searing things like flame that you never could taste but only watch. A modern inferno was in that booth, but he was no longer terrified by it; he liked it; he made it.

He alone could taste the weld; he could feel it in his fingers and his nerves and through his brain. He could smell-hear-taste-feel the heat-light-frying-itching-weird operation. It lived in him and he in it; and he could go away in it, alone in it. And there would be only the vicious, leashed, blue-white heat concentrate of the spitting arc in all the world, controlled and manned, guided and steered, ordered and made to fuse two metal plates into one by the almost ridiculously gently motion of his wrist.

Welding gave him a feeling of power, of satisfaction. Driving a cab had never been like this; not even when he was new at it and was learning to make his way among all the cluttered facts of the city and its people. Each time he dug a crater into the hard, flat surface of the base steel and penciled a weave or a series of stringer beads with the little vicious arc at the end of the melting rod, he felt the deep drama of the operation. There was always in him at such times the wonder of man coming out of his cave, dropping his primitive clubs, and mastering fire and finally metal and electricity. Not that he knew much about that or ever thought consciously of it in that way; Spark Taylor was not an educated man, but all the wonder was there just the same. As much as if he'd known about every tortuous step man had made to reach today's engineering marvels, and had a knowledge, too, of how little divided him from slipping quickly back to his primitive beginnings.

When the rod had burnt down to a stub, Spark cut the current and shook the butt into a can placed on the bench. By the number of butts at the end of a day's work, the instructors could tell how many rods each student had used.

He went out into the dim aisle and sauntered to the wash room for a smoke. In the play of the blue light that flashed through the translucent door and aided the sickly yellow glow of the one bulb dangling on the end of a cord high over head, a grin broadened in the sharpness of Spark's face. He was pleased with himself, with the school, and with the world. This is it! Tomorrow they hand me a slip of paper saying that in four weeks Richard B. Taylor has learned to do flat, vertical, and overhead jobs with a London Arc Welder. It was going to be his passport right into those shipyards.

At first glance in this fuller light, he was an ordinary guy with a big-city nonchalance; but that grin—a thing he wore like a mask—and the crow-feet pull at the outer edges of his eyes, lifting his face in a slight outside slant, made him an individual. Looking at him again, you could imagine him standing pat on a trey, six, jack, four, and a deuce and saying: "Well, this is it boys," and setting in his stack.

In a way of speaking, four weeks before, he had done just that thing, buying a $12.90 round-trip ticket from New York to Cleveland out of his last 93 bucks, staking his stack on a four-week's course in an arc welding school he'd never seen.

He'd been standing down on Broadway near 50th that afternoon, watching the hacks roll up and down the stem; and wondering how in hell he'd let himself be high-pressured into cracking a red light for ten lousy bucks to catch a train—and him hacking that town for seven years without a rap—when Tony Shapiro sauntered by, looking sharp as barber's shears. If he hadn't called out, "I'm the same fella," Tony would have never seen him.

Hearing the familiar phrase, Tony stopped and turned. He came back with his hand out. "The Spark. Boy, you look undressed without your hack. Waiting for a party?"

"Me? I'm grounded, son, as the air corps guys say. Lost my license for 30 days."

"Tough," Tony sympathized. "How'd it happen?"

"I stuck out my chin instead'a my hand." Spark looked him over. "You seem to be doing O.K. How're you playing 'em?"

"I'm a welder now," Tony explained. "Dressing uncle's battleships with armor plate. I went out to Cleveland and came back with a new angle."

After digging out the details, Spark decided: This is as good a time as any. Thinking back on it now from the window of the washroom, with the burning arcs from the practice room playing blue lightning over his face, his grin rippled. What a guy could learn in just four weeks!

The first person he had talked to after reporting at the big plant on the lake front which manufactured the arc welders and operated the welding school at a loss, writing it off to advertising, was the vice president, Mr. Travis. He was the guy, Spark learned later, who had inaugurated the school to supply operators to the purchasers of their machine.

"So you're from New York," Mr. Travis had said, looking him over. "And you used to be a hack driver. Well, that don't surprise us. We get 'em from all over. We charge you 15 bucks and don't ask questions. All we want to know is do you want to learn to weld?"

"I ain't no tourist," Spark said.

"All we can give you is the fundamentals of welding. Take me, f'rinstance. I went to Ohio State and took a course in engineering and got a degree, and you might say I was an engineer. But all I got was the fundamentals, the ground work. If I had gone into some field of engineering and specialized and worked at it, then I would be an engineer. Same way with welding. In four weeks all we can teach you is how to do plain work. Take you four years to know all there is to know about arc welding—maybe more. It would break us to give a four year course to all the men who want to learn arc welding. We'd have to turn the whole plant into a school. A four year course would damn well break the men before they got started too!"

If the telephone hadn't rung, Mr. Travis might have kept this up for a long time. Spark could see, even then, that it was his pet. While reaching for the phone, he directed, "You go down this hall and turn to your right and you'll see a door marked 'Sales.' You go in there and ask for Mr. McCarty. He'll take care of you. Travis speaking. . . . "

From McCarty who talked fast without looking at you, Spark learned that the school ran 24 hours a day in 8-hour shifts and that the pupils were required to spend 8 hours a day, 6 days a week, for 4 weeks in the course. They checked in and out each day as if working in a shop.

Situated on the fifth floor of one of the shop buildings, the school had nothing impressive about it; and he began to wonder if he had been gypped. The class room was long and narrow and overlooked a gravel factory yard. At the front was the instructor's desk, and beyond, several rows of backless benches, the purpose of which Spark never learned. A work bench, piled with shields without glasses, scraps of metal, and what then seemed to Spark a clutter of junk, extended along the windows. At the rear was a demonstration table of metal with the welding machine back of it.

To the right of the class room, looking dismal through the dingy windows of the double doors, was the practice room. Other men were straggling in now. A couple of them looked O.K. Looked like cross country truckers. The rest weren't so hot, he decided with his practiced, cynical hackster's eye. The paunchy pale one was probably a reformed bum; somebody trying to put him on his feet via the industrial course route. He lit a cigarette and wondered if it was Alcoholics Anonymous that was straightening the guy up. He'd read something about them in *Colliers* or some place; maybe the *Mirror*. Anyhow, he made a bet with himself the guy would be back in psycho ward in four months. A little Italian with sharp shoes and a waxed mustache—it looked waxed anyhow—came in next. Two or three pale little men, ex-bookkeepers or clerks, he guessed, straggled in. The instructor came in fast and began taking down names and addresses. He was bald and his chops hung like an English bulldog's. There were other instructors; Travis had said there were three for each shift. He drew the one with the chops and was assigned to the day shift. The instructor took his gang aside and told them what to buy: asbestos gloves, a glass for the shield, and heavy overalls. "Report at eight sharp," he said and shut his notebook and hustled away.

Spark was pretty sure he wouldn't like it. He thought about using the rest of his ticket to get back to the big town and to hell with welding. But he knew the best welding school in the country was supposed to be this one; he had found that out before he came, and that it would be cheaper, even with the fare thrown in, than the New York schools. Once out on the street, he decided he might as well go through with the thing. His 15 bucks was in the pot, and he could stand anything for four weeks.

Spark thought about his course in snatches. How he'd gotten to almost like the hustling little man with the chops. How the class clustered around the instructor so they could hear his voice above the noise of the machinery in other parts of the plant. How the instructor snapped out his first words to the class that morning. "The principle of arc welding is to form an arc between the rod carrying the current. . . . " The ex-bum had fidgeted. The instructors never talked more than they had to, though. Mostly the class practiced.

The practice wasn't easy. Sometimes he'd get the rod too close and it would stick to the metal. Sometimes he'd hold it too far away to make a crater and all he'd have when he was finished was a filigree of melted metal sticking to the weld. Then there was the time Spark forgot to hold the shield with one gloved hand and, instead, held the metal in one hand and the welder in the other. For a minute he thought he was blind from the searing light. Then he remembered the instructor's safety instructions: "Light blisters the eyes. Use argyrol[3]—there's some in the wash room—and ice packs." He had staggered into the wash room and one of the other pupils, an ex-professional football player, helped him until the instructor came and took care of his eyes with a practiced hand. He never forgot his shield again.

Spark decided that learning to weld was like learning to drive. The instructor could sit beside you and talk his head off, but you had to learn to do it yourself and you never really knew until you took a car down through traffic alone.

He got used to the difficult numbers of rods and learned which to use for each kind of job. In the third week he went on to the advanced instructor, and learned to make a vertical "T" joint. He was damn proud of himself when he got it right, and by then he loved welding and didn't mind the noise or the smoke or the acrid smell.

Tomorrow he'd get that paper and be a welder. Not that he'd be an expert welder. Travis was right; he could see that now. But he was going to know all there was to know about welding before he died, and in less than four years too. But for now he was a welder, according to the London Electric Company's certificate, and that was enough to get him a job in uncle's shipyards, helping build a two oceaner. No more hacking. Spark Taylor, walking out of that wash room, was a guy with a trade.

Notes

1. The refinement of arc welding technology in the first half of the twentieth century was an essential component in the development of the American industrial base during this period. Shipbuilding, aviation, and many other industries relied heavily on trained arc welders and companies like Lincoln Electric, based in the author's home state of Ohio, were essential in supplying these industries with technology and certified welders. "Welding for War and Peace," *Popular Mechanics*, June, 1943: 8–11; 166–68; Lincoln Electric, *The Procedure Handbook of Arc Welding* (Cleveland: Lincoln Electric, 1994), 1–6.

2. Refers to a taxi or, less frequently, some other type of commercial automotive conveyance such as a bus. It initially signified a horse-drawn carriage, but after the invention of the automobile, the term came to mean a taxi cab. Harold Wentworth and Stuart Berg Flexner, *Dictionary of American Slang* (New York: Crowell, 1960), 238.

3. The trade name for a silver solution developed by Dr. Albert Barnes. The solution was marketed as an effective treatment for eye injuries and other antiseptic applications. Howard Greenfield, *The Devil and Dr. Barnes: Portrait of an American Art Collector* (Philadelphia, PA: Camino, 2005), 17; Alan B. G. Lansdown, *Silver in Healthcare: Its Antimicrobial Efficacy and Safety in Use* (Cambridge, UK: Royal Society of Chemistry, 2010), 234–35.

ILLUSTRATIONS

1. Leah Balsham, *Man with Pick*, lithograph.
Image copyright The Metropolitan Museum of Art/Art Resource, New York.

2. Paul Tyler, *High Lead*, 1938, lithograph on ivory paper.
Collection of the Newark Museum, commissioned by Federal Art Project,
Works Progress Administration. Lent by General Services Administration, 1945. 45.844.

3. Michael J. Gallagher, *Black Country*, wood engraving.
Courtesy Illinois State Museum.

4. Bernard Schardt, *Slaughter House*, wood engraving.
Courtesy The Blanton Museum of Art.

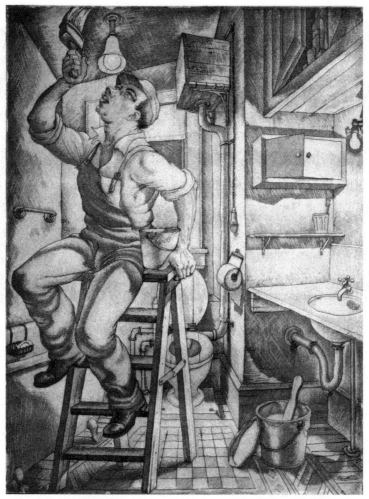

5. Hugh Botts, *House Painter*, etching and aquatint.
Courtesy Library of Congress.

6. Salvatore Pinto, *Mills*, ca. 1935, wood engraving.
Collection of the Newark Museum, commissioned by Federal Art Project,
Works Progress Administration. Lent by General Services Administration, 1945. 45.402.

7. Elizabeth Olds, *Blast Furnace*, lithograph.
Courtesy Smithsonian Institution.

8. Charles Reed Gardner, *Tapping the Furnace,* wood engraving.
Courtesy the Historical Society of Pennsylvania.

9. Michael J. Gallagher, *Last Shift*, 1937, lithograph on ivory paper.
Collection of the Newark Museum, commissioned by Federal Art Project,
Works Progress Administration. Lent by General Services Administration, 1945. 45.1202.

10. Elizabeth Olds, *Miner Joe*, lithograph.
Courtesy Library of Congress.

11. Beatrice Cuming, *Locomotive*, 1937, etching on cream paper.
Collection of the Newark Museum, commissioned by Federal Art Project,
Works Progress Administration. Lent by General Services Administration, 1945. 45.1156.

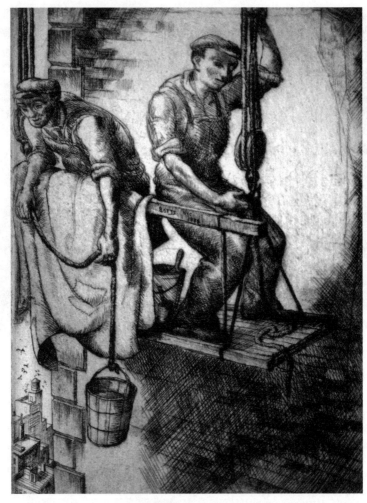

12. Hugh Botts, *Sign Painters*, 1936, Etching on cream paper.
Collection of the Newark Museum, commissioned by Federal Art Project,
Works Progress Administration. Lent by General Services Administration, 1945. 43.350.

13. Hugh Botts, *Construction Workers*, etching and aquatint.
Courtesy Library of Congress.

14. Fred Becker, *Clambake*, wood engraving.
Courtesy Smithsonian Institution.

15. Horatio Forjohn, *Defense Steel*, lithograph.
Courtesy the Historical Society of Pennsylvania.

16. Isaac Soyer, *Bacteriologist*, ca. 1935, lithograph on ivory paper.
Collection of the Newark Museum, commissioned by Federal Art Project,
Works Progress Administration. Lent by General Services Administration, 1945. 43.775.

17. Harry Mack, *Arc Welder*, etching and aquatint.
Courtesy Library of Congress.

CONTRIBUTORS' BIOGRAPHIES

Clair Anderson (*1902–1956*). The scion of Scandinavian immigrants Charles C. and Walborg (Christiansen) Anderson, Clair Anderson was born in rural Huntington, Utah. By 1910 the family had relocated to Salt Lake City. Beginning in the mid-1930s Anderson worked on several FWP projects including the "History of Grazing" in Utah. He also researched the history of mining in Utah for the state's writers' project. Five months before Pearl Harbor and at the age of thirty-nine, Anderson enlisted in the Navy. He achieved the rank of Storekeeper 1st Class in the U.S. Naval Reserve. After the war it appears he settled in Phoenix, Arizona, where he was employed as a clerk and freelance writer for magazines. Anderson married Dorothy May Reiley on 21 August 1950; he died 24 August 1956.

REFERENCES: 1910 U.S. Census, Salt Lake City, Salt Lake Co., UT, stamped p. 194, household of Charles C. Anderson; 1920 U.S. Census, Salt Lake City, Salt Lake Co., UT, p. 8, household of Charles C. Anderson; FamilySearch, Ancestral File Record for Charles Christian Anderson (Ancestral File No.: 1 WJJ-0Q), accessed 8 Jan. 2011, https://www.familysearch.org; Archived email "descendants of Norris Thomas from England," 6 Mar. 1999, accessed 8 Jan. 2011, http://archiver.rootsweb.ancestry.com/th/read/THOMAS/1999-03/0920745258; "Honor Roll," *Salt Lake Telegram*, 14 June 1941, p. 12; Photograph of gravestone for Clair C. Anderson, accessed 8 Jan. 2011, http://www.findagrave.com; Certificate of Death for Clair Charles Anderson, recorded 28 Aug. 1956, State File No. 5002, digital image, Arizona Department of Health Services, accessed 8 Jan. 2011, http://genealogy.az.gov/index.htm.

Leah Balsham (*1915–*). Born in Philadelphia, Pennsylvania, to Jewish Russian immigrants, Balsham was living in Chicago by 1930. She attended the Art Institute of Chicago, one of the premier art schools in the country. The Institute thought so highly of her that they later appointed her as a professor of ceramics. Her prints and ceramics were exhibited at the Art Institute in the 1930s and 1960s;

Hyde Park Art Center in Chicago in 1955; University of Chicago in 1962; Illinois
State Museum in Springfield, Illinois, in 1983; and at Valparaiso University, in
Valparaiso, Indiana, in 2003. Balsham moved to Beverly Shores, Indiana, in the
early 1970s.

REFERENCES: "Leah Balsham," Illinois Women Artists Project, accessed 19
Aug. 2010, http://iwa.bradley.edu; "The School of the Art Institute—1961," *The Art
Institute of Chicago Quarterly* 55, no. 2 (June 1961): 33; 1930 U.S. Census, Chicago,
Cook Co., IL, p. 24; "Honorary Members," National Council on Education for
the Ceramic Arts, accessed 20 Aug. 2010, http://nceca.net/static/about_hon-
oraries_members.php; Beverly Overmyer, "Volunteer Focus: Leah Balsham," *ICS
Newsletter*, (Spring 2006): 5.

Frederick Gerhard Becker Jr. (1913–2004). Becker was born in Oakland, California, on 5 August 1913. By 1920 his family had relocated to Los Angeles. Becker
attended the Otis Art Institute in Los Angeles from 1931 to 1933, then moved to
New York City in September 1933, where he briefly studied architecture at New
York University. In early 1934 he returned to studying art at the Beaux Arts Institute under Eugene Steinhof. During World War II he served for four years with
the U.S. Office of War Information in Burma and China. After the war Becker
returned to New York and printmaking. He worked under Stanley William Hay-
ter at his studio, Atlier 17, during this period. In 1948 he moved to Washington
University in St. Louis, Missouri, where he established a printmaking program and
served as an art professor for two decades. In 1968 Becker took a position at the
University of Massachusetts. He retired in 1986. Galleries and museums in New
York, St. Louis, Philadelphia, Massachusetts, Washington DC, London, Paris,
Rome, and Buenos Aires exhibited his work, as did the 1939 and 1964 World's
Fairs. Becker received fellowships from the Louis Comfort Tiffany Foundation,
Yaddo, and the John Simon Guggenheim Memorial Foundation. He married Jean
Barclay Morrison on 19 February 1949 in St. Louis; they had two children. Becker
died at Amherst on 30 June 2004.

REFERENCES: Peter Hastings Falk, ed., *Who Was Who in American Art* (Madi-
son, CT: Sound View Press, 1999), 2:257; 1920 U.S. Census, Los Angeles, Los
Angeles Co., CA, p. 5, household of Antony W. Becker; "Jean Barclay Morrison
Married in St. Louis," *Cranford (NJ) Citizen and Chronicle*, 24 Feb. 1949, p. 4;
"Frederick G. Becker," unpublished typescript biography written after 1965; Fred
Becker, "The WPA Federal Art Project, New York City: A Reminiscence," *The
Massachusetts Review* 39, no. 1 (Spring 1998):74–92; Grace Glueck, "Fred Becker,

90, Artist, Printmaker and Professor, Dies," *New York Times,* 12 July 2004, online edition, http://nytimes.com, accessed 1 Feb. 2010; U.S. Social Security Death Index, entry for Frederick G. Becker, born 5 Aug. 1913.

Hugh Pearce Botts (1903–1964). Born 19 April 1903 in New York City, Hugh Botts lived most of his life in either the city of his birth or nearby New Jersey. In the mid-twenties Botts ventured to London. He served as an Ordinary Seaman on board the S.S. *American Farmer* on its 6 August 1926 voyage from London to New York. He studied at Rutgers University in New Jersey, and at the National Academy of Design, the Art Students League, and the Beaux Arts Institute, all in New York City. In the 1930s Botts was employed by the WPA's New York City Graphics Program of the WPA. A man of multiple talents, Botts held patents for a number of inventions, including some that appeared in *Popular Science.* In the arts, his principle area of endeavor, Botts was not only a printmaker, but also a painter, designer, sculptor, craftsperson, illustrator, and writer. His organizational affiliations reflected his diverse artistic interests. Botts served as director of the Audubon Artists Membership Committee, he was an associate member of the National Academy of Design, and a member of the Salmagundi Club in New York City, the American Artists Professional League, the Philadelphia Watercolor Club, the Princeton Print Club, the American Color Print Society, the Connecticut Academy of Fine Arts, the Chicago Society of Etchers, the New Jersey Painters and Sculptors, the New Haven Paint and Clay Club, the National Sculpture Society, the Northwest Printmakers, the North Shore Artists Association, the Springfield Artists League, and the New England Print Association. He exhibited at many major national print shows and received a number of prizes for his work. Hugh Botts died 25 April 1964, in Cranford, New Jersey.

REFERENCES: Peter Hastings Falk, ed., *Who Was Who in American Art* (Madison, CT: Sound View Press, 1985), 68; Falk, *Who Was Who in American Art* (1999), 2:392; "Hugh Pearce Botts: Personalities, Places, and the Urban Scene," *Gallery Notes* (Memorial Gallery of the University of Rochester [NY]), May 1985; 1920 U.S. Census, Scotch Plains Township, Union Co., NJ, stamped p. 297, household of Hugh F. Botts; New York Passenger Lists, 1820–1957, digital image, ship manifest for S.S. *American Farmer,* 6 Aug. 1926, Ancestry.com, accessed 28 Aug. 2010; 1930 U.S. Census, Cranford Township, Union Co., NJ, p. 57, household of Hugh F. Botts; Rachael Baldanza, "Prints, People and Practice . . . Or How Artists Can Linger. . . ," *Gallery Buzz* (blog of the Memorial Art Gallery of the University of Rochester), 15 Oct. 2009, http://blogs.rochester.edu/MAG/?=917; "Hugh P. Botts," *Cranford (NJ) Citizen and Chronicle,* 30 Apr. 1964, p. 4.

Verne Bright (*1893–1977*). A major figure in Oregon's arts projects during the Great Depression, Verne Bright was born in 1893, in the midst of one of America's other great depressions. As a boy he moved from Missouri to Kansas with his family and then, upon being orphaned as a teenager, to Oregon. During World War I Bright served with the American Expeditionary Forces in Siberia. He graduated in 1925 with a BA from Pacific University, an institution that would later award him an honorary doctorate of letters. In 1935 Bright was made the state editor of the Oregon Writers' Project. He occupied that position until 1940, when he accepted the editorship of the Oregon Historical Records Survey. Bright worked there until 1942, when he joined the flood of men and women on the home front who took jobs in the wartime shipbuilding industry. In 1951 Bright returned to historical work as the assistant curator of the Oregon Historical Society. Bright also worked as a farm laborer, newspaper reporter, freelance writer, poet, English composition and creative writing teacher, and postmaster of Aloha, Oregon. By the time he was sixty Bright had moved to The Breakers in Tolovana Park, Oregon. He died in January 1977 at Seaside, Oregon.

> REFERENCES: Hazel E. Mills, ed., *Who's Who Among Pacific Northwest Authors* (Salem, OR: Pacific Northwest Library Association Reference Section, 1957), 61; Oregon Historical Society Research Library, entry for Verne Bright Papers, 1920–1953, OHS Library Catalog, accessed Jan. 2010, http://librarycatalog. ohs.org; World War I Draft Registration Cards, 1917–1918, digital image, Washington Co., OR, Draft Board, Aloha Precinct, Aloha, OR, registration for Verne Bright, Ancestry.com, accessed Feb. 2010, http://search.ancestry.com; 1900 U.S. Census, Fawn Creek Township, Montgomery Co., KS, p. 97, household of Leonard C. Bright; 1920 U.S. Census, Aloha, Washington Co., OR, p. 183, household of Charles E. Barkey; 1930 U.S. Census, Aloha, Washington Co., OR, p. 176, household of Verne Bright; Kenneth Fitzgerald, "Kin to the Wandery Wind," *The (Portland) Oregonian*, 18 Dec. 1948, p. 5; "Young Poet is Student," *The (Portland) Sunday Oregonian*, 23 Oct. 1921, p. 16; U.S. Social Security Death Index, entry for Verne Bright, born 15 Jan. 1893.

Lorin W. Brown (*1900–1978*). Brown was born in Elizabethtown, a New Mexico mining camp, in 1900, but after his father's sudden death in 1901, he and his mother moved to Taos, where his maternal grandparents, the Martínezes, largely raised him. They had an enormous influence on his view of New Mexico and the place of Hispano culture within it. Brown's grandmother taught him the folkways—particularly folk medicine—that she and other Taoseños practiced. Both a well-regarded healer and midwife, Juanita Montoya de Martínez claimed Taos Pueblo as well as Hispano ancestry and had connections to both communities.

Brown also spent four years living with his father's relatives and attending school in Kansas. Brown's bilingual abilities, multicultural sensitivity, and his ties through blood and experience to Hispano, Anglo, and Pueblo culture, made him, according to the scholars who know his work best, the ideal chronicler of 1930s New Mexico. Before beginning his more than half-a-decade employment for the Santa Fe office of the FWP, Brown worked for the National Recovery Administration and the Public Works Administration. In his time with the FWP he produced almost two hundred manuscripts including numerous transcribed folktales and folksongs, field reports from his travels among the Northern New Mexican villages he called home, and interpretive and impressionistic sketches of the life of the people in these places. Brown left New Mexico during World War II and did not return until the early 1970s. In 1978, Brown was laid to rest in Cordova, the village where he had spent the most time during his remarkable years working for the FWP.

REFERENCES: Charles L. Briggs and Marta Weigle, "Preface" and "Lorin W. Brown in Taos and Cordova: A Biographical and Ethnohistorical Sketch," in Lorin W. Brown, *Hispano Folklife of New Mexico: The Lorin W. Brown Federal Writers' Project Manuscripts* (Albuquerque: University of New Mexico Press, 1978), xi–xiii, 3–7, 9–10, 23–25.

John Wesley Conroy (1898–1990). "Jack" was raised in Monkey Nest, a coal mining camp in the northernmost part of Missouri. Conroy's 1933 autobiographical novel *The Disinherited*, his editorship of the *Anvil* and a number of other thirties magazines, his participation in the John Reed Club in Chicago, and his time with the Illinois Writers' Project made him one of the best-known *Men at Work* authors during the 1930s and today. "Drift Miner" makes apparent his intimate familiarity with mining life, but as the "tall tale" folklore pieces Conroy submitted to *Men at Work* indicate, he had a deep interest in, knowledge of, and affection for workers in a variety of other industries. The term "worker-writer" often used to describe Conroy reflects not just his sensibility but his own experience working on the railroads, in construction, and in the auto industry. He wrote, edited, taught, lectured, mentored, and agitated for progressive change throughout the course of his life, but his effort to foreground workers' quotidian existence was ever present. Jack Conroy died in 1990.

REFERENCES: Douglas Wixson, *Worker-Writer in America: Jack Conroy and the Tradition of Midwestern Literary Radicalism, 1898–1990* (Chicago: University of Illinois Press, 1994), 10; 96; 292–93; Jack Salzman and David Ray, eds., *The Jack Conroy Reader* (New York: Burt Franklin, 1979), 100–108; 291.

Howard Corning (*1896–1977*). A major figure in the Oregon Writers' Project
and in the state's postwar historical community, Corning first called Nebraska and
Ohio home. He did not come to Oregon until 1919, when he was in his mid-twenties. A decade and a half later Corning joined the Oregon Writers' Project. He
edited *History of Education in Portland* with Alfred Powers, published through
the WPA Adult Education Project in 1937. During World War II Corning was
employed in the U.S. Maritime Audit Section at the Kaiser Company shipyard in
Vancouver, Washington. His ties to the writers' project, however, lasted into the
postwar. In 1947 he published *Willamette Landings*, and almost ten years later
he released a new version of the *Dictionary of Oregon History: Compiled from the
Research Files of the Former Oregon Writers' Project,* for which he served as editor.
Corning was also a teacher with the Portland Center for the Oregon State System
of Higher Education, a poet and historian. He was perhaps best known as the editor of a literary column for *The* (*Albany*) *Democrat* and the "Oregonian Verse" column of *The* (*Portland*) *Oregonian*. Like many *Men at Work* contributors, Corning
held a wide variety of jobs during his life. He was employed as a window trimmer
in a department store, a publishing and advertising copywriter, a freelance writer,
a poet, and a librarian and research director at the Oregon Historical Society. He
married Virginia Wallace Runyon on 8 August 1940; they had one son. Howard
McKinley Corning died on 11 January 1977 in Portland.

REFERENCES: Oregon Historical Society Research Library, entry for Howard
McKinley Corning Papers, 1899–1977, OHS Library Catalog, accessed Feb. 2010,
http://librarycatalog.ohs.org;. World War I Draft Registration Cards, 1917–1918,
digital image, Franklin Co., OH, Draft Board, registration for Howard M. Corning,
Ancestry.com, (accessed Jan. 2010, http://search.ancestry.com; 1900 U.S. Census,
Clinton Township, Franklin Co., OH, p. 16, household of Mark L. Milford; 1910
U.S. Census, Clinton Township, Franklin Co., OH, p. 222, household of Mark L.
Milford; 1920 U.S. Census, Portland, Multnomah Co., OR, p. 143, household of
Mark L. Milford; "Writers Wed," *The Seattle Times,* 23 Sept. 1940, p. 11; "Corning
Gets Post," *The* (*Portland*) *Oregonian,* 15 Aug. 1945, p. 17; A. Stanley Coblentz, ed.,
The Music Makers: An Anthology of Recent American Poetry (n.p., Buttle, Shaw,
and Wetherill, Inc., 1945), 42; "H. M. Corning Named Editor," *The* (*Portland*)
Sunday Oregonian, 19 Dec. 1965; Hazel E. Mills, ed., *Who's Who Among Pacific
Northwest Authors* (Salem, OR: Pacific Northwest Library Association Reference
Section, 1957); Rolf Swensen, "Oregon's 'Poetry Landslide': Col. E. Hofer and the
'Lariat,'" *Oregon Historical Quarterly* 99, no. 1 (Spr. 1998): 33.

Robert Cornwall (1907–1979). Before he settled in Jacksonville, Florida, the place he would call home for almost the last sixty years of his life, Robert Cornwall lived in Iowa and Oklahoma. He was the assistant state editor of the Florida Federal Writers' Project by at least 1939. In his work for the writers' project Cornwall recorded a number of interviews and folk songs around Jacksonville and on the Seminole reservation in 1939 and 1940. He also served as assistant editor for the Florida office of the FWP. After his stint on the project but prior to his enlistment in the army in 1944, Cornwall was employed as the city editor for the *Jacksonville Times-Union*. His army service primarily involved being a newspaper reporter for the *Stars and Stripes* in Japan and Korea. He married Evelyn Baltzell in 1937, and died 26 August 1979 in Duval County, Florida.

REFERENCES: Stetson Kennedy, "Florida Folklife and the WPA, an Introduction," Florida Memory: State Library & Archives of Florida, accessed 13 Feb. 2012, http://www.floridamemory.com/onlineclassroom/zora_hurston/documents/stetsonkennedy/; 1910 U.S. Census, Sapulpa City, Creek Co., OK, stamped p. 274, household of Stephen Cornwall; 1920 U.S. Census, Jacksonville City, Duval Co., FL, p. 276, household of Steven N. Cornwall; 1930 U.S. Census, Jacksonville City, Duval Co., FL, p. 201, household of Stephen N. Cornwall; 1935 Florida State Census, Precinct 1a, Duval Co., FL, p. 2; 1945 Florida State Census, Precinct 10c, Duval Co., FL; Florida Department of Health, *Florida Marriage Index, 1927–2001*, entry for Robert Cornwall, p. 197, digital image, Ancestry.com, accessed 2 Sept. 2010, http://search.ancestry.com; U.S. Army enlistment record for Robert E. Cornwall, serial no. 34972223, Electronic Army Serial Number Merged File, ca. 1938–1946 (Enlistment Records), U.S. National Archives and Records Administration, accessed 9 Jan. 2011, http://aad.archives.gov/aad/record-detail.jsp; Margaret Pauline Rose, "Press Censorship in the Occupation of Japan: 'On a Clear Day You Can See MacArthur,'" (MA thesis, University of Wisconsin, 1950), p. 146; *Pacific Stars and Stripes: The First 40 Years, 1945–1985* ([Novato, CA]: Presidio, 1985), 7; U.S. Social Security Death Index, entry for Robert Cornwall, born 27 May 1907; Florida Death Index, 1877–1998, entry for Robert Emmet Cornwall, Ancestry.com, accessed 9 Jan. 2011, http://search.ancestry.com.

Beatrice Lavis Cuming (1903–1975). Cuming was born in Brooklyn, New York, on 25 March 1903. She studied at the Pratt Institute Art School where her talent was evident enough that she was sent to work under H. B. Snell in Boothbay Harbor, Maine. In 1924 she moved to Paris where she studied at the Academie Colarossi, the Grande Chaumière and Moderne Academies, and the Andrè Lhote Studio. In 1925 and 1926 she painted as she traveled through Italy, North

Africa, England, and Brittany. She returned to New York in September 1927 and trained at the Art Students League in 1928. In 1929 she moved back to Paris and later relocated to Tunisia. Cuming came back to New York City in October 1933, but moved to New London, Connecticut, in 1934 to work for the Public Works of Art Project, a precursor of Federal One. Soon afterward she began her WPA employment. To make ends meet Cuming also taught private art lessons and led classes in the New London public schools from 1936 to 1940. Between 1937 and 1967 she was the director of the Young Peoples' Art Program at the Lyman Allyn Museum in New London. Cuming, who became best known for her paintings and etchings, also taught at the Summer Art Colony at Sul Ross State College in Alpine, Texas, and the Parsons School Design & School Visual Arts in New York City. She was membership director of the Mystic Art Association for fifteen years and also belonged to the American Watercolor Society, the National Association of Women Artists, the Connecticut Watercolor Society, the Essex Art Association, and American Artists. The Guy Mayer Gallery, the Contemporary Artists Gallery, and the Lyman Allen Museum all exhibited her work. She died in March 1974 in New London.

REFERENCES: Falk, *Who Was Who in American Art* (1985), 142; Falk, *Who Was Who in American Art* (1999), 2:791; Glenn B. Opitz, ed., *Mantle Fielding's Dictionary of American Painters, Sculptors & Engravers*, 2nd ed., (Poughkeepsie, NY: Apollo Book, 1988), 193; "Artist Beatrice Cuming To Teach at Sul Ross," *Dallas (TX) Morning News*, 3 June 1942, p. 7–11; "Beatrice Lavis Cuming," AskArt Academic, accessed 31 Jan. 2011, http://www.askart.com; Mark Jones, "WPA Artist Beatrice Cuming Chose New London," *CONNector*, Apr. 2009, pp. 6–7; U.S. Social Security Death Index, entry for Beatrice Cuming, born 25 Mar. 1903; 1930 U.S. Census, Brooklyn, New York City, Kings Co., NY, p. 15, household of Frederick Cuming; New York Passenger Lists, 1820–1957, digital image, ship manifest for *Ilsenstein*, 15 Oct. 1903, Ancestry.com, accessed 28 Aug. 2010; New York Passenger Lists, 1820–1957, digital image, ship manifest for *Leviathan*, 20 Sept. 1927, Ancestry.com, accessed 28 Aug. 2010; *Beatrice Cuming: 1903–1974*, (exhibition 4 Feb.–18 Mar. 1990), Lyman Allyn Art Museum: New London, CT, 1990.

John Delgado. Very little is known about John Delgado. As a member of the Northern California Writers' Project, he contributed to *The Central Valley Project* and to the "History of San Francisco Music: An Anthology of Music Criticism." Delgado may have been a member of the staff of *Fore'n'Aft,* a weekly newspaper printed for and by the employees of the Kaiser Shipyards of Richmond, California, during World War II.

REFERENCES: WPA Northern California Writers' Program, comp., *The Central Valley Project* (Sacramento: California State Department of Education, 1942), p. viii; WPA Northern California Writers' Program, comp., "History of San Francisco Music, Volume VII: An Anthology of Music Criticism" (San Francisco: City and County of San Francisco, 1942), preface; Fredric L. Quivik, "Historic American Engineering Record: Kaiser's Richmond Shipyards with Special Emphasis on Richmond Shipyard No. 3, A Historical Report Prepared for National Park Service, Rosie the Riveter/World War II Home Front National Historical Park, Richmond, California," 2 July 2004, 150–52, http://www.rosietheriveter.org/home/shipyard-3history.pdf.

Ned DeWitt (1911–1984). Born 18 January 1911 in Fayetteville, Arkansas, as a boy Ned DeWitt moved with his family to Oklahoma City, Oklahoma, where at a young age he went to work in the oil fields. He briefly attended the University of Oklahoma and became a member of the Oklahoma Historical Society in 1936. That same year he both began writing for the Oklahoma Writers' Project and found himself elected president of the Oklahoma Writers' Project union. Three months after he assumed the presidency the union threatened to go on strike. DeWitt's position on rank-and-file rights did not damage his reputation with his bosses. In March 1938 he was appointed state supervisor of the writers' project. During his time working for the FWP DeWitt conducted interviews for the "Oil in Oklahoma" series, contributed to *Economy of Scarcity*, and took a leading role in producing the Oklahoma State Guide. DeWitt published his own work in *Poet Magazine,* (Oklahoma) *Labor,* and the *State Anthology of Oklahoma Poetry.* He married Alta Churchill in 1938 and died 17 November 1984 in Los Angeles, California.

REFERENCES: 1920 U.S. Census, Oklahoma City, Oklahoma Co., OK, p. 1, household of Ned T. De Witt; 1930 U.S. Census, Oklahoma City, Oklahoma Co., OK, stamped p. 85, household of Edward J. DeWitt; California Death Index, 1940–1997, entry for Ned Phillips Dewitt, Ancestry.com, accessed 12 Sept. 2010, http://search.ancestry.com; U.S. Social Security Death Index, entry for N. Dewitt, born 18 Jan. 1911; "Minutes of the Meeting of the Board of Directors," *Chronicles of Oklahoma* 14, no. 3 (Sept. 1936): 384, transcript, Oklahoma Historical Society's Chronicles of Oklahoma, accessed 12 Sept. 2010, http://digital.library.okstate.edu/Chronicles/vo14/vo14p383.html; "Strike Threatened," *Ada (OK) Evening News,* 17 Nov. 1936, p. 4; Robert Polito, *Savage Art: A Biography of Jim Thompson* (New York: Knopf, 1995), 206–14, 232, 239; Paul F. Lambert and Kenny A. Franks, eds., *Voices from the Oil Fields* (Norman: University of Oklahoma Press, 1984), xi.

Francis Donovan (*ca. 1907–?*). Francis Donovan was another *Men at Work* contributor whose life is shrouded in mystery. He was born sometime between January and April 1907 in Thomaston, Connecticut, and worked in a brass factory and likely also a clock factory as a young man. In the mid-1930s Donovan joined Federal One. He conducted a series of oral histories in Thomaston for the Living Lore of New England unit of the Folklore Studies arm of the Federal Writers' Project. Donovan was a prolific interviewer and the Library of Congress holds a significant collection of his field notes covering Thomaston's early history, the town's politics, local clockmakers, the Seth Thomas Clock Company, tramps, and numerous other subjects. After his stint with the WPA, Donovan recedes from the historical record.

> REFERENCES: 1920 U.S. Census, Thomaston, Litchfield Co., CT, stamped p. 68, household of William Aschoff; 1930 U.S. Census, Thomaston, Litchfield Co., CT, p. 20, household of William H. Aschoff; "WPA Life Histories from Connecticut," Library of Congress: American Memory, accessed 2 Feb. 2011, http://memory.loc.gov/ammem/wpaintro/ctcat.html.

Horatio Connell Forjohn (*1911/3–1943*). Also known as Horatio Connell Forgione, he was born in Pennsylvania to Felix A. and Josephine Forjohn at the beginning of the second decade of the twentieth century. We know little about his life. In 1941 he exhibited at the Delgado Museum of Art in New Orleans, Louisiana, in conjunction with the federal art project. He died in 1943 in Philadelphia.

> REFERENCES: 1920 U.S. Census, Philadelphia, Philadelphia Co., PA, p. 2, household of Felix A. Forjohn; "Dock Fight Termed Finest of Paintings in '35 Under 35'," (*New Orleans*) *Times Picayune*, 25 May 1941, p. 2–6; Smithsonian American Art Museum and the Renwick Gallery, entry for Horatio C. Forjohn, Smithsonian Collections Catalog, accessed 30 Aug. 2010, http://americanart.si.edu/collections/search/artist/?id=1608.

Michael J. Gallagher (*1898–1965*). Born on 1 April 1898 in Scranton, Pennsylvania, Gallagher studied at the Pennsylvania Museum School of Industrial Art in Philadelphia. (Some documents list 1897 as the birth year, but a granddaughter confirmed that the accepted date is 1898.) He later became supervisor of the Federal Art Project Graphics Workshop (also known as the Philadelphia Graphic Arts Division of the WPA) in Philadelphia. He served in that position from 1935 to 1941. Gallagher, who was a member of Philadelphia Print Club, developed with

Dox Thrash and H. Mesibov an "innovative graphic technique, and intaglio process" known as a carograph. He exhibited at the Philadelphia Print Club in 1936 and at the 1939 World's Fair at New York City. He also served as the illustrator for J. T. Adams, *The Epic of America,* and Bernard DeVoto, *Mark Twain's America.* Gallagher died March 1965 in Philadelphia.

REFERENCES: Falk, *Who Was Who in American Art* (1985), 222; Falk, *Who Was Who in American Art* (1999), 2:1232; "Michael J. Gallagher," New Deal/W.P.A. Artist Biographies, accessed 31 Aug. 2010, http://www.wpamurals.com/wpabios. html; U.S. Social Security Death Index, entry for Michael Gallagher, born 25 Apr. 1897.

Charles Reed Gardner (1901–1974). Born in Philadelphia on 17 August 1901, Gardner attended the Pennsylvania Academy for the Fine Arts and studied with Thornton Oakley and Herbert Pullinger. He was a member of the Philadelphia Print Club and the Philadelphia Sketch Club, and resided at Salford, Pennsylvania. A drawing specialist, engraver, etcher, block printer, lithographer, illustrator, painter, and writer, Gardner also designed book and magazine covers. He published *Historic Philadelphia: Twelve Woodcuts* in 1929. He was married to Alice R. Grosch, and died in Philadelphia in July 1974.

REFERENCES: Falk, *Who Was Who in American Art* (1985), 223; Falk, *Who Was Who in American Art* (1999), 2:1240; Glenn B. Opitz, ed., *Mantle Fielding's Dictionary of American Painters, Sculptors & Engravers,* 2nd ed., (Poughkeepsie, NY: Apollo Book, 1986), 314; "Charles Reed Gardner," AskArt Academic, accessed 31 Jan. 2011, http://www.askart.com; Charles Reed Gardner, *Historic Philadelphia: Twelve Woodcuts,* University of Washington Chapbooks, no. 33 (Seattle: University of Washington Book Store, 1929); "Wood Engravings Now Being Shown At City Library," *Springfield (MA) Daily Republican,* 6 Oct. 1937, 3.

John "Jack" Worthington Gregory (1903–1992). Gregory, who was born on 14 March 1903 in Brooklyn, New York, worked as a lithographer but was best known as a photographer. *Time* magazine and the *New York Times* both published his images, and the Associated Press distributed his work. The Smithsonian Institution named him "one of America's finest pictorial photographers" and awarded him a one-man show in 1948. Numerous galleries exhibited his work. He studied at the Art Students League in New York City and taught at Hunter College and the Butera School of Art in Boston. Gregory called Provincetown,

Massachusetts, home from around 1933 until his death. Besides his artistic labors, he found employment as an "adjustor" of Edison players in the early years of the Great Depression. He married Adelaide Elizabeth Gibbs on 10 October 1934; they had 2 sons. Jack Gregory died in Hyannis, Massachusetts, on 19 July 1992.

REFERENCES: Falk, *Who Was Who in American Art* (1985), 246. Falk, *Who Was Who in American Art* (1999), 2:1373; Commonwealth of Massachusetts Department of Health Services, "Massachusetts Death Index, 1970–2003," Ancestry.com, accessed 12 Dec. 2009; Frank William Scott, ed., *The Alumni Record of the University of Illinois at Urbana* (Urbana: University of Illinois, 1906), 101; 1910 U.S. Census, Brooklyn, New York City, Kings Co., NY, p. 188 (stamped); 1920 U.S. Census, Brooklyn, New York City, Kings Co., NY, p. 175; 1930 U.S. Census, Brooklyn, New York City, Kings Co., NY.; "Hayward-Howard-Chase-Chace-Thomas-Wixon-Wixam and Others—37 Generations," family tree submitted by "CharlesHayward23," Ancestry.com, accessed 19 Aug. 2010; Gerry Desautels, "John Gregory: Was He Cape Cod's own Ansel Adams?," *Provincetown (MA) Banner and the Advocate,* 10 Mar. 2005, online edition, accessed 16 Aug. 2010, provincetownbanner.com; "John W. Gregory, 89 Renowned Photographer," *Boston Globe,* 21 July 1992, p. 67, text online at ProQuest, accessed 19 Aug. 2010.

Sanford Hassell (1888–1970). Born the day after Christmas in 1888, Sanford "Sandy" Hassell was among the oldest contributors to *Men at Work*. (Numerous documents list his first name as Sandford. Additionally, different sources list the birth date differently, but census records repeatedly place his birth in 1888.) He was a native of Tennessee and lived in Nashville at the beginning of the twentieth century. By 1920 he had moved to Wyoming and taken employment as an electrician. In 1923, under the Stock-Raising Homestead Act, he obtained 652 acres of land about five miles south of Lander, Wyoming, near the Wind River Indian Reservation. It is unclear whether he proved up his homestead, but his experience with the local American Indian population appears to have led him to change his profession. The beginning of the Depression saw him employed as an Indian trader in Gallup, New Mexico. He later worked as a trader through the Tuba City Trading Post at Tuba City, Arizona. Hassell contributed to the New Mexico section of the Federal Writers' Project, and wrote and published *Know the Navajo* in 1949. He also published a number of short stories in *Desert Magazine* in 1951 and 1952. He died January 1970, probably in Denver, Colorado.

REFERENCES: Tennessee Deaths and Burials, 1874–1955, entry for Hellen Henry Hassell, FamilySearch.org, accessed 13 Jan. 2011, https://www.familysearch.

org; 1900 U.S. Census, Nashville, Davidson County, TN, p. 12, household of Elijah Hassell; 1920 U.S. Census, Election District 8, Fremont County, WY, p. 40, household of Sandford W. Hassell; 1930 U.S. Census, Gallup, McKinley County, NM, p. 2, household of Katherine Leyden; *Annual Report of the Public Schools of Nashville, Tenn.: Scholastic Year 1904–1905* (Nashville: Marshall and Bruce Company, 1906), 21; U.S. General Land Office, Land patent for Sandford W. Hassell, 21 July 1923, patent no. 912660, digital image, U.S. Bureau of Land Management, General Land Office Records, accessed 12 Jan. 2011, http://www.glorecords.blm.gov/PatentSearch/; U.S. Social Security Death Index, entry for Sandford Hassell, born 26 Dec. 1885; Mary May Bailey, interviewed by Karen Underhill, 13 July 1999, interview transcript, p. 9, United Indian Traders Association Project, Northern Arizona University, "Traders: Voices from the Trading Post," accessed 18 Sept. 2010, http://library.nau.edu/speccoll/exhibits/traders/oralhistories/textfiles/bailey.txt; Northern Arizona University, "Native American Traders Bibliography," Traders: Voices from the Trading Post, accessed 18 Sept. 2010, http://library.nau.edu/speccoll/exhibits/traders/biblio.html.

Gail Hazard. Gail Hazard was a rank-and-file member of the FWP for whom the historical record offers few clues. He worked for the Northern California Writers' Project in the late 1930s and authored "Tales of the Monterey Indians," which was never published, in May 1939. Hazard may have enlisted in the U.S. Army in August 1942. Nothing else is known about his life.

REFERENCES: University of California Libraries, entry for *Tales of the Monterey Indians*, typescript, 1939 May, accessed 18 Sept. 2010, http://melvyl.worldcat.org/title/tales-of-the-monterey-indians-typescript-1939-may-4/oclc/62313883&referer=brief_results; U.S. Army enlistment record for Gail Hazard, serial no. 39098984, Electronic Army Serial Number Merged File, ca. 1938–1946 (Enlistment Records), U.S. National Archives and Records Administration, accessed 18 Sept. 2010, http://aad.archives.gov/aad/record-detail.jsp.

Chester Himes (1909–1984). Born July 29, 1909, in Jefferson City, Missouri, Chester Bomar Himes was the youngest of three children. By his own account, Himes witnessed grotesque racial hatred and indifference at an early age—most especially the decision by white doctors not to treat his badly injured brother. These experiences impacted him deeply. His parents, both educators, moved the family to the Cleveland area during the writer's adolescence. Himes began writing fiction in his late teens and early twenties from an Ohio prison where he was serving seven and a half years of a twenty-five year prison sentence for robbing a

couple at gunpoint in their Cleveland home. Soon after his release he began working as a researcher for the Ohio Writers' Project. Though his time with the WPA
was brief, it helped lead him to the company of other black writers such as Richard
Wright and Langston Hughes. Himes would hold a number of jobs throughout his
life, from butler to shipyard worker, but his time in the WPA seems to have been
pivotal in that it brought about the necessary associations and training to gain footing as a professional writer. Like a number of other important African American
intellectuals, Himes moved to France in the postwar era. Acclaimed for his works
of fiction, most notably *If He Hollers Let Him Go* and his series of Harlem-based
detective mysteries, Himes was a brilliant and complex figure deeply shaped by
the turmoil of his own life. Himes died in Spain in 1984.

> REFERENCES: Gilbert H. Muller, *Chester Himes* (Boston: Twayne, 1989), xiii–
> xv; 1; James Sallis, *Chester Himes: A Life* (New York: Walker and Company, 2000),
> 22–23; 72; See also, Edward Margolies and Michel Fabre, *The Several Lives of
> Chester Himes* (University Press of Mississippi, 1997).

Irwin David Hoffman (1901–1989). Irwin David Hoffman was the son of
Jacob and Minna Hoffman, born on 8 March 1901 in Boston, Massachusetts.
Beginning at the age of 15, Hoffman trained at the Boston Museum of Fine Arts
School. Recipient of the Page Traveling Scholarship in 1924, he traveled in Europe
and North Africa for the next two and a half years. He moved to New York City in
1927 and maintained a studio there for the remainder of his life. Hoffman periodically traveled in the 1930s and 1940s through the southwestern U.S., Mexico, Canada, and Puerto Rico with his brothers who owned a mining company and were
mining prospectors. A painter, lithographer, etcher, and sculptor, he exhibited at
numerous galleries and museums across the country, including at a retrospective
of his art at the Boston Public Library in the early 1980s. He was a member of the
Society of American Etchers, the Society of American Graphic Artists, the Society of Independent Artists, and the Print Club of Albany. He married Dorothea
Geyer in 1930 and died in 1989.

> REFERENCES: Falk, *Who Was Who in American Art* (1985), 286; Falk, *Who
> Was Who in American Art* (1999), 2:1587; J. Harlan Johnson "Mining Murals to
> 'Mines' Museum," *The Mines Magazine* (Golden, CO: Colorado School of Mines,
> Apr. 1940), 165–67, 170, 176, 202; *Irwin D. Hoffman, An Artist's Life: Essays on the
> Artistic Career of Irwin D. Hoffman with Commentary by the Artist on an Exhi-
> bition of his Work* (Boston: Boston Public Library, 1982); "Irwin D. Hoffman,"

AskArt Academic, accessed 31 Jan. 2011, http://www.askart.com; *Irwin D. Hoffman* (New York: Associated American Artists, 1936).

Sam Kutnick (1908–1966). Kutnick was born to Jewish Russian immigrants on September 11, 1908, in Pennsylvania. After his father's death in 1918, he resided for a time at the Cleveland Jewish Orphan Asylum in Ohio. By the early 1930s he had moved to San Francisco, and by 1936 he worked as an editor for the California Historic Records Survey. Among his other accomplishments he contributed to the "History of San Francisco Music," published by the Northern California Writers' Program in 1942. Kutnick participated in the war effort by hiring on as a seaman on a number of ships from fall 1942 to summer 1943. He published in the *People's Daily World* during the postwar era and actively involved himself in local labor unions in the 1960s. Kutnick married Lisette "Lee" Levy in the 1930s; they had two children. He died November 6, 1966, in San Francisco.

> REFERENCES: 1910 U.S. Census, Philadelphia, Philadelphia Co., PA, p. 1, household of Bennie Kutnic; 1920 U.S. Census, Cleveland, Cuyahoga Co., OH, p. 3, Jewish Orphan Asylum; 1930 U.S. Census, Celveland, Cuyahoga Co., OH, stamped p. 287, household of Rachal Kutnick; "Around the Town," *San Mateo (CA) Times,* 29 Dec. 1936, p. 1, Obituary for Lee Kutnick, *San Francisco Chronicle,* 12 Dec. 2010; Ohio Deaths, 1908–1953, entry for Ben Kutnick, Ancestry.com, accessed 28 Jan. 2011, http://search.ancestry.com; California Death Index, 1940–1997, entry for Sam Kutnick, Ancestry.com, accessed 27 Jan. 2011, http://search.ancestry.com; New York Passenger Lists, 1820–1957, digital images, ship manifests for *AC Rubel* and *Tradewind,* 6 Nov. 1942, 4 Dec. 1942, 18 Dec. 1942, 31 Aug. 1943, Ancestry. com, accessed 27 Jan. 2011; *Fourth Report of the Senate Fact-Finding Committee On Un-American Activities: Communist Front Organizations* (Sacramento: California State Senate, 1948), 342–43; *Proceedings and Reports: 1966 Pre-Primary Convention of California Labor COPE, San Francisco, April 8, 1966* (San Francisco: California Labor Council on Political Education, 1966), 14, 22; *Proceedings and Reports: 1964 Pre-Primary Convention of California Labor COPE, San Francisco, April 8, 1964* (San Francisco: California Labor Council on Political Education, 1964); U.S. Social Security Death Index, entry for Sam Kutnick, born 11 Sept. 1908.

Harry Francis Mack (1907–?). Born 4 May 1907 in Gloversville, New York, Mack was a student at the National Academy of Design and the New York School of Applied Design. Besides the WPA, Mack found work with U.S. War Department. He lived in Baton Rouge, Louisiana. Mack's primary areas of artistic interest were illustrations, portrait painting, and etching. He was a member of the Southern Printmakers Society and the Salmagundi Club in New York City, and exhibited at the Louisiana State Art Commission in 1942.

REFERENCES: Falk, *Who Was Who in American Art* (1985), 388.

Edward Miller. We could not locate any details about Edward Miller's life.

M. B. Moser. We did not uncover any information about M. B. Moser.

Elizabeth Olds (1896/7–1991). Olds was born in Minneapolis, Minnesota. She studied architecture at the University of Minnesota from 1916 to 1918, and attended the Minneapolis School of Art from 1918 to 1921. From 1921 to 1923 she studied at the Art Students League of New York City. In 1925 Olds became the first woman to win a fellowship from the Guggenheim Foundation. She continued her training in Europe from 1925 to 1929. She subsequently returned to the U.S. and lived in Massachusetts and New Hampshire before relocating to Omaha, Nebraska, in 1932, where she learned lithography and joined the Public Works of Art Project. By 1935 she was back in New York City and employed by the Graphics Division of the Federal Art Project and the Silk Screen Unit of the WPA. Olds later traveled extensively in Mexico, Guatemala, and the U.S. She worked as a reporter and illustrator during the 1950s and 1960s, and moved to Sarasota, Florida, in 1971. Olds was a lithographer, painter, printmaker, illustrator, and serigrapher; she also wrote and illustrated a number of children's books. A founding member of the American Artists' Congress, Olds also belonged to the Artists League of America and the Serigraphy Society in New York City. She died in 1991 in Sarasota.

REFERENCES: Falk, *Who Was Who in American Art* (1985), 458–59; Falk, *Who Was Who in American Art* (1999), 2:2463; Doris Ostrander Dawdy, *Artists of the American West: A Biographical Dictionary*, 3 vols. (Athens: Ohio University Press, 1985), 3:326; Chris Petteys, *Dictionary of Women Artists: An International Dictionary of Women Artists Born before 1900* (Boston: G. K. Hall & Co., 1985), s.v. "Olds, Elizabeth"; Glenn B. Opitz, ed., *Mantle Fielding's Dictionary of American Painters, Sculptors & Engravers*, 2nd ed., (Poughkeepsie, NY: Apollo Book, 1986), 679–80; Helen Lange, "Elizabeth Olds: Gender Difference and Indifference," *Woman's Art Journal* 22, no. 2 (Fall 2000/Winter 2001): 5–11; "Elizabeth Olds," AskArt Academic, accessed 31 Jan. 2011, http://www.askart.com; Ann Lee Morgan, "Olds,

Elizabeth," *The Oxford Dictionary of American Art and Artists* (Oxford University Press, 2007), Oxford Reference Online, accessed 31 Jan. 2011, http://www.oxford-dreference.com/views/ENTRY.html?subview=Main&entry=t238.e993.

Charles Oluf Olsen (1872–1959). Olsen emigrated to the United States as an eleven year old in September 1888. After arriving at Ellis Island, he found a job as an ironworks laborer in New York City for several years. He relocated to the western U.S. in 1899 and by 1900 was employed as a blacksmith in Butte Township, California. By 1910 he had moved up the coast and taken a position as a woodcutter in Newport Precinct, Washington. Olsen settled in Oregon in February 1925 and became a naturalized U.S. citizen a little less than two years later. Olsen did not begin his writing career until the age of 47. He published features, historical articles, fiction, and poetry in local and national newspapers and magazines including *The (Portland) Oregonian, American Mercury, American Forests,* and *Poetry.* Besides his other occupations, he was employed as cook, salesman, and lumberjack. He married Elizabeth (Bessie) Thompson in 1922; they had one son. By the time of his death in 1959 Charles Oluf Olsen was considered one of Oregon's foremost poets.

REFERENCES: 1900 U.S. Census, Butte Township, Siskiyou Co., CA, p. 321, household of Charles Olsen; 1910 U.S. Census, Newport Precinct, Stevens Co., WA, p. 76, household of John F. Anderson; 1930 U.S. Census, Precinct 528, Multnomah Co., OR, p. 6051, household of Charles O. Olsen; Naturalization Records for the U.S. District Court for the District of Oregon, 1859–1941, National Archives, Washington, DC, digital copies available via Ancestry.com: Declaration of Intention for Charles Oluf Olsen, 18 Sept. 1919, no. 13001; Petition for Naturalization for Charles Oluf Olsen, 1 Jan. 1921, no. 4897, p. 98; Petition for Naturalization for Elizabeth Thompson Olsen, 1 Mar. 1925, no. 4896, p. 97; "Death Takes Oregon Poet," *The (Portland) Oregonian,* 23 June 1959, p. 15; "News Notes," *Poetry* 33, no. 5 (Feb. 1929), 291.

Aida Parker (1892–1962). Only a rough sketch of Aida Parker's life has emerged. She was born at the end of the nineteenth century in New York. She married Folsom Reed Parker probably in 1918, and they had at least four children. By 1920 they resided at Fort Jay, on Governor's Island in New York City. By 1930 the family had moved to St. Clair, Michigan. Parker relocated to Connecticut and worked for that state's writers' project in the late 1930s and early 1940s. She died 13 October 1962 in Stamford, Connecticut.

REFERENCES: 1920 U.S. Census, Governor's Island, Fort Jay, New York City, NY, p. 16, household of Folsom R. Parker; 1930 U.S. Census, St. Clair, St. Clair Co., MI, stamped p. 117, household of Aida Parker; Texas Deaths, 1890–1976, digital image, Death Certificate for Folsom Reed Parker, died 18 Sept. 1961, Austin, Travis Co., TX, state file no. 54929, FamilySearch.org, accessed Sept. 2010; Connecticut Death Index, 1949–2001, entry for Aida C. Parker, Ancestry.com, accessed 13 Sept. 2010; U.S. Social Security Death Index, entry for Aida Parker, born 14 Aug. 1892.

Jim Phelan (*1912–1997*). Jim Phelan was born in Alton, Illinois, in 1912, making him one of the younger contributors to *Men at Work*. He attended the University of Illinois in the early 1930s, moved to Chicago in 1934, and by 1938, although only twenty-six years old, Phelan became the managing editor at the Illinois Federal Writers' Project. He either authored or contributed to a number of publications in the Federal Writers' Project's "American Guide Series" including *Illinois: A Descriptive and Historical Guide; Nauvoo Guide;* and *Missouri: A Guide to the "Show Me" State*. In 1941 he obtained a job as a newspaper reporter at the (Alton, IL) *Evening Telegraph*. Phelan may have enlisted in the U.S. Army in 1942; a decade later he made Los Angeles his home and was working as a reporter for the (Long Beach, CA) *Press-Telegram*. Within a few years he was writing mainly for the magazine market. Phelan published articles in nationally known magazines including the *Saturday Evening Post, Paris-Match, Time,* and *Playboy*. His writing also appeared in *The New York Times*. Phelan was perhaps best known for his biography *Howard Hughes: The Hidden Years*, which came out in 1976. In 1990 he relocated to Temecula, California. Although he was primarily employed as a writer, he also found employment as a golf caddy, a "color tester" at an oil refinery, and an editor. He married Amalie Muriel Strauss Deran in 1945; they had two daughters. Jim Phelan died 8 September 1997 in Temecula.

REFERENCES: 1920 U.S. Census, Wood River Village, Madison Co., IL, p. 36, household of George L. McCullom; 1930 U.S. Census, Wood River, Madison Co., IL, p. 5, household of John E. Phelan; James Phelan, *Scandals, Scamps, and Scoundrels: The Casebook of an Investigative Reporter* (New York: Random House, 1982), xi, 40–41, 53, 66–68; James R. Phelan, Chicago, IL, to Lewis A. Ramsey, Salt Lake City, UT, 30 Nov. 1938, Lewis A. Ramsey, Collection, ca. 1908–1962, LDS Church History Library, Salt Lake City, UT; U.S. Army enlistment record for James Phelan, serial no. 36367579, Electronic Army Serial Number Merged File, ca. 1938–1946 (Enlistment Records), U.S. National Archives and Records Administration, accessed 10 Jan. 2011, http://aad.archives.gov/aad/record-detail.jsp;

"About the Author," in James R. Phelan, *Howard Hughes: The Hidden Years* (New York: Random House, 1976); Janet Phelan, "Happy Birthday, Agent Smith," blog post, *Janet Phelan Reporter at Large*, 18 Aug. 2010, http://janetphelan.com; *Who's Who of American Women: A Biographical Dictionary of Notable Living American Women*, vol. 2, (Chicago: Marquis-Who's Who, 1961), 781; U.S. Social Security Death Index, entry for James Richard Phelan, born 31 July 1912; Robin Pogrebin, "James R. Phelan, 85, Is Dead; Biographer of Howard Hughes," *New York Times*, 12 Sept. 1997, online edition, http://nytimes.com.

Salvator(e) Pinto (1905–1966). Pinto, born on 4 January 1905 in Casal Velino, Italy, immigrated to the United States as a child in 1909. By the age of fifteen he had already been invited to exhibit at the Pennsylvania Academy of the Fine Arts. His work would be seen there again in 1930 and 1943, and also at the Corcoran Gallery, Philadelphia Print Club, the Philadelphia Art Club, the Art Institute of Chicago, and the Whitney Museum of American Art during the 1930s. He returned to Europe at the beginning of that decade and studied there until 1933. His specialties were mural painting, etching, block printing, and drawing. He held memberships in the United Scenic Artists of America and the Philadelphia Print Club. He died in Philadelphia in 1966.

REFERENCES: Falk, *Who Was Who in American Art* (1985), 486; Falk, *Who Was Who in American Art* (1999), 2:2615; Helen McCloy, "Human Values in the Art of the Pinto Brothers," *Parnassus* 6, no. 8 (Jan. 1935): 4–6.

Ralph Powell. We found no information about Ralph Powell's life.

Leonard Rapport (1913–2008). Leonard Rapport was born in 1913 in Durham, North Carolina. Before going to work for the North Carolina FWP in 1938—a job he held until 1941—Rapport worked for the University of North Carolina Press and wrote fiction. His skill with the written word landed him in a collection of the best short stories of 1937 alongside Eudora Welty and John Dos Passos. It is also evident in the oral histories and other materials he produced for the WPA Southern Writers' Project, some of which have been republished as part of important folklore collections ("Tobacco Auctioneer" was included in a *Treasury of Southern Folklore* in 1940). Rapport served in the 101st Airborne Division during World War II. His co-authored history of the division's experiences, which built on the folklore-oriented method he developed while part of the FWP, was published in 1948 to critical acclaim. In the postwar era Rapport used the archival training he received at the University of North Carolina in his position at the National Archives. He became one of the nation's leading experts on late eighteenth-century manuscripts, especially those related to constitutional matters. He also played a critical role on the WPA historical records survey. Within archival circles Rapport established a reputation as a methodological innovator and first-rate appraiser. Among the other honors he received over his long career, the Society of American Archivists named him a fellow and the NEH and Ford Foundation awarded him grants. He retired from the National Archives in 1984, but his curiosity about the world hardly abated. Rapport spent considerable time in his retirement undertaking long journeys on foot in the United States and Europe. He died at 95 years of age in 2008.

REFERENCES: Pete Daniel, "Reasons to Talk about Tobacco," *Journal of American History* 96, no. 3 (Dec. 2009): 663–77; Matt Schudel, "Leonard A. Rapport, 95; Archivist and Author," *Washington Post*, April 12, 2008, online edition, http://www.washingtonpost.com/wp-dyn/content/article/2008/04/11/AR2008041103941.html; Brave Astronaut, "Obituary: Leonard Rapport," on "Order From Chaos" blog, March 27, 2008, http://braveastronaut.blogspot.com/2008/03/obituary-leonard-rapport.html; Maygene Daniels, "On Being an Archivist: Presidential Address Society of American Archivists," SAA website, August 30, 1995, http://www.archivists.org/governance/presidential/daniels.asp.

Edward Reynolds (1906–1976). In the "Sketch Biography" that he submitted with his short story, Edward Reynolds noted he was born and raised in Anaconda. Both of Reynolds's parents held prominent places in the community in the first two decades of the twentieth century. His father Claude was born in Kentucky but lived in the smelter city for thirty years and served for a period as the president of the Anaconda Smelterman's union. Reynolds's mother, Marie, according to the *Anaconda Standard*, was born in New Orleans and "came to Anaconda as a young woman and during her 24 years' residence here gained by her noble character and charming personality the friendship of all with whom she came in contact." Upon her untimely death she was mourned throughout the city. Suggesting the complex and often localized operation of race in the U.S., the 1910 Montana census, based on Marie's African American roots, listed her, the Reynolds' children, and even Claude as "mulatto." A former Anaconda resident confirms that locals knew about the family's racial background. That classification barred many others in Anaconda from the privileges that came with whiteness, such as bet-

ter working conditions and higher pay, but not the Reynolds. Edward Reynolds
first worked in the smelter on weekends as a high school student. Thanks to the
dominance of local codes over national ones, he was treated as a well-connected
white local when it came to securing a position there. The wages he earned at
the plant helped him complete a journalism degree at Montana State University.
He returned to Anaconda and won a job as a writer for the *Montana Standard*,
although his white-collar position did not protect him from the Great Depression.
Dismissed by his employer, like many men in the copper towns he sought government relief work and found a position with the FWP where his work was highly
regarded. Regarding his short story "Anaconda," he told Rosenberg that "it would
take a book to tell of the Micks and Slavs and Swedes and Russians; the Cousin
Jacks, the Polacks, the Italians, the Germans . . . of the varied occupations, as many
in number as the works is huge." Reynolds described the story as depicting in
detail only "a small part" of what went on at the plant, "with but a cursory glance
at the remainder." Thirty-four years old on the cusp of World War II Reynolds
decided to enlist. He was badly injured in the war but nonetheless went on to
finish an advanced degree. He later returned to journalism, but not to the smelter
town with which his family had such a fascinating relationship. Reynolds died in
San Mateo, California, on June 10, 1976.

REFERENCES: State of California Certificate of Death for Edward Brisco
Reynolds, San Francisco Area Funeral Home Records, 1895–1985, digital image,
Ancestry.com, accessed 3 Mar. 2012; *Montana Standard*, 25 Feb. 1929, 2; "Edward
B. Reynolds—Sketch Autobiography," 24 Mar. 1941, WPA Records, box 18, folder
6, Montana Historical Society Research Center, Helena, Montana; "Mrs. Marie
R. Reynolds," Certificate of Death, State of Montana Bureau of Vital Statistics,
29 Jun. 1929; "Anaconda Woman Passes in Butte," *Montana Standard*, 28 Jun.
1929; "Claude Reynolds Called by Death, *Montana Standard*, 13 Aug. 1933; *Ninth,
Twelfth, Thirteenth, and Fourteenth Census of the United States, Jefferson County,
Kentucky, Orleans County, Louisiana, and Deer Lodge County, Montana*; *History
of the United Brothers of Friendship and Sisters of the Mysterious Ten* (Louisville,
KY: Bradley and Gilbert Company, 1897); Michael Stephen Kennedy, interview
by Betty L. Hoag, 26 Nov. 1965, Archives of American Art, Smithsonian Institu-
tion. For more on Reynolds and for a detailed reading of "Anaconda" see Matthew
Basso, *Meet Joe Copper: Masculinity and Race on Montana's World War II Home
Front* (Chicago: University of Chicago Press, forthcoming), and Matthew Basso,
"Context, Subjectivity, and the Built Environment at the Anaconda Reduction
Works," *Drumlummon Views* 3, no. 1 (Spring 2009): 125–52.

Harold Rosenberg (1906–1978). Harold Rosenberg was born February 2, 1906, in Brooklyn, New York. Educated at City College and St. Lawrence University, he became a lifelong fixture in New York City's intellectual and art scenes. Rosenberg's keen intellect and his association with writers like Irving Howe, Dwight MacDonald, and William Phillips, and artists like William de Kooning, Arshile Gorky, and Mark Rothko made him one of the most influential cultural voices of the postwar era. Rosenberg is most famous for coining the term "action painters" to describe the artists others came to call abstract expressionists. For Rosenberg, "action painters" showed that a new relationship had developed between the artist and the art she or he produced. Rather than the object that was created, Rosenberg argued that is was the act of making art that was critical. For Rosenberg, that act, the moment of creation, functioned as a way for the artist to find his or her individuality. This perspective was popular with artists, but stood in contrast to that championed by the other towering art critic of the era, Clement Greenberg, who offered a formalist perspective on abstract expressionism.

Known for his ties to existentialism, Rosenberg was deeply influenced by Marxism in the late 1920s and 1930s. He joined other young New York-based intellectuals, writers, and artists to create the magazines, including *Partisan Review* and *Dissent*, that were a cornerstone of the culture of the era. In 1932 he married the writer May Natalie Tabak. Rosenberg began his career with the WPA on the Art Project, but soon transferred to the Writers' Project. In 1938, Rosenberg moved from New York City to Washington, DC, where he served as the lead expert on American Art and the editor of the art sections of the American Guide series. Following cuts to the project in the late 1930s, Rosenberg remained one of a handful of national office staff. He worked on a variety of projects—including *Men at Work* and the *Index of American Design*, which catalogued American folk art—until World War II began. During the war Rosenberg worked for the Office of War Information. He maintained ties to the Associated Advertising Council of America until 1973. A prodigious writer, Rosenberg is the author of more than a half dozen books, including the widely read *Art of the New* (1959), and countless essays. He served as art critic for the *New Yorker* beginning in 1962, and from 1966 until 1978 he was a professor of art at the University of Chicago. He died in New York City on July 11, 1978.

REFERENCES: Harold Rosenberg, interview by Paul Cummings, 17 Dec. 1970 and 28 Jan. 1973, Archives of American Art, Smithsonian Institution; "Biographical/Historical Note," Harold Rosenberg papers, 1923-1984, Getty Research Library, accessed February 17, 2012, http://archives2.getty.edu:8082/xtf/

view?docId=ead/980048/980048.xml; "Harold Rosenberg," TheArtStory.org, accessed, February 17, 2012, http://www.theartstory.org/critic-rosenberg-harold. htm.

Sam Ross (1912–1998). Sam Ross was born in Kiev, emigrated to Chicago with his family, and grew up among other Russian and Eastern European immigrants. Ross, who received a journalism degree from Northwestern, later drew on his early life in Chicago for a number of well-received novels. As one critic put it, "Ross knows his town and convincingly takes the reader there in a kind of flamboyant funky ethnic/erotic grand tour of the American '20s, '30s and '40s." Film and TV studios loved Ross's work. His first novel appeared as the film "He Ran All the Way" in 1951, and Ross later wrote for "The Naked City," "Rawhide," and "The Fugitive," among other TV shows. Before this success, Ross was a member of the Chicago Writers' Workshop and the Chicago Chapter of the John Reed Club, a national association of "proletarian artists and writers." He associated with other notable activist writers of the period such as Richard Wright and Nelson Algren. He worked for the Illinois Writers' Project at the end of the 1930s and the beginning of the 1940s, earning a salary that ranged between 85 and 125 dollars per month, and taking life histories about a number of topics including steel work, swimming, and Jazz. Ross's interviews of Arnold Freeman, Muggsy Spanier, and George Barnes are all available in the Library of Congress and formed the basis for his story, "Jazz Music: Chicago Style." Ross served in the Merchant Marines during World War II and spent most of the postwar era in Los Angeles. He died in 1998.

REFERENCES: Myrna Oliver, "Sam Ross; Author, Scriptwriter for TV Shows," *Los Angeles Times*, April 25, 1998, online edition, http://articles.latimes. com/1998/apr/25/news/mn-42854; Polito, *Savage Art*, 462; Hazel Rowley, *Richard Wright: The Life and Times* (New York: Henry Holt and Co., 2001), 75, 88–89, 108–9; Sam Ross, "Steel," "Savoy Ballroom," "Jazz Music (Chicago)," "Sports (Swimming)," and "Jazz Music, Chicago Style," Library of Congress American Memory Website, accessed October 30, 2011, http://memory.loc.gov.

Bernard P. Schardt (1904–1979). Little is known about Bernard Schardt. He was born in Milwaukee, Wisconsin, on 20 October 1904 to Fred J. or Peter S. and Catherine (Lauderback) Schardt, and had moved to Manhattan by 1930 where he worked as a graphic artist. He exhibited at the Federal Art Gallery in New York

City in 1937, and at the Art Institute of Chicago in 1937 and 1938. He died in
North Truro, Massachusetts, on 23 June 1979.

REFERENCES: Falk, *Who Was Who in American Art* (1985), 546; Falk, *Who Was
Who in American Art* (1999), 2:2914; 1905 Wisconsin State Census, 6th Ward,
Milwaukee, Milwaukee Co., WI, p. 1448, household of Fred J. Schardt; 1910 U.S.
Census, Milwaukee, Milwaukee Co., WI, stamped p. 226, household of Peter S.
Schardt; 1920 U.S. Census, Milwaukee, Milwaukee Co., WI, p. 7, household of
Peter S. Schardt; 1930 U.S. Census, Manhattan, New York City, NY, household
of William Rivler; Massachusetts Death Index, 1970–2003, entry for Bernard
P. Schardt, Ancestry.com, accessed 1 Feb. 2011, http://search.ancestry.com; U.S.
Social Security Death Index, entry for Bernard Schardt, born 20 Oct. 1904.

Isaac Schwartz. We could not locate any information about Isaac Schwartz.

Edmund Sharrock. As a member of the Florida Writers' Project Edmund Sharrock authored "Our Defense Program," in 1941. Beyond that we do not know anything concrete about his life.

Isaac Soyer (1902–1981). Soyer, who did not immigrate from Russia until 1912—
when he was ten years old—was nationally recognized as "a painter of the American Scene" by the time of his death in 1981. Soyer lived in the Bronx and studied
at the Cooper Union Art School, the Beaux-Arts Institute of Design, the National
Academy of Design, and the Educational Alliance Art School, all in New York
City. Later he also received training in Paris and Madrid. During World War II,
he was employed by the Bell Aircraft Corporation in Buffalo, New York. He also
taught at the Albright Art School in Buffalo, the Buffalo Art Institute, and the
Niagara Falls Art School during this period. Beginning in 1950 he worked as an
instructor at the Educational Alliance Art School. Late in his career he joined the
faculty at New York City's New School for Social Research and at the Art Students League. Mainly known as a painter and lithographer, Soyer exhibited at a
number of institutions across the U.S. He died 8 July 1981 in New York City.

REFERENCES: Falk, *Who Was Who in American Art* (1985), 384; Falk, *Who
Was Who in American Art* (1999), 2:3114; "Isaac Soyer, A Painter Of the American Scene," *New York Times,* 16 July 1981, online edition, accessed 10 Dec. 2009,
http://nytimes.com; "Isaac Soyer," AskArt Academic, accessed 31 Jan. 2011, http://

www.askart.com; Ann Lee Morgan, "Soyer, Raphael," *The Oxford Dictionary
of American Art and Artists* (Oxford University Press, 2007), Oxford Reference
Online, accessed 31 Jan. 2011, http://www.oxfordreference.com/views/ENTRY.
html?subview=Main&entry=t238.e1257; 1920 U.S. Census, Bronx, New York
City, NY, stamped p. 231, household of Abraham Soyer; U.S. Social Security Death
Index, entry for Isaac Soyer, born 26 Apr. 1902.

Jim Thompson (1906–1977). Thompson was born in Oklahoma in 1906, and
lived there, in Texas, Nebraska, and Kansas prior to his stint as director of the
Oklahoma Writers' Project. These years before the Great Depression gave
Thompson, who among other jobs worked in the oil fields and in a hotel, some
of the first-hand experiences that would form an important basis of his critically
acclaimed writing later in his life. During his time as director of the WPA funded
Oklahoma Writers' Project, Thompson furthered his rich awareness of labor life
and formed several key professional relationships. He become close friends with
fellow WPA writer Ned DeWitt and associated with artist Thomas Hart Benton.
Though his involvement with the Oklahoma Writers' Project was marred with
strife and cantankerousness, Thompson, with the aid of several researchers, helped
publish the *Labor History of Oklahoma* in November of 1939. It is the case-his-
tory style of documentary labor writing that appears here, much like that of James
Agee's and Walker Evans's *Let Us Now Praise Famous Men*. Thompson's skill
for writing the dialogue of everyday working life is apparent in "'Snake' Magee
and the Rotary Boiler." His ability to portray and inhabit characters became more
apparent in the crime novels like *The Killer Inside Me* (1952) and screenplays for
which he is most famous. Thompson spent his final decades in Los Angeles. It was
only after his death in 1977 that his unique artistry has been fully recognized.

REFERENCES: Polito, *Savage Art*, 244–55.

Paul Tyler. No biographical information known.

Paul Weller (1912–2000). Weller was born in Boston and later studied at the
National Academy of Design and American Artists Congress. A photographer,
painter, and designer, as well as printmaker, he belonged to the *Artists League of
America,* the *Society of Magazine Photographers*, and served as vice-president of
United American Artists. In the thirties the Art Institute of Chicago, the Pennsyl-
vania Academy of the Fine Arts, the Museum of Modern Art in New York City,

and the Art Alliance of Philadelphia all exhibited his work. He also showed at the end of that decade at the World's Fair in New York. In the fifties he worked as the art director at *Infinity Magazine*. Weller died December 1, 2000, in East Hampton, New York.

REFERENCES: 1920 U.S. Census, Boston, Suffolk Co., MA, stamped p. 121, household of George J. Weller; Falk, *Who Was Who in American Art* (1985), 668; Falk, *Who Was Who in American Art* (1999), 2:3510; U.S. Social Security Death Index, entry for Paul Weller, born 20 Dec. 1912.

Carroll Whaley (1898–1984). Born in 1898, Whaley lived in a number of Wisconsin towns and cities before graduating with a BA degree from the University of Wisconsin, Madison, in 1921. He moved to Chicago and almost immediately began playing organ at Chicago-area churches. He restored his first reed organ in 1938, the same time his association with the Illinois Writers' Project began. Whaley restored two hundred fifty reed organs over the following forty years. In 1956 he was named organist emeritus of Hermosa-Salem Methodist Church, but he kept playing actively until at least 1971. In 1976 the *Chicago Tribune* featured him for his dedication to the organ. For the writers' project he served as editor of *Annals of Labor and Industry in Illinois,* in at least 1939 and 1940. In the postwar era Whaley was primarily employed as a secretary at Stewart Warner Corporation, a tool and instrument firm, in Chicago. He also worked as a bank investment correspondent, high school teacher, and editor for the Chicago Park District. Whaley died in February 1984 in Chicago.

REFERENCES: 1900 U.S. Census, Greenfield, Milwaukee Co., WI, stamped p. 94, household of Omar Whaley; 1910 U.S. Census, Janesville City, Rock Co., WI, pp. 14–15, household of Omar J. Whaley; 1920 U.S. Census, Janesville, Rock Co., WI, stamped p. 142, household of Omar J. Whaley; World War I Draft Registration Cards, 1917–1918, digital image, Rock Co., WI, Draft Board 1, Janesville Precinct, Janesville, WI, registration for Carroll Omar Whaley, Ancestry.com, accessed 19 Sept. 2010, http://search.ancestry.com;. *The University of Wisconsin Catalogue, 1921–22,* Serial no. 1158, General Series no. 941, *Bulletin of the University of Wisconsin* (Madison: University of Wisconsin, 1922), 464, 702; 1930 U.S. Census, Chicago, Cook Co., IL, p. 21, household of Omar J. Whaley; "Organ 'Sermon,'" *(Chicago) Austin News,* 10 July 1963, p. 2A; Charitey Simmons, "At 77, He's Still Calling The Tune," *Chicago Tribune,* 4 Apr. 1976, p. 14; U.S. Social Security Death Index, entry for Omar Whaley, born 31 May 1898; "Death Notices," *Chicago Tribune,* 29 Feb. 1984.

Robert Wilder. All that we know about Robert Wilder is that he conducted a series of interviews in Northfield, Massachusetts, for the Living Lore of New England unit of the Folklore Studies arm of the Federal Writers' Project.

REFERENCES: "WPA Life Histories from Massachusetts," Library of Congress: American Memory, accessed 2 Feb. 2011, http://memory.loc.gov/ammem/wpain-tro/macat.html.

Grace Winkleman (1901–1964). Grace Winkleman lived an astonishing life. She was born in Omaha, Nebraska, in 1901. As a girl she lived in a number of the copper boom towns that dotted the landscape of Carbon County, Wyoming, (including Rawlins, Encampment, and Collins). Her father was a mining developer, a member of the Wyoming House of Representatives, and editor of one of the county's major newspapers, the *Grand Encampment Herald.* After several other moves around Wyoming, the family headed to Salt Lake City, Utah, so Winkleman's father could take a position as the manager of a mining company. Winkleman briefly attended the University of Utah where she worked for the student paper the *Humbug.* That experience helped her land a position at the *Salt Lake Telegram* where she was purportedly the first female sports editor in the United States. Her recurring column, "With the Women," ran from 1923 to 1925. During these years she also contributed book reviews for the same paper and began publishing short stories in magazines. In 1927 Winkleman married John S. Williams (alias Albert Harry Adams) in Rich County, Utah. Less than a year after their wedding the couple was arrested in Colorado Springs, Colorado, for bank robbery and murder. Winkleman was released after a brief detention, but her husband was convicted of robbery. She divorced in 1933, resettled in Salt Lake City, remarried, and then briefly went to work for a public relations firm. By the end of the decade she had found a position at FWP. She contributed to research projects on the history of grazing and mining in Utah; edited *Provo, Pioneer Mormon City* (published in 1943); and served as the last state director of the Utah Writers' Project. When the writers' project shut down Winkleman hired on as the assistant state information executive for the Office of Price Administration in Salt Lake City. Sometime around the end of the war Winkleman divorced again, got remarried again, and then moved to Denver, Colorado, when the OPA transferred her to their office there. In 1947 she returned to newspaper work, taking a position as a reporter for the *Las Vegas Review Journal.* Over the next twelve years she also served as the executive secretary of the Henderson Chamber of Commerce and wrote articles for the *Las Vegas Sun* and the *Henderson (NV) Pages.* In the early 1960s Winkl-

eman owned and operated an office equipment business in Henderson, worked
for the Nevada Tuberculosis and Health Association, and for Southern Nevada
Memorial Hospital as a personnel director. Still hard at work, Grace Winkleman
died on 10 November 1964 in Henderson, Nevada.

REFERENCES: 1910 U.S. Census, Grand Encampment, Carbon Co., WY, p. 2,
household of George M. Winkleman; Notice, (*Hudson, WY*) *Miner,* 17 July 1908, p.
2; "Personal Paragraphs," *Laramie (WY) Republican,* 8 Oct. 1910, p. 5 (semi-weekly
edition); "Novel Play To Be Staged Gymnasium Building Two Days," (*Cheyenne*)
Wyoming Tribune, 17 Feb. 1917, p. 6; 1920 U.S. Census, Salt Lake City, Salt Lake
Co., UT, p. 6, household of George Winkleman; "First Issue of Humbug Comes
Out Tomorrow," (*University of Utah*) *Utah Chronicle,* 7 Nov. 1922, p. 1; "Salt Lake
Girl Sells Her First Short Stories," *Salt Lake Telegram,* 13 Jan. 1924, p. 1 (magazine
section); "25 Years Ago Today," *Salt Lake Telegram,* 27 Sept. 1948, p. 8; Utah Mar-
riages, 1887–1966, entry for Albert Harry Adams, FamilySearch.org, accessed 19
Jan. 2011, https://www.familysearch.org; "Utah Bank Robber, Former 'U' Coed
Arrested," *Salt Lake Telegram,* 25 Mar. 1928, pp. 1, 7; "Former Salt Lake Girl Held
in Colo. on Robbery Charge," (*University of Utah*) *Utah Chronicle,* 27 Mar. 1928, pp.
1–2; J. S. Williams, Application for parole, 27 Feb. 1930, digital images, Utah Board
of Pardons, Prisoner Application Case Files, Utah Division of Archives and Records
Service, Salt Lake City, UT; 1930 U.S. Census, Salt Lake City, Salt Lake County,
UT, p. 23, household of Harriet Winkleman; "Divorces Asked," *Salt Lake Telegram,*
19 July 1933, p. 15; "Statistics," *Salt Lake Telegram,* 10 Dec. 1934, p. 12; Brigham
Young University-Idaho, Special Collections and Family History, Western States
Marriage Record Index, entry for Frank J. Haberle, (Marriage ID #529157), accessed
20 Jan. 2011, http://abish.byui.edu/specialCollections/westernStates/westernStates-
RecordDetail.cfm?recordID=529157; "Divorces Asked," *Salt Lake Telegram,* 8 Dec.
1936, p. 14; "Aid Appointed," *Salt Lake Tribune,* 4 Mar. 1944, p. 19; "Provost Saw
Lake First, Writers Hold," *Salt Lake Tribune,* 28 Jan. 1943, p. 13; Utah State Histori-
cal Society Research Library, entry for U.S. Works Progress Administration (Utah
Section) Records, 1938–1943, USHS collection register, accessed 20 Jan. 2011, http://
history.utah.gov/findaids/B00057/B0057.xml; University of Nevada, Las Vegas,
Lied Library, Special Collections, Journalism Manuscript Collections, entry for
Grace Winkleman Byrne Collection, ca. 1950s, Special Collections at UNLV registers, accessed 20 Jan. 2011, http://www.library.unlv.edu/speccol/ms_subj/journal-
ism.html; "Funeral Services Today for Pioneer Resident Grace Byrne," *Henderson*
(*NV*) *Home News,* 12 Nov. 1964, p. 1; Photograph of gravestone for Grace W. Byrne,
FindAGrave.com, accessed 17 Sept. 2010, http://www.findagrave.com/cgi-bin/fg.cgi
?page=gr&GSln=byrne&GSfn=grace&GSmn=w&GSbyrel=in&GSdyrel=in&GSob
=n&GRid=36510898&df=all&.